AN IMMORTALS OF NEW ORLEANS NOVEL

QUINTUS

NEW YORK TIMES & USA TODAY BESTSELLING AUTHOR

KYM GROSSO

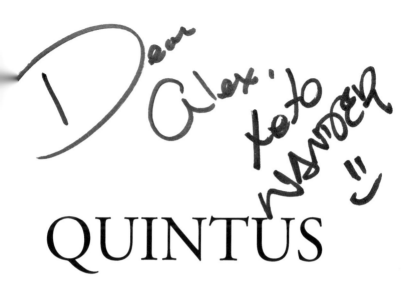

QUINTUS

Immortals of New Orleans, Book 9

Kym Grosso

MT Carvin Publishing
West Chester, Pennsylvania

Editor: Julie Roberts
Cover Design: Clarise Tan, CT Cover Creations
Photographer: Wander Pedro Aguiar, WANDER AGUIAR :: PHOTOGRAPHY
Cover Model: Colton Benson
Formatting: Jason Anderson, Polgarus Studio
Proofreading: Rose Holub, Read by Rose

DISCLAIMER
This book is a work of fiction. The names, characters, locations and events portrayed in this book are a work of fiction or are used fictitiously. Any similarity to actual events, locales, or real persons, living or dead, is coincidental and not intended by the author.

NOTICE
This is an adult erotic romance book with love scenes and mature situations. It is only intended for adult readers over the age of 18.

Dedication

I'd like to dedicate Quintus to two friends, who are both incredible strong women, people who make this world a better place, and whether they know it or not, helped me so I could write and finish Quintus. Jennifer Coll, I could not have survived my first year in California without you. You are an incredible person and caring friend, someone who has been with me through thick and thin over the years, always supporting me. I'm so proud of you and your creative, beautiful AveryRose lingerie designs. I was so excited to get my own "Kym" bra! I will never forget Paris, and our ghost hunting in New Orleans…both experiences influencing my book. Thank you so much for being there for me when I needed you the most, for being the very special person you are! You've made me laugh when I didn't think I could laugh, encouraged me when I needed someone to tell me I could do it. I mean it when I say you are an amazing friend and I'm so very lucky to have you in my life. Love you!

Karin Fox, you are a wonderful friend, mother and autism advocate. I'm in awe of your tireless efforts, helping children with autism and their families. Our path is not an easy one, but having the support of other parents has made all the difference in my life and my son's. While we may have met through the autism community as fellow autism moms, you have become a great friend. I don't think I could have gotten through this first year here without our friendship and phone calls. Thank you so much for your support. It has meant everything to me! I'm not going to stop trying to convince you to move to California! Haha.

Acknowledgments

~ My children, for encouraging me to write and supporting me in everything I do. I'm incredibly blessed to have you in my life. You are amazing, special people and I'm so proud of you both!

~ My readers, for waiting patiently while I wrote Quintus! I'm so thankful to have each and every one of you, supporting me and my books. I hope you love my sexy vampire as much as I do and look forward to writing more adventures in the series!

~ Julie Roberts, my friend and editor, who spent hours reading, editing and proofreading Quintus. As always, there are not enough words to thank you for all you do to help me. I'm terribly sorry about not giving you that log cabin, but I know someday soon I'll be visiting you in one! Haha. You seriously are the best ever!!! I can't wait for you to come visit me in California so we can do hot yoga and go to the beach!

~ Shannon Hunt, publicist and all-round assistant who gives me support! Thank you so much for everything you do to help me, your patience and friendship! I definitely think you need to reconsider going snorkeling with me to see the baby sharks. Haha. It'll be fun...I promise!!!

~ My dedicated beta readers, Denise, Janet, Jerri, Karen, Kim, Lacy, Leah, Laurie, Maria, Rose, Shannon,

Stephanie, and Rochelle, for beta reading. I really appreciate all the valuable feedback you provided. You guys rock!!!

~ CT Cover Creations, for designing Quintus' sexy cover.

~ Wander Aguiar, for taking all the gorgeous cover and teaser images for Quintus' novel. And Andrey Bahia, for helping arrange the shoot. You both are incredible people, and I'm so lucky to have you both as friends!

~ Colton Benson, cover model, for the amazing cover and teaser images. I'm so happy you're my Quintus!

~ Polgarus Studio, Jason, for formatting Quintus. You do terrific work, presenting my books so they look their best digitally and in print.

~ Rose Holub, Read by Rose, for proofreading. You are awesome!

~ My reader group, for helping spread the word about the Immortals of New Orleans series. I appreciate your support more than you could know!

Chapter One

Quintus jerked at the restraint, and hissed as the silver burned his skin. Immobilized, he struggled to breathe. As he dragged his tongue across his dry, cracked lips the faint taste of blood piqued his senses.

"Shh. You're going to be all right." The soft whispers of the feminine voice soothed him. Her nourishment was the only reason he was alive.

He shivered as she brushed her palm over his forehead. The gentle touch calmed him but the beast inside demanded to be freed. A growl tore from his lips and he bared his fangs.

"Settle now. The poison is almost out of you."

"I…" His raw throat seized and he coughed, recalling the events that had led to his near demise.

Quintus had gone with Jake Louvière, the Alpha of Anzober Wolves, to kill Kasdeya, a demon vampire hybrid. Bitten and poisoned, he'd managed to save a human who'd become caught up in the melee. Materializing to New Orleans, it had been a miracle he'd been able to get her safely to a hospital. Desperate, he'd stumbled into an underground blood bar. In the underbelly of New Orleans, Quintus had found donors with no issue, but he'd been unable to feed. Vomiting blood for days, he'd succumbed to the poison, praying for mercy as he died in the blackness of the crypt.

Quintus had thought it a nightmare but as his senses awakened, he knew otherwise to be true. The sweet trickle of blood nourished his body, the magical essence flaring his cells back to life. A siren in the distance wailed, and he blinked his burning eyes open, taking in the sight of his surroundings. Sunlight streaked through the cracks of the stone ceiling but didn't filter through the muddied stained glass windows. He ran the pads of his fingers over the cold granite bed on which he lay and glanced to the loose bricks on the ground. *A mausoleum. I'm still in the damned crypt.*

A shadow passed by him, her voice reminding him of her calming presence. He sniffed into the air, detecting only the scent of magick, but his instinct told him there was something more to her. *A witch saved me?* Throughout the years, he'd always relied on human blood, rarely indulging on other beings. The purity of his species had been strengthened by the underlying humanity genetically imprinted over thousands of years into human blood.

"Hey, how do you feel? I've got to get out of here soon," she told him, breaking his spiraling thoughts.

"Ah, bella, I don't think you need to worry. Remove the silver and I'll be on my way."

"No, if I let you go…"

"If you let me go…what exactly do you think is going to happen here?" Quintus sensed the hesitation in her voice.

"I'll just leave the key here. When we're done, I can call a friend for you. They can let you out." She brushed her long brunette hair out of her face as she paced. "You're weak. I'm sorry. I can't chance it. If I let you go now you could drain me dry."

Quintus tugged at the silver and it sizzled against his flesh. "Holy fuck. Look, if you don't get these chains off me, I very well may bite you. And I can't promise you'll like it."

As she turned to him, his gaze painted over his attractive captor. Honey-brown curls feathered around her face. Her wide blue doe eyes blinked over at him as she nervously bit her rosy pink lip. "I take that back. I promise you're going to like it. I know I will."

"I'm sorry, I can't," she refused.

Quintus glanced down, noting he'd been stripped of his clothing. "Is there any particular reason I'm naked?"

"You'd thrown up on yourself. I had to check your injury," she explained, averting her gaze.

"And here I thought I was getting lucky," he mused.

"I…I'd never do that." Her head snapped to look at him.

"How about you let me go? I don't even have my clothes on. What could I possibly do?"

"I…I need a promise," she said, her voice shaking.

"A promise, huh? Negotiation." A corner of his lip ticked upward. "This is progress."

"First I need to feed you more blood," she said, changing the subject. "I think you're ready."

Quintus' skin tingled as she ran her palm over his forearm. Magick danced through her touch. Her soothing voice continued and he listened as if an orchestra were playing, his concentration honed on her words.

"I'm sorry this happened to you. But it's okay, you're getting better." Her voice grew stronger as she spoke. "It's just when I first saw you...the wounds on your back were pretty intense. I'm guessing they were infused with black magick. What did this to you?"

"Long story. Fucking vampire bitch." He coughed, and a streak of pain stabbed through his abdomen. His thirst blossomed, his gut clenched in raw hunger. He tugged on the chains, the silver sizzling as it dug into his skin. "Get this off of me."

"I'm sorry. One more feeding. Please." She ran her palm over his forehead, not flinching as his fangs dropped.

"I swear on my life I won't hurt you. I don't know how the hell you found me. I don't know what's in your blood, but you did it." Quintus hissed as another wave of agony tore through his body. He struggled to clarify his thoughts.

"I'm sorry I can't let you bite me, but I promise this is enough."

Quintus growled, calming for but a second as the female's soft hand caressed his scruffy cheek. Her oddly familiar touch soothed his pain.

"Here you go...I'm sorry. I know it's better for you when you bite, but this is the best I can do."

The fresh scent of her blood registered seconds before the syringe touched his tongue. As his lips clamped around the hard plastic, draining the blood, his eyes locked on hers. She wore a sincere, concerned expression as she fed him. His beautiful savior cared.

He blinked, startled as her eyes flashed to a light shade of purple, her hair blonde. *Is she wearing glamour?* Quintus resisted the urge to speak and tamped down his curiosity, concentrating on healing. As her glorious essence rejuvenated his being and her vitality threaded through him, strength fired through his limbs.

Sated, he spat away the tube. His heart pounded, every cell in his body awakened. Quintus' eyes flashed to the ceiling, his thoughts clear. He clenched his muscles, snapping the chains off as if they were made of tissue paper. Feral, he lunged for his enticing savior. She ran for the door, but he was too fast, caging her against a cold stone wall. With his legs straddling hers, his cheek brushed her silken locks.

"Who are you?" he growled.

"My name is Ga…Gabby," she responded.

Quintus sniffed along her neckline, the scent of jasmine wafting into his nostrils. Delicate but strong, her palms flattened onto his bare chest. "How did you do this? I want to know now."

"My blood…please, I should get out of here," she told him.

"You're a witch?" Quintus dropped his fangs, and brushed his lips over her collarbone. Her pulse pounded in his ears. Healed with her potent blood, his body thrummed with power.

"Yes," she responded.

His instincts warned him of deception, but something about her piqued his interest. His tongue darted onto her skin, tasting the lovely beauty. She smelled delicious, and he yearned to sink his teeth into her creamy flesh. Although he'd sought to scare her, he detected her arousal.

"I don't give you permission to bite me." Defiance flashed in her eyes.

"I didn't bite you now, did I?" The firm peaks of her nipples brushed against his abdomen, and his cock stirred. "Hmm...your response, though..." Quintus closed his eyes briefly and breathed, regaining control.

"Let me go," she sighed as his lips brushed her ear. "They're coming. The others. They've sensed you've awakened. If they find me here...please...I can't stay."

"This isn't the place. But whatever game you're playing, little one, I'm not simply letting you go."

Footsteps and whispers echoed in the catacombs that connected the underground blood club to the crypt. His renewed energy was likely felt by every vampire in New Orleans. He could have cared less who found him, because he'd kill them if they so much as looked at him the wrong way.

"We're leaving," he growled. Without discussing it, he made the decision to keep her. Her palatable fear of being discovered drove him to protect her. She might be a liar but she'd saved him nonetheless.

"If you just let me go, I promise I won't tell anyone," she pleaded.

"Ah, bella. That's not how this works. You may have saved me, but it is I who call the shots."

"What?" she asked, her wide eyes on his.

"Brace yourself. This will only take a minute," he warned.

Quintus heard the faint sound of her cry as he dematerialized them out of the church. He inwardly laughed, delighted at the surge of power that pounded throughout his veins. Whatever she was, he'd find out her secrets.

"You're okay," he whispered as she shook in his arms. Quintus thought it odd she struggled with the transition, given that witches easily adjusted to materialization. With the flavor of her potent blood imprinted in his mind, he suspected she was a hybrid. She moaned, her fragile body clutched in his embrace. "Ah, bella. Your magick is strong. Why does a witch suffer like this?"

"My magick…I gave you my blood," she responded, her voice soft.

"Witches transform. But you…you're not witch?"

"I am," she protested. "My powers, they're different."

"Hmm? Should I call a coven?"

"No. No witches!" Her voice grew loud in protest. "No!"

Quintus' gut clenched with concern as her panic ran through him as if it were his own, and he wondered how her blood had affected him. Terror. Pain. All her emotions pulsed in his mind, her quickening breath soon evolving into pants as she gasped for air.

"Easy now." Quintus scooped her up into his arms and brought her to the bed. Aware he was nude, he considered covering to put her at ease, but as she continued to retch for breath, his only concern was for her safety. He lay back onto the bed bringing her with him, embracing her in his arms.

"No witches," she repeated.

"No witches," he told her, surprised at her fear.

"Promise me. Promise no witches." She clutched at him. "They'll…they'll…"

"It's all right." She attempted to push away from him, but he held tight and brushed his palm over her silken hair. Quintus closed his eyes, and attempted to send a calming energy to her. "What happened to you?"

"What are you doing?" she asked, her voice trailing off.

"Whoever did this to you? The pain. Let it go." Quintus breathed away his anger. He saw flashes of her stolen innocence yet he couldn't reach all her memories.

"Please don't let them have me." Her voice drifted to silence as she closed her eyes.

"You're safe," he assured his fragile savior. Quintus' protective streak flared. Someone had hurt her badly.

She breathed softly in slumber, and Quintus relaxed, staring up at the tin ceiling. Despite his promise to the contrary, he considered calling the high priestess of New Orleans. But he'd given his word, so for at least the night, he'd honor her wishes. No witches.

Quintus ran his palm down her arm and gently inspected her skin. His lips tensed in a straight line at the sight of the needle marks. Having tasted her blood, he knew she hadn't taken drugs. No, the telltale scars had been caused by bloodletting. *Jesus fucking Christ, what in the hell had this witch gotten herself into?* He recalled the plastic syringe she'd used to give him blood. Guilt rolled through him, aware she'd sacrificed herself to save him from death.

What trouble are you in, bella? He sighed. When she woke, they'd have a long conversation. Something about the magical woman drew him, and he couldn't deny a connection. He swallowed the emotion, surrendered to the healing calm that washed over him as he rested with the lovely witch in his arms.

❦· *Chapter Two* ·❦

The familiar nightmare stormed in her mind. Only thirteen years old, she clutched at the muddy earth. Her mother screamed as the cloaked witches tied her to the wooden stake. Gabriella watched helplessly as they set fire to the kindling, burning the only parent she'd known. Cries of terror resounded in the darkness, the stench of burnt flesh forever etched in her memory.

The clouds cleared from the sky, but they came for her once again. Gabriella had felt nothing but pain slicing through her as she'd shifted. *Run, Gabby, run,* the voice echoed in her mind. She never looked back, tearing through the woods as the witches attempted to break her with their dark magick. The moon and stars fed her strength as she escaped into the night. Lying in a cold Boston alleyway, she woke up in human form, shaking and crying for her mother.

"No!" Gabriella screamed. She jolted upward and sucked a breath, attempting to shove off the bed. Weakened, she fell backwards and curled into the warm blanket. Her eyes slowly blinked open, memories flooding her mind. *Quintus.*

As a child, her mother had told her of ancient vampires, their powers unmatched by all others. Rumors had circulated in the underground blood clubs that one of the most ancient vampires in the world had been spotted in the crypts. Poisoned. Dark magick. Some said witches had done this to him to punish him for sins of the past. Some pointed to an unleashed demon.

Gabriella had gone in search of the elusive vampire, convinced he could help her overturn the coven that sought her death. When she'd discovered him in the crypt, he'd laid unresponsive, barely breathing. Only the magick within her could save him. After the first feeding, she'd broken down in utter devastation when he'd failed to rally. Although tempted to leave him, she'd stayed by his side, talking to the handsome stranger. When he'd finally roused, she'd been terrified and elated all at once. With his help, she'd be free. But as he'd leapt and pinned her to the wall, she'd trembled underneath his touch. His extraordinary power drew her to him like a magnet, and her body had prickled with awareness.

Gabriella didn't anticipate he'd dematerialize them away from the crypt. She suspected her hybrid nature and the trauma of her own blood loss had sickened her. For the brief seconds Quintus had wandered her psyche, his warmth had saturated her mind. The infusion of his powers had worked to calm her. With the horror that danced in her thoughts exposed, she'd briefly allowed him to peer into the nightmares.

Gabriella's stomach clenched in hunger, drawing her out

of her contemplation. As her mind drifted to her responsibilities, nausea rose in her gut. Her latest torturer, her blood runner, Ramiel, had been expecting a shipment. He'd threatened to expose her location to the coven if she didn't deliver.

She glanced to the window, noting the sun hadn't broken the horizon. If she made it to Ramiel within a few hours, he'd forgive her lateness. Gabriella swung her legs over the side of the bed and prayed her head would stop spinning.

A gentle hand settled on her shoulder, and her stomach flipped as she raised her gaze to meet Quintus'. His piercing dark eyes caught her attention and she struggled to find her words. "I…I…"

"You're weak."

"I'm fine. You shouldn't have brought me here." Her bravery rose, yet she remained captivated by his penetrating gaze.

In the crypt he'd been pale as a ghost, but as she studied his face, she noted his healthy olive-skinned complexion. At six-foot-four, the commanding vampire towered over her. With wavy dark brown hair and a strong jawline, he was strikingly handsome. She struggled not to stare at his rippled abs, and averted her gaze toward the floor. A muscular arm settled around her shoulders as he sat on the edge of the bed.

"You're going to be okay." Quintus took a deep breath and sighed. "I know you're in trouble."

"What kind of vampire poisoned you?" She changed the subject, looking to her torn jeans. Her clothes reeked of the stench of death that lingered in the underground. A wave of embarrassment washed over her at her circumstances. She'd been living out of a seedy hotel room for months. With little to her name, she'd been selling herself to survive.

"She may have been a vampire," he answered, "but she had some demon mojo going on. It wasn't her bite that got me though, it was her talons. Not many things supernatural or otherwise have taken me down but this one…she was lethal. I tried to recover but I couldn't drink human blood. Kept vomiting. I was starving to death. Until you."

"I told you. I'm a witch," she said.

"Yes, but something else." Quintus leaned over her, his nose brushed her hair.

"I need to take a shower," she blurted out, her face reddening. "I smell awful. Like death."

"I only smell sweetness but I'll indulge you." He smiled. "Answers. This is what I want."

"I'll try." Gabriella sat hunched over, her forehead brushing her knees. As he ran his palm over her hair, emotion bubbled inside her chest. No one ever touched her with compassion, yet this powerful stranger treated her with kindness. She prayed he'd help her.

"Whatever has happened to you. Whoever has hurt you. This is over now." His strength reverberated in his voice.

"I don't need anything." Protection was exactly what she needed, but Gabriella hesitated to ask for the favor.

"You obviously do need help. I don't know what kind. Or how you knew me. But answers. This is what I need from you first."

Gabriella shook her head, unable to speak. Quintus could be the answer to her prayers, but she was on the run. The coven sought her. Ramiel…he waited for her blood.

"Whatever you're thinking, you're safe. My home's guarded with magick. Nothing will get you here." He paused, raising an eyebrow at her. "But you won't be able to escape, if that's what you're thinking. I'm afraid that I cannot let that happen."

"What?" Panic laced her voice as her head snapped up, her eyes flashing to his. "No. I have to go. I have an appointment. You can't just keep me here."

"Ah, bella. I'm afraid you're wrong there. I most certainly can." Quintus rose and crossed the room.

"No." Gabriella jumped to her feet. A wave of dizziness threatened but passed as she sucked a breath of fresh air.

"You shouldn't be going anywhere right now in your condition. You need to eat. Shower's in there." He pointed to an open door. "Come downstairs when you're ready. I'll make you something to eat."

"No, I need to go," she insisted.

"Doors to the outside are warded and locked. Like I said, nothing's getting in to hurt you but you're not getting out. You're not well enough to leave, and I'm curious as to what has you so scared. I'll be waiting for you."

"Shit," Gabriella uttered under her breath.

She should have known better than to think she could step into the presence of an ancient vampire and easily get out of his web. As he closed the door behind him, her stomach sank in resignation that the vampire she'd been selling her blood to would call the coven, alerting them to her location.

As she trudged across the chestnut floor planks and stepped into the bathroom, hopelessness washed over her. She flicked on the light switch, and a soft glow illuminated its emerald walls. Peeling off her tattered clothes, she took a step to cross to the shower, and caught sight of herself in the mirror. Her unkempt hair spilled over her pale skin. Faded bruises from the blood draws mottled her arms.

Gabriella closed her eyes and shook her head, inwardly disgusted with herself. She reached for the spigot and turned on the water, grateful to take a shower in somewhere other than her roach-infested hotel. As she stepped into the white marbled, glass-enclosed bath, the hot spray stung her skin. She welcomed the pain, convinced that no amount of soap would ever cleanse her. No matter how many times she told herself to be proud of how long she'd survived, the guilt of how she lived lingered in her mind. As she ran the soap over her body, she glanced to her scarred arms, a painful reminder of the price she'd paid. Like a punishment for living, the ugly marks grew more defined, and no magick or shifting would remove them.

Tears streamed down her face as she released the anguish she'd restrained. At her best, she'd saved the powerful vampire from dying, demonstrating her cunning and magick. Yet nothing could save her from the coven if they found out her location.

The one man who could help her kept her hostage, and she could sense his distrust. As she recalled how he'd gently held her, she wept for the love she'd never know. To be attracted to anyone was a futile emotion. No creature would mate with her. Witches would shun her. *Be strong. Fight.* She'd repeated her mantra every day for nearly fifteen years. She swore to herself that she'd put one foot in front of the other and keep going until she found a way to destroy the coven.

Exhausted, she slid down onto her bottom and curled her knees to her chest, pressing the heels of her hands to her forehead. *Get yourself together, Gabs. Even if it's just for today, you're alive.* A creak of the door alerted her to his presence, and she startled.

"Mi, bella." His low voice wrapped around her like a warm blanket, and she lifted her eyes. "I can feel you all the way downstairs."

"I'm…I'm sorry." Water droplets dripped down her face as she took in the sight of the handsome vampire. Confused, she wiped her eyes. No one had ever sensed her emotions after drinking of her essence. That had been the beauty of her blood. Nothing more than a short-term high, her magical blood gave vampires an energizing boost. But at no point had she ever bonded with a vampire or become tied to them.

"I know what you're thinking. Something about your blood," he said, his back turned to her.

"I'll be down in a minute." Gabriella glanced away, wishing she could hide her vulnerability, her sadness. This was not who she was. Tough. Impenetrable. Essentially invisible, she'd flash her glamour, hide her appearance and feelings.

"I promise you you're going to be all right, little witch. Whatever pains you, you'll let this go."

"I…" She lost her words in confusion.

"Come down and eat when you're done taking a shower," he told her. "Just letting you know I've put a robe out for you. It'll be a little big on you, but it's all I have. I, uh, I just didn't want you to worry about your dirty clothes. I'll see to getting you some new ones."

"Ah…okay," she replied, her voice soft. Gabriella noted how he'd been careful to avoid staring at her nudity, only briefly looking at her face. Ensuring her modesty, he'd quickly turned away. Something about this ancient vampire intrigued her. She hoped he didn't plan on feeding from her, but her gut told her to trust him. With her magick weakened, she wasn't in a position to argue.

As the bathroom door shut, she released an audible breath. She gingerly shoved to her feet, realizing that her mind had gone calm. *Quintus Tullius.* Her intuition told her that no matter what happened, her life would forever be changed. Giving him her blood had altered the course of the universe, and the Goddess would determine the future.

Gabriella wrapped the warm towel around her, and approached the window. Although the vampire had warned her he'd locked his wards, she hoped she could hijack an opening, and slip through a loophole. She closed her eyes, conjuring the magick within. Despite her weakened state, a slight spark twisted through her body. As she focused her power, her magick blanketed over the wards like water dousing a flame. She heard the crackling of the locks as she tensed, determined to break free. But her hopes were dashed as a shock sizzled her fingertips. She broke the connections, swearing out loud in frustration.

"Dammit to hell." Gabriella blew out a breath.

As she stepped into the bedroom, she spied the black terrycloth robe lying on the bed. Cream-colored walls trailed up to the fifteen-foot ceiling; an intricate crown molding edged its perimeter. She ran her hand over the cool walnut post of the canopy bed. Swathes of white linen draped over its beams and dusted down onto the floor.

Gabriella reached for the soft cotton robe and pressed her hands into the arms, then tied it tight around her waist. Lifting the lapels to her nose, she inhaled his masculine sandalwood scent. Something about this vampire…so much more than what she'd expected, both soothed and frightened her all at once. She sighed and reminded herself that this was a simple business transaction. She saved his life. He owed her. It was as simple as that.

Her stomach tightened, aware she'd been late delivering her blood to Ramiel. She'd have to convince Quintus to release her, promise she'd return to his home.

Gabriella opened the door, and peered into the hallway. Quietly, she stepped toward the landing. As she slowly made her way down the stairs, she heard the male voices and froze. Flattening her back against the wall in the foyer, she quietly listened. Her heart sped, regretting her decision to save

Quintus. He'd gone to one of his own, betraying her. Barely dressed and unable to escape his wards, she'd have to fight for her life. It wasn't the first time and wouldn't be the last.

She scanned the living room, her eyes going to an ancient sword that hung on his wall. As she reached for it and her hands wrapped around its hilt, she felt vampire magick rush into the room. Gabriella whipped the weapon toward the energy, the blade slicing through the stranger's shirt. Her gaze rose to meet his and her heart pounded in her chest at the sight of the tall blond vampire. Her eyes darted to the torn fabric, a thin red line bubbling over his abdomen. His fangs dropped, and his eyes lit with amusement as he laughed.

Terrified, she raised the sword above her head, and squealed as a muscled arm clamped around her waist. Strong fingers applied pressure into her wrist, taking her to the edge of pain and forcing her to drop the blade. The loud clank was offset by the whisper in her ear. "No, bella. What are you doing? Such a fiery little witch you are."

The blond vampire's wounds appeared to heal before her eyes and Gabriella sucked a breath, panic burning through her. She attempted to jerk free but Quintus held firm.

"Let me go," she grunted, her eyes trained on the Nordic vampire.

"Calm down, little one. This one is a friend. Gabriella. Meet Viktor. My brother."

⊷❈⊷ *Chapter Three* ❈⊷

As Quintus prepared the meal, he attempted to rein in his spiraling thoughts. Whether a coincidental stroke of luck or a deliberate act, Gabriella's gift of her magical blood had saved his life. Awakening on the cold slab in the crypt, he'd committed to repaying her. He'd sensed her pain, and suspected whatever shit she was in, she was in deep. Although the temptation to bite her had been great, he'd restrained himself. He chalked up his spiraling desire for the little witch to the poison, and grew convinced that whatever seeds of feelings had sprouted, he should ignore them.

His stomach clenched in hunger as he opened the refrigerator, searching for milk. *Shit.* Being gone for a few weeks, he'd forgotten to call on his local butler to restock the perishables. Discovering a carton of eggs hidden on a shelf, he shrugged and carried on with his task.

A feral thirst for blood twisted through him as he searched through the pantry, not entirely sure what else he was looking for. He'd already texted for a donor, and she was expected shortly. Although Gabriella required sustenance, human food wasn't a necessity for him. Rather he simply enjoyed the emotional comfort of a home-cooked meal, reminding him of his human existence.

He fired on the gas stove and set a skillet onto the burner. As he went to reach for a knife, his instincts flared, recognizing the vampire. *Viktor Christiansen.* Unrelated by blood, Viktor and Quintus had been turned within days of each other. They'd become sired brothers by chance, friends by choice. Subjected to torture by their brutal master, the fledgling vampires had survived only with the support of one another.

"What brings you to New Orleans?" Quintus asked, waving his hand in the air with a smile.

"Just coming to check on you, man. Last thing I knew you were in New York. Gone missing. Of course there're stories. Had to see for myself."

"I love a good story." He turned and smiled at him, wiggling his eyebrows, but his levity was met with a cold stare. "What? I'm alive."

"Rumor on the streets had you dead."

"Well, they're wrong. Better than ever." He sliced off a chunk of butter and tapped it into the pan. It immediately sizzled, smoke twirling up into the air.

"Cut the shit, Quint. You've been missing for weeks."

"I was busy. You knew that when I left New York."

"I called for you and you didn't answer. What am I supposed to think?" His voice went soft as he approached. "Stop fucking with me."

"Something happened," Quintus said with indifference.

"Jake said you were poisoned." Viktor craned his head to check out what Quintus was cooking.

"You went to the Alpha?" Quintus asked, shaking his head with a small laugh. He'd expected his brother would search high and low for him. Although they often fought, they'd kill for each other.

"Fuck yeah, I went to Jake. But the thing is he didn't have a clue where the hell you went. I knew you weren't in the city, so I went to the next place I thought you'd go. And here I am."

"It's always been home." Quintus shrugged. He owned several properties across the globe but he'd made New Orleans home long ago.

"How long have you been here, because before you answer, you should know that I...there was this girl."

"Yeah, I've heard that one before." Quintus grinned. "Many times actually."

"Be fucking serious for a minute. How long have you been here?" he pressed.

"I've been back here...I don't know...a couple of weeks maybe," Quintus guessed, unsure of how long he'd been missing.

"I tracked down a human a week ago. She had your scent..."

"Cassandra?" Quintus spun to face him, his face flared in anger. He'd saved Jake's friend who'd graciously fed him in San Francisco. He'd been her first vampire, and after the attack, he'd saved her life and rushed her to the hospital.

"Are you going soft?" Viktor rolled his eyes and glanced

again to the stove, the butter browned in the skillet, releasing a burnt odor into the air. "You gonna get that?"

"You'd better not have fucking touched her." Quintus shot him a glare and began to crack the eggs into the pan.

"So what if I talked to her? You staked no claim on her."

"I'm serious. This is no matter to quibble over. She's a friend of the Alpha's. She was nice. And no offense asshole, but you don't do nice."

"Jesus, you have gone soft." Viktor slid over a chair and sat down, his elbow resting on the kitchen table.

"Did you touch her?" Quintus asked.

"No, okay? Calm down. You're burning the eggs." Viktor rolled his eyes and then looked to the stove. "What ya makin' anyway?"

"What's it look like? Eggs. Nothing fancy. I forgot to call my butler."

"I can't believe you're still cooking human food after all these years. You know it doesn't do anything for you."

"I don't care."

"You don't need it."

"I enjoy it. That's all that matters. Seriously, are we having this argument again?"

"Who's the chick upstairs?" Viktor gave a sly smile.

Quintus turned off the gas and flattened his palm onto the cool granite. He had known Viktor would sense Gabriella but didn't want him to know anything about her until he had more information.

"None of your business. And before you get ready to do something extraordinarily stupid, you're not to speak to her."

"Ah…she's special. Okay, I'll bite. What is she? Hmm…she's a virgin? No, no, wait. She's a warrior of some sort. A challenge. Wild in bed, I bet." Viktor laughed, his eyes drifting up toward the ceiling. "She must be something if you brought her here."

"She's special, that much is true. It's all business I'm afraid. A witch."

"A witch? That's unusual. Didn't you have some sort of rule…?"

"I'm not fucking her. I'm feeding her."

"Yeah okay." He laughed.

"Her blood." Quintus paused, reminding himself that he could trust Viktor. "All I can say is that it's special. I don't want you touching her. Not even thinking of touching her."

Viktor laughed in response, a broad smile on his face.

"No joke. You're in for a world of hurt if you touch her."

"I thought you just said you aren't fucking her. What is this possessiveness? We share everything."

"Correction. We share most things. She is not one of them." Quintus struggled with the jealousy that boiled within him. Aside from drinking her blood, he had no other ties to the girl.

"She's something special, huh? Should I be worried?" Viktor leaned back into his chair and put his hands behind his head.

"No need to worry, my friend. She's mine. As long as you don't touch her, you'll be fine. Am I clear?" Quintus slammed the spatula onto the countertop in frustration and shook his head. *What the hell am I saying?* He couldn't believe he just told Viktor the witch belonged to him.

"Tell me brother, what's so special about the blood of a witch? If anything it would be less potent than a human's."

"There was a vampire. I had a run in with her in California. I've only been attacked a few times in my life by one, but this didn't go so well. Poisoned talons."

"Got it. But you should be able to bounce back."

"I managed to jump from San Diego to New Orleans carrying Cassandra. But when I flashed I wasn't even sure where the hell I was taking her. Thank fuck I landed close to St. Mary's. I didn't have the energy to go anywhere else, so I ended up in that shit underground club around the corner." Quintus released a sigh. "You want some breakfast. Coffee? I got the pods in here somewhere."

"I just ate. You know I don't eat that human crap."

"I was poisoned a fair amount," he continued, ignoring Viktor. "I couldn't feed. Whenever I drank human blood, I got sick. Couldn't keep it down."

"Maybe you got a few junkies in the mix. You know they sell in there for drug money."

"No way would I drink that shit. I'd scent that out before they ever got within ten feet of me. These donors were top shelf. None of it mattered. Whatever I ate came right back up. I thought...this is it. I wasn't sure what to do. I didn't want some fucker thinking they could kill me while I was weak, so I retreated, holed up in a crypt. I thought...it was the end."

"But here you are. We're tough stock."

"I was dying. The Goddess was near. I'm fucking telling

you, it wasn't good. I didn't think I was going to make it."

"You got some drama going on there," Viktor mocked.

"Fuck you, V. I'm serious. I could have fucking died down there. I don't know how she found me…she's not what she appears to be."

"Let's just hope she didn't put some kind of hex on your ass. She's a witch."

"I think she's in trouble. I'm not sure what it is. I sensed it. She's a fighter but there's something I can't figure out…"

Quintus stilled as he heard the patter of water from the shower taper off into silence. When he'd checked on her, she'd been crying. Her pain filtered through him as if they'd been truly connected. Although he sometimes sensed others' emotions, hers were clear and unfettered. The unusual sensation took him off guard, but he buried the nagging feeling.

"What does she want?" Viktor asked.

"Ah, that is the million-dollar question."

"No one goes to you without wanting a favor."

"She didn't ask a favor though. Not yet." Quintus raised an eyebrow and scooped the eggs onto a plate.

"Still, she must have gone to great lengths to do that. It's not like that club is exactly a beach resort. It's more of a shithole." Viktor sniffed the air, his eyes falling to the eggs. "I know there're tunnels that lead to the cemetery and crypts but she'd have to know how to get there through the club. Did you ever meet her before?"

"Never in my life. But I'm telling you, that poison took me down. When I first came to, I couldn't really see her.

She was feeding me her blood. As soon as I rallied, well then…that's when she got really nervous. I scared her."

"I can't imagine why. Did you bite her?"

"No." Quintus recalled his body pressed to hers, her delicious scent calling to him. "It's not like I didn't want to. But I'm not an animal. Jesus."

"Tell me, oh, great one. If she was scared, how'd you get her to agree to come to your house?" Viktor picked a fork up off the table and spun it with his fingers.

"I didn't exactly ask. Let's just say it was strongly recommended we leave." Quintus shrugged.

"So let me get this straight. Said witch feeds you her blood, saves you in a crypt. She expresses regret and then you kidnap her?" Viktor laughed. "Okay then. Going old school, I see."

"I didn't kidnap her. I prefer to think of it as saving her. Yeah, that sounds about right." Quintus turned to his friend, a devilish smirk on his face. "Eggs? You sure you don't want some?"

"You totally kidnapped that chick."

"She needs help. Besides, once I roused, I could tell there were people coming. We had to get out of there. Eggs?"

"Did you ask her if she wanted to come here? What the hell, Quint? It's not like we didn't pull that shit when we first turned, but it's been centuries. We…no, correct that, you don't need any trouble with her coven."

"She doesn't like witches."

"Bullshit. All witches have a coven. I'm not sayin' we don't bite a witch every now and then, but fuck. You can't just take them. You ever hear the expression you catch more flies with honey?"

"Eggs? They're getting cold," Quintus replied, ignoring him.

"Okay fine. Give me the damn eggs. Jesus, you have issues." He waved the plate towards him. "You know I'm not going to eat this shit."

"That's a good vampire," Quintus teased, setting it on the table. "Food is good for the soul. Reminds you of who you once were."

"Yeah, yeah." Viktor stabbed at the food with the fork and then set the utensil down on the plate.

"I did not kidnap Gabriella," Quintus stated.

"Gabriella is it? Ah, the witch has a name."

"Yes she does." Quintus placed another plate of eggs on the table and sat. Lifting a forkful of the fluffy goodness to his mouth, he ate it and sighed. "Hmm…it's good."

"The scent…it does remind me of being human. You're always fucking right."

"You know that I am. I'm older."

"By three weeks." He rolled his eyes.

"This witch. There is something…" Quintus hesitated to share his concerns about how he'd read her memories. "We have some sort of a connection. I'm not sure why or what it is. It could be her blood. I don't know."

"The plot thickens."

"I don't know what's going on but I do know she's not just witch. Like maybe she's a hybrid of some kind. I've tasted witch blood on occasion. It's never done anything particularly special for me."

"Maybe you just haven't bitten the right witch. I know I've tasted quite a few. Their magick. You often can taste it. It has a distinct flavor."

"It's more than that. I was dying. And now…" Quintus set his fork on the table, his gaze meeting Viktor's. "You know, we often can sense things from blood. But this…I could read her."

"You can do that. You're a vampire."

"This was different. All I know is that she's in trouble. I owe her my life."

"Is she hot?" A mischievous smile broke across Viktor's face.

"What the hell is that supposed to mean?" *Hot as fuck.* Quintus stabbed hard at the eggs.

"She *is* hot. All right. Now we're talkin'. Or your dick is talkin'. Yeah, pretty sure this is all related to your dick. Let me see her and let's see what my dick says."

"Fuck off. It doesn't matter how she looks." *It's how she feels.* "She's scared of other witches. I know that much. Whatever is going on, my instincts tell me it isn't going to be good for any of us."

"Witches, baby. They can be trouble, all right. Have you heard from Ilsbeth?"

"Ilsbeth." Quintus stretched his neck side to side, releasing the tension. The mere mention of the bitch caused his blood pressure to rise. "Look at what she did to the wolves. You heard she's playin' a game now. Saying she's not a witch. Calls herself Zella. It's some bullshit."

"At least the coven down here's run by Samantha now. They won't have as many issues. At home though…"

"What's going on?" Quintus asked, his eyes trained on Viktor. "What aren't you telling me?"

The creak of the wooden floor above drew his attention and he jumped up from his seat. He read the flicker of mischief in Viktor's eyes and gave him fair warning. "Leave her be, brother. She belongs to me."

"Why must you be so selfish? Sharing is caring."

"There is no sharing. She's mine."

"Yours, huh?" He laughed.

Quintus heard footsteps coming down the staircase, and as she approached, his body quickened in awareness of her magick. His eyes flashed to Viktor who gave a smirk.

"No," told him.

"Yes."

Quintus cursed as Viktor dematerialized out of the kitchen. "Goddammit."

The blade sliced across his brother's abdomen, and Quintus gave a muffled laugh. With his arm wrapped around her waist, his eyes lit in amusement as his little witch vowed her vengeance.

"This is what you brought home?" Viktor chuckled and wiped the blood from his healing skin. "She's feral."

"Fuck off, V. She's special. And you deserved it." She attempted to jerk from his arms but he held tight. "Sorry bella but you'd best relax. Make nice."

"Fuck you. I will not make nice. I should have never helped you," she yelled at him.

"Feisty." Viktor's lips curled upward. "Ah my friend. Is it her blood or her spirit you're after?"

"Neither," he lied, aware he craved her blood like air.

"Definitely her blood. You don't normally go for women with spirit. Demure is more your type."

"Would you shut up?" Quintus demanded, his voice calm but terse.

"Go to hell. Both of you," she spat. "Let me go."

"This is going to be fun." Viktor nodded his head in amusement.

"This is going to be an obligation I fulfill. Nothing more, nothing less. I need to get back to New York before shit goes down." Quintus maintained a nonchalant tone.

"Shit is already going down." Viktor shook his head and walked toward the kitchen.

"Let me go," Gabriella grunted, wrenching out of his arms.

"Easy now."

"I want my clothes."

"I'm having some things sent over but if you insist, there are clothes in the closet you can wear."

"I want my clothes not something that belongs to a girlfriend. And I want the wards lifted too. I've got to get out of here."

"Demanding little thing. You picked a winner," Viktor's voice carried from the other room.

"I didn't pick her. She picked me." Quintus smiled.

"This isn't a joke. I have commitments." Her eyes widened at his audacity. "I saved your sorry ass. You need to trust me. I do need your help but I...I..."

"Whatever is after you, we can discuss it. But you must understand...look at me." Quintus gently placed his hand on hers. She stilled at his touch, her fingers relaxing into his. A defiant fear shone in her eyes as they drifted to his. "I'm going to protect you. I don't know what you owe." His anger roused at the thought of anyone hurting her, holding her hostage for debt. "But I'll repay it. You'll be free."

"It's more than that. I mean...I owe someone something." A single tear rolled down her face. "And there's the witches..."

"I want to know what's exactly going on so I can protect you."

"I can't talk to you..."

"You can trust me."

"I can't trust him." Gabriella trembled, craning her neck to peek down the hallway into the kitchen.

Quintus had had enough. He wanted to know exactly what was going on and who was after her. He made a split-second decision, aware that neither Gabriella nor Viktor would like it. *Fuck the eggs.* "Hold on."

Transporting her away into his bedroom, Quintus held her tight as she trembled in his arms. It was the only place in his house where even Viktor couldn't hear them. Gaining her trust was the only way to get her to tell him what in the hell was going on and who was trying to hurt her. He trusted Viktor with his life but his brother and Gabriella hadn't exactly gotten off on the right foot.

"You're okay," he told her. She didn't move to break free but instead molded into his embrace. "Witches don't usually get dizzy. Ah, what's going on with you? Please, bella. You're safe in here. Viktor won't hurt you."

"I'm not safe," she said through her tears.

"He can't hear you in here. I promise." Quintus held her in his arms, gently cradling her head to his chest. What in the hell had happened to his little witch?

"You need to eat." He was beginning to regret his decision to leave the kitchen. He knew she needed actual food to survive.

"It's not that...I just can't stay. The moon is coming soon. And I'm going to..." Her words faltered as he sat onto his bed.

Quintus lay back onto his pillow, bringing her with him, not willing to let her go. "Gabby, I'm the one in your debt. I could have died if you hadn't intervened. I don't know why you did it but you did. So let me help you."

"I can't stay here. I swear I'll be back. I'll tell you anything you want to know."

"Whatever you think you need to do, it'll wait." Quintus sighed. "Even if you gave me your blood because you needed a favor, I might have helped you anyway."

"You're not known for helping with no reason."

"It depends on the situation." While it was true that he'd been merciless in his ways, ruling with an iron fist, he would occasionally help those he deemed worthy. Both supernaturals and humans alike were a disappointing lot. He didn't have time for insolent idiots calling on favors.

"They're after me. They've always been after me," she replied, her voice calm. Quintus glanced to her eyes which were glazed over in an icy haze.

"Who's after you?"

"If you'd let me go, I could have got the product to him."

Quintus' fingertips grazed over her silky smooth skin. His anger spiked as his eyes drifted to the needle marks. "And I take it you are the product. You sell yourself."

"Don't judge me, vampire. There was no other way. I'm surviving."

"I'm not judging you." His stomach clenched at the thought of her sharing any part of herself with others.

"Blood," she whispered. "Nothing else. I would never do that."

"I didn't say that you were selling your body, it's just…" Quintus' words faltered as he reconsidered his thoughts. He released a silent breath in relief. Something about her. He didn't want to know if she'd had sex with anyone, let alone for money. "Why though? You're a witch. You could work at a variety of places."

"I can't practice the craft." She raised her eyes to meet his. "I'm running. This is my life."

His stomach twisted at her words. "Do you have a home?"

"Yes. No. Sort of." She laid her head onto his chest, and relaxed into his arms.

"How long have you been in New Orleans?" Quintus asked.

"Five months. Before that I'd been in Seattle for seven years. Lucky number seven." A sad smile formed on her lips, her eyes wet from her tears.

"Why'd you leave? Why'd you come here?"

"Because they found me. They always do," she said, her voice soft.

"Who?" His question was met by silence. "You can trust me. Look, I know we just met but when I give my word, I don't break it. I swear to the Goddess. If there is anyone here in the city who can protect you it's me."

Her magick buzzed under his fingertips. *What the hell? How is she doing that?* The fortress of the wards in his home, especially his bed chambers, had been specifically designed to block any magick, except for his own. Although she trembled in his arms, her strength was apparent.

"I'll keep you safe," he promised.

"I've never been safe," she admitted.

"You can trust me," Quintus assured her, sending his calming energy to her.

"The daughters of Salem. Circe coven," she whispered.

"Circe? As in Greek mythology? Helios' daughter?"

"Yes. She was a witch. The coven is named for her. Bloodline and rituals are everything. In all they do, they are pure with intent," she said in a low monotone voice as if repeating a mantra.

"And if you're not pure?" He'd suspected she was hybrid. "I imagine that's frowned upon."

"Justifiable death," she said, her voice without emotion.

"What are you?" He suspected wolf, but couldn't be sure.

"It doesn't matter what I am. What matters is that I'm not pure. I'm tainted." She curled her fingers onto the fabric of his shirt. "The coven, they won't stop until I'm dead. The impurity must be removed."

"Circe? I haven't heard of them. Tell me more about these witches."

"They're orthodox. There can be no mixing of the blood. My parents…" Her voice went silent. "It doesn't matter. I've been on the run for as long as I can remember."

"How long Gabby? How long have you been running?"

"I was thirteen when I first started so yeah, about fifteen years now I've been on the move. But it might as well be a thousand. And it won't ever end. Not unless I do something about it."

"Jesus. You were just a kid." Quintus heard the hopelessness in her voice. "No one deserves to be hunted like an animal."

"When someone tells you something's wrong with you over and over…it's hard to shake. Maybe I'm cursed."

"Your blood is special. Far from cursed. These witches. Whatever antiquated rituals they follow, they're wrong, not you."

"Morality doesn't matter. They're powerful. And they always find me."

"I've handled witches before. I'll admit it's tricky.

Depends on the power of the coven. But whoever is after you, we'll deal with them."

"I met this creature in LA once. She said she was a mystic. She told me that I needed the help of an ancient vampire. And it's funny because my mom, she'd told me about the existence of ancients too. That there're only a handful of you on the earth."

"Did she now?" Quintus kept the secrets of his kind close to the vest. They certainly didn't control other species but they were powerful.

"You bend the rules of the universe. Atoms. Disappearing from one place and reappearing in another."

"It's true I can materialize. There're a few witches I've met who can conjure the same sort of magick."

"True, but this woman said…" she hesitated.

"Do tell." He gave a small chuckle.

"You can make people believe what you say as truth. You can conjure the magick of Heaven and Hell."

"My powers are as any other vampire, I assure you," he lied. It was true that he could create an alternate truth, blinding the victim into believing something they otherwise knew as false.

"You saw through my glamour," she challenged.

"I'll admit I saw you flicker for a few seconds in the crypt. It's true. I see through your magick. I see you."

"No one has ever seen through my glamour except for Lilitu."

"And I take it she's from your coven?"

"The high priestess. But you see, some things, no matter

how impure they deem me, my magick is no different than theirs."

"Your mother was a witch?"

"Yes. She was beautiful. Powerful. All creatures were drawn to her light. She would not be bound by the coven."

"And your father?"

"I don't know who he was. She told me he was warlock."

"But he wasn't?"

"No, no he wasn't. He couldn't have been. And now, I don't belong anywhere. I am the hunted."

Outcast. Alone. Gabriella's emotions danced over his mind. As much as Quintus wanted to block the pain, he suspected she knew of the connection, was allowing him to read her. In the heat of the moment, he held her small form against his and wished he could keep her safe forever.

"That woman I met. She said something about a spell that can be done to break the coven. But I need help. Which okay…like duh. I could hardly do it on my own. Because, believe me, if I could I would. I've been running…running so damn long."

"They won't find you here." He pressed his lips to her hair, her enticing scent drifting around him.

"You don't understand. Ramiel. He knows about me. I don't know how he found out."

"Ramiel?"

"He's the guy who's expecting my blood. A vampire. He sells it in the underground clubs." She blew out a breath and continued. "It's not like I want to sell my blood. I want you to know that. It's just that I needed money. I don't usually go in the clubs either. You know, like the night I found you. I was only in there because I was supposed to meet Ramiel. When I go, I always have to use my glamour. But for the most part, I try to stay away from those places. I can't risk doing too much magick in the open. The coven always finds me. Always."

"How did you know I was in the club?"

"I didn't. Like I said, I was just in there to meet Ramiel. But people talk. Everyone was saying you'd been in there. That you weren't leaving. Before that, I'd been working up the courage to go to Kade for help. I figured he's the head vampire. He'd know you."

"But I'm usually in New York." Quintus stilled as she ran her palm onto his chest, desire twisting through him. He took a deep breath, willing his arousal to cease.

"I didn't want to go to you directly. People say…"

"People say what? I'm sure I've heard it all." A corner of his mouth ticked upward.

"You're dangerous." She bit her lip.

"I am," Quintus answered honestly.

"You kill people."

"I do." *Not without reason.*

"I was afraid."

"You weren't afraid in the crypt." Quintus recalled how she'd chained him. "You do not fear me, pet?"

"Yes. No." Gabriella grazed her leg against his and went still as if she knew what she'd done. "Maybe…it's just…I couldn't leave you in there."

"You needed me alive," Quintus said, disappointment in

his tone. Why was it important to him that there was another reason? He didn't even know her.

"I needed to try to save you. I know what my blood does. It's why I sell it. It makes people feel good."

"But this Ramiel. He knows too."

"He also knows…about the coven."

Quintus brushed a lock of hair from her face, his pinky trailing over her soft skin. He sensed her fear. "What has he done to you?"

"He…he's a thug, you know. But this?" She glanced to her arm, trailing her fingers over the raised scars. "I did this to myself. It's ironic that I can heal others sometimes but I can't heal myself. I'm supernatural yet these marks aren't going away."

"He's hurt you. I can feel it. Don't lie to me."

"I can't tell you…" She sighed.

"He's threatening you now?"

"No, this is my fault. I should have never told him…"

"Anyone who takes advantage of an injured witch is a predator. He hurt you. Look at your arms." Anger roared through his gut.

"I don't want to talk about him." Ramiel had beaten her once. She'd missed a delivery. The shocking blow to her jaw had been unexpected. Shaking and bleeding, she'd been unable to see clearly and her magick faltered. As his foot connected with her head, the world had gone dark. When she'd woken, he'd texted her, warning that she'd receive worse the next time, that he'd expose her secret.

"I can promise you this. If this guy comes anywhere near

you, he's a dead man. From now on you are under my protection."

"But he'll call on the coven," she replied. "They'll know I'm in New Orleans."

"Let them come for you. I'll destroy them."

"You don't understand. They're not to be trifled with." She pushed up onto his chest.

"Nor am I." Quintus heard her pulse race faster.

As her finger brushed against his chest, he resisted looking at her delicate neckline. Her breast spilled out of the robe but she didn't move to cover herself.

"I'm not scared of you," she breathed, gazing into his eyes. "You're...you're..."

At the hint of her arousal, Quintus rolled her onto her back. She gave a breathy cry but didn't struggle as he pinned her wrists to the bed. His lips moved to her ear.

"You should be," he growled.

"I...are you trying to scare me?" she whispered.

He dropped his fangs in response, his lips brushing over her soft skin. "Perhaps you should be scared?"

"Maybe I should be, but I'm not now," she confessed.

"Something about you..." Quintus pressed his lips to her collarbone. The taste of her stirred an instinctual response. There had only been one other time he'd sensed a connection with a woman, and she'd been ripped away from him. He swore to never to let himself be torn open again, yet as Gabriella's fingertips brushed over the scruff on his cheek, he nearly lost control.

"Quintus..." she said, her voice husky.

"Shhh," he murmured.

"But I'm not…"

"You don't listen well, do you?" Quintus fought his burning desire, holding on by a thread.

"I do, but…" Gabriella's mouth parted as she lost her words.

Fuck it. Unable to resist, his lips crushed onto hers, commanding her attention. She moaned as his tongue swept against hers. Arousal coursed through him, and his cock turned to concrete as she kissed him back. Tearing his mouth from hers, his lips trailed kisses down her neck. Quintus released her wrists and tugged her robe open, exposing her. His tongue lapped at her rosy peak, eliciting an erotic moan. His teeth itched to slice into her enticing flesh, her blood tempting him.

She trembled, her hips rocking upward, grinding against his hard length as he sucked her taut tip into his mouth. His hand glided between her legs, his fingers delving into her slippery folds. *Jesus Christ, she's so fucking wet for me.* He questioned going further, aware she still kept secrets.

"Quintus, yes…please," she begged.

"Ah, bella." *Just one little taste.* Quintus delved a thick finger into her tight core, stretching her.

"Oh my Goddess…I…I…" Gabriella arched her back, her hips tilting into his hand as he fucked her pussy.

"Do you have any idea how much I want you?" His primal instinct urged him to bite her but he resisted.

"Please…ah yes," she cried as he drove another digit inside her tight channel.

As he drove his fingers inside her, his rigid shaft ached, yearning to make love to the enticing witch. Quintus' mind spun in arousal and he fought the impulse to drink her blood. *Do not bite her. Do not fuck her. This will only complicate things. Control, Quint. Get fucking control.*

In the split second he'd regained his will, Gabriella speared her fingers into his hair, pulling him to her breast, and his fangs nicked her skin. Her sweet blood trickled into his mouth and he sucked at her essence. Gabriella screamed his name as he relentlessly penetrated her hot core, his thumb flicking over her swollen clit.

"No…don't stop. Please," she cried as he licked over the wound, lifting his head.

Quintus, determined not to fuck up the situation any further than he had, placed a kiss to her breast, and reached for the edge of her robe.

"What are you doing?" Gabriella panted.

"We can't. As much as I want you, we can't do this. It's not right." Quintus shoved off the bed, cursing in pain. He sucked a breath and adjusted his throbbing dick. *Fucking idiot. Now look what you've done.*

"Quintus." Her eyes filled with moisture as she protectively wrapped her arms around her waist.

"I'm sorry, Gabby. You need to eat something. I'll be right back." Detecting rejection in her eyes, he turned his back to her. He should have never touched the witch. With the taste of her blood on his tongue, he'd forever crave what he couldn't have.

As he walked out of his room, he didn't look back. For

the first time in his life, he couldn't simply take what he wanted without remorse. Gabriella had come into his life, igniting a fire that should have stayed dimmed.

Quintus bounded down the stairs, plowing his fingers through his thick hair. Jesus, he couldn't resist the attraction to the brunette beauty. He struggled with the temptation, aware he'd sworn to protect her.

A laugh from the kitchen drew his attention from his spiraling thoughts. *Viktor.* As Quintus rounded into the kitchen he caught sight of his brother leaning toward a pretty young brunette. Ravenous, the sight of the donor should have pleased him, yet anger coursed through him instead. She was not the one he craved.

"No playing with the food, Viktor. She's mine. If you want some, get your own." Quintus looked to the woman and pointed to the hallway. "Second door on the left. Sit on the red sofa, not the white leather."

"Ah, specific as always. Ever the master." The corner of Viktor's mouth drew upward in a wry smile.

"In a world full of chaos, we fill the void with rules." Quintus snapped his fingers and the woman jumped to her feet, her eyes wide as he raised his eyebrows. "Be quick. I don't have a lot of time."

"Jesus, Quint. Could you treat this anymore like business? Feeding is for pleasure as well as sustenance."

"Eating is pleasure. You enjoyed the eggs, didn't you?"

"Don't be an asshole. You need to make it pleasurable for her. Even a cold-hearted bastard like you wouldn't hurt a donor."

"I don't need advisement on this." Quintus carefully watched the girl as she entered his office, and continued speaking to Viktor. "Gabriella is upstairs. I need you to help me with something."

"I thought you said you didn't want me touching the witch."

"I'm not asking you to bite her, asshole. She needs something to eat. Now," he growled.

"This is exactly why you shouldn't harbor humans without a nanny."

"Humans aren't children. Besides Gabby's a witch and she doesn't need a babysitter." Quintus rolled his eyes, and opened the pantry. "She needs food. Maybe...oatmeal? It's nutritious, right?"

"Sort of." Viktor shrugged. "What the hell do I know?"

"Good enough for now. I'll get her a proper meal when we get to New York."

"You're bringing her to New York?" Viktor scoffed. "You're joking?"

"Do I sound as though I'm joking? She's going." Quintus snatched a mug out of the cabinet and filled it with water.

"We shouldn't be taking stray witches to New York. We have enough issues as it is." Victor stared at the oatmeal box.

"It'll be fine. Absinthe deals with her coven. Jax keeps his wolves on their leashes. For the most part anyway."

Quintus set the cup into the microwave and pressed the start button.

"Speaking of New York witches. There have been rumors of attacks."

"There're always rumors."

"The vampires are restless. They're thinking the witches are starting a war."

"I'll talk with them, set them at ease. They'll fall in line." *Or die.* It was true that he'd been gone for far too long. His presence in New York was imperative.

"A few witches have gone missing the past week. As far as I know, none of our vamps were involved."

"It happens. Not our problem." Quintus retrieved the mug from the microwave and set it on the counter. He tore open a packet of dry oatmeal and poured it into the steaming water. "Do you think she likes it sweet?"

"What?" Viktor wore a look of confusion.

"The oatmeal. Brown sugar? Honey? What do you think?"

"Are you for real? What the hell is wrong with you, Quint? Didn't you just feed from her?"

"Feed from her? No. No I didn't." Quintus blew out a breath in frustration. There was nothing else he could think of but sinking his cock and his fangs into her. If he didn't feed soon, he worried he'd lose control.

"Jesus Christ. What is so special about her?"

"She needs food. You can't feed from a human or witch when they're already compromised; you know that as well as anyone…" Quintus shook his head and opened an overhead cabinet, retrieving a small plastic bear. "Sweet. Definitely sweet. Thanks for your help by the way, asshole."

"Who the hell cares? She's just a witch."

A flare of anger lit and Quintus spun in a flash, shoving Viktor up against the refrigerator. "She. Is not *just* a witch."

"What the hell, man?" Viktor pushed at Quintus' chest but he was unmoved. "There is something special about her. I'm not even going to say it out loud what I think is happening here. But you'd better get your fucking hands off me, bro. Not cool."

"You will not cross me on this, Viktor," he growled, releasing him.

"Fuck you too."

"The witch goes to New York." Quintus popped the lid off the honey and squeezed it into the porridge. "And before you say another word, you are wise not to speculate on her place in my life."

"Ah ha! And she does have a place, doesn't she, brother?"

"That's not your concern at the moment. No, what you will be concerned with is bringing her a meal."

"So you're avoiding the same witch you're planning to bring to New York? Brilliant plan."

Quintus sighed, his eyes going to Viktor's. "I promised to help her. She's in danger."

"From what?"

"More witches. It's complicated." Quintus grew irritated he hadn't pressed her for more answers.

"It always is. Hey, I'm not even going to ask. Not now anyway." Viktor's eyes went to the living room. "You want me to take this upstairs?"

The thought of Viktor alone with Gabriella in his bedroom shot a spear of jealousy through him, and he grit his teeth. "Maybe it's better if she eats in the kitchen. Call up to her."

Quintus rubbed the back of his hand across his lips and gave a final warning before heading toward his office. "Don't touch her."

"No worries. How 'bout you do me a favor? Eat something. You get mean when you're hangry."

As Quintus entered his office, his stomach turned at the sight of the naked woman who lay waiting for him on the sofa. She smiled at him, and he forced the corners of his mouth upward. He'd never gone to feed while thinking of another woman, yet as he drew closer his mind flooded with thoughts of Gabriella.

"Put your clothes on," he commented, aware extras were included with a feeding. His bite, a natural aphrodisiac, elicited arousal, orgasm, ensuring the donor's pleasure.

She abruptly sat upward. "Are you not pleased with my body? I can call another donor for you."

"You're fine." Quintus registered the flash of hurt in her eyes and quickly recovered. "It's not you. You're lovely. I'm short on time. I need to make this quick."

Quintus sat back into the sofa and laid the back of his head onto the crushed velvet. He gave a sigh as she fumbled to pick up her dress. He closed his eyes, picturing his lovely witch, recalling the succulent taste of her rich blood. Quintus dropped his fangs, the bitter hunger seizing his chest. His eyes flashed open, trained on the donor's neck.

"Leave it," he ordered, and she promptly dropped the garment. "Stay right there."

She slowly reclined back onto the sofa, her knees spread open, exposing her pussy. The sight of her laid out didn't as much as stir a twitch of blood to his dick, but her pulse fueled his hunger. He reached for her, bringing his lips to her neck. "Just relax."

As his fangs sliced into her skin, he attempted to ignore the sound of her moaning in ecstasy. He gorged on the tasteless fluid, his body regenerating itself with the healing essence. Quintus lapped at the wounds, racing to finish. Her hand wrapped around his wrist, bringing his fingers to her fleshy breast. The scent of her arousal filled the room and as his eyes opened, she writhed in orgasm beneath him.

The high-pitched sound of her cries for more were drowned out as Quintus sensed his witch. His eyes flashed to meet Gabriella's. Her jealousy flared over him like fire, and quickly shut off, as if she commanded her emotions with a spigot.

"I need to feed," he explained, his voice calm as he concealed his rage. *Where the hell is Viktor?* How did she get into his office without him hearing?

"I…I…we were just…" Gabriella stared at the woman who lay beneath him. With her legs spread wide open, the donor fingered herself, still reeling from her climax. "I should have never been with you. I've got to get out of here."

Quintus stood, and strode toward her. His gaze painted

over her body, noting she'd dressed in his clothing. Her figure swam in a button-down shirt, a pair of boxer briefs peeking through the bottom. "This is not how it appears."

"No, I think it is. I don't know what I was thinking…" Gabriella shook her head, and stared at the donor. "Whatever. You're a vampire. I should have known you were like all the rest. Go ahead, fuck her. I'll find someone else to save me. I need an ancient one. It doesn't have to be you. I'll ask Viktor."

Jealousy tore through him at the mention of his brother. He materialized to her, coming within inches of her skin. He dropped his fangs and hissed. She bravely faced him, the pounding beat of her heart echoing in his ears.

"I told you I'd help you. Not Viktor. This." His eyes went to the donor who struggled to pull her dress over her head. "She's nothing but food. I am vampire. I cannot change what I am."

"You could have…No. Forget it. I've never let a vampire bite me. Never will." Gabriella went to turn but he flashed behind her, blocking her from leaving.

"What's happening here is nothing," he said, his voice raised.

"Are you for real? Um, yeah. I'm pretty sure she just came all over your couch. And you know what? It doesn't matter. Whatever we just did upstairs…" Her cheeks turned red and she shook her head. "Whatever. It doesn't matter. You still want to help me? Fine, but don't ever touch me again."

"You do not wear jealousy well, bella."

"Stop calling me that. My name is Gabriella. And if you had wanted to eat…ah Goddess, it really doesn't matter. I'm the one who saved you, so fine, you think you owe me? Then just help me. I just can't. I just thought that you…and me…I told you things…"

"Things are not always how they appear. You will understand this one day."

"Viktor was right about something. I need to eat. I'll take my food upstairs. And then I'm getting out of here. You can help or not. I don't care."

Quintus didn't stop her from leaving his office. As she brushed by him and her arm grazed his, guilt weighed heavily upon him. She deliberately kept her emotions open to him. The pain emanated from her, pulsing through him like poison.

He blew out a breath, and tore off his t-shirt, desperate to eradicate the scent of the donor from his nostrils. "Viktor!"

His brother immediately materialized in front of him. "What's up?"

"What the fuck? I told you to feed Gabby. And she was just in here."

"My bad. I needed to flash for a sec. Ya know I got my own shit. But I did feed her. As soon as you left, she came down to the kitchen."

"What the fuck could be more important than my witch?" he growled, angry with both himself and Viktor.

"There's someone I know. She's uh…she's in trouble. I'm helping her with something. And before you ask, she's got nothin' to do with New Orleans. Or your witch. I was only gone for a few minutes. Gabby was fine. It's not like I've got to watch her put the spoon in her mouth."

"Gabriella."

"Gabby," he challenged with a stare, "is well guarded in here. This place is like a fucking prison."

"She's vulnerable and in danger. She's my responsibility."

"She's a witch. She's trouble."

"She's mine." As the words left his lips, Quintus sucked a deep breath at the realization of his connection to her.

"Possessive, brother. You don't normally become this way with women."

"It's her blood. I told you of its power."

"If you say so. But you know this could be something else." A corner of his lips raised in a sly smile.

"Don't say it. Because it's not so. Her blood incites this attraction. I owe her my life. That is all. I need to make a few calls and then..." Quintus stilled, listening for movement. The deafening silence throughout the house confirmed his fear. "Do you feel it?"

"Your wards...how would she have..." A noise sounded from above and they both looked toward the ceiling.

"My bedroom. She must have picked up some of the power in its wards."

"Perhaps a spell to hide her heartbeat."

"No. She's gone." Quintus clenched his fists, enraged she'd escaped. His sweet little witch was clever but he'd track her within minutes. Her punishment would be swift and sweet, and in the dark recesses of his mind, he reveled in the chase.

Chapter Four

"I'm so stupid. So fucking stupid." Gabriella's thoughts raced as she tore down the sidewalk.

Escaping his home had been a serendipitous surprise. She'd always known of the mystical power that thrived within her blood. She'd toyed with the idea for months, suspecting if her blood could heal, it, too, could destroy. Using her fingernail to prick her wrist, she'd drawn blood and let it drip onto her hands. With her palms on the French doors, she'd released her energy, ripe with jealousy and hate, inciting the destruction. Safety glass shattered into bits onto the balcony. She'd carefully navigated the tiles, and hoisted herself over the railing and down the pole to the street.

Spotting a familiar building in the French Quarter, she took off running and attempted to orient herself. As she rounded the corner, she tripped over a broken brick in the sidewalk and tumbled to the ground. Her hands scraped the pavement, its rough texture shredding her palms. Waves of shock and pain rolled through her as she shoved to her feet.

She struggled to run, smearing her bloodied palms across her shirt.

Gabriella gasped for breath, clinging to the stitch in her side. *Where am I?* She ducked into an alleyway. With her back against the cold brick wall, she doubled over and heaved for breath. She lifted her gaze and spied the old apothecary. Two more blocks and she'd be at her hotel.

Self-doubt threaded through her mind, tears filling her eyes. Finding Quintus with the blood whore had been like a knife to her gut. Even after he'd callously left her in the bedroom, she'd thought he'd been interested in her. It wasn't rational, she knew. A man like him probably enjoyed a different woman every night, but there was just something about his erotic touch that woke her heart. Lying in his arms, his lips on hers, the embers of arousal had been stoked. With the exception of a one night stand here and there, she'd never indulged in carnal desires. On the run, she couldn't afford to get attached to anyone.

He's a vampire. What were you thinking? She blew out a breath and wiped the tears from her eyes. Regret boiled in her stomach. Impulsive and fueled by jealousy, she'd escaped with no plan. Logic told her she should have stayed but seeing him with the donor pushed her over the edge. *I shouldn't have left. He's the only one who can help me.* She'd never be safe unless they worked together to destroy the coven.

It's going to be okay. Just keep moving, she told herself. She'd collect her meager belongings, deliver blood to Ramiel, and return to Quintus. If she was lucky, she'd escape New Orleans before the coven arrived.

The wind whistled, and she raised her face to the dark sky. An icy raindrop stung her forehead, and she wiped it away with her hand. Thunder rumbled in the distance and she took off running towards her home.

Gabriella stepped out of the shower and screamed as a cockroach the size of a small dog scurried across the room. She loathed this dump, but the seedy hotel studio apartment, tucked into the corner of a courtyard, had been the best she'd been able to afford. Gabriella had given up dreams of a normal life long ago. This was the reality she'd come to accept.

She quickly dried herself with a towel and stepped into her panties. Gabriella snapped on a bra and slung a black t-shirt over her head and reached for her jeans. With a glance to the clock, she realized she'd been gone for at least twenty minutes and she suspected Quintus would come looking for her.

Reaching for her drawstring backpack, she tugged it open. Her chest tightened in a sentimental knot as she looked to her desk. Scattered spells on shreds of cocktail napkins littered its surface. A brass locket lay curled at the base of a lamp. She brushed her fingers over its embossed surface. As she'd done a hundred times, she picked open the brass heart with her fingernail, revealing the picture of her mother and father. They sat on the sea rocks, her mother smiling as her father placed a kiss to her cheek. When she'd been ten, it had been a secret gift. No one could see it or know the truth. Mama always told her she wanted her to remember the love from which she'd been created.

Gabriella closed it and brought it to her lips. Too afraid she'd lose the memory, she slipped it into an inside pocket and zipped it shut. Gabriella reached for her spell book and stuffed the torn papers inside it. Old and new spells, they all served a purpose. One to levitate objects. One to bring love to a friend. One to change the color of her hair. Although she didn't know how to use each one, she'd collected them like memories, with the possibility that someday she'd learn to perfect her imperfect craft.

Gabriella's power waned as the full moon approached, her beast demanding to shift and renew her magick. After gathering one last scrap of paper, she reached for the small stuffed animal she'd been carrying around since she was five years old. The tattered kitten was the closest thing she'd ever allowed herself to have as a pet. Although the high priestess was bestowed a companion, it was forbidden for others to own or communicate with animals.

Gabriella tossed the childhood toy into her bag along with her wallet and cell phone, and cinched it shut. She considered taking clothes but didn't have time to start packing her things. If she had to wash her underwear in the bathroom for the next week she was prepared for what she had to do.

Time had run out. Thunder rumbled outside, and she startled. The southern storms often grew violent, but as the familiar sound of hail pinging the roof began, she grabbed her hoodie and headed toward the door. As she flung it open, her breath caught at the sight of the dominant vampire, his dark brown eyes penetrating hers.

"I...I had to get my stuff," she stammered. Gabriella had suspected he'd come for her, but hadn't anticipated the sheer anger that poured off him like the rain. Soaked, his black t-shirt clung to his body, revealing every contour of his muscular chest.

"What the hell do you think you're doing?" he growled, scanning the shabby interior of her room.

"I told you...it's just...you and that girl." *Jesus Gabby, get it together.* She vacillated between fear and arousal as he reached for her wrist.

"How the hell am I supposed to protect you if you just take off on me? You're going to get yourself killed before I have a chance to help you."

"You were busy. Eating." Her tone dripped with sarcasm and she hated herself for the jealousy that bubbled in her chest.

"You." Quintus tugged her toward him. Closing the gap, he stepped forward. He towered above her but kept his eyes locked on hers.

Gabriella gasped, not out of fear but desire, her breasts brushing his chest. "I...I..." Words failed her as he leaned his head toward hers.

"Don't leave again. Do you understand?"

"You can't tell me what to do. I'm not a child." Gabriella's voice wavered, her mind demanding she speak.

As his arm went around her waist, drawing him toward her, her heart pounded. The cold rain pelted her face, droplets clinging to her eyelashes.

"Do. Not. Leave," he repeated, his tone firm. With his gaze upon hers, Quintus brought his lips within inches of hers.

"Why are you doing this? I'm nothing to you." The warmth of his body on hers flared her arousal.

"Si, bella. You're under my protection. You're mine."

As his lips crushed onto hers, excitement rushed through her body. She molded into his embrace, returning his searing kiss, and moaned as he pulled away, his lips still touching hers as he spoke.

"We'll finish this later, pet." Quintus straightened, his head snapping toward the street. "The magick grows thick."

"We've got to go somewhere safe. They must know I'm in New Orleans by now. Ramiel…"

"We're going back to my house and then New York," he told her.

"New York? Quintus, I can't go to…"

Gabriella sucked a breath as they dematerialized. Her knees buckled as he settled her into his kitchen. The faint scent of smoke drifted in the air and she coughed.

"Is something burning? I smell it. What have they done?" *The coven.* They'd burn her to ash like they'd done to her parents.

Quintus sniffed the air, his fangs dropping. "Nothing's burning in here. It's just a thunderstorm, bella. It's possible it hit a tree." He wrapped his arms around her, tugging her close.

"They're here," she whispered. Dark magick swept over her like a thousand centipedes crawling on her skin. She shivered, and coughed into her sleeve.

"Where the fuck is Viktor?"

"I'm here, dear brother." Viktor brushed a fleck of dust off his black tailored shirt.

"Where have you been?" Quintus asked.

"I keep telling you we're having some problems in New York. The others, they look for your guidance. I need you to get back now. Shit is going down at the club."

"Very well. New York it is. The vampires will get what they need." Quintus turned to Gabriella. "I'm sorry but we've got to go now. You're coming with me."

"New York? I just told you I can't go to New York. I think what I need is in New Orleans. I picked up some spells." Gabriella wrenched out of his grip and shoved her hand inside her bag, fumbling for the small book. Psychics and rogue witches had given her various spells over the years; some she'd tried to no avail. A strong arm wrapped around her shoulder and panic tore through her body. "No...Quintus. I can't go to New York... you don't understand..."

No. No. No. What is he doing? Gabriella screamed as she landed on the black velvet sofa. Tiny lights flickered through her blurred vision. A hand reached for her and she screamed, "Get away from me!"

"Gabriella, you're okay."

"What is wrong with your witch?" Viktor asked, annoyance in his tone.

"She's not all witch. I told you she's a hybrid. Gather the others," Quintus ordered.

"I'm not his witch," Gabriella spat, brushing his hand out of the way. How could he have taken them out of New Orleans? She was convinced she needed something for the spell, something that could only be found in the Big Easy. "Let me go. I have to go back."

"I'm afraid you aren't going anywhere right now. Stay here in my office. I'll be back in a few minutes and we'll go home."

"I have no home. Where are we anyway?" She scanned the gothic room, taking note of a faceless figure in the corner, bronzed bands stacked on its armor, its head topped with a domed hat. The statue held a long metal spear in its hand as if it were readying for war. Fixated on the walls, her mouth gaped as she caught sight of an array of axes, swords, knives, sickles and clubs. Although in shock, she forced her voice, speaking slowly. "What is this place?"

"This is my office," he told her, shoving to his feet. "Rest here."

"Rad, isn't it?" Viktor ran his finger over the blade of a sword.

Gabriella's stomach rolled at the sight of all the ancient weapons. Their dark energies vibrated throughout the room. "New Orleans. Take me back now."

"I'm afraid that's not possible. I need to deal with some business. We'll discuss your coven sisters later."

"They're not my family," she interrupted. Her hands gripped the arms of the sofa, and she sucked a breath in an attempt to regain her equilibrium. "I tried to warn you."

"I have a city to run. You aren't the only one with witch problems. The coven up here is causing conflict. I'm expected at an event tomorrow night. While I have every intention of helping you, I have things here I need to deal with. I'm not entertaining a war in my town."

"Where are you going?" Gabriella's head spun as he spoke. An underlying beat bled into the room and her eyes went to a huge wooden door.

"Don't even think about it. You're not leaving."

"You can't keep me here." Her fingernails dug into the fabric of the sofa as she attempted to stand but dizziness overcame her, forcing her to rest again.

"I'm sorry, Gabby, but I most certainly can." Quintus crossed the room to an intricately carved mahogany armoire and opened the door.

As he stripped off his wet t-shirt and tossed it onto the floor, Gabriella struggled not to stare at his muscular chest. *What is he doing?* She stole a glance at his ripped abs which left her pulse racing. She quickly averted her gaze, struggling to ignore her burning attraction to the vampire.

"You're wet. While I'm gone, you can change into one of my shirts if you want. I'll keep a guard at the door. You'll be safe in here." Quintus reached for a tailored shirt and slipped it on, buttoning it as he spoke.

"I can't stay in here. I hear music. Where is this place? Where are we?"

"New York, of course."

"Of course," she repeated, her deflated tone matching her expression.

Quintus stood in front of a rectangular wall mirror. Looking into the reflection, he glanced at his brother. "I'll take care of your coven issue, but first I must attend to my own. We have…"

"Complications." Viktor completed his sentence and turned the doorknob.

"Yes. My followers. Vampires. They're extremely dangerous should they be left unattended for too long. And I have been gone for quite a long time." Quintus looked back into the mirror, and finger-combed his hair.

"I'll meet you out there. Liam can keep watch." Viktor swung open the door, and music blared. As it slammed shut, the din dialed back to the beat of a bass.

"This is Sekhmet," Quintus offered.

"Like the goddess?" She sighed and shook off the confusion.

"Si, you know of her? Although she wasn't vampire, she thirsted for blood. I think of this place as a sanctuary for the wild souls that inhabit Manhattan. Sekhmet is more of a playground."

"You live here?" Gabriella ran her palm over the cold stone wall.

"Occasionally I sleep here but it's not my main place."

A dark magick buzzed under her hand, and she contemplated how hard it would be for her to conjure an escape spell. "Something about this is different. Why are there no windows?"

"We're underground. The earth. It rejuvenates us." Quintus blew out a breath and turned to face her. "This place is special. But it's also very dangerous. These vampires are lethal. It's not safe for you to be out in the open."

"What kind of vampire are you?" Her heart pounded in her chest as her eyes drifted over the sexy and charismatic vampire. Every bit as attractive dressed in a shirt and jeans, he dripped with sex. *Lust. Fear. Desire.* A kaleidoscope of emotions flashed through her mind, and she settled on anger in an attempt to focus.

"Tonight, I need to take control. Set things straight. There is business that must be attended to."

"And what about me?" Gabriella trembled as she managed to stand steadily onto her feet. "We have business."

"You." Quintus crossed the room, towering over her. "You are not business. You are...mine."

"But..." Her breath escaped her lungs as he closed the distance.

"Do not leave. I'll be back."

As she placed her palms to his chest, he disappeared underneath her fingertips, and her stomach dropped in disappointment. *Fuck this. Does he seriously think I'm going to stay in his office, like a dog in a cage waiting on its master? Hell no.*

Gabriella put her hand on the wall. The energy she'd felt along the surface was strong but porous. She suspected other supernaturals, and perhaps humans for feeding were allowed into the club. If she simply walked out the door, he'd sense the loss of her presence. But if he were distracted, perhaps she'd find a way to leave, disappear into New York City and find her way back to New Orleans. Gabriella's magick waned but she suspected she had enough power to pass the guards. If there was one thing she was good at, it was hiding.

Gabriella tore her sodden shirt over her head and threw it on the sofa. She reached into the armoire and selected one of his shirts. After she shoved her arms through its sleeves, she sniffed the collar. *Quintus.* A fresh clean scent held a touch of his cologne, and memories of his embrace. Confusion swept through her. Domineering and lethal, he'd surely killed many in his lifetime, yet her attraction to the vampire was inexplicable and undeniable.

Her beast recognized him, and each time in his presence, she demanded more. Tomorrow night, she'd shift and bathe in the light of a full moon, renewing her magick. He'd discover her secret, and see her for the impure mongrel she truly was.

A simple immobilization spell paralyzed the fledgling vampire who guarded the office. Gabriella's damp jeans clung to her thighs as she navigated the dimly lit hallway. Through a curtain of fringe, lights flashed to the throbbing music. As she approached the iridescent silk fabric that dangled from the ceiling, her pulse raced. She sniffed the blood-tinged air, her beast stirring at the sound of a human's scream. Gabriella resisted the urge to intervene, aware whatever was happening might be consensual.

It wasn't as if she hadn't been in a club before, she knew

the deal. *Keep quiet, fly under the radar.* She'd deliver her blood. Get in and get out. The screams haunted her dreams. The humans, naked and desperate, begging for release, for the addictive orgasm only the vampire could bring.

As she stepped through the curtain, she sucked a breath, the dank air curling around her body. Gabriella summoned enough magick to flick on her glamour; a raven-haired grunge chick blended into the abyss of darkness. In the corner, a tall bearded vampire carefully tied a blonde to a hook that dangled from the ceiling. The naked girl smiled, her bare feet precariously perched on a platinum ottoman. While a small crowd watched, a heavily tattooed man ran his hand in between her legs, driving his fingers deep inside her. She screamed in pleasure as his teeth sunk into the soft flesh of her belly.

Gabriella turned away, and made her way through the sea of people. Their energies, consistent with vampires, were intermingled with the familiar hum of humans. As she drew closer to what she'd thought was the entrance, she realized it was another room. She glanced up to the limestone ceiling. A metallic sculpture, lined with miniature lights, was embedded into the stone. The distinctive sound of violins harmonized with the heavy metal music and as she passed into an arched tunnel, the string instruments grew louder. Her eyes drifted to a stage where a female string quartet played. The musicians, dressed in black satin tuxedos, appeared to be in trance, their eyes closed and bodies in motion with the melody.

Gabriella gingerly made her way toward the music,

scanning the room. Quintus' voice registered before she saw him. With a commanding tone, a slight Italian accent blended over his words. His face tightened with disconcertion as he spoke to a woman. Dressed in a scarlet leather corset and miniskirt, the striking female lowered her eyes in submission. Her blonde locks were pulled tight into a ponytail, and Gabriella noted the desire in her gaze as she shifted her hip and flipped her hair, giving Quintus a flirtatious smile.

Gabriella attempted to tamp down the jealousy that flared in her chest. *Breathe, Gabby.* As she stepped forward, Quintus' gaze snapped to her darkened corner. She ducked behind a portly man who was very much involved in a political discussion, touting statistics over the lilt of the cello's smooth notes.

She backed against a pillar, her head resting on the cold stone. A bearded vampire passed, baring his fangs with a nod. She cringed as she glanced across the room, spying several human donors who lay on a round bed. They slept on bloodstained satin sheets, their nude bodies on display.

Gabriella summoned her courage and poked her head around the piling. *Where is Quintus?* Her heart pounded as a deafening crescendo filled the arena. The piece ended, and the musicians went limp, their faces devoid of expression. Applause roared in response.

Gabriella jumped, his warm breath on her ear before she ever heard his words. "Fireworks Rejoice."

"Quintus." She sighed, closing her eyes as his arm circled her waist.

"Fireworks Rejoice. Handel," he offered.

"What?" Her fear was replaced by arousal at the brush of his lips on her shoulder.

"The music."

"It was…" She struggled to find the words that eluded her.

"You should be afraid, my lovely little witch."

"I'm sorry…" She attempted to turn around but he kept a firm hand on her waist, his erection prodding at her back.

"These creatures. They struggle to hold onto their humanity. Like the humans they feed off of, the war of good and evil rages in their souls. But make no mistake, they are the bold ones who enter my club. They are the ones who seek power. The influencers of the masses." He released her waist and spun her to face him. His fingers trailed down her temple to under her chin. "I ordered you to stay in my office. And while I'm impressed with your ability to incapacitate Liam, I'm afraid you really are going to have to learn to obey my orders. Perhaps the best lesson is experience."

"What do you mean?"

"Rules exist for a good reason. In this realm, you're only as safe as I say you are. But you think you know best? Let's test it, shall we?" Quintus gave a sly smile as he brought his fingers to his lips. A shill whistle pierced through the space, all conversations ceasing to silence.

Chills danced over Gabriella's skin as the lights lifted and curious eyes drifted her way. Her magick tingled within her chest and she struggled to keep it in check as a well-dressed female whipped her head around, flashing her fangs.

"This, my friends, is a witch," Quintus declared, nodding towards Gabriella. He snapped his fingers and a young woman dressed in a white transparent bodysuit appeared in front of him.

As his palm settled on her shoulder and the girl gave a sigh, Gabriella's stomach tightened. *Why is he doing this? A fucking test? Because I disobeyed his instruction?* The icy stares of the patrons bored through her chest, and she balled her fingers into fists in response.

"Witches. They're difficult. Humans on the other hand," he paused and dragged his palm over the woman's chin and she bared her neck, "we exercise control over. They listen. On your knees, pet."

Gabriella's breath caught as the woman dropped obediently to the floor, her hands brushing his feet. As if in a trance, she hummed in pleasure as he stroked her collarbone with the pad of his forefinger. As the female's hands traveled up his shins onto his thigh, Gabriella gave a low growl.

Mine. Her breath quickened, the beast clawing at her psyche. She envisioned her beautiful black animal lunging at the female, tearing at her flesh. Gabriella suppressed the urge to shift and bit her lip, distracting herself with the pain. Her body tingled, the magick bursting from her skin. *Don't shift. Don't use magick. Keep it together.*

Quintus gave a laugh, his eyes trained on her the entire time. "Do you see? This witch, she's harmless to us."

"The others! They're planning to attack," a voice called from the darkness.

Gabriella froze, sensing movement behind her. Quintus calmed her beast with his swift response.

"You, Ravi. Keep quiet with your thoughts. I've warned you and the others more than once. Disobedience will have consequences." Quintus' eyebrows narrowed in annoyance at the antagonistic vampire's outburst.

No, no, no, she silently repeated, the odor of stale cigarettes swirling into her nostrils as the vampire stalked behind her. Her beast growled, warning him away but she lost focus as her eyes were drawn to the girl on her knees, who began tearing at her clothing, revealing her bare breasts.

"How would you know what's happening, Quintus? You've been in New Orleans. California. While you've been gone the witches grow stronger. And now," Ravi paused, nodding toward Gabriella, "you've brought a witch to your club. It makes me wonder. Perhaps she has a spell on our fearless leader."

"The next word you speak will be your last," Quintus promised, his face tense with ire.

"This witch here. How do we know she isn't working with the others?" Ravi baited.

Gabriella gasped as the vampire rushed her from behind, his strong grubby fingers clasped on her shoulder. Quintus lunged at Ravi, shoving him away from her. As she tumbled toward the ground, her fall was broken by a stranger. Out of her peripheral vision she caught sight of Quintus, his hands wrapped around the vampire's neck. Before Ravi had a chance to speak, Quintus crushed his trachea. Droplets of blood sprayed onto her face as his head rolled across the floor. Terrified, Gabriella struggled to breathe as Quintus' eyes burned red, glaring at the others.

"Shh, little one. My brother must settle things," she heard Viktor tell her, his voice soft with concern. He took her by the hand, and gently helped her to her feet.

Paralyzed by the violence, Gabriella took a heaving breath, the taste of blood-tinged air on her tongue. Gooseflesh surfaced on her arms, the magick building a charge beneath the surface of her skin.

"This is a lesson to all of you here tonight. Go tell your children. Your friends. This isn't a democracy. New York is mine and mine alone now. Should you decide to challenge me, there will be consequences." He glanced to Gabriella who lay sheltered in Viktor's arms and quickly refocused his attention on the crowd. "Tomorrow night, the Arronick witches are holding their solstice ball. Those who have been invited to attend will do so with caution and respect. Should they be colluding with other covens, I will deal with them. But this witch…" Gabriella's heart pounded against her ribs as he reached for her.

Gently he pried her from Viktor's arms and cradled her into his embrace. *What is this man?* Fear and arousal threaded through her, unable to process what she'd witnessed in his world. Terrified, she blinked up at him, clutching his bloodied shirt. His penetrating gaze held her captive.

"This witch," he repeated, "she's mine. If anyone touches her, they're dead."

Mine. Gabriella's head spun with the words that claimed

her soul. She screwed her eyes tight as the dizzying portal opened, darkness claiming her as they dematerialized into nothingness.

·❧· *Chapter Five* ·❧·

"Don't even give me that fucking look," Quintus snarled, reaching for a bottle of one-hundred-year-old scotch. "Ravi's had it coming for months."

"No judgement, man. I'm just saying, you sort of…no, yeah, you ripped off the dude's head. Now, call me crazy but that's not the exact kind of thing women go for." Viktor crossed the room to the bar and slung his leather jacket onto the sofa. "I like a good bloodbath as much as the next guy but…"

"If she's going to be in my world, she's got to accept me for what I am. And this city, you know there is no other way."

"Tame the savages?"

"This world. Our world. Eat or be eaten. It's not just a saying. Don't play like you don't know this." He uncorked the bottle and spilled the liquor into the glasses. After sliding the drink across the granite, he gave a sigh and raised the rim to his lips. "Ravi. He's been stirring on the others for a long time. Even a small uprising is enough to cause chaos.

I've got enough shit on my plate right now."

"But the witches…"

"You and I know they can be as evil as the demons. But our coven here? We haven't had that many issues. Sure we've had a killing every now and then." He shrugged and shook his head. "This is the city after all. Can't be avoided."

"Perhaps you're right."

"I'll know better tomorrow night. The one thing Ravi got right is that I've spent too much time away from New York." Quintus stared down at his blood-spattered t-shirt and took a deep swig. "Gabriella. She's strong. She'll get over what happened. Ravi would have killed her."

"The dude doesn't think twice about killing when he gets pissed." Viktor raised the glass to his lips.

"Gabriella's special," Quintus said, his gaze meeting his brother's.

"She's a witch." Viktor shrugged with a roll of his eyes. "Nothing special about that. Ravi still would have killed her. She was frozen like a deer in the headlights. You saw her."

"I don't know about that. I felt her. She was readying to attack him. I saw the flicker in her eyes tonight. She was fighting it."

"Fighting what?"

"She's a shifter."

"No way, bro. If she'd been wolf, there would have been a serious throw down when you brought Daisy on stage. That human is like a cat in heat…can't keep her legs shut. She's totally into you. I could see your little witch didn't like it, but if she was a wolf? Hey, wolves don't mess around. And Ravi? It'd be likely she'd shift before he had a chance to go for her."

"I know her. I'm telling you, she was going to shift. What she shifts into is an entirely different question."

"I don't get it. Why not just tell you what she is?"

"I don't know. She's scared. It doesn't matter to me what she is. She could be a wolf. Any kind of shifter, really. This coven. It killed her only parent and is after her. She's been on the run since she was a kid. She keeps telling me I need to help her find something for a spell, but I don't know. I don't think she really knows how to stop them. Either way, I'm going to put an end to it."

"Interesting you bring up wolves, being that they're the possessive types, because I noticed…" Viktor gave a laugh, his eyes meeting Quintus'. "It's, uh, you kind of sounded pretty possessive back there yourself. You do realize you claimed her in front of everyone?"

"Of course I did." Quintus' expression remained impassive, recalling his words. *Mine.* He'd deliberately declared his intention, yet as he spoke, he sensed there was more to their connection. He could have easily let her go at any time, he reasoned, but there was something about her taste, her smile. *Fuck.* He grimaced, displeased with his growing attachment to his witch.

"Of course you did? That's all you've got to say?"

"Don't be an asshole," Quintus growled, tearing off his shirt.

"Someone catch feelings?"

"Correct that. Don't be more of an asshole than you already are." Quintus slung back his scotch, a smooth burn coating his throat.

"I think there's a cure for that. You might want to go fuck little Daisy. Get it out of your system."

"Fuck off."

"I am right about this. The best way to shake her from your system and get over her is to get under someone else."

"I'm an asshole for leaving her upstairs."

"Yeah about that. I was kind of surprised myself."

"Every time I flash her. She's out of it."

"But she's a witch."

"I'm telling ya. It's the shifter in her. That's why she doesn't do well."

"Where'd you put her?"

"I put her onto the sofa. I was hoping she'd sleep it off."

Viktor laughed and reached for the bottle. "This is going to be good."

Quintus blew out a breath and set down his empty glass. "What?"

"Hmm…" Viktor gave a closed smile, raising an eyebrow at his brother.

"Just fucking say it. I've gotta get upstairs." Quintus glanced down to his bloodied jeans.

"You left her upstairs? Covered in blood? Then come down here for a stiff one?" Viktor took a swig of his drink and exhaled loudly.

"What's your problem?" A sickening guilt twisted in his stomach. His brother wouldn't let it go, whereas he'd prefer to bury his feelings where they belonged, in a pit of indifference. The flicker of delight in Viktor's eyes told him he'd dredge the baby up no matter how deep he'd hidden it.

"This little creature has you out of sorts."

"No shit. I'm indebted to her," Quintus replied. It had been the perfect excuse for keeping her in his life.

"You like her."

"Well, yeah. I've liked many people."

"She's a beautiful woman."

"I've liked many women. Jesus Christ, Viktor. I don't have time for this shit. I've gotta go."

"Ah, but a choice, my dear brother. You chose to be indebted."

"She saved my ass. It happens."

"You could have given her money. That you do not lack," Viktor challenged.

"Money for my life? Really? Since when have I ever…"

"Since when has anyone ever saved your life?"

Quintus glared at Viktor. *Only once.* As a new vampire his brother had saved his life from their master, and he'd since saved him tenfold.

"So you see this happenstance isn't mere serendipity. You've made a choice to protect her. You've declared her as yours."

"I already told you. It was for her protection," Quintus insisted.

"Was it now?" Viktor laughed, shaking his head. "So easily you fool the others, making them believe a lie. Your powers are impressive, indeed. But you never could lie to me."

"I haven't lied." *Stretched the truth perhaps.* It was true that Viktor was impervious to his ability to make others see as he wished. He was careful in his use of the power, aware it drained his magick.

"Did you consider it's possible you might bond with her? You are drawn to her, after all. It would be unusual. She's not even human, but…"

"I'm not having this conversation." Quintus turned his back to leave. Her blood had been intoxicating but he'd reasoned it was her magick.

"You need to taste her," Viktor suggested.

"I've already tasted her." *And I want her more than ever.* Quintus knew the truth, but denied it to himself.

"Bite her. It's the only way," Viktor encouraged.

"I'm done talking. You're welcome to stay. We'll discuss a game plan for the ball tomorrow."

"You could be her mate. You won't be able to resist forever, Quint. The Goddess, she always gets her way," he called out, a rumble of laughter following.

"Night, V." Quintus strode out of the living room and quickly ascended the steps. Although he'd refused to engage, Viktor's comments plowed through his mind.

It was rare to bond with a witch. Even rarer to do so with a shifter. Yet long ago, he'd discovered that it was indeed possible. *No, this isn't happening again.*

As he made his way to the bedroom, he slowed at the door. He stood still with his eyes closed, sensing her. *Fear.*

Confusion. Arousal. He smiled, aware she'd deliberately remained open despite what he'd done at the club.

When Ravi had touched Gabriella, he'd gone feral. Tearing off his head was nothing compared to the slow torture he'd have inflicted had she not been watching. It had been a lesson to the others. No one could have her, touch her…no one but him.

The possibility that there was another creature on this earth that belonged to him terrified Quintus. The only other woman he'd ever loved was dead. Yet his brother's advice was sound. *Taste her*, his instinct agreed. It was the only way.

Her fiery eyes lifted to meet his as he strode into the room. Quintus slowed, taking in the sight of his fragile witch. Slumped over, she'd partially undressed, her bloodied clothes piled next to her feet. A wave of overwhelming sadness washed over him as she revealed her emotions.

"Gabriella."

"Quintus," she whispered.

"Are you okay, bella?" He approached slowly as if she were an injured animal.

"Okay?" She gave a small laugh, shaking her head. "That place."

"I told you to stay in my office. You don't listen." He took a deep breath and reined back his temper. When she'd ignored his direction, he'd sought to teach her a lesson. "What happened in the club…"

"You…you tore off his head. I…It's not like I didn't know what vampires do. I've been in clubs…"

"I'll protect you with my life, but this is who I am. I warned you. I told you stay…"

"Stay? I'm not a dog. I can take care of myself. I just…" Her words trailed off as tears sprang to her eyes. "Look. You don't need to help me. I'll figure it out. I need to do a spell before they find me."

"I'm not going anywhere." Anger rolled through him at the thought of her leaving.

"I've got some spells. I just need a few days to figure it out. I could go to others. No, no, no I've got this…" She went to reach for her clothes, and he knelt, placing his hand gently on her wrist.

"Gabriella," he said, his voice soft. "You've got to trust me. No more running. No more lies."

"How am I supposed to trust you? You keep flashing me anywhere you want. I get sick. Then you leave me alone. That woman in the club…" She sighed.

"You can trust me because I haven't left you. Because I know what's best…" As the words left his lips, he questioned his approach. He sighed, running the pad of his thumb over her wrist. "Gabby. I'm vampire. The donors…"

"Women…"

"Yes, the ones you've seen. I must have blood. This is my existence. There is no other way." He'd held onto his humanity with a thread some days, but always made a point to remember what being human was like. "I love to cook. Do you know why?"

"What?"

"I cook because it reminds me that once upon a time I was human. I wasn't born into magick like you. You're so close to being human but you aren't. You're a magical creature, walking among them as if you were." Quintus lifted her hand in his, bringing her to her feet. He closed the distance, his hand drifting to her cheek. "The day I turned, I had no choice but to feed."

"That girl in the club. You feed from her?"

"Daisy? No, she's not my type."

"But you want more?"

"Yes, I need to eat."

"Do you want my blood?"

Quintus gave a small laugh, unsure of how to respond to her question. He hungered for her blood with each moment he spent with her, yet he was becoming increasingly certain that if he bit her, he'd bond to her. "If that's something you want, there's no going back, sweet bella."

"What is this between us?" she whispered, her eyes set on his.

"You have to trust me. There can be no other way."

"I've never let anyone bite me," she confessed. "None of them. My blood. I've sold it but I've never…"

"What are you, Gabriella?" Quintus had to know her secrets if he was to help her.

His question was answered by silence.

"I told you you can trust me. But if I'm going to help you…"

"Please…you won't want me if you know."

"I already want you," he told her.

"No, you…"

Quintus brushed his lips to hers, silencing her protest. He opened his mind, sending his calming power through her. Reluctantly he broke the gentle kiss, his forehead resting upon hers.

"I promise I won't reveal you to others," he assured her.

"Tomorrow night I'll change," she admitted. "It happens on the full moon each month. My magick weakens as the month drags on but when I shift, it renews it."

"What are you?"

"Promise you won't leave me. Promise that you won't be repulsed."

"Jesus, Gabby. I'm not going anywhere."

"I'm a wolf." Tears rolled down her cheeks, and she turned her face away from him.

"Ah, lupine. But why? Why are you so ashamed?" Confusion danced in his mind at her response.

"My magick will never be pure. The coven will kill me, and I don't know. There's times when I doubt myself. I'm not like the others. I never will be."

"You're perfect, do you hear me? As for the coven, I'll never let them have you. I'll keep you safe as you shift. I'll talk to Jax."

"I've never run with another wolf. I have no pack. I always shift alone. I can't let anyone see me."

"You're wrong. Look at me, Gabriella." His fingers trailed under her chin, lifting it until she met his gaze. "You have me."

"I won't ever belong to anyone. I'm a wolf. Vampires. Wolves. It doesn't matter how I feel about you. I mean back at your house...we...I kind of liked it. I probably won't ever be able to mate, just so you know," she rambled.

"You have me. I'm not going anywhere," he repeated.

In silence he took her hand and led her to the bathroom. The urge to take her escalated and he resisted with all his will. The stench of the other vampires lingered on their skin. No other being would be in their minds when he made love to her.

This creature was far too important to him. Centuries had passed and he'd never bonded with another. For so long he'd thought he'd been cursed for choosing someone other than a human. Yet it was the blood of a hybrid wolf that had healed him, the one he'd been craving ever since he tasted her.

He didn't bother to turn on the lights as his hand reached for the spigot. Her mouth parted as if to say something and he shook his head no. No more arguments. No more talking. Tonight he'd make love to her, and tomorrow he'd help her disappear from the coven. He'd strike a deal with the witches he knew. They'd help her. He'd get her settled with Jax Chandler or Logan, finding her a home within a pack where she could mate.

He unbuttoned his pants and kicked them off, standing nude before her. Her fingers went to her bra, and Quintus reached around her back, easily unhooking it. As it fell to the floor, his eyes remained fixed on hers. She exhaled softly, allowing him to take the lead. Although he wasn't wolf, he'd demand her submission.

Steam rolled through the air as his palms drifted over her shoulders. They lingered briefly before trailing down her arms. As he settled his hands on her hips, he slid his fingers under the sides of her panties. In one swift pull, the fabric tore away, leaving her bare to him.

"Quintus." She backed into the hot spray, her gaze painting over his body.

"Si, bella. You're trouble." He took a step forward, looming over her fragile form.

"What do you want?" she whispered, water beading over her body.

"Something about you…your blood…it's special. That's true."

"So all you want is my blood?" Her defiant eyes met his.

"Your blood saved me. But something about you. Your spirit…" He placed his palm onto her chest. "This is the person I want to know."

"I…don't date. I don't…"

"Your disobedience will get you killed some day. You must learn to listen." Quintus kept his eyes locked on hers, brushing the back of his knuckles over her taut nipples. Blood rushed to his dick, and he breathed, restraining the urge to fuck her right then.

"I'm not a human. I've been on my own for a long time…you can't just expect me to take orders…"

"But that is the thing, little one, I do expect." He leaned toward her, his firm chest brushing her nipples. His lips teased over her collarbone and she sighed, her back flattening against the cool tiles. "I'll teach you. Is this what you want?"

"Quintus…it's not in my nature…"

"Ah, ah, ah." He sniffed her skin, taking in her delicious scent. "I disagree. You're wolf. Your submission will be mine."

"I…" she began to protest but instantly went silent as he dragged his tongue over her neck.

"Tell me you want this, Gabriella." Although he knew he'd just fed, her blood called to him, but he denied their true connection. There was no way the Goddess would send him a wolf. He'd fuck her out of his system, sating his hunger, he lied to himself.

"You and I…" Her fingers grazed his chest, reminding him that her wild nature was in need of taming.

"I'm going to fuck you right here. Tomorrow we'll figure out the rest." His palm drifted between her breasts and down onto her stomach.

"Quintus, please." As his fingers delved between her legs, she sighed, her head lolling back against the tiles.

"Tell me you want this." His dick went rock hard as he teased his fingers inside her slick sheath.

"I…that feels so…" Her fingers gripped his shoulders as he stroked inside her.

"But pet, if we do this, there will be no going back. I want to hear it now. Do you want this? Answer me or I'm going to walk away." It'd kill him but she needed to do as she was told. For as much power as she held, her impulsivity could get her killed.

"Yeah…I just…please, Quintus." Her hand moved to grip his shoulder.

"Say it," he pressed.

"Yes…I want you…I…" Gabriella panted as he withdrew.

The temptation to bite her mounted. *Fuck her first*, his gut told him. Once he tasted of her during sex, he'd forever be tortured if she didn't belong to him.

Lust twisted through him as his eyes lingered on hers. The emotion of what she might be to him was too much in the moment. He spun her around, shutting off his feelings. She moaned his name as he bent her forward, kneeing open her legs. He ran his hand down her slippery back, teasing his fingers over her bottom, spreading her cheeks open. A chill ran through him as he stroked his dick, his crown prodding her entrance.

"Keep your hands on the wall." As he eased inside her sensitive flesh, her magick danced through him and he gave a loud sigh.

"Quintus," she exhaled, pressing back onto him.

He withdrew and thrust inside her, wrapping his hand around her stomach. His other palm moved to her throat, and he fought the urge to come inside her.

What the fuck? Over a thousand years had gone by and he'd never felt so connected to someone. None of it made sense. The urge to taste her blood surged yet his mind warred against it. He laid his cheek upon her shoulder, his fangs dropping, itching to bite her. Careful not to draw blood, he glided the edges of his fangs over her skin. She moaned in response, her core contracting around his dick.

Don't bite her. Fuck her. Help her. Leave her be. A wolf,

she'll have a true mate and you're not it. He'd never been as conflicted in his entire life, his thirst mounting as he fucked her.

Quintus wrapped his hand around her neck, his little witch trusting him as he took control. *Fucking hell, she's submitting.* As the pad of his forefinger glided toward her mouth, his strength wavered as her lips sucked it.

"Please. You can bite me. Do it," she encouraged. Her tongue teased his finger as if it were his cock.

"Jesus Christ, Gabby." Quintus increased his pace, stroking in and out of her, his fangs burning to slice into her flesh.

"Please, do it. Ah Goddess...I can't stop...I'm...I'm coming," she screamed.

Quintus cursed, unable to control himself as his climax slammed into him. He struggled to rein in his primal urge, his fangs retreating as his lips kissed her shoulder. "Holy fuck...I..."

She panted, begging him to bite her as he gave a final thrust, but he restrained himself, refusing to do it. Her emotions plowed through him like a freight train, but as quickly as they'd rushed over him, they ended. Gabriella sealed off her thoughts and Quintus knew for certain he'd have to let her go. He couldn't bear to fall for a wolf whose mate would wait for her, or lose another woman like he'd lost Mao.

As he eased out of her, she softly moaned, averting her gaze. He pressed a kiss to her shoulder, words failing him in the moment.

"I need a minute," she whispered, turning her face into the spray.

Quintus backed out of the shower, reaching for a towel. The intimacy had smothered him, the space bringing air to his lungs. *Jesus fucking Christ, what have I done? I'm a selfish bastard.* The chaos of his thoughts would not settle. As he left the bathroom, he caught the sight of her chest rise in a subtle sob. He shook his head in disgust, aware he'd rejected her blood. *It was for her own good,* he told himself, yet the lie bored a hole in his gut.

Chapter Six

Gabriella shook with anger. Opening herself, being vulnerable to the vampire, emotionally, physically, had been a mistake. *Jesus, what kind of a fucking idiot am I?*

She breathed slowly, recalling how he'd made love to her. He hadn't even looked at her as he fucked her, let alone bit her. Yet he'd played her body like an instrument in a symphony with the magic of his lips and his hard-as-fuck cock stroking every inch of her pussy. She'd sensed the raw attraction threading through his psyche but he'd abruptly shut down, never tasting what she'd offered.

Gabriella shook her head and leaned back into the shower, her body still sizzling from the mind-numbing orgasm. The droplets teased her taut nipples, ripe with desire. Her traitorous body yearned for the vampire, who'd denied her.

Impure. Inbred. The taunts ran through her mind and she shoved them aside, reminding herself that Quintus wasn't the coven. He was vampire, which perhaps, made it worse. Her blood had been good enough to save him yet now that he knew she was wolf, he wouldn't drink from her.

Gabriella's chest ached, recalling how she'd begged him to bite her. The refusal had been a slap in the face. Her wolf had nearly submitted, crawling to the forefront of her psyche. Convinced the dominant vampire had somehow played with her mind, she attempted to cut off her emotions and ignore the hunger, but the beast stirred, howling, demanding it be let loose.

For so long, she'd restrained her wolf, keeping it at bay. Ashamed of her lupine blood, she'd only shifted on the full moon, aware her magick would falter if she didn't. But tonight, the wolf had grown increasingly restless. She'd always maintained control, but making love to Quintus had awakened her feral instincts. She craved his touch, ravenous for the man who'd resisted her blood.

Humiliation and frustration boiled in her gut. Exhausted, she balled her hands into fists and spread her fingers wide, allowing her claws to extend. As she stepped out of the shower, beads of water spilled down her body, and she caught sight of her wild eyes in the mirror. *Let her free*, an inner voice whispered. *Yes,* she responded.

A tornado of emotion swirled in her chest as Gabriella released her wolf and she surrendered to the transformation. As the pads of her feet hit the cool marble floor, the strength of her feral beast replaced the weakness of the witch. The vampire would not lie with her ever again once he saw the power of her wolf. She'd sleep alone, soundly, awaiting the magick of the moon.

The scent of her vampire permeated the air, but as

Gabriella loped into the bedroom, she immediately sensed his absence. Although the witch inside her mind immediately flared with both pain and desire, the wolf ignored the emotions, and stalked toward the bed. Its power would protect her by healing her from within, strengthening her magick and readying her for a fight.

She jumped onto the bed and settled onto the plush white comforter. With the house quiet and her wolf on the watch, Gabriella closed her lids, succumbing to the nurturing sleep. *In the morning,* she told herself. *In the morning, I'll get answers.* Her whole life had been nothing but pain. Tonight was a lesson in trust and acceptance. No one ever wanted her, not even Quintus. But she'd choose herself and know that she was enough.

Her dream was interrupted, and she went on alert, hearing the footsteps in the hallway. As her lids slowly opened, she caught sight of her magnificent vampire. A towel slung low around his hips, shadows of the candlelight danced on his sculpted abs. As he stepped into the bedroom, a low growl rattled in her throat.

"You're a...you've shifted." Quintus held a bottle of wine and two glasses in one hand and a tray in the other.

Gabriella grew louder, protesting as he took a deliberate step toward her.

"We have to talk, Gabby," he said, his voice soft. "Let me just...I want to see you."

She let out a loud bark as he drew closer, her hackles raised.

"Your color, it's unusual. Your fur. It's black with tones of red and grays…you're beautiful."

Her heart softened at his words. She'd been called all sorts of hideous names but never beautiful. *No. Don't listen to him. Let him go. You'll get hurt.* Protecting her heart was paramount if she ever were going to be free.

"I thought the full moon was tomorrow," he said, not as much as a question but a statement. He glanced at the New York City skyline through the floor-to-ceiling window then drifted his focus back to Gabriella. "What just happened in the shower…ah, bella. I know you wanted me to drink from you, but I couldn't."

She bared her fangs in response, daring him to come closer. It was her who would draw blood if he touched her.

He passed her on the bed, keeping his focus on her ebony eyes as he crossed the room to a sleek rosewood desk. As he turned his back to her, Gabriella noted her surroundings. With twenty-foot ceilings, the enormous master bedroom's stark white walls contrasted with the deep cherry hardwood floors. Its contemporary furniture was a vast departure from the old world décor of his home in New Orleans.

The sound of the glasses settling onto the wood refocused her attention, and she cautiously watched him pour the red wine. As he turned to her and lifted the rim to his lips, he gave a knowing smile. Her stomach flipped, his sexy gaze washing over her. In an attempt to ignore him, she shoved her humanity to the recesses of her mind, shifting all power to her beast.

"The thing is my lovely little wolf, you've never been bitten." Quintus slowly took a sip, his seductive eyes locked on hers. "I could lie and say I don't want your blood."

Quintus made his way toward Gabriella. She snarled in response, her claws extending into the fabric.

"Easy there, no need to tear up the bed. I mean, I'd be happy to do it the old-fashioned way but…ah well, perhaps that shouldn't happen."

Gabriella glared at him in contempt.

"Did you not feel my fangs on your skin?" he asked, his lips forming a sexy smile.

She cocked her head, still baring her teeth at him. Of course she'd felt the scrape along her shoulder, teasing her into submission.

"I wanted it every bit as much as you, but I have my reasons. I'm not ever going to lie to you. Even if I could, I wouldn't use compulsion to make you think I bit you when I didn't. My guess is that you wouldn't be susceptible to my ability to do it anyway. Do you know how special that is? There have been very few people in my life who are immune. Viktor. But of course, he's my brother. He has the gift, as well, as did our sire. And then there was Mao," he stated, turning to gaze out the window.

Every muscle in her body tensed at the mention of another woman on his lips. Jealousy flared but she smothered the negative thought while remaining on alert.

"She was a special creature. A pixiu. It doesn't matter to

say much more but she…well, I suppose she was somewhat of a shifter as well. Not in its true sense of the word like you, but she wasn't human. I'm not sure if you realize but, although there're certainly exceptions, vampires typically feed off of humans."

Gabriella recalled the humans at the club, aware he'd fed off of them, most likely using them for sex as well. She loathed the blood clubs, donors desperate for an experience and shifters seeking more of the same. Although she'd felt like a whore selling her blood, she'd never let them have more, not her flesh. The temptation of the orgasm incited by their bite lingered in her thoughts but she'd never been willing to give herself to anyone…until Quintus.

"Humans have never been anything more than food, a simple necessary means to an end. Perhaps some more enjoyable than others. But there has been no one in my life like Mao…no one who I've bonded with…until…" He sighed, and turned toward Gabriella. "You're an unexpected complication. I keep saying that there's something about you, but you see, I've suspected it's so much more."

Quintus approached the bed, drawing closer to his wolf. "Easy, bella. I'm just going to sit down here. No fighting. Just talking. Now, I'm not sure what made you shift before the moon or if this is something you can just do on demand, but you can't stay that way forever."

Gabriella gave a soft whine as he sat gently on the mattress, coming within inches of her lupine form. The scent of her vampire called to her, tempting her to shift.

"What happened back there?" He gave a loud sigh.

"Your blood saved me in New Orleans. But I suspect that when I bite you…there is no going back once I do it. You're a virgin, si? Never been bitten?"

Her wide eyes blinked, acknowledging his statement. Never allowing the vampires who bought her blood to feed directly had been essential to her survival. Mostly working through third parties, she remained anonymous. Her magical blood was a rare commodity. Permitting them to bite would have relegated her to the ranks of a donor. Gabriella didn't seek the rush of being bitten by strangers, or the sex that would have followed.

"There's nothing wrong with that. But this connection between us…"

She refused to change, although she desperately yearned to touch him.

"On an average day, when I bite someone, there's sometimes a slight tie to the human. For at least that moment in time, I can feel their emotions, but it ends there. With you, you must understand, this is not something I can take back. If I bite you and we bond, it could be permanent. I can't be sure if you're the one until I bite you, but instinct tells me…"

Mate. The word danced in her thoughts. Although aware that wolves mated, she never suspected it could happen to her. Not being of pack, it'd been unlikely she'd meet anyone.

"I know what you're thinking. Wolves mate with wolves. And this is true. It's crossed my mind that although we have this connection, perhaps your mate is out there somewhere waiting for you. And if that's so, that you have a mate, someone other than me, then I suppose I'm simply just enamored with you." He took a sip of his wine, gently setting the glass on the night table. "The only way to test this is for me to bite you. To see if the bond is there. Of course it sounds easy enough, but bella, you've never been bitten. This is not a choice to be made lightly. I could not allow myself to bite you, no matter how much I wanted to. It would not be wise or honorable."

Gabriella's heart squeezed at his words. As he reached for her, she stilled in anticipation of his touch. Her body sizzled with magick as his palm ran over her head and down her flank.

"You're beautiful, Gabriella. As a wolf. As a witch. This coven, these people who called you impure, they're wrong. You're unique. Any pack would have been privileged to have you."

As Quintus shifted off the bed and crossed the room, the loss of his warmth saddened her. She'd never been told she was beautiful.

"You must be hungry," he said, reaching for a tray. "I apologize but with all my travel as of late, I'm not fully stocked. But apples and cheese do stay well."

She whined, not for food but for his touch. As if he'd read her mind, he returned to the bed, setting the tray next to his wine.

"I can feel you, Gabby. Even as wolf, I feel you inside me. This isn't natural for me. I don't want to hurt you. I won't hurt you. So I'm sorry, but we cannot do this."

Anger burned hot inside of her. Why did he get to make the decision about whether she was bitten? The magick blistered bright, forcing the transformation. She gasped for breath as her shift completed, her eyes set on his.

"I'm no different than the other donors. I wanted this. Do you have any idea what I offered you?" she stated, her voice raised.

"You are different than the others," he challenged.

"So what is this between us? You fuck me but you feed from humans. You tell me we're connected but you won't bite me to find out if I'm supposed to be with you because I'm a…haven't ever been bitten." Gabriella shoved up to sit, fury in her eyes. "Jesus, I should have never asked you for help."

"I told you I would help you and I will. I helped you right now. Don't you understand what could happen if I bite you?" Quintus' intense stare held hers as if daring her to move.

"I get that you bite thousands of women. Fuck them too. That's what I get. But me, what? I'm good enough to save you but not good enough to drink from. And your reasoning is that we might be bonded? You don't want to risk doing that with someone like me." Gabriella blew out a breath, and shook her head, averting her gaze. "Nope, you know what? I shouldn't have had sex with you. I shouldn't have asked you for help. And I shouldn't be here."

"Do you want a bond with someone who will need to feed from you? Let's say I'm right. You're my mate. That somehow, the Goddess sees fit for me to bond with a witch, a shifter, never a human. Do you know what it means to be food? Because I can tell you this, feeding off others, it's intimate. If you don't like it, I still need to eat. Would you want to bond with a male who feeds off strangers? Is that what you want? Because that's where this is headed."

Gabriella leapt off the bed, running towards the door. Naked, she hadn't given a thought to where she was going. She only knew she needed to escape the pain of rejection. Craving Quintus, wanting him to bite her wasn't rational, yet the obsession grew by the second. All the other women had been good enough. *Not me.*

Within seconds, he flew across the room. Firm hands spun her shoulders around, pinning her naked form to the wall. The heat of his body emanated onto her skin as he caged her with his palms planted firmly to her sides.

"Let me go," she demanded, releasing her magick. His body brushed hers and her traitorous nipples stood erect in arousal.

"If we're bonded, this is not something I can undo. I'm powerful. Lethal. Ruthless. You don't even know me, Gabriella. It would be hard but I could let you walk away now. But if I bite you…once this starts…"

She gasped as his fangs dropped, the sight of them inciting exhilaration deep in her belly. Without thinking, she reached for his face, her palm on his cheek, but his expression didn't soften as he continued.

"I crave you like no other woman. But if you choose to be mine and bond with me, you'll either allow me to feed from you, or I will have to have others. I can't force this decision on you."

"I'm not supposed to have a vampire as a mate." Sliding the pad of her finger down his fang, she met his gaze. Gabriella's chest rose as she inhaled and released a deep breath. "I never expected this could happen. I don't know what it means to be bonded to another, yet my beast...she wants you."

"I can choose not to bond, Gabby. It would be hard, but I could do it. If I bite you and I'm wrong about us, if I'm not your mate, your wolf...she may find someone else who is. After you're safe, you can still walk away from me and this life of mine."

"I...I don't know why I want this...no, I need this," she whispered. Arousal twisted through her as she stroked his sharp fang. With the brush of his erection against her stomach, she shivered in anticipation of his touch. "Quintus. Be clear on this. If you're my mate, there will be no others. Only me."

"Be aware you play with fire, pet. I am thousands of years old. I've killed more men than I can count. The power within me is held by few who roam this earth. And you're but a child. The bitter darkness in my soul, it craves the light within you."

"The energy between us...I can't explain it. I want you to be my first. But there are times..." Quintus terrified her with his sheer power, yet her magick, her very soul craved to breathe the same air with him. "Tonight in that club. Those people..."

"My people..."

"They scare me. They do as they wish, only complying

with society's rules because a leader makes them." On the rare occasions she'd been forced to go into a vampire club, she'd witnessed ruthless acts of violence. "If you weren't there tonight, Ravi would have killed me."

"If you say yes, and you're mine, you're going to be part of my world. I'll protect you but you must learn to submit. Your wolf knows this." Quintus sucked her finger into his mouth and released it, the sharp tip of his pointed tooth scraping over its pad.

"I'm also a witch," she countered. As he rocked his hard cock against her hip, her pussy clenched in arousal. "I…I'm not like the others."

"Tell me, mi bella. Do you understand what it would be like to be food? To make love and be bitten, to be only mine?" His mouth brushed a rough kiss to her chin, and he sucked her bottom lip.

"I…" Gabriella's knees grew weak, the painful ache between her legs growing as his hands settled on her shoulders.

"Surrender is power. Yin and yang. My dominance to your submission."

"My wolf…I don't know if she will," she sighed.

"You must be sure this is what you want." His hand reached between her legs.

"Ah…I…" She lost her thoughts as he speared a finger deep within her core, his hot breath on her neck.

"Your blood. It's the most delicious I've ever tasted. But I will walk away if you don't want to be in my world. I'm far too old for complications," Quintus told her as he withdrew his finger.

She gripped his shoulders, her mind and body spinning in arousal. Commitment to someone she'd only just met was incomprehensible. Whatever street smarts that told her to run seemed to disappear as the call of her wolf grew louder, urging her to make love to him. Earlier, she'd simply wanted to be bitten, an urge to satisfy a carnal desire. But with a full understanding of the ramifications, her beast grew impatient. To be mated for the rest of her immortal life to a vampire, to surrender to the slice of his fangs, to submit to a man forever…logic told her to run. Yet as his lips pressed to her skin, her core tightened with desire and she gave in to the yearning.

"I want this. I choose…I choose you." Her pulse raced as she committed to her vampire.

"Stand still my little wolf. Your lesson begins," he growled.

His towel dropped from his hips, revealing his proud erection. As he stepped away from Gabriella, she sucked a deep breath, anxious to touch him. She attempted to go to him but froze like a frightened rabbit, his voice commanding her to stay.

"Patience. It's a skill that must be practiced. Seconds. Minutes. Hours. Centuries we may wait for exactly the right moment."

Gabriella's nipples tightened in anticipation, excitement dancing over her bare skin.

"I want to see you." His gaze slowly painted over her body from head to toe. "Fuck your pussy."

"What?" her eyes widened at his words.

"Touch yourself, Gabby."

Her heart pounded against her ribs as she raised her hand to her chest. Trailing her fingers over her aching breasts, she trembled, her tender nipples begging to be touched.

She knew he demanded submission but it wouldn't come easily. She'd been independent far too long. The seduction continued; a slow torturous dance. Drinking in the sight of his glorious body, she imagined his cock thrusting inside her as she glided her fingers through her wet folds.

"That's a girl…fuck, you're so beautiful," Quintus groaned, stroking his palm over his thick cock.

Gabriella's eyes locked on his, his sensual energy sizzling through her as her fingers plunged between her legs. Her other hand went to her breast. Taking her sensitive tip between her fingers, she tugged gently, the pain distracting her from coming.

Quintus crossed to the bed, his cock in his hands. "Over here. Now," he growled.

The demand shot through her, but she didn't move. Her spectacular vampire stood tall, the candlelight dancing over the contours of his skin. She drank in the sight of his broad muscled chest and his ripped abdomen. She imagined licking wine off his entire body, tasting every hard line of him.

"Now," he demanded, breaking her contemplation.

Her focus snapped to attention, her fingers slowly withdrawing. The painful ache between her legs caused her to suck a breath as she slowly made her way towards him.

Her magick crackled, an aura of glowing sparkles flittering into the air. Like a magnet, she was drawn to the domineering vampire, her beast pacing.

"On your knees, little witch."

Gabriella's heart skipped a beat at the request. She found herself obeying. Her knees brushed the cold hardwood floor, wakening her body. She settled in front of him, the heat from his thighs emanating onto her face.

"Open." His expression heated as her pink lips parted.

Gabriella lost her words, her mouth wide as he drew closer. She reached for him but he swiftly reprimanded her. "No touching."

As Quintus guided his cock over her tongue, she closed her eyes, savoring the delicious taste of her vampire.

"I'm going to fuck your pretty little mouth. I'm going to fuck you in ways you've never been fucked." He withdrew and pressed back into her. "Once I drink of you, you're mine."

Gabriella opened her eyes, her gaze settling on his as he slid into her mouth. She'd never felt more vulnerable or more powerful as he groaned, her lips closing around his shaft. Her tongue lapped over the slit of his broad head.

"Your pussy. Your ass. In all ways, in all places. You'll become mine and no one else's unless I choose to let them see you with me."

The dark fantasy swirled in her mind and she moaned in pleasure, the salty taste of him in her mouth. As his hands cupped the back of her head and he increased his pace, she ran her hands up the back of his thighs. He threw his head back in ecstasy, groaning as she swallowed his shaft down to its root.

Gabriella sensed the surge in his energy, so close to coming. She sucked harder, her tongue swirling over his slick cock.

"Ah…fuck, you're amazing," he growled, threading his fingers into her hair.

As he tugged her head backward, a sweet twinge of pain danced across her scalp. Panting, she licked her lips, a sensual smile on her face.

Quick as lightning, he reached for her. She gasped as his hands clasped her waist and threw her onto the bed. She pushed up onto her elbows in anticipation, and her eyes widened at the sight of his glorious cock. Quintus crawled onto the bed, his fangs dropping as he pressed between her legs. Detecting the feral energy in his eyes, she stilled, aching in arousal for her lover.

His palms pried open her thighs, and her knees fell apart, revealing her glistening pussy. She licked her lips as his fangs scraped over her sensitive skin.

"Ah, so beautiful." Quintus rested onto his forearms, his mouth settling onto her mound. "Your blood calls to me…but first I feast."

Gabriella cried out as his devilish tongue lapped through her slick folds, flicking over her swollen clit. "Oh Goddess."

"La tua figa è così deliziosa," he murmured, sucking her swollen nub into his mouth.

"Please…I'm on fire…" A fresh rush of arousal threaded through her, her pussy throbbing as her orgasm mounted.

"You're so fucking delicious," he groaned.

"No, don't stop…" Gabriella shivered, stilling as a sharp point trailed across her flesh. Her wolf howled in submission at the sensation, desperately awaiting the slice of his fangs. As he plunged two thick fingers inside her, she moaned, arching her back. Pressing her hips up to his mouth, she urged him to bite her.

The tip of his tongue lapped over her clitoris, and she gasped, the heat of her body increasing with each lash. Her entire body thrummed with arousal, his strong fingers pumping inside her tight pussy.

"Please…" she begged, her thoughts bordering on incoherent as her magick danced in the air.

"You're so beautiful," he told her, his voice breathy. "Easy, bella. It's time."

As his teeth sliced into her mound, he drove his fingers deep into her core. Gabriella screamed, her climax rocking through her. Quintus' thoughts merged with hers, every cell of her body alive as she bucked upward into his bite. His emotions twisted through her mind, memories of a lifetime flashing before her eyes. The pain of dying and being reborn, the great sense of loss and loneliness…her own connection with the vampire sizzling in clarity as her wolf celebrated, giving her lifeblood to her mate.

Mate. Gabriella's eyes flew open at the silent sound of the word. She was shaken with surprise as Quintus withdrew both his fangs and his hands, leaving her with a desperate sense of need.

"No, please…" she pleaded, panting for breath as he

flipped her onto her stomach. As his hand returned to her mound, she sighed.

"Si, bella…I never thought this could happen…" he breathed.

Gabriella braced herself, presenting her bottom, open and receiving. As he slammed his thick cock into her pussy, she grunted, pleasure spiking through her. Fisting the sheets, she braced herself as he gripped her hips, slamming inside her tight core.

"Quintus," she cried, his hard cock stretching her open.

"You're mine," he told her, wrapping a hand around her waist. "Do you feel this?"

Gabriella pushed upward onto her knees, the palm of his hand guiding her as he fucked her. With her body on fire, she submitted to his wish, accepting every hard inch of him. She mewled as his fingers pinched a nipple, a twinge of pain sharpening her focus.

"You're beautiful. I've never wanted someone so much in my life….ah, yes," he grunted, thrusting hard inside her tight channel.

"Yes," she cried as he bit into the soft flesh of her neck, grunting as he came inside her. The wave of her orgasm tore through her, leaving her shaking in ecstasy. Relinquishing control to the ancient vampire, she opened her mind, receiving his energy, allowing him to read her, to know her pain and her joy as he drew her lifeblood into his body.

As he withdrew his teeth, licking over her wounds, she went limp, overwhelmed in sensation. Her wolf crouched in submission to her mate. Quintus eased himself out of her, swiftly cradling her to his chest, his gentle kiss brushing her forehead.

Shocked in the realization that this creature, this man, this dominating vampire was hers, she trembled, both terrified and exhilarated at once. She couldn't say she was in love but knew without a doubt that she belonged to Quintus and her life was forever changed.

Chapter Seven

Quintus leaned back into his chair, sitting at his desk and sighed. Making love to Gabriella, tasting her blood had been extraordinary. He was her mate. It seemed incredible yet true; she was his, and he'd begun bonding with his little wolf.

He fingered the golden figurine as he reflected on his life, emotion seizing his chest. Thousands of years had passed since he'd been turned. His master, Baxter, had sired hundreds of vampires over the centuries, but only a handful had survived. The skilled sadist bastard took pleasure in the art of torture. He'd skin his victims, bringing them to the brink of death and then reviving them. Inflicting brutal punishments thrilled the malicious vampire. He'd kept a menagerie of creatures at his beck and call, as no supernatural was immune from his fury.

Quintus ran the pad of his thumb over the ridges of the winged metal creature. Although he'd never seen Mao shift, he'd memorized every contour of her human form, making love to her for hours. He'd tasted of her blood, certain he'd been her mate. While he'd never communicated with her telepathically or completed the bond, Quintus had absorbed her vibrant energy, immersed in their special connection.

When his master discovered he had fallen in love with his beautiful Chinese lover, he'd kidnapped and raped her. Mao's bloody screams had echoed into the night. Quintus had attempted to save her but was too late. By the time he reached them, he watched in horror as his master hoisted her limp body into the Daduhejinkou Grand Canyon. A fledgling vampire, his ability to materialize on a whim hadn't been cultivated, so he'd been helpless to save her. Swearing retribution, Quintus had waited patiently, growing more powerful through the centuries, until the day he'd been strong enough to destroy Baxter. But his master's death had never relieved the crushing grief that haunted him.

The notion that he'd ever love again had been a dream he'd never anticipated. Instead, he'd filled his time amassing his wealth as a mercenary, killing for money and his enemies alike, bedding women on a whim. He'd deliberately remained elusive within the vampire hierarchy, preferring to wield his great powers as he saw fit.

Quintus glanced again to the dragon-like statue in his hands, and his thoughts drifted back to Gabriella. It had been much more likely he'd bond with a human. But like the rarity of lightning striking twice, another shifter had connected with him. The pure energy connection he'd shared with Gabriella had taken him by surprise. But moreover, when he'd bitten into her soft flesh, his mind had blended with hers, experiencing her memories, her emotions, her hopes.

For the first time in over a thousand years, he'd been terrified. Losing Mao had broken him. Gabriella had burst into his life like a bright star, shining like the sun. When he'd bitten her, he'd known there was a possibility he was her mate. But now all had changed. The bond had begun. There was no turning back, except to refuse her his blood, to deny the completion.

Both guilt and fear rushed through his thoughts. He'd loved Mao, and she'd died a horrific death because of him. While Baxter was long dead, a few of his legacies remained hidden in the far corners of the world. Like dormant volcanoes, they could reignite their fire, turning them deadly with the news of his new bonding. If Gabriella died because of him, he'd never forgive himself.

The creak of the wooden floor sounded, and Quintus' eyes flashed to the entryway. Viktor stood dressed in a tuxedo, tapping his fingertips on the doorjamb.

"You think too hard, brother," he commented as he stepped into the office.

"This has been a good life, si?" Quintus set the figurine onto his desk. "You're dressed already?"

"Why yes. I'm not going to be late to this shindig. The witches be bitchin'. Vampires…well…they suck." He gave a laugh, seemingly fake.

"A few thousand years on this planet and you still have the worst jokes. But looking stylish as always." Quintus chuckled and leaned backwards in his chair, resting his head and closing his eyes. "There were times I'd wish I'd died. If it weren't for my desire for revenge…"

"Baxter. He haunts you tonight." Viktor glanced to the bottle of cognac. "1858 Cuvee Léonie?"

"Mao." Quintus sighed. "He killed her for no reason."

"Jesus Christ. All these years…" Viktor threw himself down onto a white leather chair. "You know it wasn't your fault."

"I didn't say…"

"He was a bastard, Quint."

"If it were only that…" Quintus opened his eyes, his energy drained from reflecting on her death.

"This world, it breeds both good and evil. And he sure was from Hell. I didn't think we'd survive."

"Nor did I."

"Mao was your happiness. That's why he killed her. He killed your happiness."

"As he did yours."

"We survived, though. He didn't. So fuck him."

"The good. That light within us. I've held onto it with a straw at times. To turn to his dark ways…it could have been easy." Quintus reached for his glass, and brought it to his lips, the smooth cognac coating his tongue.

"True. Our brothers and sisters…some chose his way," Viktor reflected.

"A few are still out there. I feel them at times but they dare not stay within a thousand miles of me." His sister, Amelia, was especially dangerous, but it had been many years since their last encounter.

"Gabriella's yours?" Viktor asked, brushing lint from his red velvet jacket.

"I don't know how it's possible." Quintus considered denying the bond, but as the minutes passed, his psyche continued to absorb her unique magick.

"So she is yours." Viktor raised a questioning eyebrow, his lips curving upward. "You're bonding."

"She's not human."

"A witch, though. It happens."

"She's hybrid. A wolf."

"But of course the Goddess pairs you with a shifter," he laughed.

"You should see her. She's beautiful. She shifts into this gorgeous black wolf." Quintus blew out his breath and shook his head. "It's still hard to believe this is happening."

"Hey, I can't say I've had experience in this area but you can't shake this bond. She belongs to you. I know that much."

"I can choose to walk away," Quintus lied. It would be nearly impossible.

"So you say, my friend. But why…"

"I have enemies. She's vulnerable. I cannot allow her to be killed. Mao…"

"That was a long time ago. We were young. Weak. Now, you're one of the most powerful vampires in the world."

"The only thing I can do is protect her from the coven. Do what I need to do to break whatever hold they have on her. She's already in enough danger."

"Tonight's the full moon. Does she have a pack?"

"No, but you are right on the moon." She'd be forced to shift. "I'll make arrangements but we've got to straighten out the witches. There must be peace. Jax will control his wolves."

"You plan to pawn her off on the Alpha?"

"She will have no other master." His eyes snapped to Viktor, who wore a sly smile.

"Ah, but she's wolf. If the bond is not completed…" He stood and stretched his neck from side to side.

"She doesn't belong to Jax. I'll simply see to her safety." A stern expression crossed Quintus' face, his pulse racing at the thought.

"So you'll keep her then?" Viktor gave a chuckle and gazed out the window.

"She doesn't belong to Jax," Quintus replied without directly answering his question.

"And tonight?"

"If there is one thing I've learned in all these years it's not to be impulsive. We have many things going on of importance. The vampires have concerns regarding the witches. There hasn't been this level of unrest in hundreds of years. From the minute we arrived in New York, I sensed the rumblings. What happened in the club was just a taste."

"Surely what you did to Ravi will make an impression?"

"Perhaps. But other vampires from outside the city could be involved, possibly from Louisiana."

"You'd think Kade would have some info," Viktor guessed. "How 'bout Jonathon?"

"He's an amateur but I wouldn't discount him."

"He's hungry for power. He knows Kade's got a tight hold of New Orleans, and if there's nothing in Baton Rouge for him, it wouldn't surprise me. Takes balls, but never underestimate stupid." Quintus set the glass on his desk.

"They really could come from anywhere."

"Unlikely they're from out of the country but they'll come from strongholds. Either way it doesn't matter. The only way to feel this out is to attend the event. It's possible the witches have been influenced by outsiders as well. This coven that's after Gabriella...from Salem. They're unusual. Purists."

"Since the beginning of time, these purist cults have existed. For every species there is another that dislikes others. Idiots."

"Hybrids exist but are rare. I'm not sure how a witch breeds with a wolf...it's impossible really. The wolves...they must be hybrid."

"Perhaps her father was hybrid."

"Or she's an undiscovered diamond. Nature changes life. Evolves."

"There's always been something special about you, Quint. It's how you've survived. The fact that there are two women you've come across in your lifetime...this is an opportunity."

"Or a curse. Mao's dead. Gabriella is at risk from her coven and my enemies." Quintus shook his head. "Ironic that we have all these women throwing themselves at our feet. Blood whores who live to be bitten. Yet the loneliness, we ignore it to the point where we forget it even exists. It's a weakness in our humanity. And now…"

"And now you have a shifter. But you're not alone in this unusual path. Look at Leo. He enjoys his fish."

"Naiad." Quintus gave a small smile, amused with his brother's simplicity.

"Naiad. Fish. Whatever. She breathes underwater. She's like a dolphin."

"Technically that's a mammal."

"Seriously? A shark then. Because she seems to be able to take care of herself." Viktor laughed. "Not so much a mermaid? I still believe they exist…but she's got no tail."

"You're lucky Leo can't hear you. He'd kick your ass," Quintus laughed.

"Pfft. I'd kick his ass, and you know it. Your child isn't as strong as me."

"Let's not try to find out. But about tonight…"

"It's important," Viktor finished his sentence.

"It's critical to put an end to any trouble. Jax is always trying to establish his own dominance. Plays games. I won't have it."

"Ah, but you've known the wolf many years."

"That may be so. I'll grant him his due but nothing more. Apparently he and his beta are off on some other business tonight and sending in Hunter Livingston," Quintus said.

"What the hell?"

"I don't expect any issues from him. I met up with him out in California."

"Yeah, well, no offense, but look how that shit show turned out for you," Viktor replied.

"The bigger issue is that the wolves are simply just that. They're wolves. Jax. Hunter. Alphas control packs not witches. There are others in this city, ones who would gladly start shit with Jax."

"Absinthe?"

"Don't speak too loudly. My wards are strong but that damn witch has this uncanny ability to sense her name in the air." Quintus shoved to his feet, his gaze set on Viktor. "She's been around long enough to know if there's been a shift in the magick. Any rumblings of new covens…she'll know. She might be able to help with the Salem coven that's been chasing Gabriella."

"You know her better than I."

"Perhaps, but that's only because you're a rolling stone."

"I'm here when you need me. That's what counts." Viktor smiled broadly.

"True, but when you flash, I expect your ass with me. No spur of the moment trips to Egypt, V. This is one of those times I need you there and on time."

"What else do you know about the coven that's after her?" Viktor asked.

"Not much. Gabby's been on the run for years."

"She's a child in the supernatural world."

"Yet another concern."

"She's an adult with you, though. I smell her on you."

"Not so much on me but in me. Her blood. She's like pure magick. I've never tasted another like her."

"Not even Mao?" Viktor challenged, turning to give his brother a sly smile.

"It's been many years. Mao…she wasn't at all human." Quintus considered the years that had passed; he barely recalled the taste of her, leaving him wondering if she had been but a dream. "She wasn't a witch. You know full well that although most witches are born, they can be created under unique circumstances. Look at Luca's woman. She was human."

"Are you trying to say that Gabriella's human?" He gave a disbelieving laugh.

"I'm saying anything is possible. She's hybrid. There clearly was something special about her mother that allowed her to mate with a wolf. You know as well as I do it's impossible. Witches have gone mad attempting to mate with their lovers. Look what happened to Ilsbeth. No, no, no…" He scrubbed his hand over his hair. "Something broke the spell. Perhaps her father had been hybrid as well…something within his bloodline…it wasn't pure."

"And you're saying Mao was?"

"What I'm saying is that I was young, and it was a very long time ago. And Mao was a rare creature."

"You were her mate, though."

"But we didn't complete the bond. She never took my blood." Quintus had begged her but she'd refused, afraid of turning. From a rural village, she'd been young and believed the superstitions spread by her elders. He'd always believed that if she'd had his blood, his master wouldn't have been able to kill her as easily.

"All I'm saying is that Gabriella is every bit as much of a shifter as Mao was, maybe less pure but she shifts." Viktor shrugged and glanced at his reflection in the wall mirror. "Do you think this red velvet looks too...I don't know....vampirish?"

"Are you for real?" Quintus shook his head.

"I'm just saying. Red. Blood. It's kind of stereotypical. Maybe I should have gone with purple. I'm thinking of dyeing my hair."

"You've got issues."

"You've got no room to talk. Blue satin? Don't get me wrong. It works on you."

"The red does scream 'vampire'. Maybe you should change." Quintus rolled his eyes.

"Are you fucking with me?" Viktor's eyes widened and he craned his neck to get a better view of himself in the mirror.

"What do you think, asshole? We're about to go shake things down at this supe fest and you're worried about whether or not you look like a vampire. You're a fucking vampire."

"Well, yeah." He shrugged and looked at himself once again, smoothing a stray hair from his forehead. "But that doesn't mean I need to let other people know. Always keep them guessing. I don't want to be predictable."

"You're a fucking idiot, you know that?" Quintus sidled up to Viktor, his hands moving to his own silk bow tie. He straightened the fabric, his thoughts drifting to Gabriella. She was beautiful, a glorious sexual creature created just for him.

"You look fine," Viktor said.

"Jesus, would you stop talking. A little silence." Quintus closed his eyes briefly and opened them.

"I can hear you, bro." Viktor laughed. "You're into her."

"Turn me the fuck off then. I can't help it. She consumes me. There're no words to describe it. I've got to get things sorted for her so she feels accepted. Fuck Jax if he doesn't help me. I'll find another pack that will. Hunter. He's always been friendly with the witches. Or maybe Logan."

"Quint, man, I don't know about this plan of yours but you're right about one thing. We've got to sort the mess here with the witches. The vampires are starting to freak the hell out and Jax? Jax is Jax. We've been together long enough to know you're gonna do what you want."

"So we focus." Quintus released his tie, a firm hand settling on Viktor's shoulder. "Don't discuss Mao in front of Gabriella. I don't want her involved too much with my history."

"I hear you but..." Viktor went silent and Quintus raised his fingers to his lips.

Quintus should have sensed her far quicker than he had. He suspected the blood exchange had affected his judgement. At the sight of his gorgeous witch, he struggled to appear composed.

The sheer fabric of her dress hugged every curve of her body. Although her nudity was concealed by wisps of royal blue silk leaves, Quintus recalled every inch of her creamy skin. Thick curls spilled over her shoulders, accentuating her delicate neck. She might as well have been wearing nothing, deliciously alluring in the couture dress.

Blood rushed to his cock as her intense gaze met his. Quintus rooted his feet to the ground, determined not to reveal his excitement. Goddess, this woman could get him killed. His body and mind lost their logic, summarily immersed in her presence.

"I…" Gabriella glanced to her feet. "Do I look okay? The things you bought. I'm not used to dressing up."

"You're stunning," he responded in awe of her humility.

"I…I've never worn anything like this," she admitted, running her palms over her hips.

"It's not the dress, it's you." Quintus reached for her hand, the ambrosial floral perfume filling his senses. Gently turning her wrist, he brushed his lips to her delicate skin. Her magical essence tempted him. His fangs ached to release but he restrained himself.

Quintus gently released her, and his eyes lifted to meet Gabriella's. "Tonight we shall be in dangerous company. I'm hoping you've learned your lesson. Don't repeat your defiant behavior from the other day, pet."

"I know tonight is important, but you remember I'm going to shift tonight, right? I can only fight it for so long." Her soft expression turned tense. "You can't tell me what to do."

"But I can. And I will." It was much too dangerous for her to disobey. Although he could flash them away, he couldn't predict what others would do within the confines of the event.

"Just because we…you know, we did what we did…you can't boss me."

"Tonight, at this event, I most certainly can. You're mine." The thunderous words reverberated in his chest, claiming her. He sucked a breath, his gaze darting to Viktor and back to his witch. "You're a novice, untrained."

"How am I supposed to hide? If I use glamour, the witches will probably detect it."

"They'll sense your magick as soon as you walk in the room, but don't say a word about being a witch."

"What are we going to tell them?" Her face flushed in anger.

"We'll lie. Correct that. I'll use compulsion, they'll believe me. I'll tell them that you're a wolf."

"I don't know if that'll work with the wolves. They'll know I'm not from their pack."

"I've already texted Jax. Anyone in attendance will not question your presence. I'll say you're with Hunter Livingston's pack. He's a friend." Viktor gave a chuckle and Quintus' lips straightened in displeasure, refusing to respond. "He's more of an acquaintance really." They weren't friends at all but they'd both fought as allies.

"I'm sorry to intrude on this little tête-à-tête, but he doesn't really like you. You know that, right?" Viktor gave a sly smile. "It's true. He's kind of…well, how would you say it? Hmm…"

"An Alpha," Quintus replied.

"A dick," Viktor joked, a lilt of amusement to his voice.

"But he's a wolf. And so is Gabriella."

"I still don't believe a word of it. She looks to be all witch to me," Viktor said as he buttoned his jacket. "Not sure I like my women with fur."

"Seriously? You don't need to worry about it. She's not yours," Quintus growled, his eyes fiery.

"Ah, you see that there, Gabby. He's possessive." He laughed and smiled at himself in the mirror.

"Would you please shut up?" Quintus turned to Gabriella, his gaze settling on hers. "Tonight you're wolf. They'll sense your magick. But sometimes it can be difficult to discern the type when there are so many supernaturals in one place. The energy will be high. No mentioning Salem. You can say we met in New Orleans. That Logan Reynaud invited you to visit the city. He's the Alpha of Acadian wolves. I'll make up some bullshit story about you needing warmer weather."

"I bet ole Hunter freezes his furry balls off in the winter," Viktor chirped.

"What the hell is wrong with you tonight?" Quintus shot him a look of annoyance.

"I kind of like the snow. Reminds me of home," she responded.

"This isn't a joke, you two. Wolf. You belong to Hunter." Quintus blew out a breath.

"What about the vampires who met me at your club? They'll know I'm witch."

"But do they?" Quintus rarely discussed his powers, but the ability to make a lie into a truth was a gift. "The vampires in that room are under my control. What they once knew to be true is no longer. Again, you're a wolf."

"Yes, fine. But I'm worried the coven…they can track me. Wherever I've gone, they've followed. What if they come?" Panic laced her voice.

"We'll deal with it if they come but there's going to be a lot of supernatural energy. It may cloak whatever signal they have on you. We'll take the limo."

"What no flashing in? The witches love that shit," Viktor said to Gabriella.

"They don't," Quintus told her, a small smile on his lips. "Less is more. This is a formal event. A few humans could be in attendance as well so it's best not to make a scene. That being said, I'm not taking any shit from anyone so if things get tense, Viktor…you keep her safe."

"No one's getting Gabriella," he replied, his tone serious. "I'll fucking rip their heart out."

"And that is why he's my brother." Often impulsive and lethal, Viktor was quite capable of killing. With every year that passed, Quintus often wondered how long he'd remain in control.

"Would be a shame to ruin this suit though. You like the red?" Viktor asked Gabriella, a broad smile crossing his face.

Although his brother's demeanor had changed, Quintus detected the blood thirst that flickered in his eyes.

"It's…it's a lovely color. You look…" Gabriella's eyes went to Quintus and he sensed her concern. Her emotions rolled through him as she raised her walls, a twinge of fear in her mind. "Very handsome."

"You can trust him to protect you," Quintus told her, his voice calm.

"But the coven…"

"Let's deal with these New York witches first. There's someone I know here. Someone who might be able to help us."

"I have some spells. I've been told there's something I need that will help me, but I'm not sure how it works or what it is." Her breath quickened.

Quintus resisted the urge to take her in his arms with his brother's watchful gaze upon him. Instead he reached for her hand and brought it to his chest. "You need to trust me, Gabby. You saved me once. I promise you, I have every intention of saving you right back. Look at tonight as one more step toward your freedom. We both have something to gain. But I know my city. They do not play. You need to follow the rules. My rules."

She returned his statement with silence. While he respected her spirit, and considered the fun he'd have spanking her ass, tonight's event was no time for defiance. He understood her reluctance to submit. The trials of her abandonment had born her independence. He considered that she'd likely resist her submission to an Alpha, yet she'd need to obey him as well.

"Come…it's time to face the witches and wolves." Quintus nodded to Viktor as he led Gabriella out of his office towards the door. Tonight he'd get answers, and kill anyone who crossed him.

"Do you see the full moon?" Gabriella asked, her voice in a whisper.

"You can go for a run after the event," Quintus assured her. "I know a wooded area outside of the city."

"Okay. Just take me there. I can run by myself." She stole a glance at Viktor who tapped at his cell phone, seemingly not paying attention.

"It doesn't seem particularly safe to run alone in New York. Tonight, I'll be there with you." Her confession didn't surprise him, given she'd been in hiding.

"I stay away from supernaturals whenever possible. Especially wolves and witches. I could navigate the vampires. I'd wear glamour. My energy is usually weak. I could have easily been human or psychic. They didn't know the difference."

"You may have done a good job avoiding the wrong vampires…most of them anyway. But I knew within seconds you weren't human. Or psychic." He placed his hand on her thigh, and but for a second, he recalled her taste on his lips, making love to her. Blood rushed to his cock at the thought and he sucked a breath, willing his erection to subside.

"My wolf. You're the first person I've ever shown," she admitted.

"You're beautiful."

"Is she?" Gabriella asked.

"You're always beautiful. Both as witch and wolf. You don't have to hide anymore."

"I'm not so sure," she hedged.

"It's up here," he interrupted. Quintus glanced to Gabriella whose eyes widened at the spectacular stone building. "It used to be a sugar refinery. Built in the 1800s."

"The get together is in there? It's so big."

"Whatever happened to renting a ballroom at the Four Seasons?" Viktor commented with a smirk.

"Not exactly the right crowd." Quintus looked to Gabriella. "It's not that certain groups don't meet in…how would I say? A more typical establishment."

"These partyers are anything but…I mean a few of the wolves are well cultured but you see, many of us…paranormals, we prefer a setting where we can let our inhibitions loose," Viktor added.

"You've seen my club. They crave the darkness of the night and in their souls," Quintus explained.

"Yeah, I'd say everyone's going to be revved when they see Quint tonight, so buckle up, sweetheart." Viktor raised his eyebrows and gave a devious smile.

"What's that supposed to mean?" she asked.

"It means my boy doesn't get out often and when they do see him, they all know some shit's about to go down."

"Is he serious?" As the car slowed and the dim factory lights lining the entrance came into view, she reached for his hand.

"I prefer my solitude. I keep my vampires in line. That's all that matters," Quintus explained.

"He's what they call in celebrity circles…reclusive."

"I'm not into the bullshit. I'm good without it." Quintus didn't see the point of mingling on a regular basis with supernaturals who weren't friends.

"How long has it been since you've gone to one of these things?" she asked.

"Twenty years give or take. New York City isn't that old

when you look at it in the grand scheme of things. Look…up there. That's where we're going." Quintus slid his arm around her, and pulled her close. "Just breathe."

"What is that?" she gasped.

The body of a beheaded man sat on a barrel, illuminated by red candlelight. Rats scurried around the body as partygoers milled toward the entrance.

"If it's a vampire, he's rogue. Not one of ours," Viktor said.

"They just leave him out there?" Her face wrinkled in disgust.

"It's a warning. Although it's a party, there're dangerous individuals in attendance," Quintus told her.

He sensed her fear as it rolled off her, and although he wished he could comfort her, the emotion would serve her well. They needed to exercise extreme caution, and this would provide a lesson in her practice, controlling impulses when faced with danger.

The car rolled to a stop, and he nodded at Viktor. "An hour tops. I address the community and speak with Absinthe. Got me? Stay with Gabriella."

"You ready?" Quintus asked her. She nodded and he briefly brushed his lips to hers, tasting her honeyed mouth. No time to be distracted; he wore a mask of indifference and readied to exit the car.

The limo door creaked open and the driver stood solemnly waiting in silence. Quintus stepped onto the black macadam, and extended a hand to Gabriella. She instantly broke out in gooseflesh as an icy wind gusted, and clutched her velvet shawl closed. He walked quickly past the guards, giving them a nod. They acknowledged the ancient vampire with respect, bowing to them as they passed.

Quintus sensed Viktor close behind. His jovial brother had switched his light demeanor to the dark persona that often cloaked his mind. Tonight was business. As he'd done over the centuries, Quintus stepped into battle willing to employ diplomacy, knowing the reality was he'd be lucky not to kill someone within the hour.

◦◦◦ *Chapter Eight* ◦◦◦

Shivering masked the fear causing her to tremble. Gabriella took a deep breath as they walked, spying the dead body out of the corner of her eye. *Act nonchalant. You can do this. No, fuck no, I can't. Yes...get out of here alive.* Her emotions bordered on explosive as they reached the tall purple wooden doors.

Sensing danger, Gabriella's wolf howled, itching to shift, but she forced her back into the recess of her mind. She'd suspected all the wolves would do the same. With the full moon, it would be nearly impossible to last more than a few hours. Although she hadn't told Quintus, she worried about her ability to control her beast around the other wolves.

A low scratchy voice drew her out of her contemplation. Gabriella raised her gaze to the tall thin man who extended his hand, ushering them through the door. She struggled not to stare at his white tuxedo which had been stained in blood. Her heart pounded in her chest, recalling the body that sat only a few feet away from the entrance.

"Sir," he greeted them, his focus settling on Gabriella. "I

do hope you and your young lady friend have a lovely time."

She nodded politely as he smiled at her, revealing his brown decayed teeth.

"We won't be staying long," Quintus growled at him and protectively wrapped his hand around her shoulders. "Viktor."

"Right behind you."

"Did you see that guy? What was he?" she whispered, her nose nuzzled against his lapel.

"A ghoul."

"A ghost?" she asked, clutching at his arm.

"Yeah, sort of. He's more or less a lower level demon. Not quite dead but no longer alive."

"How?" Gabriella kept her voice low, attempting to conceal her shock.

"The witches…he was human."

"Emphasis on was," Viktor added, his lips brushing her ear.

"A few hundred years ago. A witch put some sort of spell on him," Quintus explained.

"Name's Trev. Poor bloke's been stuck like that for a while," Viktor said.

"Not much of a life. They let him out for the occasional haunting. He's got this gig of course, but he's on a tight leash."

"Not tight enough. That man outside missing his head…he did that?" Gabriella asked as the din grew louder.

"Most likely. Or had a snack before he attended," Viktor confirmed.

"No, he doesn't. He eats them?" Shock rolled through her at the thought.

"Sometimes people. Sometimes animals. The guy out front? It was probably done with good reason," Quintus stated in a matter-of-fact manner.

"Easy, bro. Your girl isn't up for ghoul talk."

"It's not like you see them every day. Not all witches can make them. To be fair, there's a world out there beyond witches, wolves and vampires. Our numbers are the strongest, but there are others...shifters, fae, demons … other nasty things. But tonight, our three groups celebrate together."

"Is that what this is?" she asked.

"Positive thoughts." He gave a small chuckle, his hard exterior showing a crack as a corner of his mouth turned upward.

"A unique opportunity to see special creatures?" Gabriella suggested with a smile. She stayed close to him as they talked.

"That's the spirit," Viktor quipped.

"May I take your shawl?" a squeaky voice asked.

Gabriella startled at a tap to her shoulder. As she swung around, she caught sight of a curvy female, her balayage-colored hair spilling over her shoulders in shades of the rainbow. She wore an orange latex corset and white tutu, her large bosom spilling over the tight fabric like an overbaked muffin. She blinked her red eyes, turning them to purple as she reached for Gabriella's wrap.

"Thank you," Gabriella managed, detecting the

distinctive magick that only came from witches.

She forced herself not to stare at the girl as Quintus led them down a darkened brick hallway. Unable to contain the shock, she leaned toward her vampire, whispering, "I felt her. I don't know the coven…she's strong. That magick…"

"Don't worry about her. She's harmless. A basic witch."

"But her energy," Gabriella protested.

"My sweet little wolf. I'm afraid you haven't been around many witches lately. You're going to be okay. Take a deep breath. It will be all right. No more talking of this once we get in the ballroom. This section has been warded to protect wandering ears from listening but it's free game in there. Mind your words. Stay with Viktor."

Gabriella did as he said, inhaling deeply as they approached a stairwell. They passed through the entryway, and the walls appeared to close in around them. The narrow, brick, spiral staircase twisted up several stories. The suffocating tunnel morphed into a claustrophobia-inducing nightmare, their steps illuminated only by a dim string of twinkling lights on the ceiling.

When they finally emerged into the ballroom, a flickering neon green light blinded her. She caught flashes of men and women engaged in conversations. A Celtic rock band played on a raised circular stage while a line of young women danced in unison. Long blonde braids grazed over their bared breasts, red silk skirts hung low on their hips and brushed the ground as they moved. Masked in white leather, they floated rhythmically at a frantic pace, their eyes glazed over as if they'd been drugged.

In a far corner, Gabriella spied a stunning woman dressed in a bright green satin ball gown. Vines adorned with tiny reflective flowers topped her bun like a crown of glass. She spoke with a small court of young women who appeared bespelled, their attention solely focused on the grand female.

Quintus' voice rumbled through the noise, startling her. "Gabriella."

"Ah, yes. Sorry…what?" she asked, unable to focus.

"Champagne?"

"I'm not sure…what if…"

"Blood for vampires. Champagne for everyone else." He waved at a pair of waiters. One stood with his eyes lowered, holding a tray of empty glasses, waiting on another who poured the effervescence from glittery golden bottles.

Quintus accepted a glass, gently setting it into her hand. His fingers deliberately brushed over hers, sending a tingle up her arm. Her body went on alert, her wolf seeking her mate. *Mate.* Gabriella blinked her gaze away, quickly sealing off her emotions. Confusion twisted through her, but she didn't have time to linger on her thoughts as the music went quiet and the screech of a microphone tore through the ballroom.

"Good evening," a female voice with an earthy tone resounded and the room went silent. "Welcome witches, wolves and vampires. Please show your appreciation to your fine leaders. Quintus. Please come up and say a few words."

"Stay with Viktor." Quintus brushed a kiss to her cheek and released her hand.

Gabriella's heart pounded as Quintus strode toward the stage. Cheering and whistling sang in her ears. She startled, as a firm hand clasped hers.

"Easy sweetheart," he said.

"Why does he have to go up there?"

"Business is business. Her name's Absinthe. She's the high priestess of the Celestine coven. She can quell all this dissension by showing solidarity with Quintus. You know how it is…every now and then you've got to pull out the big guns."

"But where's Jax again? The wolves?"

"That big fella over there. Hunter Livingston. He's an Alpha from Jackson Hole."

Gabriella's heart raced as his eyes locked on hers. Even with her shields up, the call of his wolf spoke to her. Her beast stirred, scratching at the surface to run free. *No, no, no. This can't happen. Look away. Look away.* She sucked a breath and brought the champagne to her lips, drawing a deep gulp.

"He's powerful," Viktor commented.

She coughed and gazed up at the blond vampire. "I'm sorry. It's just…I haven't been around many supes. Especially not wolves. The Alpha…he…" She shook her head.

"It's going to be all right. Hunter doesn't exactly love Quint but he's solid. Nothing happening to you tonight."

Quintus approached the stunning witch, and Gabriella's stomach twisted in a knot as she embraced her vampire and held tight to his hand. Absinthe appeared far too familiar with him, and Gabriella's wolf growled in response.

"The ways of our tribes are different, but we live peacefully with each other," the witch continued, a broad smile plastered on her face.

Gabriella released a breath as Quintus freed his hands, holding them towards the crowd. He spoke with determination, the entire room silent.

"There is only one true and powerful coven within New York. The Celestine coven has held leadership since the days this country was founded. And while we've had our disagreements over the years, we've protected vampires, the coven, the pack. There will always be outsiders. As long as they bring flavor not dissension, they're welcome. Our leadership is far too cohesive for division. Tonight is a reminder. So please, tell your children, and heed my words. There will be no trouble in New York." Quintus' line of focus drifted to Hunter who stood with his arms crossed. The Alpha nodded in agreement. "The wolves. You'll have no issues and should you cross paths with an enemy, Jax will take action. Tonight is a celebration."

The room exploded in applause and Quintus held a hand up to silence them. "Tonight is also a warning. A warning to others wishing to try their hand at taking down the coven. A warning to those who spread false rumors. There's no trouble here, so don't go seeking it. If you do, this is the face you will see."

Gabriella's heart fluttered at the sight of Quintus. His fangs dropped as he gave a lethal glare to the crowd. Fear filtrated through the room, the dark energy spearing through her mind. His anger and strength didn't scare her, but his commanding presence reminded her that her vampire was indeed lethal, an ancient creature, powerful and alpha.

"Wise words darling," Absinthe said, her voice firm. "We have a few more surprises for tonight so please do stay for a few hours."

Music blared to life reanimating the crowd. Quintus leapt from the stage onto the floor and stalked toward her. His feral energy blasted through her and she sucked a breath. As he took her hand into his, Gabriella hoped they were leaving.

"Let's dance," he growled, his fangs still bared.

She lost her words as he tugged her toward him and released her glass of champagne to Viktor. A slow sensual beat pulsated throughout the open space, and Gabriella surrendered into his arms as he pulled her toward him. With his chest pressed tightly to hers, she relaxed into his embrace.

"Are we going?" she whispered.

"You're beautiful tonight," he told her, loud enough for others to hear.

"I…thank you," she replied.

"Jesus Christ, you're fucking hot, do you know that?"

"Quintus…" She lost her words as he rocked his erection against her belly. Her nipples tightened in response.

"I'd fuck you right here. I want them all to know you belong to me. Do you understand?"

She gasped as he tugged at her dress, exposing her

shoulder. His lips brushed her bare skin.

"Look around here. I'm an animal too. This body. Your soul. It's mine," he claimed.

"Ahhh…." The sweet prick of his fangs teased her skin as he dragged his lips lazily over her collarbone. "But I've never….It's public…"

The lights dimmed, flashes of red and white light strobing in the darkness. She caught sight of others crowding around the dance floor.

"I want to be in you," he told her, his voice rough with lust.

She clutched his shoulder as he brushed the fabric of her dress aside, his hand slipping through the slit of her dress. She bit her lip, the touch of his fingers dancing over her mound. "Quintus…please…"

"Are you begging me to stop or are you begging me to finish?" he asked.

A jolt of arousal twisted through her, and she whispered. "Quintus…there're people watching." Her forehead rested on his shoulder as he plunged a finger deep inside her pussy.

"You're so fucking wet."

She rocked her pelvis as he fucked her with his hand. The ache between her legs blossomed, and she rubbed her breasts against his chest, her body on fire.

"What's happening?" she breathed in confusion at her uncontrollable desire. She caught flashes of faces surrounding them as the lights pulsed overhead.

"They'll all know you're mine."

"Quintus…please." Through her lust-driven haze, her

beast clawed to be with her mate. Her words failed as he slid a second finger inside her heat.

"Tell me, did you enjoy my bite?" He gently nibbled her shoulder, without breaking the skin as he held her in place.

"I'm going to come…" Her orgasm rose, his fingers thrusting in and out of her slick core, his thumb playing at her clit.

"Tell me…tell me who you belong to…"

"I can't…this is crazy…" Her eyes flashed open but she couldn't see, the lights blinding her.

"Say it," he demanded.

"Yours…" She contracted around his fingers as he pumped in and out of her. The sweet insanity of the moment called to the wildness of her wolf. "I'm yours…just fuck…please…"

Gabriella cried out at the sting of his fangs slicing into her shoulder, "Ah Goddess…" Her fingernails dug into his shoulders, her body shaking, coming hard as he sucked at her essence. She didn't care who watched. She hadn't lied; she belonged to this vampire, and had no control but to allow the waves of ecstasy to roll through her body.

He lapped over her skin and withdrew his fingers. She stood mesmerized as he sucked them into his mouth. With her gaze locked on his, she panted, attempting to catch her breath. Quintus captured her lips, his seductive tongue danced with hers. Tasting herself, she surrendered to his intoxicating kiss. Gabriella returned his passion, publicly claiming him. This vampire was hers, no other's.

His dominant thoughts filtered through her mind, the

rabid thirst to declare her as his own. She sucked a breath as his guilt slammed into her, and he shut down his energy.

"Jesus, Gabby," he whispered, pulling her close to his chest.

Safe within his embrace, Gabriella struggled to process what the hell had just happened. They'd just had sex in front of everyone, he'd bitten her.

"I just…you make me lose control. I want them all to know you're mine," he whispered.

"It's okay…" Gabriella began but was interrupted by a tap on her shoulder. She swiveled her head to face Absinthe. The cool witch grinned from ear to ear, and Gabriella struggled to regain her composure.

"Ah, a young couple in lust. Such is the way of wolves." She sniffed into the air and grinned. "You aren't from here. Are you sure you aren't a mix of some kind? You're magick…I can't tell but it seems like you are…"

"She's wolf," Quintus assured, interrupting her.

"Hmm…I don't know. Hybrids can be a peculiar sort."

"We've got to get going. Full moon," Quintus told her.

Gabriella's mouth went dry, Absinthe's power washing over her, probing, seeking a way into her mind. She closed off her walls, refusing the high priestess access.

"Very interesting, Quintus," she sang, eyeing Gabriella from head to toe.

"She belongs to me and is none of your concern," he told her flatly.

"Yes, I was privy to your little show. Protective I see. But where is her Alpha? I assume she's not one of Jax's."

"I'm Hunter's." The lie rolled off Gabriella's lips, and inwardly she cringed, shocked at her own words.

"Really? Well then…I'm surprised at this," Absinthe said.

"She's new to my pack," a low voice rumbled.

Gabriella's eyes blinked up to gaze upon the familiar handsome Alpha. Her walls fell in an instant, his wolf commanding hers. She resisted his call, aware she had no pack. Yet her wolf betrayed her, crouching in submission.

She looked to Quintus who kept his focus trained on Absinthe. *Easy, bella.* A wave of calming energy flowed through her as he squeezed her hand.

"So the Alpha owns the little wolf." She laughed and turned to Hunter. "You're okay with the vampire claiming her as he does?"

"Affairs of the heart are not my concern. She does as she wishes. She's not my mate," Hunter replied.

"And Jax?" Absinthe asked.

"As you know, he and Finn are otherwise engaged. He trusted me to lead this event on his behalf. Dissension in the Big Apple isn't good for any of us. I'd hate to have to send some of my wolves to help Jax kick ass in New York. So here I am. Besides, who doesn't enjoy New York City? Perhaps I'll take in a show."

"You're an interesting lot, I'll give you that," Absinthe said, raising a disbelieving eyebrow. "Well, it's good that little wolf has her Alpha, because Quintus is going to be quite the busy bee."

"What's that supposed to mean?" Viktor asked as he

approached, his tone cold.

"It's a surprise," she cackled with a tilt of her head. "I'm afraid junior won't be very happy, but Quintus? Let's just say you'll be quite happy. And busy."

"Enough with the games, Absinthe," Quintus growled.

"Look, I know your coven must have some super witchy, voodoo, get out the cauldron and dance naked kind of thing to do, so a little less chatting. Full moon and all. Gotta go soon," Hunter told her.

Gabriella's heart pounded in her chest. *What the hell did the witch have for her vampire?*

"One question before we leave. The outside covens. There's no chance you might miss one of these witches? Maybe, let's say, they blend into your coven. New witches. Things go on in the underground all the time…even with the vamps. Rumblings. Rumor is that there's a particularly rough coven from Salem. Circe."

Gabriella froze at the name, taking note that Quintus didn't mention the high priestess. Absinthe smiled broadly in response, her eyes cold as ice.

"I have a private table in a blood room. Care to join me?" she asked.

"Let's go," he agreed.

Gabriella's focus darted to Viktor and Hunter who both moved to follow.

"We all have a stake in this. Agreed?" Quintus asked, but his tone commanded.

Absinthe gave a subtle eye roll, a hiss escaping her lips. "Yes. This way."

Gabriella held tight to Quintus' hand as they navigated through the sea of gyrating bodies. The scent of burning sage and sweat drifted in the air. The heat from strangers' bare skin emanated onto hers. Tunneling through the crowd, she breathed in relief as they approached an open area in the corner. She caught sight of a tattered white linen cloth swaying, light pricking through the porous fabric. Cold air rushed into her lungs as she pressed into the stark white hallway. The walls reflected bright light that shone down from the ceiling. Gabriella calmed as the pounding music went silent, their footsteps echoed as they made their way through an endless labyrinth of winding tunnels.

"Ah, here we are," she heard Absinthe announce, the hallway abruptly flashing into a red haze.

Gabriella's pulse raced, an intense magick rushing over her. *Easy, little one.* She blinked, realizing he'd communicated to her again without speaking. She shoved the uncomfortable realization to the back of her mind, her wolf warning her of danger.

"We've arrived," Absinthe declared.

Gabriella steeled her nerves and straightened her spine as she strode through the threshold into the dimly lit room. Lined with faux leather sofas and white candles, the cozy room appeared innocuous until she spied the sanguine-colored tubes that sprouted from the circular teak coffee table.

Quintus nodded, and she slowly inched her way onto the royal blue cushion, keeping close to her vampires. The door slammed shut, and Absinthe reached for a chilled glass of champagne that sat near an ice bucket to her left.

"Too many prying ears out in the open."

"Agreed," Quintus said. "The Circe coven. What do you know?"

"They're purists. Have been in the U.S. for nearly three hundred years but have mostly flown under the radar."

"They must have a special kind of broom." Viktor gave a half smirk, his eyes not revealing a hint of humor.

"Funny, pretty boy." Absinthe took a deep breath. "They mostly keep to themselves. Inbred some say. In my opinion, they're dangerous. Always have been. I'm not saying my coven comes without drama but Jesus, you don't need to sign up with a cult that won't let their witches even look at another breed. And when I use the term cult, that's exactly what it is."

Cult. Gabriella had always thought them evil killers, but she'd never considered that she'd grown up in a cult. Scared, intimidated, it was all she'd ever known. *Don't trust them. They'll kill you.* No outsiders were ever welcome. She began to question her deep-seated fear of other covens.

"They're violent," Quintus commented.

"Well yes. I suppose. Now wait…are you trying to insinuate it's them who's causing the fuss?" she asked, her voice raised.

"I'm not saying anything. I'm just asking questions. Questions that perhaps only a high priestess would know the answers to."

"I'm not hearing any questions," she challenged.

"Let's just say that perhaps it was their coven. That

maybe they had a spell of some sort that was riling the supernaturals. And maybe they were threatening certain members of their organizations. How would one most quickly go about..." Quintus went silent and shrugged, raising an eyebrow at her, "ridding themselves of such a problem?"

"Theoretically?" The corner of her mouth upturned slightly.

"Theoretically." Quintus gave a squeeze to Gabriella's hand but kept his focus on Absinthe.

"I suppose you'd need an artifact to disable the high priestess. It's her direction that steers the cult. For example, if you had a car that had been totaled, there would be no other choice but to replace it."

"Replace it?" Gabriella failed to hold her silence as her emotions bubbled to the surface. The coven had already killed her mother and was trying to kill her.

"Yes, I'd prefer to think of it as replace."

"But do you honestly think that will be the end...it will never end as long as she's alive. You need to kill her."

Absinthe burst out in laughter and soon after Viktor joined her, amused by Gabriella's statement.

"This isn't a joke. She needs to die." Gabriella grew annoyed at the conversation. She pressed down her heels, readying to leave, when Quintus settled a strong arm around her shoulders and placed a kiss to her head. Fucking hell, she was about to lose her shit. She shook her head, glaring at the blonde witch.

"Ah, your wolf is bloodthirsty." A pregnant pause filled

the room. She gave a cool smile, her gaze slowly moving from one person to the next until she settled on Quintus. "But of course, she's correct. I prefer to remain politically correct but yes, I don't expect she'd take to her replacement well. Therefore, it must end in her death. Only then do you have a chance to change the followers. But you must be careful, because there will be stragglers who never change their minds. Who will seek retribution."

"How do we do it? What do we need?" Quintus asked.

"Although they settled here in the States, they've been around for quite some time. The origin of their coven is Paris. Dated back to the Middle Ages."

"How did they manage to fly under the radar? I was in Europe during the Middle Ages and I don't recall their name."

"They were in their infancy. I heard they use bone dust in their spells. But if you ask me, it's why they are the way they are."

"How's that?"

"Twelfth century. There were only a handful. They embrace earth's magick, keeping their powers on the down low."

"What happened to them?" Quintus asked.

"What happened to anyone back then? You know the way of the inquisition." Absinthe sipped her drink.

"We were on the move. We couldn't stay in groups. The idea of what we do today would have been a death sentence. No more than three or four of us traveled at a time, often hiding in tunnels, the woods." As he spoke, Quintus' gaze went to his brother, recalling the difficult times.

Gabriella watched Viktor intently. His curved smile disappeared, his expression solemn. Quintus held an ancient power that had been earned through centuries of solitude. She considered that it was only recently he'd been able to build his network of vampires, to connect openly with other supernaturals.

"Yes, well. No one's really sure when they left but some say they hid the body of the first witch in the catacombs among the millions of other bones. They say she's so well hidden no one will ever find her. As you know, humans are limited to the areas they are allowed to access. In the darkest tunnels even supernaturals steer clear of the evil that lurks under the earth. Speaking of which…" Absinthe fished a cell phone from her bustier and tapped on the glass. The door creaked open, but the stranger kept his face turned until it hinged shut. "Everyone. I have a delightful surprise."

"Witches sure know how to throw a party," the newcomer commented.

As he turned toward the group, the lights flicked onto his face, and Gabriella caught sight of his devilish smile. She sucked a breath as his dark energy smacked into her. The fiery spirit danced over her skin, leaving a distinctive tingle. *Demon*, she heard Quintus say, but as her eyes flashed to him, he hadn't spoken out loud. He remained focused on the mysterious guest.

"Everyone's so quiet…cat got your tongue?" The handsome stranger strode across the room with confidence and sat in a chair to the left of Absinthe.

"We may not have many rules, witch, but you know damn well demons aren't welcome. What the hell is this?" Hunter asked, his voice raised. He went to push onto his feet but went still as Quintus held up a hand.

"Demon. You're something else, though, aren't you?" the dominant vampire guessed.

"This is some bullshit, Absinthe. I don't know what you're trying to pull but we're all out of here," Hunter said.

"Your power holds a unique energy. Hybrid, perhaps. Si?" Quintus continued. Although he spoke in a calm manner, Gabriella noted the tick of his jaw as he cocked his head in distrust.

"Clever vampire," he responded.

"Explain. Now," Quintus demanded.

"No need to get testy. True, I'm a demon, but I still harbor human tendencies. As you can imagine, I'm not popular in Hell. Something about killing for fun doesn't quite appeal to me as it should. Doesn't stop me on occasion but just doesn't do it for me if you know what I'm saying. Can't seem to shake those pesky human attributes. I'm a lesser level demon. Technically I'm half demon. So no need to fly into a bat over my presence." He stared at Quintus in defiance.

"I'd like to introduce Thorn Rachille." Absinthe ran her palms over her lap and smoothed her dress, raising her gaze to establish eye contact with each person in the room. "You see, he's been having his own set of difficulties, and I did what any self-respecting witch would do."

"Kill him. That's what you should have done," Viktor

commented, his brows furrowed in disbelief.

"But of course she wouldn't kill him, would you?" Quintus asked her, his mouth drawn tight. "He has something on you. Perhaps one of your witches. He's not particularly powerful by demon standards but he could serve a purpose. Witches." He blew out a breath and shook his head. "Hoarding."

Gabriella's head spun, considering her own mother's tendency to collect. Absinthe must have needed him.

"Exactly. You collect it all, don't you? Wolf hair. Scales from the rarest fish. Vampire fangs. Ingredients saved for a spell you don't even know you're going to use."

"A girl has to be prepared," Absinthe admitted.

"You know, if I wasn't so incredibly talented, I might be insulted," Thorn commented, a wry grin on his face. "Your group is quite interesting. A wolf, a witch and a vampire walked into a bar. Do you know that one?"

"What is he doing here?" Hunter asked, his fists clenched.

"But her…" Thorn's attention settled on Gabriella. "She's very unique, isn't she?"

Gabriella's stomach clenched as the demon pointed at her. A rush of hot energy blasted towards her, and she closed her eyes, ramming a shield up, forcing it back onto him.

"Ah…that's lovely. Look what she can do," the demon laughed. "She's something all right."

"She's a wolf. Now leave her the fuck alone or you're going to be leaving here in little pieces," Quintus growled at Thorn, and then turned to Gabriella. "Are you okay?"

"I'm fine," she replied, anger pulsing through her veins. Whatever this creature was doing here was evil. She sensed the wispy edge of a dark intention, but she couldn't tell if it was truly coming from the demon or from an outside force. The trace amounts of energy lingered around her, and she scented hints of rose petals, leaving her with the impression of a feminine owner.

"You're not as weak as they perceive you…" Thorn's words trailed off, waiting on her to provide her name.

"Don't do that again. Ever." Gabriella gritted her teeth, refusing to introduce herself.

"You seem quite close to the vampire," the demon noted. "Come on now, love. Tell me your name."

"You don't need to know who she is. All you need to know is that she belongs to me." Quintus stood, taking Gabriella by the hand. His gaze went to the high priestess. "This meeting's jumped the rails. Absinthe, I'm going to give you a little piece of advice. Stay away from demons. They're not good for your health."

"Half-demon. It's cool though." He shrugged, giving a roll of his eyes. "Haters gonna hate."

"You're a demon. It's not like there's a middle ground. You're from Hell," Gabriella shot at him. Her beast paced, her pulse raced faster.

"Thanks for pulling together this party but we're done," Quintus told Absinthe. "I'll make sure mine play nice. If you hear anything at all about outsiders, whisperings of the Circe coven, I want to know yesterday."

"I have a gift. Thorn has brought it," she replied coyly.

"Absinthe. Whatever it is, I'm sure it's a lovely thought but totally unnecessary." Quintus shook his head and turned to leave.

"Of course it is," she responded as she rose and stepped toward the door. Her gown trailed behind her. "But you know when you happen to trip upon the perfect gift for someone...well, I simply couldn't say no. As much as I appreciate your advice about demons, Thorn is his own beast."

"We've got to go," Quintus insisted.

Gabriella squeezed his hand. *Please. My wolf.* As she closed her eyes and spoke, she prayed he'd sense her desperation. Her eyes widened at his response.

"Tonight's full moon," Quintus said. "Hunter. Your wolves need to run."

"Tru dat, brother. I'm so over the show tonight. It's been real." Hunter shoved to his feet and crossed the room, not bothering to shake the demon's hand. He stopped in front of the witch, his fiery eyes on hers. "For the record. I'm with Quint on this one. There is no such thing as a good demon. You're gonna get burnt."

"Patience, lovelies," Absinthe commented. With a firm grip, she grasped the handle, swinging the door wide open, sharing her surprise.

Gabriella's breath caught at the sight of the petite female standing in the hallway. A rush of Quintus' emotions slammed through her...shock...grief...guilt. As fast as it came, it disappeared, his shields shutting her out of his thoughts. *He knows her.* Although he held tight to her hand, his eyes remained focused on the woman. His heavy breath gave away his emotion. *Love. He'd loved this woman.* Stunned, Gabriella yanked away her hand from his.

"Mao," he whispered and quickly focused his attention on Absinthe. "What the hell is this? Is this some sort of sick spell? Who is this woman?"

"You know who she is, my dear Quintus."

"Mao is dead. I watched her fall to her death."

"Ah, well, apparently she's not," Thorn commented.

"What the hell do you have to do with this?" Quintus demanded.

"I don't take trips to Hell often. Was there on unrelated business. Purely out of necessity. I haven't been in a while and took a wrong turn. Can happen to anyone. Opened up the wrong dungeon door and there she was." Thorn gave a loud sigh, raising his eyebrows. "I found her in a rather unsavory place. Eighth dimension of the court of demons."

"If she's in Hell, did it ever occur for you to leave her there? Maybe she's not who she says she is," Viktor suggested.

"You don't understand. She was in a section where the innocents reside. And she was asking for you. And so…I contacted Absinthe. No offense, but you're not the kind of warm and fuzzy vamp I'm looking to help. To be honest, this could have gone either way. I could have easily left her there, but I owe Absinthe a favor."

"A favor for what?" Quintus asked.

"Ah well, you know we all need a bit of witch's help every now and then. It happens. Debt's clear now. She seemed to think you were in love with this waif but it all seems a little anticlimactic now."

"Quintus." The female lifted her eyes to the vampire. "Please…what's going on? I'm…"

"Mao…" Quintus shook his head in disbelief.

Gabriella's stomach turned hearing the woman's name on her mate's lips, yet it was the softening of his eyes that stirred her beast. This intruder threatened to destroy the fragile relationship she'd built. She closed her eyes willing her wolf to retreat. *Mate.* The territorial urge warred with her humanity.

"I've been to Hell," Mao said, her hands outreached. "Please…I need you…"

As she fell to her knees, Quintus rushed to her side. Gabriella held her breath as he scooped the female into his arms.

"Mao…" Quintus gazed at his old lover then looked up to the demon.

"She needs comfort. Give her blood," Thorn suggested. "Shifters. They're practically as vulnerable as the humans."

"What?" Gabriella gasped, shock rolling through her body.

"The trip from Hell. It's not exactly first class. More like being in the back of the bus." Thorn brushed his palm over his sleeve. "Suit held up well though."

"You mean you left her there after you found her?" Quintus growled, his focus on Mao.

"What did you expect me to do? I don't know who took her or how she got there. For all I know she deserved to be there. Demons aren't exactly the most forgiving people. I only took her once I knew I could deliver her to a reliable owner."

"Quintus doesn't own her," Gabriella protested. Her blood boiled in anger. A vampire couldn't have two mates. Her beast clawed to emerge. She closed her eyes, breathing deeply. *No shifting. No shifting.*

"Sorry, love, but look at them. Clearly they were supposed to be together."

"Knock it off, demon." Viktor placed his hand on Gabriella's arm but she shoved him away.

"Don't touch me," she hissed, her eyes glowing red. Fire burned hot in her belly. Her wolf desperately scratched at what remained of her human psyche. Nothing could keep her beast at bay. "I've got...I've got to get out of here." Gabriella scanned the room, planning her escape, her chest heaving.

"Viktor, take Mao," Quintus ordered, cradling the lifeless woman in his arms. "I've got to get Gabriella outside."

"No. I can't do this. You have another mate...no, I don't want..." Gabriella's vision blurred as her wolf emerged. Rage drove the feral beast toward the surface, her claws extending.

"You try to do a nice thing and it all goes to shit. Good intentions." Thorn shrugged with a sardonic smile.

"Shut the fuck up," Quintus spat at the demon. "Viktor, come take her. Now."

The room spun as her wolf emerged. Gabriella clawed at the fabric of her dress, the full moon compelling her to shift.

She lost control, helpless to thwart the change. The possessive nature of the animal drove her, and within seconds, the pads of her feet hit the ground. With the transformation complete, Gabriella pressed to all fours, her attention set on Mao.

"Easy, bella. You don't want to hurt anyone," Quintus warned.

A ripple of his power danced over her fur, but Gabriella reflected it and sent his energy dissipating into the air.

"Settle, Gabby," she heard Hunter say. Gabriella twisted her head to face him. His commanding voice resonated, yet he wasn't her Alpha. The only one who she'd given power to had been Quintus.

"What the hell is going on here?" Absinthe asked, rolling her eyes. "I bring you a gift and you shit on it. All of you. I'm done."

"Where do you think you're goin', Princess Pineapple?" Thorn shook his head at the sight of the wolf and shrugged. "Well I suppose it's time for me to fuck off as well."

"Who shifts during an event? No control whatsoever. Pfft…and to think I suspected she was a witch. Look at her." Absinthe took off toward the bar and gazed in the mirror, smoothing the fine hairs around her temples.

Gabriella growled at Mao. Despite the female's frail disposition, her instincts warned her of the danger. *Evil. Deception.*

"Quintus…" The female trembled as she roused. "Who is she?"

Gabriella stalked toward Mao, a low growl rumbling in

her throat. Sensing Quintus' disapproval, she sealed off communication with him. She crouched low to the ground and prepared to attack.

"Gabriella, no." Quintus nodded to Viktor, who knelt next to him, taking Mao into his arms. He lifted his palms, slowly backed away and stood. "I'm not touching her. No one's going to hurt you."

Lies. Gabriella snarled.

"Damn, I didn't think wolves cared about vampires. You learn something new every day." Thorn opened the door, and paused.

"I don't know how the hell this can be," Hunter commented. "Vampire, she's really yours?"

"Of course she's mine," Quintus answered.

"Even the wolf didn't know you're mates." Thorn smiled as he turned, giving a wave with his hand as he walked into the dark hallway.

"Jesus Christ, Quintus," Hunter mumbled under his breath.

With her hackles raised, Gabriella poised herself to pounce. She snapped her jaws, a loud growl reverberating throughout the room.

"Gabriella, I'm ordering you to back off now," Quintus told her.

It wasn't as if she didn't hear her vampire command her, but incomplete, the bond he had wasn't strong enough to bend her will. The wolf drove her decision. Mao threatened a mate she'd hadn't yet claimed. Nothing else mattered.

"Gabby, as Alpha, I'm commanding you to retreat," Hunter said, his voice stern.

Electricity shot through Gabriella as the Alpha spoke. She'd never been commanded by another wolf, submission wasn't in her nature. The unrelenting order constricted her, but she fought him. *Not my Alpha. Not my pack. Lone wolf.* She crouched to the ground, whimpering as pain tore through her body.

"Jesus, Hunter...leave her be," Quintus said, stepping forward to help her, but she went wild, gnashing her teeth together.

"She's out of control. How the fuck can you have two mates anyway?" Hunter kept his eyes trained on the black wolf.

Gabriella glared at Quintus, refusing to allow him into her mind. *He never cared about me*, she thought. If he already had a mate, there was no way he belonged to her. No matter what he'd said about bonding, he'd been wrong. She never developed a mating mark. *Stupid Gabby. He was never yours.* Without giving warning to the others, she made the decision to run.

Charging through the door, she tore through the darkened hallways. The scent of sandalwood incense filtered through the air, and she suspected the witches were spiking the air with a spell. Instinct drove her escape, recalling her way out of the building. She dodged bodies in the darkness. Shadows and magical energy blended together in a kaleidoscope of colors. The blood-scented fragrance coated her nostrils.

Sensing no wolves in the din of the crowd, she suspected they'd already left to run. Distraught, she'd find solace in the moon's healing light. Her magick renewed, she'd have the strength to fight to keep hidden from the coven.

Feral with grief, she burst through the open doors, her claws gripping the gravel as she tore into the darkness. She'd never run in a city but it hardly mattered. A clear night, the bright streaks of moonlight bathed the streets. Jealousy burned hot in her soul, her wolf mourning the loss of her mate.

She pressed on hard with no regard to the few humans who stood warming their hands around a steel can fire. Like a flash of lightning, she disappeared into the shadows.

Running, running, running. Her spirit soared, the flare of anger still fresh in her mind. The wolf ducked into a park, and she imagined the forest, the leaves rustling, but the blare of a train's horn reminded her she was in the city. Cool air carried a hint of moisture, drawing her toward the river. When she finally reached its pebbled beach, she loped to a slow pace. Panting for breath, her head tilted toward the stars. Releasing a tortured howl, her wolf lamented until her throat grew raw.

Her magick renewed by the moon, Gabriella shifted to human form and collapsed onto the sand. Hot tears streamed down her face as she curled onto her side. *Why did I trust him? He lied. Just like the coven. Just like everyone I've ever met. No one cares. I'm alone.* With an unexpected fervor, she heaved for breath, crying, her stomach cramped in knots.

"He has a mate. He has a mate. I can't do this. I can't do this," she repeated.

She'd tried to deny it, but her connection to Quintus had been strong. Confusion swept through her as doubt seeded in her mind. *How could he not have known she was alive? How could he lie to me?*

A cold breeze iced over her skin, but she barely noticed. She coughed, lying naked, trembling and curled into a ball. Simple spells she'd used to conjure clothing eluded her as her thoughts raced. *Why is this happening?* Tragedy followed her wherever she went, and she couldn't seem to shake it. Her mother's horrifying murder. Running from city to city. Imminent death had come and gone so many times she'd lost count. Discovering she had a mate who wasn't wolf. Losing him before they'd completed the bond.

Gabriella reached inside, determined not to give up, grasping the only strength she'd ever known. Moonlight bathed her bared body, infusing her with renewed courage to face another day. Her wolf rested, calmed by the soothing lunar energy that radiated around her.

I'll do it without him, she told herself, fresh tears brimming from under her lashes. She didn't know how she'd become so close to Quintus. She knew wolves could walk away from their mates, but she'd heard it drove them mad, forcing them to go rogue.

The crackle of broken branches caught her attention, and within seconds his familiar dominating presence registered. Her attempts to block his energy were thwarted as he drew closer, her name on her vampire's lips.

"Gabriella, you're going to be all right," Quintus said, his voice calm.

"Go away," she managed. With her forearms pressed to the cold sand, she lifted her head. Her wolf howled with pain as he continued to approach. She yearned for the mate she'd thought was hers.

"Please. Gabby. We'll figure this out. Let me take you back home."

"No, don't come closer. I'll shift. I'll run."

"I'm not certain she's really my mate. Once upon a time, yes…a very long time ago…"

"No, don't say it. I don't want to hear about her. I don't care. I should have never come to you. Just so you know, I would have done it anyway. Saved you. But I'm so stupid asking for your help…all this. I let you bite me…" Her words faltered as she began to cry.

"I just need a little time to sort this. It's possible she isn't…"

"No!" Gabriella pushed away from the earth but struggled to stand. She fell to her knees, defiantly staring at him. "Don't touch me."

"I didn't want to do this the hard way, Gabby, but I'm taking you home one way or another," he told her, his tone stern.

"No…I'm not…" Gabriella went silent as the Alpha's power unexpectedly washed over her. Hunter approached through the brush, infusing her with his healing powers. Her wolf cowered in submission.

"Gabby." Hunter gave Quintus a nod as he crouched down so he was on eye level with Gabriella. "It's all right. What you're feeling right now…that energy. It's me claiming you as my pack. I know you're hybrid but your wolf feels me and I feel her. I can't say I know all of what's going on between you and the vampire, but I do know you belong with pack. I'll protect you."

"Like hell you will. Gabby, we're going home…" Quintus' focus shifted as Viktor materialized.

"Hey Quint. This sitch is getting a little…uh, complicated." His brother glanced to Gabriella then back to Quintus.

"Can't you handle things? I've got my hands full here."

"Yeah, she's not in good condition. I really think you need to get back here. Hunter and I will take care of Gabby."

Quintus blew out a breath. "Goddammit. Okay, look, Gabby, we've got to go. Just let me flash us both out of here. You can't stay here."

"You mean *she* needs you." Gabriella gave a soft sigh, then a laugh, and shook her head. "You can't have two mates. It's okay. It didn't make sense anyway."

"I'm going to give you three seconds," he warned.

"And what?" She gave a sad smile. "I'll go back to your house to get my things, but I'm not going with you." Her eyes landed on Viktor's. "I'm not going with you either." Rubbing the back of her hand against her mouth, she sighed in defeat and nodded toward Hunter. "The Alpha. I'll go with him."

"What the hell…" Quintus began.

She gave a sad laugh, her eyes finally settling back on Quintus. "I'm a wolf. You saw me. You all saw me. This is my nature."

Quintus reached for her but she flinched, quickly transforming to wolf. She released a low growl, warning him away.

"Hunter," he said, never taking his sight off of Gabriella. "You can bring her to my home. I don't give a shit what the rules say about mates. This woman, this wolf…she's mine, are we clear?"

"You haven't completed the bond," Hunter challenged. "If she doesn't want you, that's her choice."

"We've already begun the bond."

"You have a problem on your hands, my friend," Hunter said.

"Don't worry about me," Quintus replied. "Just bring her back to my house safely."

"I'm offering her sanctuary with my wolves. Jax's pack would seem logical but he's not here and I am."

"Look at her. She's scared, but she's not yours." Quintus' face softened as he gazed upon his angry she-wolf. "Hunter…just bring her back. I need some time to deal with this situation. It's only a matter of time before the Salem witches catch up with Gabby and I'm not leaving her."

"But if you're not her mate…"

"I am," Quintus insisted, his voice certain.

"But…"

"Don't test me Alpha. I'm not a fight you're looking for."

"I'm Alpha for a reason, vampire. You're not a wolf. Gabby is."

"I don't give a shit where you think she belongs. I know where she belongs and it's with me. She's confused..." Hunter's lips tightened with anger.

Gabriella growled, incensed by Quintus' insistence she was his. None of it mattered if he had another mate. She forced her feelings for him away, refusing to let them influence her. She turned to bolt when the call of the Alpha seized her, thwarting her escape. *What is happening?* As she attempted to block Hunter, Quintus' voice played in her head. *Little wolf. It's time to go home.*

"You can't run forever, Gabriella," Quintus told her, his voice softened.

"You can't block both of us at the same time," Hunter cautioned. "You might be getting more clever with Quintus but he's not a wolf. What you're feeling is just a sliver of my power."

"I told you not to hurt her," Quintus warned.

"I'm going to shift now, and then we're going back home," Hunter said to Gabriella. "It's not a good idea for you to be around Jax's pack."

Quintus sighed as the wolf stripped off his clothes. "Don't touch her, wolf. As much as I appreciate your help, I won't think twice about killing you if she's harmed."

As Hunter shifted, Quintus' focus went to Gabriella. "You get a pass tonight, but this conversation is far from over. Next time there will be no running. The only things saving you are the moon and the Alpha. I don't care what you think just happened back there, but you belong to me."

Gabriella set off running into the brush, his anger

sweeping over her. *Run little wolf run...you'll always be mine.* She shoved his words to the recesses of her mind, unwilling to give her heart to someone who'd never be hers. As the Alpha joined her, she gave in to her feral nature, forgetting everything and everyone except the call of the moon.

·❦· *Chapter Nine* ·❦·

Quintus had grieved Mao's death for centuries. The guilt had nearly caused his own demise, but he'd prevailed, finally accepting that life went on without her.

"Goddammit," Quintus growled under his breath as he flashed into his living room. The second his feet hit the floor he caught sight of his brother's face mere inches from his.

"Hey brother," Viktor quipped, materializing directly in front of him.

"Jesus. I told you not to do that."

"You'd think after a few hundred years of annoying your ass, it'd get old." He shrugged with a smile. "But no. Just as good as it was the first time."

"Contrary to what you believe, tonight isn't a fucking joke." Quintus strode behind the bar and retrieved a bottle of whiskey. "You're supposed to be watching Mao. Where is she?"

"She was taking a shower last I saw her. She's a hot chick but I didn't think you'd be down for me sticking around to watch. Room's warded so she can't get out if that's what you're worried about."

"She's a fucking pixiu. If she wants to get out, she's going to tear the damn house apart." Quintus blew out a breath, slid two glasses across the bar and began to pour. "Well that night certainly went to shit pretty fast."

"Gabriella," Viktor said, accepting the drink from Quintus.

"I can't believe she went with Livingston." Quintus took a long draw of the liquor, exhaling as the golden nectar burned down his throat. "Fuck."

"I'm surprised you let her go with the Alpha." Viktor raised an eyebrow and cocked his head.

"Don't fucking say it." He poured another shot.

"So let me get this straight. Your girl turns into an animal. You guys find her and then let her run off with the wolf." Viktor laughed, shaking his head. "An Alpha at that."

"Don't be an asshole."

"What the hell are you doing? No don't tell me. Look, Quint. You're one of the toughest mofo's I've ever known. This woman is turning you inside out. There's no way in the past you'd have ever given up on a woman...let alone one who's your mate. What the actual fuck is going on?"

"You saw her tonight. I know it seems like the wrong thing to do but I'm telling you, she's losing it because she's a wolf. I'm her mate..."

"Mao is your mate."

"No, she's not. I mean, yeah, she was once. But that was a long fucking time ago. I've bitten Gabriella, tasted of her. The bond. I know it's begun."

"So Gabriella mated with you? She's got the mark?"

"Well, no. I mean, I guess it didn't even occur to me until tonight."

"She probably doesn't even know to look for it. She hasn't been raised in the pack." Viktor downed the whiskey and slammed the glass on the bar. "But what about Mao? You started the process…I don't know when. Fuck. I can't even remember how long it's been but I sure as shit know she was your mate. When she died…" His words trailed off and he continued to shake his head, staring into his empty glass, and then sent his gaze back up to meet Quintus'. "You almost died."

"I'd bitten her, but we hadn't completed the bond." Quintus plowed his fingers through his hair and sighed. "Look, I don't know how this shit works. I mean if she survived the fall, why didn't I feel her life force? I didn't. It may have been a hell of a long time ago but I remember it like yesterday. It felt like my guts were ripped out. There was nothing. She was nowhere."

"But she's not dead. She's upstairs in the west wing guest room."

"It's been a long time, and I'm telling you that whatever bond we'd started…it's gone. It's just gone. I don't know what's going on. That woman looks like Mao, but I don't trust the demon or Absinthe for that matter."

"And our dear little Gabriella? You send her off with an Alpha? What the hell were you thinking? She might never be back."

"She's a wolf. She needed to shift tonight. And despite her doing it like she did, shifting right there in front of everyone, I wanted this for her. It's the first time in her whole life she's ever run with another wolf." Quintus grabbed his drink off the bar and made his way over to an oversized black suede chair and fell down into it, propping his feet on an ottoman. The scent of the Kentucky whiskey filled his nostrils as he brought the rim of the glass to his lips. "She's been alone for a long time. She trusted me to bite her. And more importantly, her wolf, she trusted me. And now this thing with Mao…Jesus Christ, I feel like an asshole for saying this, but I've already mourned the loss. She's no longer my mate. I don't know how I know this but I just do. Today…"

"Today you were in shock. And truth here…I was not expecting to ever see her again. I mean…she looked fine too. Your girl was in Hell and she looks like she's been to Cabo, taking a chill on vaca."

"She's not my girl." Quintus' head snapped up, his focus on his brother. "I need more information about how she survived. That woman upstairs looks like Mao. It doesn't mean that's actually her."

"She's twinning, that's for damn sure."

"Her scent…aside from the slight burnt odor, it could've been Mao."

"Hell. Can't get the smell out of the skin." Viktor sunk down into the plush sofa and rested his head back onto one of its pillows. "Well, I don't know what to tell you. She's here. In your house. In the flesh. Not dead. Very much alive and my guess is she's going to be gearing up for making up some time in the next few hours."

"No. Absolutely not. That isn't happening." Quintus shook his head.

"I didn't say you. I said her. I can just tell by the way she looked at you back there, she's got lovin' on her mind. No joke."

"You need to shut the fuck up because Gabriella's going to be strolling through that door any minute and I want her to stay."

"Stay where?" Viktor looked around the room, and gave Quintus a sly smile.

"Here, of course." Quintus dragged his forefinger around the rim of his glass. "It's not like I didn't love Mao. I did. But I grieved. I moved on. And now...Gabby's a..."

"A complication?" Viktor's smile disappeared, a serious expression washing over his face. "It will happen to all of us eventually. I can't say I ever tire of being single but the Goddess...she does what she wants."

"I've tasted Gabriella. I can feel her. The bond has begun. I could deny it...maybe."

"Vampires have done so. It won't be easy. No other will satisfy you."

"Leaving Gabby to Hunter tonight..." He shook his head and lifted his glass to his lips. "It was so Goddamn hard. She needs to submit to me...not the fucking Alpha."

"She submitted to him?" Viktor asked, surprise in his voice.

"No. Well, how the fuck am I supposed to know? All I do know is that there's bones in France that can possibly be used to lift the hold on the Salem witches. Whatever's going on with those bitches is spooking everyone in New York City. They're coming for Gabriella. I want to get this thing…whatever the hell it is and get back to New Orleans. It's time for all this bullshit to end."

"And Mao?"

"I don't know. She could go back to China. Or stay here…" Quintus blew out a breath in frustration. There was no way Gabriella would ever accept his ex-lover living in the same city.

"Yeah, probably not the best idea."

"I'll figure something out." Quintus' thoughts drifted back to his little wolf. "Gabriella shut me out tonight, but I'm not going to let her do it again. This business of running. She's going to learn submission."

"Well, that should be interesting because even I could feel her power tonight. She's not the shy little wolf she pretends to be."

"Witch."

"Whatever. I'm just saying, that there's something about her power."

"I've felt it too. She's young. She's learning her power." Quintus looked to his brother. "This thing with Mao. I need to deal with this tonight."

He set his drink on an end table, and retrieved his phone, tapping on its screen.

"What's next?"

"Paris is what's next. Taking the private jet."

"The PJ? No flashing?"

"If it were just you and me? Yes. With Gabriella? No.

She's just getting used to…" Quintus stopped short of finishing his sentence as she entered his building. *Gabriella.*

As the elevator door slid open, Quintus caught sight of Hunter, the sheen of his sweat on his bared body. The small black wolf trailed behind him.

"Thank you for returning her safely," Quintus said, his attention on Gabriella.

Viktor remained seated and rolled his eyes as Hunter approached, a small smile forming on his lips. "You know I'm down for commando any day of the week, but I never get how you wolves give zero fucks about strolling around buck naked in front of other people. Just letting it swing free in the wind. Nice."

"I'm a wolf, jackass."

"Yeah, I get that. Windmill away."

Quintus ignored both his brother and Hunter, transfixed as Gabriella shifted back to her human form. Her long caramel locks tumbled over her shoulders, brushing over her nipples.

"I'm here," she said, her voice steady.

"That you are, bella."

"These wolves are…" Viktor began but Quintus cut him off.

"Not a word, brother. I can assure you this isn't the time." Quintus reached for Gabriella but she stepped backward, avoiding his touch.

"I need to go shower. Then I'm leaving. I know I asked you to help me but…"

"You're not going anywhere. We're flying out in the morning."

"You don't need to help me," she insisted. "No, it's more than that. I don't want your help anymore. I'll go myself. I'll get the bones of the first witch. I'll learn the spell or ritual or whatever it is I need and then I'll go."

"Gabby." Quintus stepped forward, removing his jacket.

"No, please…" Gabriella held up her hand.

"I'm just going to…" Quintus' chest tightened, sensing her confusion and pain. Pain that he'd caused. *Mao.*

"I can't stay here anymore," she whispered. Her voice shook.

"Gabby." Quintus gazed into her teary eyes, his heart heavy.

"I'm leaving."

"I promise you it's going to be all right." His lips grazed her hair as he set his jacket around her shoulders. "I'll deal with this situation and then we'll go to Paris."

"Quintus…I can't."

"I know you need some time, little wolf. Take a shower. Get some rest. We're leaving in the morning."

"Okay, fine. I'll sleep in the guest room."

"No, you'll sleep in my room where you're best protected." Although tempted to flash her away, he didn't want to traumatize her any more than she already had been. Quintus set his palms on her shoulders and closed his eyes, sending his power to her, attempting to calm her wolf. She didn't shut him out, yet her thoughts remained clouded.

"I can find it by myself," she said.

"I'll be up in a few minutes," Quintus told her, opening his eyes. He knew it was a lie; he'd need time to talk to Mao and send her to safety. "It's going to be all right, Gabby."

"I…Quintus…" she sighed, without finishing her thoughts. "Forget it."

Quintus released her shoulders, and she averted her gaze as she stepped around him. Her sad smile hinted at her disagreement, but he refused to let her simply walk out of his life. Refuting the bond would be difficult for him, but for Gabriella, a shifter, she'd likely not survive the loss of her mate.

He watched in silence as she walked away and headed toward his bedroom, his thoughts interrupted by the sound of Viktor's voice.

"Quint, I hate to be the bearer of bad news but Mao…you'd better get up there."

"I'm going to go talk to her now." He blew out a breath and looked to Hunter. "Alpha…"

"I've gotta get back to the pack," Hunter began.

"I need a favor. I'm leaving in the morning, and I hate to ask you this but I'm thinking Mao isn't safe here in New York. I could ask another vampire to take care of her but she's a shifter. I'm thinking if we can get her to Kai…maybe she can help her through this transition."

"I'm going out west in a few days. I'd be happy to keep her at the pack house. Finn's coming back tomorrow so between the two of us, we can keep an eye out."

"I'll text Jake to make sure it's okay but I'm thinking after everything Kai went through, she might benefit from being around another pixiu. I know they don't have packs but she's new to the whole shifter arena."

"Look Quintus. I know this might not be easy for someone like you. As old as you. But ya gotta go easy on Gabriella, okay? She's nearly a pup. You did the right thing letting her run with me. I'm sure you could feel it but just in case you vamps can't, I didn't ask her to submit to me. That's your place, not mine."

"I don't want to see her hurt any more than she already is," Quintus responded, his face serious.

"Hey man, I'm not mated but I know the score. When this shit happens, the last thing a wolf, Alpha or not, wants to do is get in between unmated wolves." Hunter's eyebrows rose as he shook his head. "But you've gotta tread lightly, vamp. Because that girl of yours...something about her. She's young but the magick is strong. I could feel it tonight and there's something...I can't put my finger on it."

"She's a hybrid." Something about her magick was special. Quintus kept the thought to himself and continued, "It doesn't matter. I know what you're saying. I owe you one for helping her. And I'll owe you again for Mao. But the thing is, with her..."

"I'll do my best but you know she's not wolf, right?" Hunter asked.

"A very long time ago, she was my mate. We'd begun the bond but didn't complete it. Our pairing was rare."

"It's rare for a vampire to mate with a wolf. Or a witch," Viktor interjected.

"Everyone has been misled to think we only bond with humans, but it happens. We find other supernaturals every now and then. All I know is that I don't want to see

Gabriella hurt," Quintus said, reflecting on his choice to help her.

"I've got to tell you, I'm not sure how or if Mao was your mate before…it just seems like, with wolves anyway, that bond, it's not something that simply goes away. Not for a minute. Not for one thousand years. Wolves only have one mate."

"I don't have answers. All I can guess is that something may have happened to her in Hell. I've been walking around on this earth for years and never once after she went over the cliff did I sense her. My guess is whatever found her…"

"Whatever took her," Viktor corrected.

"They must've done something to her. Or the bond. Something happened. I need time alone with her to know for sure. Back there with Absinthe…I knew it was Mao from the second she walked in, but I can't explain it…my craving, everything about the pull on my soul…this bond…it's Gabriella, not her."

"If it's any consolation, wolves go through this shit all the time. Take me for example, I've gone a long time without complications. I've been lucky. Tristan. He went down like a deck of cards. But that's usually how it happens."

"I can't say what's happening or why. All I do know is that Gabriella belongs to me. Whatever happened with Mao, it's over. I feel like we all need to be cautious. Both of you need to be careful around her."

"She might hear you," Viktor cautioned.

"I want her to hear me. The Alpha's right. Bonds…

matings…they don't just get broken out of nowhere. I have a lot of questions about what she's been doing in Hell. I'm not saying it was her fault, but I'd like to know who put her there. Something off about this whole situation."

"I'll be back in a few hours," Hunter said as he turned toward the foyer.

"Thanks for your help tonight," Quintus acknowledged.

"You'd better go talk to Mao. I can stay here if you'd like," Viktor offered.

"No, I'll handle things."

"I've gotta shower." Viktor sniffed. "Fucking demon. I can smell him on me."

"Thanks for tonight." Quintus gave a sigh and walked away, turning down the hallway.

He'd detected a hint of sulfur in the air. *Mao.* When Absinthe and Thorn had presented her, he'd been shocked at the sight of his former mate, but the love he'd once felt had been dulled. A distant memory, she wore an emptiness in her teary eyes. The connection they'd once shared no longer existed. He neither sensed her thoughts or emotions. Bonds could be ignored to a point but never broken.

Years ago, he would have trusted Mao with his life, but as he reached for the door handle and Hell's scent grew stronger, his suspicion spiked. Even though his wards prevented demons and black magick, he'd willingly brought her to his home.

The hinges creaked as Quintus turned the knob and opened the door. He stepped into the room, concealing his disgust at the distinctive odor lingering in the air. He caught sight of Mao's small figure in the corner. With her eyes lowered, she slowly turned to face him.

"You don't trust me." She raised her gaze.

"I don't trust what happened to you," he responded, studying the contours of her face. Her damp black hair brushed over her pale cheeks, deep brown eyes staring at him. Her small body swam in the white terrycloth robe. She was exactly the same as he remembered her, yet altogether different.

"I haven't forgotten," she began, her voice soft but steady. "That day...your master..."

"I'm so sorry. I couldn't hear what he was doing to you." Guilt haunted him. He'd been tasked with watching over another one of Baxter's fledgling vampires in the forest and hadn't been in her village. When he'd heard the screaming from afar, he'd gone to save her but was too late.

"I'd thought after he raped me, that would be the end."

"I was weak. By the time I reached you. Fuck, Mao. I've thought about that day a million times and what I could have done differently. It was my fault. Baxter. He was a sadist. I knew that when I got involved with you. I knew how he tortured others. Hell, he tortured me for as long as I was with him. When he threw you over that cliff, I died that day with you."

"After I fell into the canyon, I shifted. I began to fly."

"You died," he countered, stepping closer.

"My kind is rare. The demon who traded me to Hell claimed he'd made a fortune on me."

"I failed you." Quintus' instinct warned him away, but

his heart propelled him forward as he took each step toward her.

"There was nothing either of us could do. He was stronger than both of us."

"But I should have protected you. We'd almost completed our bond." As he said the words, he was reminded yet again that he felt nothing. Although tempted to comfort her, take her in his arms, doubt rooted in his mind. "I saw your body hit one of the rocks. But then you disappeared. I couldn't reach you."

"It was the first time I'd shifted. I don't remember much. I flew into a web of magick. The demon took me that very night." Mao licked her lips, and closed the distance, coming within inches of Quintus. "For over a thousand years I've been locked away. Tortured. But I never forgot you. Or us."

As she reached for him, Quintus accepted her into his arms. Her small figure fit into his embrace, the memories rushing over him. Their first glance. First kiss. Making love. But even with her close to him, no emotion curled in his chest.

"Mao…" Quintus shook his head, pulling away from her. "I'm sorry…you must know…our bond…"

"I can feel you." Mao untied her belt, revealing her bared breasts. She reached for Quintus' hand and brought it toward her chest. "They tried to break me…to break our bond. But it's still there…feel me."

"Mao…" Quintus tugged his wrist away. "I can't. I'm sorry. The bond. If this is…" *If this is really you.* He stopped his errant thought, cautious not to hurt her any more than she'd already been. "You've been traumatized."

"Make love to me. Take my blood," she pleaded.

"I can't." Quintus reached for her lapels, gently pulling her robe closed. "I loved you Mao. I grieved your death. And when I say that I mean my gut was ripped out…" *It almost fucking killed me.* "I grieved every single day for over a thousand years. And now here you are. But Mao, I've got to be honest with you. There's someone else."

"I never would expect you to wait for me," she insisted.

"I'm bonding with another," he confessed. "Please, Mao. I'm so fucking sorry. If I'd known you'd been taken…Jesus, you know how things were back then. It was impossible."

"You'll come to me, Quintus," she told him, her eyes hopeful. "Whatever this is…I assume it's that wolf. She's not the real thing. We were. We will be again."

"We've got to get you to safety." Quintus changed the subject, doubting her words. It was normal to expect denial, he reasoned. "The Alpha. He's going to take you back with him. Last month, I met another pixiu. She's in California. I doubt you're related, but she's of your kind."

"I don't need protection. I want to stay here with you." She shook her head, and her eyes filled with tears. "I know I'm damaged but you have to give us a chance."

"I'm sorry, Mao. I've got some things I have to do. Gabriella…she's in danger. I can't explain it, but I've got to take care of this situation. When I return, when things are settled, I'll come visit you. I promise I won't leave you by yourself."

"Please don't leave me here," she begged. "I don't even know where I am."

"Mao. Think about this. Whatever you went through

changed you. We aren't even speaking in Chinese. Did you think of that? How do you know how to speak English? You smell like…the scent of a demon's all over you."

"I can't explain any of this. It's a blur…but I'm me. It doesn't matter what language I speak. I'm the girl you met from the village."

"You are…" *Maybe yes, maybe no.* "Look, at the very least, you're traumatized. Once whoever put you in Hell finds out you're missing, they might go looking for you again. I have to go to France. Hunter's an Alpha. A shifter. He can keep you hidden and protected until I get back. He'll be back in a few hours."

"No, I'll go with you."

"No, Mao. You won't. We may not be bonded but I'm not allowing you to go."

"You can't make me go with him. He's a stranger."

Quintus took a deep breath, considering the situation. He wasn't convinced the woman in front of him was Mao. She looked like her…talked like her, but whoever she was, she was no longer his. Perhaps Hell had changed her or something worse, but caution warned him to go slowly. Still her fragile state pulled at his heart. He'd once loved her, would have died to save her.

"I can't stay with you…" He sighed, plowing his fingers through his hair. "Viktor. You remember my brother, si?"

"Of course. He helped us so many times. He brought me here."

"If you won't go with Hunter, you can stay with him until I return."

"I should go back to China. This country of yours…this is not mine," she told him.

"No matter where you go, you're going to have to start over, start a new life. I think it's best to stay here but I can't stop you from going back to your homeland. This demon who took you? Is he still alive?"

"I don't know," she said.

"Then it's possible he'll be back for you. You can't leave my home. It's the only thing that will protect you."

"How long will you be gone?" she asked, a demure tone to her voice.

"I don't know…a few days," he told her. After they found what they needed in Paris, they'd go to New Orleans. Quintus didn't trust Absinthe, yet he had no choice but to pursue the only lead they had. He questioned her motives for sending them to France. Witches notoriously sought rare ingredients for spells, and he suspected she was sending him on a wild goose chase.

"The wolf?" Mao asked.

"What?"

"The wolf at the party. She consumes you?"

"Yes." It was of no use to lie. "We've already begun the bond."

"She's in trouble?" Mao asked, touching his arm.

Quintus' gaze fell to her hand, still confused that he wasn't stirred by her touch. "Yes, but…" He looked up to her, searching her eyes for deception. "Gabriella is no concern of yours."

"I could help."

"No, Mao. This bond, our bond…nothing should have broken it. Something, I don't know what it is just yet, it's not right. You've spent a long time in Hell and I think we'd be stupid not to think it didn't have an effect on you. The sulfur…"

"I was in Hell…"

"Exactly but it's still all over you. And the bond…" *You died.* He refrained from using the words, but kept speaking. "There's nothing that should have broken my bond to you. You hadn't completed yours, but you were mine. I couldn't live without you. When you died…" he sighed, "I thought I'd died too."

"Quintus."

"I grieved. Over a thousand years passed and no one entered my life…not until last week. And then magically, Thorn rescues you from Hell. I can't say exactly what's going on, but I know this much…something isn't right."

"Of course it isn't. I've been in Hell. Look at me. Really look at me. The things I've endured…" Tears welled in her eyes. "Those bastards stole everything I had. My life with you. My body. My mind. My soul. I wish I'd died."

"Mao." His voice softened yet he resisted touching her. "I would have traded places with you. I'm sorry…but…" Quintus paused, searching for his words. "You stand before me as the woman I loved, but you've changed. The bond is gone."

"It hasn't changed for me," she insisted.

"I'm not your mate. And you know how it is for a vampire. We can make love to many, drink from many, but when we form a bond with someone, it's nearly impossible to resist. The call of their blood…no other will satisfy us. Your beast, she knows. I'm no longer her mate." *Fuck, I sound like a dick.* Quintus inwardly cringed at his words. If only it was as simple as him not being her mate, but he feared she had a far greater problem. Death, Hell…the aura grew more intense. If he hadn't known any better, he'd guess her to be a demon.

"Maybe it's just delayed. You aren't even giving us a chance."

"I'm sorry. I have Gabriella. We'll soon be bonded. I'm her mate." Quintus' thoughts drifted to his little wolf. She needed him, and he needed her. He'd spent far too much time with Mao.

"I'll stay here until you return but I'm going back to China. I don't belong here." Her tone went cold, her eyes flat as she turned her back to him.

"I'm sorry." He sucked a breath, backing away toward the door. "I can't tell you where to go. But please stay until I get back. At the very least you're safe here. I'll help you."

"Your wolf is more than she pretends to be." Mao's monotone voice filled the room. She remained with her back to him, staring out the window.

Quintus went still at her statement. He could have sworn he detected a hint of dark magick. He feigned indifference, answering with a nonchalant tone. "My wolf is of no concern to you. She's mine. That's all you need to know."

"She lies to you," she continued. "Her magick is strong."

"Mao." He paused as a flurry of magical currents zipped through the air. Even though he resisted, it drew him toward her. "Whatever you're doing…"

"I'm a pixiu. Nothing more."

"I don't know what went on down in Hell, but don't think of stirring trouble in my home," he warned.

"All I can promise is that I will wait for you. But I could change my mind. And if I do, I'll be gone."

"China won't be the same. It's likely your village is gone."

"I'll find my ancestors. I'll begin anew." She turned to face him, dropping her robe. "And this flesh," she cupped her breasts, "this belongs to you, Quintus. What I feel…all those years ago when we made love. You've tasted all of me. Make love to me again and we'll reunite."

The scent of her arousal spun into the room, the magick pulling him toward her. Although his mind warred against it, he stepped toward her and she rushed into his arms.

"Feel me," she told him. "Remember."

"Mao." As she brought his hand to her breast, he recoiled. His fingers brushed her nipple, and he pulled away as if he'd touched fire. "I don't know what's happening but…no. I can't do this."

He backed away, his face without expression, concealing the shock that plowed through him. *Dark Magick.*

"It's our bond. You feel it, don't you?" she asked, her voice demure.

"No. This won't happen. Viktor will help make arrangements for you. I've got to go."

"I know you feel it. You cannot lie to me."

"Viktor will see that you are kept comfortable in a secure location until I return. I highly suggest you consider going to California where you could be near another pixiu."

"I'm not a pack animal like the dog you lay with. I'm a great lion."

"There're many creatures in this world and the underworld that can take you down. Need I remind you that you just spent lifetimes in Hell? Just take a few days here in New York."

"My blood will call to you again."

"Viktor will be up soon." Quintus shut the door behind him, drawing a deep breath as he walked away.

He strode down the long hallway, his mind racing. As he stepped into his office, he heard the pattering of water running above in his master bathroom and thanked the Goddess that Gabriella was settling.

The flicker of attraction that had spiked through him earlier dissipated and his head cleared. He looked at his hand, recalling his touch on Mao's breast and cursed. "Fuck."

Viktor, he silently reached for his brother.

"You called?" Viktor appeared before him, wearing purple pajama bottoms.

"I need a favor." Quintus glanced to his attire. "Nice."

"I know, right?" He smirked.

"We have a problem." Quintus rubbed his face with his hand and stretched his neck.

"Seems like they're racking up. What now?"

"Mao. Something…she's…I don't know exactly." He paused and blew out a breath. "I touched her."

"That seems kind of normal to me. I know you've got it for Gabby but Mao? She was your first. Jesus, it took you centuries before you'd even kiss another woman. I was there."

"Yes, but this thing with Gabriella. I can't explain it."

"It's her blood."

"No, it's more than her blood. I almost died in NOLA. That fucking demon vampire bitch from San Fran almost took me down. And then comes Gabriella, like this breath of fresh air in my life, saving me in the darkest of places. She was scared but still brave as hell."

"The bond?"

"I know I wasn't looking for this. But this attraction to her…I can't ignore it. I don't want to ignore it."

"Okay, but you loved Mao. You just met Gabriella," Viktor challenged.

"I was a fledgling vampire back then. Aside from our asshole sire, there weren't any predators. Things were simple. Mao and I had time to get to know each other. Things with Gabby are different. I just want her." Quintus shoved his fingers through his unruly hair and began to pace. "I told you…I can't explain what's happening."

"What's going on with Mao?"

"It's not just her scent. Something's off. She's not right."

"She was in Hell for over a thousand years. A little soap isn't going to wash that shit off."

"True, but the bond we had is broken. Something or

someone broke it. She claims she still feels it, but I think she's lying. Her eyes…" Quintus paused mid-step and glanced up to Viktor. "I touched her."

"I don't think that is going to go over too well with the woman you want to bond with."

"She did something to me. It was almost like a compulsion."

"Well yeah…I mean your hand didn't just float there."

"Would you stop fucking around, V? I'm serious. I was walking out the door and I sensed the dark magick."

"Did she have any clothes on? Because you might be sensing something all right."

"No she didn't but that's what I'm saying. I felt nothing, but then for a split second…it was dark. I wanted to resist but then I started to feel aroused."

"Yeah, that's kind of how it works, Quint. A pair of titties generally does that kind of thing. What the hell did you expect?"

"No, that's not how it works when you're not bonded with someone. Right now, all I ever crave is Gabriella. Like I'm seriously looking forward to spanking her ass later and…"

"Hold on there, bro. If there's spanking involved, I'd be happy to lend a hand."

"Not fucking happening, Viktor. Just stop talking…let me finish."

"Fine." Viktor rolled his eyes and sighed. He strode over to a leather desk chair and sank down into it.

"She did something. And before you ask, no I have no

idea how anyone could practice dark magick in my house even if I invited them here. I've got this place warded tighter than a nun's panties. No way is any demon crossing through. I'm worried that whatever changed her broke the bond, and it's part of her now. It doesn't make sense, but my instinct is telling me that woman upstairs…she may look and talk like Mao, but that's not her. At the same time, I can't let her go until I do right by her."

"Okay, let's just say she's wielding some dark mojo. She could have already done some damage." Viktor shrugged. "She looks the same. It's just that smell. But she was down there a long time."

"Yeah, she looks like Mao. Talks like Mao. The magick was subtle but it was there for sure. I wasn't going to touch her…"

"Maybe we ought to be callin' on Thorn to pick her ass up," Viktor suggested.

"That day she went over the cliff…" Quintus plowed his fingers through his hair.

"It wasn't your fault."

"I've thought about that day a million times. I couldn't see her. I couldn't sense her. She was gone. But she told me she shifted. She'd never shifted while she was with me. She says a demon, one who she doesn't know the name of, picked her off. Sold her to Hell."

"It's possible." Viktor nodded.

"I tried to get her to go to California to meet Kai but now I'm not so sure it's a good idea. Maybe if she wants to go back to China, I should just let her go. The very least I can do is get her set up monetarily."

"Again. Maybe we just ship her back to Thorn."

"Maybe." Quintus released an audible exhale, his emotions torn.

"So what are you going to do with Mao?" Viktor asked.

"I want you to stay with her for a couple of days while I go to Paris," Quintus replied. "Maybe if she has time here on earth, in our realm, she might be different. I don't know."

"Well fuck. You go to Paris and I get stuck with your ex?" He laughed. "You're just going for the croissants, aren't you?"

"Croissants are delicious." Quintus gave a smirk. "I hate to ask you to do it but you're the only one besides me she knows. I was going to ask Hunter to take her out west, but she refused to go with him. Like I said, I'm starting to think it's best she go back to her homeland. It's far away from New York. There's no way she can stay here. As it is now, Gabby is freaking out."

"And the Alpha?" Viktor raised a questioning eyebrow at Quintus.

"I'm going to ask him to come with us to Paris. I might need an extra pair of hands."

"Fucking wolf. If you need any extra hands with Gabriella, I thought they'd be mine." Viktor gave a devious smile.

"Not this time."

"This bonding shit is cramping my style." Viktor scrubbed his shortened beard with his hand. "I'll watch

Mao, but the second she pulls any dark magick shit on me, she's going back to Thorn. I'll have his ass on speed dial."

"Fair enough. My suggestion is that she stays in her room, but in case she thinks to go snooping, I'm locking the door to my bedroom and my office. Your room is protected, as always."

"On any other occasion I'd be thanking you for leaving me alone with a hot chick, but this is like the ultimate in sloppy seconds."

"I said watch her, not fuck her. Jesus, you're sick."

"Got ya." Viktor smiled, cocking his head. "As if I'd do the love of your life."

"You're an asshole." Quintus shot at him. "Si, I loved her. But now, she's a memory. You and I have lived thousands of years. We've met all sorts of creatures in our lifetime. If Mao were truly Mao, I'd know. The bond, even if it had been broken, I'd feel something for the woman in that bedroom. I felt nothing. Not until the magick. And it wasn't strong enough to hold me. No, there's something going on with her. Either she's simply changed or possibly something worse. I can't tell just yet. I'll keep her safe, but I have to focus on finding the bones of the first witch."

"When are you leaving?"

Quintus retrieved his cell phone and glanced at the time. "The jet leaves in three hours. It won't leave much time for Gabby to rest but she can sleep on the plane. I've gotta text Hunter and Jax."

He quickly tapped out a few messages to the Alphas, pleased at their quick response. "Ah, good. Jax said Finn is already in New York. His beta's got his pack. Hunter agreed to come with."

"It amazes me how you snap your fingers and the wolves come running like a couple of Chiweenies wearing diamond-studded collars. You're like the wolf whisperer." Viktor stood and glanced at himself in a long wall mirror, running his hands over his stomach. "Do you think these pajama pants make me look fat? Hmm…maybe I should have bought the yellow ones."

"No, but you're pale as fuck," Quintus responded.

"What can I say? I eat clean. Blood only. Stay out of the sun. This look works for me. Chicks dig it." He smiled and patted his abs. "I keep it tight. Don't look a day over twenty-five."

Quintus coughed. "You look every bit the ripe age of thirty." He shook his head and gave a small chuckle. "There's really something wrong with you. You know that, don't you?"

"My keen sense of humor makes life interesting."

"Real food makes life better. You need to remember your mortality."

"Overrated."

"I've got to go talk to Gabby." Quintus blew out a breath. "She trusted me before this."

"She'll forgive you." Viktor exhaled a loud breath.

The patter of water in the shower above drew Quintus' attention. *Is she still in the shower?* He reached for her, aware she'd grown stronger, blocking him from her emotion.

"I think there might be something…" Quintus went

silent as he detected the scent of smoke. "What the fuck?"

"Fire," Viktor said, his eyes wide.

"Get Mao! I'll get Gabriella!" As Quintus dematerialized into the upstairs bedroom he spotted Gabriella underneath the covers of his bed. He ripped off the comforter, revealing the pillows beneath it. He tore across the room into the bathroom and glanced to the empty shower, the water still running.

"Goddammit!" Quintus pounded an angry fist to the wall, shattering a nearby mirror.

He quickly flashed to each room in the house, searching for her, as plumes of toxic smoke billowed into the air. He sensed Viktor had gone and materialized onto the street below. Viktor stood barefoot, his arm around Mao.

"What the fuck is going on?" Quintus asked, directing his anger toward her.

"A fire. Your wards aren't as good as you think they are," she countered.

"Where's Gabby?" Viktor asked.

"She's gone."

"What do you mean she's gone?" he asked.

"I mean she left." Quintus scrubbed his palm over his scruffy cheek.

"She did this," Mao accused.

"What the hell are you talking about?" Quintus asked. He clenched his sweaty palms and dropped his fangs. "There's no fucking way Gabriella would hurt me or anyone else for that matter."

"I told you. She's more than what she's telling you."

"Stop talking," he yelled.

"She's a wolf. She's jealous. She'd do anything to keep her mate. She's losing you to me."

"Viktor, take her to the compound. Stay underground until I get back." His club in Central Park had been fortified after a supernatural attack shook through it like an earthquake. He'd installed several holding tanks that could be utilized to house unruly customers. Although he hated to take drastic measures, Mao could be safely locked away in a comfortable but secure cell until his return.

"You sure?" Viktor asked. "I could go to my place."

"Do it." A pixiu, it'd be likely she'd attempt a formidable escape, but it was the best he could do under the circumstances to keep her in New York.

"Sorry, Mao. It's time to go." Viktor placed his palms onto her shoulders and they dematerialized away.

Quintus blew out a breath as the firemen stormed into the high-rise building, its occupants spilling out into the streets. Although Mao had attempted to plant seeds of doubt in his mind about Gabriella, there was no way in hell she could've done this. He detected dark magick in the smoke, ashes drifting in the air like snowflakes. *Fucking hell.* He prayed it was the Salem witches, Absinthe…anyone but Mao.

He retrieved his cell phone and tapped a text to his friend who worked at the airport. Gabriella was resourceful but she underestimated his ability to track her. She'd go to the nearest airport, hop a plane to Paris. Although she had no money, he suspected she'd wield her magick to secure a ticket and get through security.

Your girl's booked a 5:30 flight to Paris. But Q, there's no record of her passing through security. She's using magick. His little wolf was resourceful, he'd give her that. But she'd put herself in considerable danger. He'd have to meet her, then later, he planned to spank her ass red.

"Hey." A voice broke his contemplation and he looked to the tall wolf approaching through the chaos. Now dressed, he blended with the humans.

"You New Yorkers sure do know how to throw a party," he commented, scanning the crowd.

"Gabriella's gone." Quintus restrained the fury that burned through his body.

"I won't ask how she managed to escape but I'm not surprised. The energy on that girl is fucking sick." Hunter sighed. "I don't know what kind of witch she is but she's not your average wolf."

"Our bond…it's affecting her. Her magick is growing stronger but she's green. She doesn't even know the spells to harness her power."

"Your New York witch. She didn't seem to let on that she knows about the Salem coven."

"Absinthe? She's kept the peace here. That's the most I can say. Her allegiance blows with the wind. Every favor comes at a cost. Don't get me wrong. I'm no different. And Jax? He's as tough as they come. We coexist but we don't trust."

"You're going to need to trust someone."

"Samantha maybe." Quintus shrugged.

"Luca's girl?" the Alpha guessed.

"Si. She's new but she's bonded with a vampire of my lineage. Ilsbeth?" Quintus gave a sardonic laugh. "She used to be a formidable ally but she's been compromised."

"Sorry about your place but it doesn't look too bad," Hunter said.

Quintus closed his eyes, concentrating on the life force within his building. "No one has died."

"You live with humans? Now that's a surprise."

"I have many homes, wolf. But since you've agreed to come along for the ride, I'm going to let you in on a little secret. There're things necessary to being a successful vampire, living thousands of years and not getting staked. Number one. Live among humans. I won't ever forget what it's like to be one. I've survived on them, but I live *with* them to remember where I came from."

"Number two?" Hunter looked up toward the flames.

"Don't ever trust an ancient. We have many secrets." Quintus wished he had the patience to travel any other way, but he didn't have time to mess around. He'd ask for forgiveness later.

"What's that supposed to mean?" Hunter asked.

Quintus placed his hand on the Alpha's shoulder and closed his eyes, dematerializing them across the Atlantic. *Charles de Gaulle Airport.* First, he'd trap his little wolf. Somewhere in the City of Light they'd find the bones of an ancient priestess and free Gabriella of the Salem witches.

·❦· *Chapter Ten* ·❦·

Gabriella clutched at the trench coat, pulling it tight across her waist. The icy rain brutally lashed at her face as she held out her hand to hail a taxi. As the car slowed, she reached for the handle, swinging the door open and slipping inside its warmth. Gabriella shut it behind her, speaking in fluent French to the driver.

"Villa Adrienne et Avenue du Général Leclerc s'il vous plait."

"Quel hôtel allez-vous?" he answered.

"Pas d'hôtel. Aller au parc pour rencontrer un ami." The lie rolled off her tongue. While it was true she was going to the park, she wasn't meeting a friend. Nor was she going to a hotel.

"Oui."

Gabriella stared out the window, disconnected from the conversation. Determined to get the bones of the first witch, she'd left on her own. After leaving the shower water running, she'd employed a simple cloaking spell, disappearing from Quintus' home.

On her way out the temptation was too great, and she'd followed voices. But as she approached, she heard the female and sensed the magick. In a stolen glance, she'd seen Quintus touching her breast. She'd fought the nausea, her wolf itching to shift, to attack. But she'd prevailed, taming the beast, and took off unnoticed. Quintus had guarded his home, but she'd easily passed through the doors. She suspected that since he'd drank her blood, the wards been compromised, allowing his mate free exit and entry.

As soon as she'd reached the lobby, she'd conjured suitable clothing for Paris. Although she'd booked a commercial flight, she'd realized he'd easily track her. Always selling her blood, she didn't have much money, but she'd kept a credit card in case of an emergency. She'd broken the bank, and arranged for a private flight to Paris. She'd paid the pilot to divert the landing to a small private airport instead of Charles de Gaulle.

Momma, please help me, she prayed. Gabriella saw her mother in dreams, and was certain she still guided her magick. Although as a child she'd only learned simple spells, she'd meditate, and new magick would spill into her mind. She'd wished at times she'd grown up practicing her craft under the loving guidance of a knowledgeable witch, but alone on the streets, she hadn't been afforded that luxury.

As the cab rolled to a stop, Gabriella steeled her nerves. Lightning flashed followed by a booming roll of thunder. She glanced outside at the ominous weather. Although she'd be protected from the elements underground, she'd hardly be safe.

"Merci." Gabriella handed the driver several bills without confirming her fare and shoved out of the cab into the driving rain.

She scanned the area for paranormal activity but didn't sense active magick. Pedestrians buried their heads under umbrellas ignoring Gabriella as she stepped onto a path that led into a city park. She tugged at her collar, attempting to shield her face from rain. Cold drops pelted her mercilessly as she searched for an entrance.

As she turned a corner, she noted the manhole next to a fountain. *Thank Goddess.* While on the plane, she'd researched different entry points into the catacombs. Although tourists entered into a formal cordoned-off area, others frequently trespassed through unconventional means.

Drenched, she fell to her knees and placed her palms onto the manhole cover. She fingered the keyhole, attempting to lift it, but it wouldn't budge. *Try to use a spell, Gabby. Be smart.* As a child, opening locked objects had been fun, but under stress she struggled to remember how to do it.

"Come on. Open for me." In her mind's eye, she imagined it levitating. As if her hands were magnets, they pressed to the cold metal. She blinked away the rain, and blew out a breath as the heavy cover lifted inches, allowing her to wrap her fingers around its rims.

"Oh thank you!" she exclaimed, shocked that it had moved. With both hands gripped tight on the edge, she flipped the lid over, exposing a dark hole.

A knot formed in her stomach as she stared down into the darkness. Danger waited below, but the bones of the first witch called to her like a siren. Daughter of a witch, from a long line of witches, she was destined to end the coven's hold on her. She'd break the cycle and take down the high priestess.

Courage filled her chest as she swung a leg into the pit, her toe catching a rung of the steel ladder. *Please Goddess, protect me*, she prayed, slowly descending into the abyss. Hand under hand she gripped the cold metal bars. As she lowered herself into the ground, dank air wafted into her nostrils. *How much longer?* She estimated she'd descended three stories when her foot finally hit solid earth.

Gabriella reached inside her jacket and flicked on a small flashlight she'd purchased at the airport. As her eyesight adjusted to the dim light, she scanned her surroundings. Graffiti painted the limestone walls of the open bunker. An empty wine bottle and cigarette butts littered the floor. Four arched tunnels led into the darkness, and she sighed, unsure of which one to follow.

She closed her eyes, concentrating on her childhood, opening channels of her magick she'd long kept closed. The joyous celebration of the moon she'd enjoyed as a child had turned deadly once she'd shifted. But long before her wolf surfaced, her mother had included her in her rituals, exposing her to witchcraft. Gabriella smiled and pictured her mother happily adding various items to her altar such as herbs and candles.

As Gabriella's eyes blinked open, a sparkle of light

flicked in the far-right tunnel. She cautiously stepped inside, careful not to trip on the crumbled pieces of stone in her path. In the 1700s, millions of corpses had been moved from cemeteries and put into the catacombs. Although most of the bones had been meticulously arranged in the ossuary during the late eighteenth century, the museum was only a small portion of the labyrinth. With hundreds of miles of tunnels, she hoped her intuition guided her well.

Gabriella passed through an antechamber and stilled as she approached a gate. Through iron bars, she spied thousands of bones, the femurs and skulls artistically lining the tunnel. She detected whispers on the lips of those who she suspected were humans touring the museum.

As she moved into the darkness, the hum of a familiar energy sizzled over her skin, and she detected the life force of her ancestors. Although recognizable, she didn't sense danger as she deliberately trekked toward its source. Like a repeating mantra, it called to her. Minutes morphed into hours as she put one foot in front of the other, moving toward the energy. Lost deep within the labyrinth, Gabriella lost track of time and space as she sought out the bones.

She passed into a chamber, noting large swatches of black paint haphazardly splashed across the walls. Gabriella placed her palms onto the cold stone, and startled as the energy jolted through her. Like watching a movie, picture frames flashed in her mind's eye. *Blood. Sacrifice. The face of a priestess slitting the throat of a human.* Her eyes blinked open, her heart pounding in her chest. *The first witch.*

But as she went to step further into the tunnel, her hopes

sank at the sight of the dead end. A small opening in the stone wall caught her attention, and the energy zipped through her once again. Murmurs echoed her name, and she found herself moving toward the hole. *Why though? Dammit, I don't want to go in there.*

As she hoisted herself inside, she sucked a breath and prayed nothing creepy crawly touched her. A dead spider for an ingredient was fine every now and then but she'd lose her shit if one decided to make a live appearance. The walls tightened around her body as she shimmied through the roughened limestone, her pant leg tearing as it caught a jagged edge. She breathed in relief as her head breached the wall into an open space. Her palms reached for the floor and she slid downward and tumbled onto the ground.

Gabriella shoved to her feet and shone the flashlight into the darkened alcove. Negative vibrations rolled over her, a dark ancient energy bouncing in the air. There was no escape from the triangular room, its peaked ceiling forming a pyramid. Unlike the Louvre, not one speck of light entered, its walls unmarred by intruders. As she ran her fingers over the smooth stone, she noted a rupture in its surface. Upon closer inspection, a thin marble inset intersected the seam of two walls.

Drawn to its vibrations, Gabriella reached for the stone, but as her fingers brushed over its etching, a familiar energy seized her. *Quintus.*

"You're in trouble, little wolf." His deep voice echoed in the chamber.

"I…you…I…" Although his scent soothed her wolf, the

fire in his eyes ignited panic in her chest.

"Cat got your tongue? You seemed quite brave, leaving my house back there. Did you really think you could escape me?"

"I saw you with her. You touched her." Courage blossomed in her chest, white-hot anger flaring as she recalled seeing his hands on Mao's bare body.

"What you saw wasn't of my doing. She used black magick. There's nothing between us. But you, Gabriella? You're mine. We are bonded," he told her.

"Not yet. I'll walk away." Her wolf cringed, whining as she issued her threat.

"I've indulged you far too long, bella. We're doing things my way now. We'll discuss what you did later and the repercussions for leaving." Quintus took two broad steps, closing in on her.

"You have another mate," she accused.

"There will never be anyone else but you," he promised.

"But I…" Her hands trembled as her traitorous wolf threatened to submit, but she stood firm.

"Not another word. This isn't the place. Do you understand?"

"Fine," she spat through gritted teeth. She'd run again the first chance she got. There was no way she'd stay with a man who cheated on her, who belonged to another woman.

Quintus reached over her shoulder, placing his palm onto the wall. Her body prickled in awareness of his touch, the heat of his body emanating onto hers. She sighed as his lips brushed her ear.

"This is far from over," he warned.

She blinked, a rush of air to her lungs as a rustle sounded behind Quintus. Out of the shadows, Hunter pressed up onto his hands and knees, his glowing eyes set on hers. With Quintus surrounding her, she hadn't noticed him in the darkness.

"You never run from your Alpha." Hunter shoved to his feet, brushed off his hands on his pants, and looked to Quintus. "Fuck me, that was a hell of a ride."

"Hell is exactly where we're at," Quintus said as he fingered the triangular design. "This is Lucifer's mark. Whoever did this was powerful. If they were alive, they most certainly used black magick, but more than that…Goddess, can you feel it?"

"The limestone generates its own energy, but something is in here," she said.

"Something evil."

"I feel it but it's not overwhelming me."

"It's because whoever created it is tied to you. You're the legacy," Quintus surmised. "These markings. Sanskrit. You see? Asrik. It means blood." He removed his hands, and blew out a breath. "Whoever did this made a sacrifice. I can feel it in these walls."

"A shit ton of bodies were dumped down here. Maybe it's just some leftover bad juju," Hunter suggested.

"No. This…this is really dark shit. Demons were summoned. Maybe Lucifer himself," Quintus guessed.

"I can feel her bones. She's here." Gabriella scanned the room.

"Looks empty to me but ya know witches can hide their shit like nobody's biz." Hunter's boots crunched over the graveled floor as he inspected the area.

"It's in the message. Your blood," Quintus said.

"I should have known the bitch would want my blood, but still, why me?" Gabriella pressed the heel of her hand to her forehead, attempting to figure out what kind of spell they'd need to find the bones.

"Very good question. If it were so easy to take down the high priestess, I'd assume others would have tried," Quintus said, continuing to finger the words. "But this isn't just blood. No, this says *rudhirapāyin*."

"I'm not going to even ask how you know Sanskrit. But from the way you just said that, it doesn't sound good," Hunter said.

"Rudhirapāyin. That word…I don't know. It sounds familiar. Like maybe…" Gabriella's words trailed off as she closed her eyes, hearing the words of her mother play in her mind. "Rudhirapāyin. Blood drinking."

"Or demon," Quintus said, exhaling loudly. "This isn't good."

"So, let me get this straight," Hunter began. "I'm just going to ballpark a guess at what's going to happen. You need someone's blood to find this thing."

"Mine," Gabriella said, placing her fingers onto the triangle.

"Yours?" Hunter asked.

"Rudhirasāra. Roughly translated means a person with blood. That's Gabby," Quintus said.

"I'm assuming the other word…what was it?" Hunter paced as he spoke.

"Rudhirapāyin." Quintus repeated.

"You're the blood drinker. But who's the demon? The only demon we met recently was that dude back at the party. Thorn. And he strikes me as being on the fence. No, this is badass straight from hell shit. And we're about to open a portal to get to the bones. Tell me we aren't summoning a demon to get it," Hunter said, his voice tense.

"No…I don't think…" Gabriella stuttered, unsure of what they needed to do.

"I'm going to draw your blood," Quintus stated in a matter-of-fact tone.

"Okay… you're not part demon or, hell, whole demon, are you?"

"Jesus, Hunter. Of course, he's not a demon. How could you say that?" Gabriella defended her vampire.

"Just sayin'."

"Ignore him." Quintus rolled his eyes.

"She can't ignore me. I'm an Alpha. Remember? Big bad wolf." A broad smile broke across his face.

"Not her Alpha," Quintus corrected.

"Yeah well, y'all need to get your shit straight, because unlike you, I'm not lovin' our current accommodations. I know you vampires are all about a good dirt nap but I'm a wolf. This air isn't good for my fur."

"As if I like it?" Gabriella asked. "I'm a witch."

"You're hybrid," Quintus told Gabriella and then focused on Hunter. "We don't sleep in the dirt."

"Sure thing, fang boy. Oh that's right. Where'd y'all meet? Yeah, pretty sure it was an underground club. A crypt or some shit." Hunter tilted his head, raising his eyebrows. "I'm seeing a pattern."

"It wasn't under the ground," Gabriella replied.

"Stop fucking around. We've got to get this bone or bones or whatever the hell we are looking for and get the hell back to the jet."

"I'm not going with you." Gabriella shoved up her sleeve, exposing her wrist. "This is my problem, not yours."

"Goddammit if your ass isn't going to be bright red by the time I'm done with you. You're not going anywhere." Quintus' eyes lit with intensity.

"You're not spanking me. I don't belong to you."

"Look, I said I'm not up for crypts, graves...pretty much anything underground...but that ass? Well, that's another topic. I'm all for a spankin'."

"I'm not...you're not..." Gabriella lost her words at the thought. A quick flash in her mind's eye of his palm on her bottom caused heat between her legs. She shoved away the sensation, aware they'd both read her emotions. "No."

"I think my little wolf might enjoy this." Quintus gave a small smile. "Ah, but this is a punishment, my sweet bella. Not a pleasure. And the way you sass the Alpha, I'm leaning toward letting him help."

"Now that's what I'm talking about." Hunter gave a small laugh. "You've pushed all kinds of boundaries tonight, Gabby. Sorry, girl."

"Fuck you...both of you." She gave a side eye to

Quintus and continued. "Can we please stop with this talk and get out of here?"

"I'm in agreement with that. What's up on the menu? Spooky spell? Maybe start seeing if there's a loose rock? If the girl says it's here, then let's find this shit and go home."

"We're going to New Orleans," Quintus replied, dropping his fangs.

"I'm down. NOLA was my first home." Hunter stared at the vampire's fangs. "I thought I was going to at least get a croissant out of this Paris trip but from the looks of those teeth of yours I'm guessing that's not happenin'."

"I'm going to have to bite you," Quintus warned.

"Just do it," she snipped, extending her arm. As he stepped closer, she pulled it back to her chest. "Wait. I don't want it to hurt."

"Gabriella. I will repeat it a million times. I'd never hurt you." He reached for her hand, and brought her palm to his lips.

Her body sizzled in awareness, his warm breath on her skin. *Mine*, her beast whispered. She closed her eyes briefly, letting his energy flow through her. *My vampire.* Even three stories underground, in the midst of death, she craved him.

"Do it," she said, her voice soft.

His fangs sent a rush of desire through her the second he pierced her wrist, but it was gone as fast as it came. She released an audible sigh, her body flushed with arousal.

"You okay?" he asked, still holding her arm.

"Yes." Gabriella forced herself to concentrate on her surroundings, expelling desire and replacing it with a sense of purpose. *The first witch.*

"I'm not sure what to do, but I'm thinking your blood is the key." Quintus released her.

"I am the Rudhirasāra. I am the witch. The legacy." Gabriella pressed her fingers to her wound, and then swiped the blood across the markings. She closed her eyes, repeating a simple protection spell. *Goddess and angels, keep me safe from all evil. Bring to us what we seek.* Despite her effort, the hum beneath her fingertips never altered. While certain the bones were near, her words did nothing to conjure their location.

Gabriella blew out a breath and blinked open her eyes. Her lips tightened in frustration. "It's not working. Something's wrong."

"It needs something else. I am the Rudhirapāyin. The blood drinker." Quintus swiped a finger over his bloodied fang and pierced his own flesh. "This."

As he smeared their mixed blood on the wall, Gabriella's eyes flew open, a lightning bolt of supernatural light spearing from the fissure in the wall into her chest. The power of the first witch channeled through her, the high priestess' soul reaching to her psyche. Unable to control her own movements, her mouth opened, light beaming from her lips.

Her body frozen, her focus went to Quintus and Hunter who attempted to reach her. Blinded by the field of bright white light surrounding her body, they also became immobilized. Oddly, she remained calm as the stream poured through her lips, its light searing the stone across the wall. Rumbling sounded throughout the small chamber, rocks and dust raining upon them.

Goddess no, she prayed as her body drained of its energy. The light extinguished in an instant, and she collapsed to the ground.

"Gabriella." Quintus' smooth voice wrapped around her as she roused. Exhausted, she rolled onto her side, embracing his touch.

"Are you all right?" he asked.

"Hmm…yeah. I'm just a little tired."

"Can you sit up?" He knelt, taking her into his arms.

"I…I still feel…ah." As she glanced up to Quintus, she blinked. A rainbow-colored aura surrounded him, and she struggled to regain clarity.

"Hey boys and girls," Hunter called. "Lookie, lookie."

"The first witch." Gabriella's eyes widened in excitement. She attempted to push up onto her feet, relying on Quintus to guide her upward.

"What is it?" Quintus asked, not leaving his mate.

"It looks like…I don't know. It fuck…I can't believe that of all the bones in a body, this is what we got."

Gabriella glanced at Hunter who held up a knife-like object. "Is that it?"

She reached out to finger the cold rough item. Smooth on one side and rough on the other, the thin flat bone was nearly six inches long. Dark vibrations bristled on its surface, and she jerked her hand away. "This thing…this bone…it's evil."

"Gabriella, look at me," Quintus told her, cupping her cheeks in his hands.

"But that bone…" Gabriella lost her words as her gaze caught Quintus'. *Are you all right?* she heard him ask, aware his lips hadn't moved. Her body tingled from the light of her ancestors, but his energy began to overshadow the other. "I…yes. I'm okay."

"Hunter," Quintus said, all the while keeping his focus on Gabriella. "Can you wrap that in something and put it away?"

"You bet. This is some creepy ass bone."

Gabriella startled as a quickening flipped her stomach. "They're here."

"Who's here?" Hunter asked, stuffing the artifact in his coat pocket. He pushed to his feet and stilled as a flash of light swirled in the chamber. "What the fuck?"

"They're here." Quintus scooped Gabriella in his arms.

"Again, people. Who the fuck is here?"

"Lilitu. The witches," she responded.

Gabriella screamed as the high priestess appeared before her. The witch's neon orange hair trailed over her shoulders in two thick braids. Her white pupils burned through the darkness.

"Little Gabriella. We've been waiting for years and here you finally are." With fire in her eyes, the witch sneered.

"No, no, no," Gabriella repeated, panic twisting through her. She froze, her hands clutched to Quintus' shirt as the distinctive odor of her mother's burning flesh registered in her mind.

"I'm going to give you this one warning. Stay the hell away from Gabriella or you'll die, witch," Quintus growled.

"Wrong, vampire. You have something that belongs to me. Gabriella. She's one of us."

"Lilitu." Horrifying memories of her mother's murder flashed through Gabriella's mind.

"Stupid half-breed. Did you really think you were avoiding us?" The high priestess cackled, and licked her lips. "But before we take you back, give me the bone."

"Orange hair, huh? Doesn't seem to really work for you." The Alpha gave a sharp laugh. "Don't get me wrong. I like a girl who stands out in a crowd."

"You know what I like to do to wolves?" she asked.

"Is this a proposition? Because I'm sort of on the fence with this one. You're kind of hot in a psycho killer sort of way."

"I'll chain you in silver and skin your fur from your body while you beg for mercy. I could use a pair of wolf testicles in my next spell." She gave Hunter an icy smile.

"Okay, maybe once. If you're really into me, I could take one for the team. Those braids are a turn on. I could wrap my hands around them. This is a tough decision." Hunter shrugged, and put his hand on Quintus' shoulder.

"Give me the bone," she demanded, her voice screeching. "I'll spare you, wolf. Give it to me now."

Gabriella's heart pounded in her chest as Lilitu drew closer. *Quintus, get us out of here.*

"Ya see now, that's a turn off. Hey, Quint…how about you do your thing?"

"You can run, but you'll never get away!" Lilitu screamed, her arms outstretched.

Gabriella's head spun as she dissolved, dematerializing out of the catacombs. The last thing she saw was the high priestess, her cold eyes burning a hole through the darkness.

She rolled onto the bed, coughing back her nausea. Sweat beaded on her forehead and she clutched her stomach. She reached for her wolf, but the mighty beast hid in the dark recesses of her psyche, afraid of what she'd seen.

"Are you okay?" A comforting hand swept over her hair. "Gabriella."

"I'm sick. I…I can't do that."

"I'm sorry, bella. The effects on wolves…it's something you'll have to get used to."

"I can't do any of this." Anger boiled inside her, frustrated. She wasn't a vampire. She'd never be one. He had a mate, one who was alive and well. "I've got to get up."

Gabriella attempted to shove off the bed, but her head spun and she flopped back onto the mattress.

"You need to take a few minutes to recover," he told her.

As Quintus' palm touched her back, she went still. She reluctantly accepted the calming energy he sent through her body. Her heartbeat slowed, and she exhaled a breath.

Gabriella had been on the run for years, but never in eighteen years had she come as close to being killed as she had tonight. The high priestess had waited, claimed she'd known where Gabriella was all along.

Ramiel had threatened to expose her on more than one occasion. He often would tell her something that only a Circe coven witch would know about Lilitu. She often wondered how he'd become privy to such exclusive information. *Had she known where I was the entire time? Why didn't she kill me?* A flash of the high priestess twisted through her head and a fresh rush of nausea rolled through her again.

"I've got to go to the bathroom." She pushed onto her elbows, and scanned the room, noting the red lacquered wood walls. Blue water twinkled in the distance and her face crinkled in confusion. "Is that a pool?"

"Si, let me help you."

"Why is there a pool?" Gabriella gave a moan as she sat upward, a dull pain shooting through her spine. The force of the energy from the relic had left her muscles aching. "What is this place?"

"It belongs to Viktor. He's got a condo in a protected building. We're safe here until the both of you are ready to travel. I'm thinking you both should rest up before I flash us over to the jet. We can leave in the morning." Quintus put his arm around Gabriella's waist. "Let me help you up. Please."

She gingerly touched her feet to the floor. "I've got this."

"You sure?"

"Yes." Gabriella teetered as she stood, the scent of her vampire all around her. She struggled to balance on her feet. As she finally found her footing, she glanced up to Quintus, her heart squeezing in her chest. She didn't want him to stop touching her but she had to learn to go on without him.

"The bathroom is there, over in the hallway. I can help you," he offered, releasing his hands from her arms.

"No." Gabriella carefully began to make her way across

the room. She stilled as she heard the Alpha rouse. She glanced to the floor where he lay on his back.

"Holy fuck," he groaned. "This flashing shit is getting old."

"Wolves…" Quintus stayed within arm's reach of Gabriella.

"Gabby. You okay?" Hunter asked.

"Yeah," she lied. Another wave of nausea slammed into her. Vomit rose in the back of her throat, and she willed it to stop. "I've gotta go. I'll be fine."

Gabriella released a breath as her hand reached the doorknob and turned it. She quickly went inside and locked it behind her. Tears sprang from her eyes, a cacophony of emotions pouring through her. Quintus had said all the right things, but it couldn't erase the memory of seeing him touch Mao.

It shouldn't matter, she told herself. She'd only known him for days. The attraction they'd felt had been but a primal instinct, driven by her beast. Any sane person wouldn't fall for someone as dangerous or ancient as Quintus. She blamed her infatuation on her loneliness. It had been so long since she'd been with a man and in truth, she'd never been in love.

Easy come, easy go had been her motto up until a week ago. On the run, she couldn't afford to get attached to anything that didn't fit in a backpack. Whatever feelings she'd caught for the captivating vampire would go away over time, she told herself.

She flipped on the light and gripped the sink counter,

staring in the mirror. *You will be okay*, she repeated and brushed away her tears.

Her stomach calmed, but her temples throbbed with stress as she considered her next steps. *How am I going to get the bone from Hunter? How can I escape Quintus?* There was no way she could stay and watch him with Mao. She reasoned she could catch a flight to New Orleans and go see Samantha herself. The thought of running caused her chest to tighten, but she couldn't keep relying on Quintus to help her when he had a mate waiting for him at home.

The heated floor warmed the pads of her feet as she crossed the room. She opened the glass shower door and turned on the spigot. Making quick work of removing her jacket, she peeled off her clothes. As she turned to look at her gaunt face in the mirror, she sighed. Her white bra and panties nearly blended with her pale skin.

"When I'm safe, I'm going somewhere sunny," she mumbled. Gabriella pictured her wolf relaxed, lying in an open field, warmth radiating onto her fur. Someday she'd be free. Happy.

Gabriella removed her underwear and unsnapped her bra, letting it fall to the floor. Steam wafted into the air, and she stepped into the hot spray. The tension in her shoulders released but her mind raced. If she was to walk away from Quintus, she'd have to get the first witch's bone away from Hunter. They'd watch her like hawks, aware of her desire to leave. If she could somehow get her hands on the object, she might be able to conjure a confusion spell.

She leaned back into the water attempting not to let her

thoughts drift to Mao. The devastating loss was simply too much emotion for her to bear. No matter how much she wanted Quintus, she had to let him go. Her heart crushed, coming to terms with the fact that she'd have to live without him. She'd pray to the Goddess for another mate. It was the only way. *I'm leaving forever.*

Calm and warm, Gabriella nuzzled into the lapels of the fine terry cloth robe. She reached for her bra, but stopped short of getting dressed as the scent of cinnamon and apples drifted into the bathroom. Her stomach rumbled, reminding her that it had been hours since she'd had food. Deciding to put off the inevitable, she opted to eat first before escaping.

As she turned the knob, Gabriella heard their voices. She softly padded down the short hallway, and caught sight of an enormous platter of pastries on the coffee table. Hunter leaned back on a sofa, his feet propped on an ottoman. His gaze settled on hers, and she swore she detected desire in his brown eyes.

"Hey, darlin'. Come eat." He patted the sofa. "You've gotta be hungry."

"I'm starving." As she stepped toward the Alpha, she startled. A loud splash drew her attention to the pool. Her jaw dropped in awe as she caught sight of her muscular vampire gliding across the surface of the water. "He's swimming?"

"Yes, he is. Quint and his brother have expensive tastes," the Alpha responded. "Sit."

This time his words struck her as an order, not a request. She heeded his tone and gently sat down next to him, her focus still on Quintus.

"Have a croissant. These cinnamon and raisin ones are the bomb."

"Thank you." She reached for a pastry and bit down into the heavenly delight, her gaze rising to meet his.

"You can thank Quint there. He's an interesting sort. For as city badass as he is, and he is one bad motherfucker, he seems to do the right thing." Hunter stared over at the pool. "He's as old as they come, but he's got this human way about him. He ordered this food, but it's not like he needs it. He thought of you and me. Some paranormals, they lose their way. Their power is so great, they lose sight of morality. Right and wrong. Loyalty. These aren't just human values." Hunter lifted a china teapot off the tray and filled two cups. "Have some."

"Thank you again." Gabriella stopped eating and held the pastry. "For everything. I don't mean just tonight, but for running with me. It was my first time."

"Listen Gabriella, I know you're not pack, but as far as I'm concerned, it's my job as an Alpha to look after those who need a place in our world. It's true that some wolves go rogue on purpose. Maybe they run from their mating. Or their Alpha. Something serious happens to divide them from their pack. But with you…you're not a typical rogue wolf. You never had pack."

"I don't know who my real father was. The coven. If they'd known my mother had been with a wolf, they would have killed her. I don't know how I was conceived."

"Maybe they were mates. And if they were, he probably died somehow, because I doubt he'd ever leave her. I don't know. But regardless, you're here now. You're a witch and you're a wolf. The power you have to shut me out. To shut him out." Hunter glanced to Quintus. "That's real strong stuff. So whatever you are, however you were made, the Goddess brought you to where you are for a reason."

"I've got to get away from the witches."

"And you will. But you're going to need help. Like tonight." Hunter sipped his tea and then set it down. "We needed you and you needed us. I'm just sayin' that you're going to have to accept who you are. As pack, we rely on each other. There is no solo act. And now, you have a mate."

She nearly choked on her food as his words pierced through her like a knife. "I had a mate. As in past tense. Quintus already has a mate. Mao."

"That's not what he says, and I think he'd be the first to know. I'll be honest here, I'm an unmated wolf so I don't know what it's like personally but I've known plenty of wolves. You can't turn away from a mating. It'll break you."

"I didn't say I didn't want him." She glanced to the pool, captivated as his face broke through the surface, water beading down his chest.

"As far as I can tell, he wants you. But you're going to have to submit, darlin'. I'm just tellin' ya now. That man there isn't going to take any less. He's your mate. Your

Alpha. And runnin' like ya did." Hunter shrugged and gave a half smile. "That shit's gonna get you in some deep ass trouble."

"But I…" Gabriella lost her words as Quintus ascended like a phoenix out of the blue water.

"I'm gonna go take a quick shower, because I think y'all need some time alone. But don't you worry now, I'll be right back because I wouldn't want to miss the show."

Gabriella's breath caught as Quintus stepped out of the pool. Droplets beaded on his flesh, rolling down his ripped abs. Bared, every inch of his rock-hard body displayed for his mate.

Stop staring, Gabby. Her eyes caught his and he gave her a wry smile. *Oh shit. Stop looking.* Her eyes dropped once to his half-hard cock and back to his face. *Stop fucking looking. What is wrong with me?*

"You like the croissants?" he asked.

"Um…yeah." *It's not the only thing I want to eat. Jesus, stop thinking. He's going to hear me.* "Um…the croissants are great."

Quintus gave her a broad smile and closed the distance, standing naked before her. He lifted his towel to his face, not bothering to cover himself.

"We're going to spend a few hours resting here before we go to New Orleans." He dragged the terry cloth over his muscular chest. "I'm thinking this would be a good time to set some ground rules. Discuss next steps."

"I…um…well…you can give me the bone and I'll go get help. I mean now that we've found it, you don't need to…"

Gabriella licked her lips, struggling to keep her eyes on his. As he took his cock into his hand and ran the towel over its length, her body ignited with desire, her wolf awakening.

"You see that's the thing. What you did the past twenty-four hours…running away? Twice. That's never going to happen again." Quintus stroked his dick in his hands, his voice firm. "I've said it nicely and now we're about to have a lesson."

"But…" Quintus raised an eyebrow, instantly stopping her from speaking. *I'm in trouble. So much fucking trouble. In so many fucking ways.* Gabriella couldn't decide whether to beg him to fuck her or run for her life.

"I hear your thoughts. No more, Gabby. No more running. Tonight you'll learn submission." Quintus towered over her, his voice commanding. "Tonight we'll complete the bonding and when it's done, there will be no room for doubt that I'm your mate. That woman back at my house. I'm not bonded to her. You're mine. There is no one else for me."

"I…" Gabriella's nipples tightened in arousal as he came closer and stroked his cock.

"Hear me, Gabby. I want you in my life. I'm your mate," he told her.

"Quintus," she breathed.

"Open your mouth," he instructed, his tone serious.

"What?" Gabriella's heart pounded as he straddled her legs and placed his palm onto the wall behind her. She yearned to touch him but resisted.

"Tonight, I'm going to fuck you so hard you'll never

forget who your mate is. But before that…submission. This is your lesson. You will learn. I am your Alpha. Your mate. Now open your mouth."

Gabriella's palms settled onto his muscular thighs as he dragged the tip of his cock over her lips. Helpless to say no, she craved her vampire like no other. He widened his stance, and glided his shaft into her warm mouth. She sucked him deep, moaning as he withdrew. He tempted her with his tip that lingered on her tongue.

"Tonight you will do as I say. You will accept your punishment for running. You will accept the pleasure. And I will accept yours."

She panted as he lifted his dick, exposing his tightened balls. She brushed over them with her lips. Her tongue flitted over his velvety sac and she sucked it into her mouth. Closing her eyes, she reached for him. His body tensed under her hands as she released him, continuing to lap at his balls.

"Fuck," he exhaled as she dug her fingernails into his thighs.

"Hmm," Gabriella moaned, her wolf roused. Her pussy tightened, and she squeezed her legs together, aching for him to fuck her.

"That's it…ah yeah," he said, sliding his shaft between her lips.

Gabriella opened her mouth wide as he plunged into her, the salty taste of her mate on her tongue. She slid her hands around to cup his ass, pulling him to her, accepting his hard length down her throat.

She gasped for air as he withdrew, and gave a squeak as he lifted her by the waist and brought her to her feet.

"You're mine, bella. Don't ever doubt this," Quintus told her, his intense eyes locked on Gabriella's.

She nodded, melting into his embrace as his mouth crushed onto hers. Her tongue swept against his, probing, tasting her mate. She returned his bruising kiss, surrounded by his warmth. She went to reach for his cock and he wrapped his strong fingers around her wrist, denying her her prize.

"Submission," he growled.

Gabriella panted as he tore his lips from hers. Her pulse raced as he tugged at the lapels of her robe, revealing her bare skin. The fabric pooled at her feet and cool air brushed over her full breasts. She shivered in arousal, the darkness in his eyes warning her she'd pay dearly.

"You took off twice. You put Hunter and me in danger but most of all, you put yourself in danger. Never again will that happen."

Gabriella squealed as he reached for her waist and lifted her into the air. "Goddess…"

"Not a Goddess but more like a God. There're a few things we need to discuss."

"But I…" As Quintus settled her over the side arm of the wide sofa, her face brushed the sofa cushion. Realizing her precarious position, she slammed her thighs together.

"Ah, ah, ah…I want to see all of you." Quintus slid his hands between her thighs and spread open her legs, revealing her glistening pussy. "I promised you a spanking."

"A spanking?" she exclaimed, her toes dangling onto the floor.

"Yes, my sweet little wolf."

"But…no…ow," she cried as his palm landed a stinging blow to her bottom. As he rubbed the soreness away, she shook her head side to side.

"You will submit, Gabby. Running from me," he landed another firm swat to her other cheek and she yelped in response, "is not an option."

"Quintus…" Gabriella lost her words. Her ass stung, the slap of a palm to her flesh echoing in the room. She cringed as her arousal bloomed at his firm touch. The cool air brushed her wet pussy, and she moaned as another blow landed on her bottom.

She breathed through the overwhelming sensations, her body on fire with both pain and desire. As she blinked open her eyes, her vampire came into focus. He knelt and stroked her cheek, pressing his lips to hers. She surrendered to his searing kiss, her palm on his cheek.

"Quintus…please," she begged.

"Ah bella, as much as I wish I could take you right now, I'm afraid you owe Hunter an apology for your antics."

Gabriella's heart stopped as she caught sight of the magnificent Alpha standing above them. Water beaded over the hard ridges of his chest, a towel hung low on his hips.

"Well, darlin', can't say I didn't warn you." The corner of his lip tugged upward.

"What do you think of my mate?" Quintus released Gabriella and stood next to the Alpha.

His smooth voice rumbled in the room as his palm cupped her bottom. His hand delved in between her cleft and his forefinger stroked the edge of her labia, leaving her core aching in desire. She moaned, pressing her forehead into the sofa cushion. Her face heated as blood rushed to her cheeks. She should be mortified, given her precarious position, the Alpha's eyes on her as Quintus fingered her, but her nipples tightened into hard points, her traitorous body responding to his presence. *Oh Goddess, what's wrong with me?*

"Ah little wolf…you enjoy having the Alpha see you like this? Spread wide open for me."

"No…" Before she could finish her statement, her lie was rewarded with the sting of his palm.

"No lying,' Quintus scolded, his voice firm. "She's in training, I'm afraid."

"Jesus," she breathed, her core quivering in response to the spanking. Gabriella sucked a breath as his finger circled her core and plunged deep inside her.

"You need to trust me, Gabby. No running. No arguing. Tonight we will bond but first…Hunter has earned a place with us. You ran from him too. Put him in danger. This is not how you treat an Alpha."

"He's not my Alpha," she moaned as he slid two fingers inside her, his thumb brushing over her swollen pearl. Gabriella turned her head, catching a glimpse of the Alpha behind her.

"You see she's very defiant." Quintus nodded at Hunter, his eyes focused back on his mate.

"This is a lesson, my sweet Gabriella."

"Ah," she cried as the Alpha's palm landed on her ass. "What are you doing?"

"I'm going to teach you a lesson in submission. And the Alpha is going to help you learn. Pain."

"Ow…" Her fingers clutched the sofa, she turned her head, spying Quintus. Her heated channel quivered around his fingers in response, the sweet sting of pain twisting through her.

"You can't move. You have no control right now. I will do with your body as I wish. Do you understand?" Quintus asked her as he withdrew his fingers and licked them.

"Oh Goddess," she breathed.

"Do. You. Understand?" He plunged two thick fingers back into her pussy.

"What are y…" Gabriella lost her words as the Alpha smacked her other cheek.

"Darlin'. Seems like you might want to answer your vampire. As much as I'm enjoying spanking your lovely ass, it's getting pretty red."

"Jesus, yes. Yes, I understand," she spat out, hating that her body flamed in arousal with each swat, instinctively responding to the sexuality of the Alpha.

"You will listen," he told her.

"Please," she pleaded, grunting as the Alpha spanked her twice more.

"Do you see how well my mate stays in position?"

Gabriella panted, her body lit on fire. Her core ached, desperate for release. She caught a glimpse of Quintus as he made his way to the front of the sofa. She attempted to grind her hips at the sight of the powerful vampire. The ambient light reflected on the sheen of his ripped abs. She pushed onto her elbows, to better see him. He stroked his magnificent erection as he approached.

"I know you want this in you but as I said, I control your pleasure." His eyes briefly went to Hunter then he refocused his attention on her. He cupped her cheeks in his hands, sliding his fingers into her mouth.

"But Quintus…" she began to protest. Her pussy tightened as the Alpha palmed her mound, his index finger giving the slightest pressure onto her clit.

"You want us inside of you, don't you?" Quintus gave her a sexy as sin smile. "Don't lie, now. I read your thoughts, my dirty little wolf. Someday I may even share your body with the Alpha but not tonight. No, right now you're mine."

"Fuck, she's so wet," Hunter said, sliding his fingers through her folds. "She really likes this."

"Please…hmm," she begged.

"He'll watch. I want the Alpha as witness to our bond."

"I…" Gabriella ached, a flood of arousal pulsing through her at the thought of him watching. *What the hell is wrong with me?* she thought to herself. She'd never had public sex, but as the Alpha lightly stroked his finger around her sensitive bead, she knew that she'd never be the same. She'd be safe with Quintus, living her dark fantasy.

"I want to taste you now." Quintus released her face and moved in front of Hunter, rubbing his cock up into her ass.

He spread her cheeks with his hands, tracing his thumb around her back hole. "I'm going to fuck you here too, Gabby. All of you, every inch of you is mine."

Overwhelmed in sensation Gabriella exhaled as Quintus slid a firm arm around her waist and lifted her into his arms. Within seconds he'd placed her on the bed. She landed on her back and curled her hands into the sheets as he pressed her thighs open and settled between her legs.

Her beast crouched in submission to the dominant vampire, and her heart crushed at his touch. Had he always known what she needed? It seemed impossible this man belonged to her, yet her instincts told her he was hers.

Gabriella caught a glimpse of Hunter, who sat on the sofa stroking his cock as he watched them. The Alpha's eyes locked on hers, and her pulse raced, knowing he could see everything they were doing. Her head lolled back onto the bed as Quintus nibbled her thigh, his mouth inching toward her pussy.

"That's right, Gabby. He's going to get off while I fuck you. You like him watching, don't you?"

"Yes," she cried, unable to lie.

"This," he whispered. Quintus plunged his fingers inside her. "Your pussy."

"Oh Goddess." His devilish tongue lapped over her clit. She trembled in arousal, her core tightening around his fingers. As he withdrew them, she moaned, begging for his touch. "Please, don't stop."

Quintus slid his palms under her bottom and cupped her ass, tugging her toward his mouth. She gripped the sheets as his tongue stroked deep inside her.

"Ah, yes." Her breath grew ragged as her orgasm inched closer.

"You taste fucking amazing," he growled.

"Please…I can't…I need to come," she pleaded, tilting her hips upward. The sweet ache drove her delirious and she squirmed, attempting to make contact.

Quintus obliged, lapping at her swollen bead and driving his fingers back inside her pussy, teasing over her sensitive strip of nerves. Gabriella writhed underneath him as he sucked her flesh, the tip of his tongue furiously flicking at her clit.

She speared her fingers into his hair, pressing her hips upward into his face. His pinky inched toward her back hole and the dark sensation twisted through her. As he inched it into her anus, a shiver ran through her.

"Ah yeah, that's it. Don't stop, don't stop," she cried.

Her orgasm slammed into her as he relentlessly licked over her clit, his fingers buried deep inside her. Rippling waves of energy flickered through every cell in her body.

"Quintus." The faint call for her lover whispered from her lips. Gabriella shivered, a roll of ecstasy flowing through her. *This vampire is my mate.* The words floated through her mind as she heaved for breath.

As he rose above her, her legs fell open, welcoming him. His lips brushed her hip, a trail of kisses peppered over her abdomen. When he raised his gaze to meet hers, Gabriella's heart caught. His intense gaze bored into her soul. She knew once the bond was complete, she'd spend eternity with this man.

"The first time you gave me your blood, you healed me," he said, dragging his tongue over her skin, his lips grazing her ear. "And tonight I give my blood to you."

Her beast roused, howling in pursuit of her mate. *Mine.* The wolf paced, itching to shift.

"Ahh…" Gabriella squirmed, her core brushing the thick crown of his cock. Her channel ached in anticipation.

"You're mine, Gabby? Si?"

The question rocked her, but the answer lay true in her mind. She belonged to him. Accepting fate, Gabriella claimed the vampire she craved.

"Yes…yes. I want this." She bared her throat in submission.

"You belong to me, bella. Now and forever." Quintus' fangs dropped.

Gabriella's skin blossomed in gooseflesh as her vampire hovered the sharp points of his teeth over her neck. Her breath became ragged as she pleaded. "Please, Quintus. I'm yours."

She cried out loud as his fangs sliced into her flesh, his thick cock thrusting inside her pussy. Her wolf growled, giving her power to take her mate. She dug her fingernails into his back as he rocked in and out of her tight channel. A braid of their magick twisted through the air as he made love to her, drawing her essence.

Her gums ached as she released the fangs of her beast. Wrapping her legs around his waist, she accepted every long inch of him as he slammed into her, stretching her open for his pleasure. He slowed, grinding his pelvis against hers and stroked her clit.

"My vampire," she claimed, biting into his flesh.

Quintus grunted as her fangs broke his skin. "Ah fuck....Jesus, yes...Gabby."

Gabriella swallowed his blood, his pure magick enveloping her as her hips bucked wildly to meet his. She shuddered as her climax rushed at her. Taking a final deep draw of his blood, she released him, surrendering as she came. Quintus funneled his fingers into her hair, capturing her mouth. She moaned, tasting the mix of their blood on her tongue and reveled in the passion of his kiss.

Tears streamed from her eyes, emotion pouring from her soul. Her life would never be the same, she knew. She willingly accepted the bonding, their hearts and minds intertwining as one. The Goddess had put forth her wishes, destiny predetermined.

As he rolled onto his back, and gently removed himself, she rested her head on his chest, clutching his arm. She'd never told another soul she loved them. To do so would've made her vulnerable. Yet Quintus was an unexpected rush, a game changer. She'd have to trust him, trust herself, that she'd given herself a gift. Her wolf howled in approval, her mate finally in her arms.

Gabriella floated in the comfort of his loving thoughts. As she drifted off to sleep, she smiled, bonded to her mate forever.

⤐ *Chapter Eleven* ⤏

Quintus' mind raced. In thousands of years of his existence, he'd never felt more alive. Connected to another being, his heart pounded in his chest. Gabriella was his, forever more. Her power hummed in his body, her energy like a lightning bolt. Dangerous and beautiful, she matched his lethal nature.

She mewled, and wrapped a leg over his. He inhaled, smiling as he nuzzled his nose into her hair. She smelled of sweet honeysuckle and the dash of her white magick tingled over her skin. Gabriella's hair spilled over her shoulder, revealing an intricate design on her skin. *My mark.* Quintus' heart squeezed as he held her tiny hand in his, drawing circles onto her palm. He never thought he'd allow another woman into his heart, yet as he brushed his lips to her forehead, his soul craved hers.

His thoughts drifted to Mao. There would have been no way he could have completed the bond with Gabriella had she been who she said she was. At best, the woman Absinthe had presented was merely a shell of Mao, her spirit long dead. At worst, the dark magick he detected belonged to that of a demon, once masquerading as his former lover. Regardless, he planned to bring her back to the witch who found her.

The creak of the door opening broke his contemplation, and his eyes went to Hunter. No words needed to be spoken. The Alpha knew they'd mated, had watched but left them in privacy to go dress. Hunter gave him a silent nod and padded across the room to the sofa. He quietly lay back on it, his feet propped in the air.

Quintus speculated they could rest a few hours before flying back to New Orleans. It was only a matter of time before Lilitu found them again. He suspected that not only could the bone kill her, it could bring down the entire coven, so she'd come for them soon. While Gabriella didn't know how to use the artifact, Quintus was certain they'd find answers in New Orleans.

Fucking Ilsbeth, he inwardly cursed. The New Orleans' high priestess had been the most feared and powerful witch in the country before her accident. But the last time he'd seen her, she'd lost her mind, disassociating herself from her former name and life.

Quintus prayed like hell Samantha could provide guidance and help them kill Lilitu. Although she was rumored to be powerful, she didn't have much experience. Spells, both white and dark magick, were passed through the lineage of witches. Because Samantha was bonded to a vampire, sired through him, Quintus trusted her more than he'd ever be capable of with Absinthe.

As he closed his eyes, Quintus relaxed into the embrace of his little wolf. For but a few hours they'd safely rest, then they'd make their way to the Crescent City. They'd bring the bone of the first witch to New Orleans and find the spell. In the meantime, Quintus swore his life to protect his mate.

"Stop messing around, Viktor," Quintus told his brother over the phone. He stood and walked to the back of the private jet, keeping his voice low.

"I'm not fucking around. I don't know how the bitch got out. I did as you asked. Put her in one of the holding cells at the club," Viktor said, exhaustion in his voice.

"Are you sure she's not there?" His blood pressure rose, a tick in his temple. "Maybe she's just hiding or something."

"Sorry, she's gone."

"She's a pixiu. Or at least she was. They've got rare powers. It's possible she could've used demon magick to escape. Or maybe one got in to help her."

"Or stole her back. Who the fuck knows? I'm so over this bullshit."

"Hey, I've got to tell you something. I bonded with Gabby. I'm her mate." Quintus' declaration was met by silence. "Did you hear me?"

"Yeah, yeah, I heard you. I mean, I thought maybe you might wait for me. I feel like I might cry...always a bridesmaid, never the bride."

"Fuck off." Quintus heard laughter from his phone and took a deep breath, tempted to throw it across the plane.

"You're so touchy. I'm just fucking with ya, bro. Congrats. I just...I don't know...I guess I wasn't sure if it would ever really happen. The Goddess...that bitch sure does take her sweet time. I guess the first one doesn't really count. It's kind of like you took a mulligan."

"Listen, Viktor. Because I need you to pay attention. Whoever this woman is...it's not Mao. It's as if someone is wearing her like a mask. Even her skin felt different. There's something about her. The more I think on this, the more I think she might be a demon."

"Fuck me. You know what this means?"

"It means she could be more powerful than you think. Just stay where you are. Call Thorn and let him go find his mess. He brought her here. Make her his problem."

"It also means we've met two demons in the course of a week. This isn't exactly good luck."

"We can't know for sure what the hell she really is, but I think it's safe to assume she's driving on black magick fuel."

"I was tempted to tell her to get some holy water to clean off the Hell stink. But if she's a demon, she's going to need more than a few spritzes. I'm thinking more like an underwater baptism."

"You're not going to get a demon anywhere near a church."

"Maybe a river. Ah, the good old days."

"The good old days weren't that good." Quintus raked

his fingers through his hair and turned to walk toward the pilot's cabin. "I need you to focus. Do as I said. Call Thorn. If you can't reach him, call Absinthe. Then meet me in New Orleans. We'll go see Samantha."

"Damn. Just when I was getting to enjoy babysitting," he quipped.

"You don't even own a plant," Quintus challenged. "You don't cook."

"I like my blood fresh. I'm more of a farm to table sort of vampire. I'm minimalistic like that."

"Get your ass to New Orleans. Make the call and get out, you hear me? I don't want anything happening to you."

"You almost sound like you care. I'm feeling like I need a hug right now, but I'll get it when I see you."

"I'm gonna smack you in your fat head if you don't listen to me."

"Hug time. I've got something to look forward to."

"Fuck off with your damn hugs."

"It's going to be a moment. I can feel it now. I'll pick a song before I get there." Viktor laughed.

"I'm going now. Call Thorn."

"I hear you," he assured Quintus.

"Oh and Vik?"

"Yeah."

"Be careful. I'm not fucking around. Keep your eyes open and get to my place as soon as possible."

"Got it. See ya."

Quintus clicked off the call and turned to see both Hunter and Gabriella staring at him.

"He lost her?" the Alpha asked.

"She gave him the slip. If she's a demon...you know it's hard to control them." Quintus crossed to sit in front of Gabriella and fell back into his tan crushed leather seat.

"She just left then? Just like that?" Gabriella asked.

"Yep. She'd said she wasn't staying in New York. So who knows?" Quintus shook his head and shrugged. "There're a lot of kinds of demons and creatures out there. My concern is that if she's demon, she's up to something else. I don't want Viktor going after her."

"My bet is on demon," Hunter said.

"What else could she be?" she asked.

"You've got your basics. Vamps. Witches. Wolves. There're an infinite number of possibilities for the hybrids. You've got the outliers like the naiads and pixiu. Although technically they're shifters. Mao was pixiu but I'm with Hunter, she's probably a demon mix."

"So you're saying Mao's...she's not really, um..." Gabriella hesitated to finish her sentence.

"It's okay, Gabby." Quintus' eyes softened, aware she didn't want to hurt him. "Mao died a long time ago. That woman...no, that thing we brought home, it isn't Mao."

"I don't understand how none of us knew. I mean, she's outsmarted a high priestess. A demon. You. An Alpha." Gabriella's focus drifted to Hunter.

Quintus gave her a knowing smile as her sexy thoughts spun through his mind. "There'll be time later to explore that."

"I'm just saying." She coughed, her cheeks heated in

embarrassment. "Something like that has to be special. Powerful."

"Maybe yes. Maybe no," Quintus said.

"You've got your hands full with that one," Hunter commented, the corner of his mouth tugging upward. "I'm happy to oblige."

"Focus, people." Quintus steepled his fingers in thought. "I think Gabriella's point is well taken. The question is, 'What is Mao?' Why didn't any of us notice she wasn't Mao at first? She looked like her. Talked like her. Holds her memories. Witches, demons…both can wield glamouring spells."

"True. Even I can do that, but you saw right through it," Gabriella said.

"What I saw was no glamour," Quintus asserted.

"You sure?" Hunter asked. "No offense, but you're emotionally involved. It's possible she got one over on you."

"No way. I'm telling you. I knew her. And that isn't Mao." Quintus sighed, choosing his next words carefully. He refused to hurt Gabriella more than he already had. "I met her many, many years ago, but this demon, this thing…it mimics her voice, her mannerisms. It's almost as if it's retained part of her DNA but it's compromised. And her story isn't straight. The day she went over that cliff, Mao died. That woman, that thing, at my house told me that she shifted. I never saw her shift. At the moment of Mao's death, there was simply nothing. I felt nothing."

"So what you're sayin' is we're dealing with a zombie?" Hunter asked with a disbelieving laugh. "No way. It happens but they don't look nearly as good as she does."

"Listen, I've seen all sorts of crazy shit in my lifetime. I never thought of this possibility until now. It's a stretch but there's a myth. Mao told me of it once. She said the elders had been threatened with black magick. It's possible she's a Jiangshi."

"You mean a vampire? Like you?" Hunter asked.

"No. Yes. Well, it's more of a zombie."

"Like the things you see in the movies? Video games?" Gabriella asked. "Aren't they vampires?"

"Pop culture has worked the myth over. They perpetuate their own ideas. But in this case, the more I think about my interactions with her and what's happening, I believe Mao did die that day. I suspect a demon, or someone who wields dark, dark magick…they took her corpse. They created a Jiangshi."

"But Thorn found her in a part of Hell. He said it was for innocents," Gabriella challenged.

"Maybe, maybe not. That demon is an interesting sort, I'll admit, but you can't trust him."

"Maybe someone put her there on purpose to find?" Gabriella suggested. "A Trojan horse."

"Or she may have just been waiting for the right moment in history to work her way back into your life," Hunter suggested.

"Why wait though? I mean, I don't know much about taking a corpse and making it into a zombie, but I imagine it doesn't take too long. It doesn't make sense. Not unless she's been waiting for something specific. Something that belongs to you." Gabriella's gaze went to Quintus.

"More like someone," Hunter suggested.

"Maybe both," Quintus added. "Gabby is a special hybrid. Born into this unusual coven."

"Evil coven." Gabriella's blood ran cold at the mention of them.

Quintus nodded. "Si. They killed your mother. Possibly your father. We're not sure on that one. They've certainly tried to kill you. Or at least made it seem so. But maybe they were waiting? It seemed that way from the way Lilitu spoke in the catacombs. Maybe she was waiting for our bonding. The bones of the first witch. We both used magick to get those bones. Maybe she was waiting for us. Maybe it was all meant to happen at a particular time."

"How do we kill it?" Gabriella asked with a tone of indifference.

"I like your girl," Hunter laughed, slapping his palm down onto his armrest.

"So do I," Quintus said with a raised eyebrow. "Obviously we should consult Samantha but if I recall correctly, Jiangshi are pretty tough to kill. Technically they're already dead. I remember something about them eating their own flesh. She won't be able to maintain her living figure forever. If she's a zombie, eventually she will rot. That smell on her. It might not be Hell. It might be her decomposing from within."

"Ooookay. Well, on that note, let me just say that I want you both to know I enjoyed that little spankin' last night. Paris always delivers. Us wolves enjoy a bit of sharin' every now and then but you vamps are usually possessive," Hunter said out of the blue. "Just lookin' on the bright side of this mess."

"What the hell are you going on about, wolf?" Quintus narrowed his eyes on the Alpha.

"Hey, this has been a fun ride. We've got some crazy-ass high priestess looking for a fuckin' bone. Another New York witch servin' up a demon who looks like a game show host. He gives you a replica of your high school sweetheart. But she's really a Suzie-zombie wind me up doll...the 'I won't die' edition. They're all lookin' to kill us. Yep, it's been a helluva ride. You vamps sure know how to have a good time." Hunter leaned backwards onto the head rest, a half smile on his lips. "I'll go back to Wyoming and they'll be like, 'Hey Alpha, did you have fun on the east coast?' Yeah, it's been a party all right."

"Stop complaining. You did have a good time. It sure felt that way last night," Gabriella spat back at the Alpha who wore a smile.

"It appears this one liked her punishment a little too much last night." Hunter raised an eyebrow at them.

"Don't encourage him, Gabby." *Jesus, this woman is going to kill me.* Quintus loved the way his feisty witch sent the Alpha off kilter with her quick wit. She'd responded, aroused by both spanking and being watched. He hadn't truly considered sharing her with the wolf but her adventurous spirit tempted him. He sighed, bringing his thoughts back on topic.

"This Jiangshi." Hunter said. "What else do you know about them?"

"Some say they're similar to vampires but I beg to disagree. Unlike what has been portrayed in movies, I'm not a corpse. I was close to death but never died. In that thin veil, we are transformed by the magick of our ancestors. The Jiangshi. They are dead. There are many myths about how they are created, what they can do but these are all just interpretations. Stories. Folklore. My guess?" Quintus shrugged. "It's like any other rare creature created by dark magick."

"Necromancy?" Gabriella asked.

"Yeah, but she's not your typical zombie. My guess is she's capable of maintaining her human form for longer as long as she feeds on blood," Quintus agreed. "Witches. Demons. Both own the toolkit to create these kinds of things."

"And just when you think the zombies were so last year, they make a comeback. Who knew?" Hunter laughed.

"Jiangshi are rare. I've only heard of them," Quintus said.

"Do you think Lilitu had something to do with this?" Gabriella asked.

"Can't rule her out. Could be a demon. One that's laying low. They aren't usually the social types. Thorn's hybrid so he doesn't count. Witches like to be known. It's possible it's a new player. A witch or a warlock, but they haven't made an appearance."

"What about Absinthe? She's a slippery one," Hunter said.

"Yes she is. But I doubt she has the power." Quintus looked to Gabriella. "When we get back to New Orleans, we'll head straight to Luca's and meet up with Samantha."

"And Viktor?" Hunter asked.

"I'm going to text him again," Quintus replied. Attempting to hide his concern, he stared out the window. He knew his brother all too well. Despite his warning to avoid her, Viktor would attempt to find Mao. She'd challenged him by breaking his wards.

"He's going to be okay," Gabriella whispered.

Although he didn't hear her voice, it was her fingers brushing his cheek that drew him out of his deep thoughts. As he turned, she straddled his legs and his hands found her waist. Her intense gaze held his and his heart tightened.

His eyes fell to her lips and he leaned in, capturing her mouth. His tongue swept against hers, tasting and probing. She kissed him in return, her hands cupping his face. She tasted of honey, her familiar feminine scent wrapping around him. Blood rushed to his cock, and he groaned as she sat on his lap and rocked over his erection.

His hand slid up her shirt and cupped her bared breast. "Fuck, you're not wearing a bra," he groaned.

"I'm not either." The voice of the Alpha broke Quintus' concentration.

He reluctantly tore his lips from Gabriella's, his forehead resting on hers.

"Don't mind me. I don't want to sit out on the game but if I can't play, I'm good with watchin' y'all again. But hold on a minute, lemme grab something to eat. Where did the co-pilot say he kept the snacks again? Up front right?" Hunter stood and walked toward the cockpit and began to rummage through the cabinet. "Damn. You didn't tell me they were fully stocked."

"Seriously wolf," Quintus exhaled loudly and lifted his head, catching a glimpse of Hunter waving a small bottle of vodka.

"Stuff's top shelf, vamp. Want some?"

"No." Quintus focused on Gabriella, whose heated gaze churned his desire. "There's only one thing I want to drink right now but that will have to wait until later."

"And here I thought I was getting another show." Hunter poured the clear liquid into a glass and held it to the air.

Quintus ignored the Alpha. As Gabriella moved to stand, he pulled her back onto his lap so that they both faced Hunter. "We should talk about the bone."

"Really? The bone?" Hunter began laughing, walking to his seat. "You mean like the one you're hiding in your pants right now?"

"He's like a thirteen-year-old boy," Gabriella commented.

"Wolves." Quintus rolled his eyes. "I'm sorry. This is your lineage."

"Hey, I'm part witch," she protested.

"The first witch. Her bone," Quintus clarified.

"Oh yeah. Right. Sorry, got distracted there for a minute with the PDA. It's over. I'm good." Hunter sipped his drink, exhaling loudly. "Look, I don't know what we are supposed to do with it, but I'll go with weapon."

"I agree with you. We either have to physically use it, which if that's true, we've gotta be in pretty close proximity to Lilitu. Or maybe there's some sort of potion. And again, that involves close contact."

"Growing up, I saw Lilitu and the others doing spells with no contact," Gabriella said.

"True but I'm with Quint on this one. I've been around a lot of witches in my time and while they can do spells on people without contact, they usually need something that belongs to the person they are using the spell on. The more personal the better. Hair plucked from the scalp. Blood. A personal item like a ring or bracelet would work too. Clothing."

"Yes, it could be used in a spell. But sometimes the artifact is simply a weapon infused with magick. That sternum? My guess is that it could be used to slit a throat. Possibly deliver a fatal stabbing." Quintus stroked the inside of her palm with his thumb.

"When I touched it…" Gabriella recalled the dark magick that stung through her body. "Its energy is strong."

"I've got it in my coat pocket, but I think we should keep it under wraps until we get it to Samantha," Hunter suggested.

"I agree. That thing is carrying some heavy vibes. Thirty thousand feet over the Atlantic isn't the best place to fuck around with magick," Quintus said.

"The energy. It was familiar but toxic. It's really dangerous." Gabriella leaned back onto her vampire, resting her head on his chest.

"Absinthe says it'll kill Lilitu. Let's hope there's not a catch," Quintus said.

"There'll be a catch," Gabriella stated, her voice almost hypnotic in its soft and even tone. "There's always a catch. I know I'm supposed to embrace what I am. Practice the craft. But for me there is no sisterhood. Even if they weren't trying to kill me, I wouldn't be in the coven."

"You're probably right, but we'll deal with it," Quintus agreed, pressing his lips to the top of her head. "If I could change what happened to you, I'd do it in a heartbeat. But you're never going to be alone again." Emotion coiled in his chest, and it took him by surprise. Quintus had almost forgotten what it had felt like to care for someone so much. The bond had been inevitable, a force far greater than his own. But opening his heart to Gabriella was unexpected. "I'll protect you."

"You're not alone anymore. You'll always have a place with my pack," the Alpha told her.

"I'm not sure if I can go with a pack." Her fingers slipped underneath Quintus' shirt.

"No one's pressuring you, but I want you to know you'll have the support of a pack if you want it," Hunter assured her.

"If you want to run with the wolves again, you will. As far as the witches, let's talk to Samantha. You've had a lifetime of Lilitu. I want you to meet a different kind of witch. She's the polar opposite of the likes of Lilitu or Absinthe. Or Ilsbeth for that matter."

Her silence told Quintus she didn't believe him, and he considered after everything that had happened to her, she deserved to be skeptical. He'd underestimated the extent of the trauma she'd experienced. Torn from her parents, living on the edge of death day after day, fight or flight was her only way of surviving. Anger boiled inside his gut, but he cloaked his emotions from her.

He grew determined to give her a better life, filled with light and love. It would be Gabriella's choice if she chose a pack, but living in fear, selling her blood to strangers was a thing of the past.

Quintus had always understood the technical aspects of bonding, yet he'd underestimated the amplified level of connection between two beings. As he wrapped his arm around Gabriella, her nervous energy sizzled through his body as if it was his own. Contrary to the sexual tension on the plane, Gabriella's mood in the limo had turned to anxiety.

The car rolled to a stop as they pulled up to a set of old pillars. The driver punched a code into a metal keypad, and the intricate metal gate slid open. He'd originally planned to meet Samantha at the coven's mansion in the Garden District, but Quintus suspected there'd be far too many witches living there, overwhelming Gabriella.

It had been over fifty years since Quintus had been to Kade Issacson's estate. Sired by his child Léopold, the leader of New Orleans had never quite taken to Quintus. He supposed it had rubbed Kade the wrong way that he'd come and go in New Orleans as he pleased, never informing him of his agenda. Every now and then, Quintus exacted his own justice, and he didn't have time for long discussions or explanations. Far older than the others, he'd grown to do what he pleased.

Tonight, however, he'd contacted Kade directly, ensuring Luca's compliance. Although Kade led the vampires in New Orleans, it was well known that his trusty acquaintance was far more cantankerous. They needed the help of his fiancée, Samantha. The witch was known for being powerful yet benevolent. Luca, on the contrary, was known for killing first, asking questions later.

As they pulled into the grand Garden District property, Quintus took note of the enormous mansion; a guest home stood majestic in its shadow. He glanced to the sidewalk, which was covered in brightly colored chalk drawings and smiled, recalling that a child lived in the residence.

The limo rolled to a stop, and Quintus issued a warning. "Luca Macquarie doesn't care much for others who aren't vampire."

"Excuse me…what?" Gabriella nervously pulled her hair back into a ponytail.

"It's just Luca's more of a purist, so to speak. It's not like he's my direct child. If it weren't for Viktor…let's just say I don't think he'd still be alive."

"What do you mean?" she asked.

"There is this thing." He hesitated. "It's very easy to become lost. To forget who you were. The humans who walk among us are fragile. They're living day to day…knowing all the while their time is limited. But if they do it right, they love, live, experiencing all that is offered on the earth. But immortals? We live year after year, often taking for granted all that the Goddess offers us. We become cold, indifferent to the plight of others."

"But you aren't like that." Gabriella reached for his hand, her attention briefly drawn out the window as the car stopped.

"I was human once, but the reality is thousands of years as an immortal can change you. You reach a point where you no longer value humans. You see them as nothing more than food. They're weak, a liability." Quintus brushed a kiss to the back of her hand.

"And Luca?" Gabriella held tight to Quintus, watching as the driver got out of the car and circled toward the back.

"He's distant. He sees humans as weak. It's his way of adapting. He's not especially fond of wolves either, for the record." Quintus' gaze went to Hunter, a corner of his lips upturned.

"Yeah well. He can take a number. I knew Luca way back when he was just a little baby vamp. Before I went to Wyoming to make my way. It didn't take him long to ditch the human routine and go full on dick. No offense but if I had a nickel for every vampire who had a beef with wolves," he laughed, "I'd be a rich man. Oh yeah, I am anyway. Look, life is hard. But you just have to accept things. Human today. Vamp tomorrow. Live and let live."

"True. But you were born as beast. We weren't. We were human once. When we transition, our loved ones and friends still live on. We watch them die. While we're both immortal beings, we take far different paths."

The car door opened, and Quintus stepped onto the cobblestone driveway. He sensed Gabriella's hesitation, but she feigned confidence, her chin held high. The Alpha exited the car, protectively shielding her from behind.

The scent of roses lingered in the air. The fragrance triggered childhood memories, momentarily distracting him. Shoving the thoughts to the back of his mind, he refocused on their task. He sensed Luca seconds before the front door opened, but it was Quintus' child who surprised him, materializing onto the driveway.

Léopold Devereoux. France. 988AD. During a drunken celebration with his fellow warriors, he'd been badly beaten. A mercenary, loyal to no man or king, Quintus wasn't bothered about humans, but the broken soldier had bought him a drink, befriended an Italian stranger in a foreign place. In a brief conversation that Léopold would never remember, the vampire had confessed his grief; his family had been murdered whilst he'd been at war. Later in the evening, Quintus had found him beaten, dying on a filthy stone floor. In a desolate alleyway, Quintus offered immortality to the pitiful stranger.

Quintus had given Léopold enough instruction to live but he couldn't afford to bring a fledgling vampire with him on the road. Living under the radar, he traveled the world, taking on dangerous missions, killing his marks. He'd known Léopold harbored resentment, but the new vampire would have died within the year had he taken him. The benevolent action had cost him a friendship, but was a price well paid, considering how the vampire had flourished on his own.

"Quintus." Léopold flashed directly in front of him, blocking his view of Luca.

"Léopold." He nodded, shielding Gabriella with his body.

"What are you doing here? You could have gone up north, no?" The vampire eyed him, letting his gaze drift to Gabriella.

"We're here to see the high priestess," Quintus explained. Far too many years had passed to ease the anger of the French vampire. "It's complicated."

"You bring wolves?" He tilted his head, his gaze falling upon Hunter.

"Si. Like I said. Complicated."

"What do you need with Samantha?" Luca interjected without greeting him.

"Where's Kade?" Quintus asked, annoyed with the Spanish inquisition.

"I'm here." The tall vampire stepped out of the doorway onto the porch. He made his way down the steps and extended his hand. "Quintus."

"Kade." Quintus shook his hand but didn't mistake the gesture as weakness. "I realize this is an imposition but I'm in need of Samantha's services."

"What are you doing here? New York is a big city. Go see Absinthe," Luca growled.

"You best mind your manners around me, Macquarie. Remember your place." Quintus narrowed his eyes on the

British vampire. He balled his fists, his fangs itching to drop.

"He's only saying what we all think," Léopold said, shaking his head. "You're one of the most powerful vampires on the east coast. Absinthe is skilled. Why Samantha? Why do this here? There's no…"

"I've got this, Leo," Kade interrupted. "Quintus. Clearly we have our reasons for questioning why you're here. To Luca's point, you have resources in New York."

"Absinthe can't be trusted," Quintus responded. "You know full well I used to consult Ilsbeth every now and then, but she's far gone. Samantha is pure. She's Luca's. This is Gabriella. She's mine. We're bonded."

Kade's expression softened, his attention going to Gabriella.

"There's a coven in Salem. Circe. They're trying to kill her. We have an artifact. Samantha is the only one I trust to help us figure out what kind of spell we need to protect her."

"Samantha's new in her role as high priestess. We have a daughter," Luca stated. "I don't want you upsetting either one of them."

"I'm new too," Gabriella said, her voice soft.

Quintus sensed her pushing her energy at the vampires. Although protective of his witch, he squeezed her hand, encouraging her to advocate for herself.

"I need help. I'm a novice witch. A wolf. A hybrid. I…we have an artifact, but I need the help of another witch." Gabriella lowered her gaze. "Lilitu. She's going to kill me. More than anyone standing here right now, I have something to lose. But I'm still standing here pleading for your help."

"What in the world is going on out here?" a female voice asked.

A corner of Quintus' lip turned upward as the diminutive redhead stepped outside onto the porch, hands on her hips.

"Luca? Why are our guests standing outside?" she demanded.

"We're just having a little conversation, darlin'. Be right in," he explained.

"Let's not be rude. We can do this in the court yard," she said, as she stepped down the stairs.

"Just making sure you're safe," Luca said, keeping his eyes on his fiancée.

"Nothing and no one here is going to harm me." Samantha reached for Gabriella and took her hand. "Come, little witch. Don't let these big bad vampires scare you. We're every bit as powerful. You just need to learn how to harness your talents."

"What do you think you're doing, Sam?" Luca asked.

"What does it look like I'm doing? I'm taking my guest inside our home. Your friends are invited too. See how that works?"

"Sam…" he began to protest.

"Hurry, dear. I hear the baby. Would you mind giving Sydney a hand with Kate while I attend to our guests? Thank you," she said, giving Luca a slight smile as she raised an eyebrow at him. Her focus went to Gabriella. "I can feel your fear as if it were my own. Don't worry now. We'll figure this out."

Quintus released Gabriella's hand, allowing Samantha to lead his witch into their home. He gave Luca a knowing smile, and the vampire returned it with a disgruntled nod. Quintus inwardly laughed. The red-haired witch clearly had a hold on the prickly vampire. *Women.* Powerful as you may be, the right one will turn your world upside down and you'll enjoy every second of it.

Where the fuck is Viktor? As the thought crossed his mind, Quintus retrieved his cell phone and glanced at the time. He'd texted him again while he was on the plane, instructing him to meet at Luca's. His brother should have been there by now. As he followed Luca and walked through their house, he quickly tapped out a message.

Quintus slid his phone back into his pocket and refocused his attention on Gabriella, who'd stopped to admire a painting on the wall. While Samantha explained its origin, he scanned the room, noting the Picasso and smiled.

"What's with you vamps? Y'all are fancy." Hunter nudged Quintus from behind, and rolled his eyes.

"It's a beautiful collection, I'll give him that." Quintus' lips tightened, his thoughts lingering on his brother. "Luca always had taste for fine arts and antiques."

"Luca's just as grumpy as I remember him as a youth."

"He doesn't care much for others. His human chip is missing."

"The witch sure has his number though." Hunter smiled.

"Someone's going to have your number someday," Quintus replied, giving Kade a nod as he waved them towards a set of opened French doors.

"I'm good. Things in Jackson Hole are exactly how I like them." Hunter followed him through the doorway.

"You can run but you can't hide." Quintus reached inside his jacket and slid on a pair of Ray Bans, the bright sun nearly blinding him.

"Yeah, we'll see about that," he commented.

"If Viktor doesn't get here soon, one of us is going to have to go after him." Quintus lost his words as he took sight of an adorable toddler running circles around a blonde female who sat in the grass smiling. The spitting image of her mother, the little girl squealed in delight as the woman blew bubbles. Her strawberry curls bounced as she jumped, clapping her hands onto the iridescent bubbles.

Quintus' chest tightened as Luca lifted the giggling child, a broad smile on his face. The brooding vampire's hard exterior had softened. So far from the battle-scarred man, Luca appeared human.

Children. They change a man, Quintus thought. He'd never been the greatest sire. The grief from losing Mao had been far too great. The unimaginable pain had taught him the consequences of growing too close to another, to loving someone. He'd sired less than a handful of vampires in his lifetime, always leaving them to fend for themselves. In every instance, he'd taken pity on their human plight. With death looming, he'd saved them, gifting them with eternal life.

Gabriella had rushed into his life like a hurricane. Unable to escape her winds, he'd given in to the inevitable. As each hour passed with their bonding, the emotional ties began to weave a fabric around his heart. Seeing the child brought a reality to his eyes that Quintus had long ignored. Under most circumstances, vampires couldn't have children, yet Luca's witch, with her unique human qualities meshed with her magick, brought life into this world.

Quintus glanced to Gabriella, who caught his gaze. She sat in a shaded gazebo with Samantha. He slammed down his shields to hide his emotions but the sad smile she gave him told Quintus she'd already detected his mood. He cursed his selfish nature, insisting they bond. He'd never once asked her if she'd wanted children, all the while assuming he'd never have any. Under normal circumstances, a wolf or a witch could procreate, yet with a vampire, the odds were unlikely. Luca was an exception, not a rule. Quintus shoved away the seed of jealousy that planted, and refocused his thoughts.

As he went to move toward Gabriella, Kade stopped him, placing a hand on his shoulder. "It's hard for me too."

"Sorry?" Quintus' lips drew into a tight smile.

"Katrina. Kate. She's named after a wolf," he said, giving a nod to Hunter.

"She's beautiful," Quintus acknowledged.

"Sydney…she didn't ask to be vampire. She could have had kids when she was human, or if she'd married someone else. But now…"

"You saved her, si?" Quintus had felt her presence after

she'd been reborn, but he'd never discussed it with Kade.

"A demon. She'd always been a fighter. A tough one. She almost died. She'd begged me to not turn her, but I couldn't lose her."

"She's happy?" Joy emanated from her face as she blew the bubbles, playing with Luca and Kate.

"We might adopt some day. The child would have to be a supe. Maybe a wolf or a witch. It's hard to believe but sometimes they lose parents or are abandoned. They need homes too. Watching Kate...she brings us hope," Kade said.

"I'd heard he had a baby, but seeing Luca with her like this...clearly it's changed him." Quintus didn't admit the feelings that stirred within him. *What the hell is happening to me?* Since being turned, he'd never given a thought to having kids until this very second.

"You don't have to say anything. I know how it feels. That's all I'm saying." Kade sighed. "Perhaps we should talk business. Even though this place is warded, I don't want to risk fate. You know the way of demons. Come. Sydney and Luca will stay with the child."

Quintus glanced at Hunter, his expression hidden behind his sunglasses. The Alpha had overheard the conversation and said nothing, making him curious as to why. The quick-witted wolf had gone silent upon the conversation of children.

"Where's Léopold?" Distracted by baby Kate, he hadn't realized the vampire had vanished.

"He only stopped by for a few seconds, because he heard

you were in town," Kade told him. "He travels often. Spends quite a bit of time in France. The woman he's bonded with is still there on holiday."

Quintus crossed the lawn and stepped out of the sun into the lattice-covered structure, taking a seat next to Gabriella. Hunter and Kade followed. Samantha turned to address her guests.

"Gabby has been telling me about her coven. But to Luca's question, why come to New Orleans? I haven't met Absinthe, but I've heard of her and she's a very powerful priestess."

"The short of it is that something happened recently, and I don't trust her," he replied.

"But she told you about this artifact, yes?" Samantha questioned.

"She did. But I have good reason to question her motive for doing so. To be honest, if I had a choice, I would have gone to Ilsbeth with this kind of thing." The last time he'd seen the ancient high priestess of New Orleans, she played as if she couldn't remember her own name. But Quintus didn't buy her convenient case of amnesia. "I take it she still isn't practicing?"

"She's indisposed at the moment." Samantha's demeanor fell flat as she looked to Kade.

"What is that supposed to mean?" Quintus asked. *Fucking Ilsbeth.*

"It's okay. You can tell them." Kade nodded.

Samantha's gaze went to Luca whose smile faded momentarily in agreement.

"She's missing," Samantha admitted in a whisper.

"What the fuck?" Quintus shook his head and balled a fist. He took a deep breath, his face tense. "I knew that bitch was faking it the last time I was here. What happened?"

"She just disappeared one day. You have to understand. She was living in the coven house. It's been converted but structures like that hold energy. I'd personally set a spell to keep her in place but one day...Holly, her keeper."

"Yes, I met her the day I last saw you. With Jake and Kai." Holly. The bubble-headed neophyte witch had been tasked with caring for the former high priestess. "I'm surprised you'd let a novice watch Ilsbeth."

"Holly was newer at her practice, but all the witches took turns keeping watch over Zella."

"Zella?" Gabriella asked.

"It's the bullshit name she's given herself. Jesus, I can't even believe she walked out of here," Quintus fumed. "You know how dangerous she is."

"She tried to kill Dimitri's wolf. Involved up to her eyeballs in the shit with Jax," Hunter added.

"She was neither all good nor all bad. But I think we can all agree she was powerful," Kade added.

"We did our best. But you know the reality. Ilsbeth is one of the oldest and most powerful witches. Holly..." Samantha blew out a breath, placing her palm onto the cool wooden table. "We found her dead in Ilsbeth's room."

"Perfect. She killed her," Quintus commented.

"Yes." Samantha paused, her lips drawn tight in a line. "Look, the truth is that although it's easy to say she killed

Holly, I'm not convinced. I was in the room. It stank of Hell. Sulfur. Could it have been Ilsbeth? Yes. She was involved with the demon up in New York. But I have this feeling whatever killed Holly actually was a demon."

"Jax said the demon in New York was contained," Hunter said.

"Maybe yes. Maybe no. From what I hear, that cave was open for a while," Quintus said. "It doesn't really matter. We all know that Ilsbeth had her finger in more than one pot. It's not like that demon up in New York was the only one she knew. That may have been the demon she lost a deal with but there have been plenty others on her dance card over the centuries."

"He's right," Samantha agreed.

"We all went to Ilsbeth at one time or another," Kade said. "You play with fire, you get burnt."

"Speak for yourself. Dimitri may have played with witchy woman but not me," Hunter said.

"I recall a few nights I've seen her in your arms," Kade challenged.

"Hold the train, vamp." Hunter held his palms upward. "I may have danced with her a hundred years ago…" He turned to Gabriella and shrugged. "And by that I mean…really it was over a hundred years ago. I was a wolf sowing my oats. And Ilsbeth? She's some exotic hot magic all right. But dancing is a whole lot different than fucking, and I steered way clear of that mess."

"Jesus," Quintus shook his head and rolled his eyes. "Ilsbeth has been around a long time and she's not going down without a fight. The last time we saw her, I'll admit I almost believed her little 'my name is Zella act' right up until she did that channeling thing she did. That was pure Ilsbeth. Her magick was there. Now to Samantha's point, I'm not sure she's a coldblooded killer. She's misguided for sure. I know you wolves will argue she tried to kill Dimitri, but she doesn't generally go after someone without reason. The issue is that she's fucking gone."

"I'm sorry. We did the best we could. I'm telling you that there was no way she could have gotten out on her own," Samantha said.

"We'll deal with Ilsbeth later. Right now, we need your help figuring what to do with the first witch's bone and more importantly, how to kill Lilitu."

"We also have a little problem with Mao. She's his ex," Hunter added. "She's a sort of zombie vampire thing. We're not exactly sure but Absinthe, the good witch of New York, gave her as a gift to the big guy here. Demon was involved."

"Another demon?" Samantha asked, her surprise apparent in her tone. "And he's out?"

"Si. His name's Thorn. He's a half-breed so not the regular kind." Quintus scrubbed his chin, frustrated. The more he spoke the worse it sounded but the situation was what it was. "Mao. She was…I was partially bonded with her, but I'm not anymore."

"A pixiu, correct?" Samantha asked.

"But I saw her die. This thing. It's not Mao."

"We've completed the bond," Gabriella confessed. "I bear his mark."

"There's no way we could have bonded if Mao was still alive. She looked real. But it wasn't her. My best guess is that she's a Jiangshi. My brother Viktor was watching her. Like with Ilsbeth, I had wards set but she escaped. Thorn claims he found her in Hell, but I suspect that she was put there as bait."

"You trust this demon?" Kade asked.

"Hell no," Quintus answered.

"Where's your brother?" Samantha asked.

"That's the fifty-million-dollar question now, isn't it? The last I talked to him he was supposed to call Thorn and then get his ass down here. I specifically told him not to look for Mao, but I'm worried he went after her."

"I haven't heard from him," Kade said.

Quintus glanced at his phone, noting his previous message had gone unread. Although concerned about him, he redirected the conversation. "We need help with the bone. How to use it."

"The bones of the high priestess of a coven can kill her successors. So as you can imagine, they are usually well hidden. Only a few witches are trusted with the entombment of a body. Sometimes there is agreement to have it burned upon death," Samantha told them. "Our covens are beautiful mystical places, where sisters and brothers learn and practice magick. But every now and then we have an outlier."

"Lilitu," Gabriella whispered, her eyes drawn to the dark cloud forming in the sky.

"Circe has had a reputation for years, but you must

understand, witches mind their own. Ilsbeth was unusually active in other cities. She often traveled to New York, Philadelphia, Vegas. She was somewhat of a free spirit. A very powerful one. She didn't play well with others. While witches like Absinthe tolerated her presence in their sandbox, they only did so out of fear."

"What about everyone else?" Gabriella asked.

"Circe is known as purist. Much like my husband." She paused and glanced to Luca and Kate playing in the grass, a smile blooming in her eyes. "He was quite a purist when I met him. He didn't like humans. Didn't care for witches either. Wolves have their purists as well."

"It's true. Some frown upon hybrids. Most of the time, packs are open minded but not all," Hunter added.

"Some covens, they very much want to keep their circle tight. They won't accept anyone but pure witches. Our coven here in New Orleans is open to others, ones who aren't deemed pure. Although my magick is more powerful than the other witches in our coven, I wasn't born a witch. There was a period of adjustment when I joined. I'm human. I'm engaged to a vampire. My child is hybrid. I know for a fact there are people who don't agree I should be here." Samantha sighed and brushed a thick red lock of hair from her eyes. "My point is that we can't take on other covens and their issues. I'm truly sorry about your parents. But if you have the right artifact, you have a chance of setting things straight."

"When I held it, I could sense the energy. It was…" Gabriella shivered, "surreal."

"Who has the bone?" Samantha asked.

"I've got it. Thought it best to keep it, since they're bonded. We didn't want to risk having something happen to Gabby through Quint."

Hunter reached inside his leather jacket and retrieved a red-checked handkerchief. He carefully set it on the table, unrolling the fabric.

As he revealed the bone, Quintus noted Gabriella's body straighten, her back muscles tensing under his fingertips. Her eyes widened at the sight of it.

"You okay, si, bella?" he asked, circling her back with the palm of his hand.

"Yes…it's just, there's something about it."

"May I?" Samantha reached for it, her fingers brushing over the stone as Quintus nodded. "It looks like a knife."

"It's a sternum," Quintus told her. "It looks like a blade, but the bone is thin. It could easily break."

"It's inconspicuous. It was easier to hide than other bones." Samantha held the artifact.

"Unless it's got some special mojo, it can't be made into a traditional weapon," Quintus said.

"I've only been doing this for a little while now. I'm sure Ilsbeth would have the answers but mine is more like a best guess based upon my current knowledge of the situation. This bone here." She held it up to the air, carefully inspecting it. "My gut feeling is that it must be ingested. So maybe it's ground into a powder and blown into the face, breathed by its victim. Or ground and used as a poison. I'm going to need more time to research to be sure. I think for now…if I could have it…"

"I feel something," Gabriella said, her voice shaken.

"Maybe just half of it," Samantha suggested.

Quintus heard the rumble of the wind, the clouds darkening. "Maybe we ought to hang onto it?"

"I really think…" Samantha began but went silent as the sky erupted.

Quintus snapped to his feet as his brother appeared in the garden. His face pale and bruised, he'd been beaten. Before Quintus had a chance to speak, Viktor shouted, a hint of fear flickering in his eyes.

Mao.

❈· *Chapter Twelve* ·❈

Gabriella's mother had been the only kind witch she'd known. Yet Samantha spoke to her as if she were family, a fellow sister practicing magick. She guessed the witch was about her same age, but her words held the wisdom of elders. Within their home, Gabriella had felt safe, and her heart bloomed in warmth, listening to Samantha gush over Luca and baby Kate.

Home. Goddess, it had been so many years since she'd been in a safe place, where the scent of home-baked cookies lingered in the air. As Samantha described her coven, Gabriella watched the female vampire play with the child. Laughter and bubbles. A father lost in the joy of his daughter.

A thread of guilt twisted through Gabriella. She'd been afraid of vampires ever since she'd stepped into her first blood club. Keeping her head down, she simply sold her blood, steering clear of the vampires. On the rare occasions she'd interacted, they'd proven dangerous, with little regard for others.

Although this group of vampires had initially challenged Quintus, they'd exhibited a great level of trust, bringing them into their inner sanctum. These people were his sired family. As Quintus spoke to Léopold, her heart broke for him. She sensed the regret, aware that crushing grief and danger had kept him from mentoring the French vampire. Like many fathers and sons, they cared for each other yet lacked the communication needed to mend old wounds.

Gabriella struggled to concentrate on the conversation as the darkened clouds congregated above. *No, no, no.* She prayed Lilitu hadn't found them. Her racing thoughts screeched to a halt as Viktor materialized before them. The suave vampire had been beaten, his clothes torn. He held out an arm, warning them away.

"Get Gabby out of here," Viktor yelled.

Gabriella sucked a breath as Mao materialized in the courtyard, her eyes glazed over in an orange haze. Her beast went on alert, dark magick swirling around her.

"Quintus, darling." Mao's sickening sweet voice trilled, blood dripping from four-inch talons extending from her fingertips. "I want the she-wolf."

"I'm sending you back to Hell." Quintus stepped out of the gazebo, shielding Gabriella from her.

"You belong to me," she insisted.

"Mao's dead. And you're going to be too."

"I want the girl."

With all focus on Mao, Gabriella's stomach flipped as the familiar energy of Lilitu jolted through her. She jumped to her feet, staring up into the sky. "Goddess, no."

Black ash descended onto the lawn, streaming down like snow. Gabriella's breath quickened, fear and loathing churning inside her chest. "It's her, it's her, it's her."

In the chaos, Mao flashed to a weakened Viktor. She strangled an arm around his neck.

"No!" Gabriella screamed, tearing at her clothes. Her beast itched to shift.

Quintus made a move toward Viktor, and Mao bored her long talon into his neck.

"Let him go," Quintus' loud voice boomed through the chaos.

"Give her to me," she hissed. Mao's eyes flashed to the table. "The bone."

"You're dead, Jiangshi. I can smell your stench from here. Without blood, you'll die," Samantha told her. She snatched the sternum off the table and held it with both hands.

"I'll have the wolf and the bone." She laughed wildly.

Gabriella clapped her hands over her ears as a loud grinding sound filled the air. The demon from the party appeared before them. *Thorn.*

"Yeah, uh. I'm not one to usually crash but you see…I'm trying to fix something here," he responded.

"Who invited this douche bag to the party?" Hunter asked.

"You knew she'd do this," Quintus accused. "You'd better get her back to Hell before I drain you, demon."

Thorn held a finger in the air, raising his eyebrows. "Half-demon. Half. It's a technicality, I know. But it's kinda important."

"What an asshole." Hunter tore off his shirt.

Viktor screamed, struggling as she stabbed another black talon into his flesh. A forked tongue extended between her lips, lapping at his gushing blood.

"Enough of this shit." Quintus flashed toward his brother but was blocked by a bolt of lightning. Lilitu appeared in his path, her lips drawn upward in an icy smile.

Gabriella's heart pounded at the sight of the high priestess. She steeled her nerves, swallowing her fear. The draw of the Alpha spurred her beast to shift. She caught a glimpse of the blonde female, protectively shielding the child. Luca rushed in from behind, scooping baby Kate into his arms.

"Little half-breed. Go ahead and shift. I'll kill you anyway." Lilitu's brunette hair twisted wild in the wind like Medusa's snakes.

"I'm going to kill you." Gabriella's inner child told her to keep running but her beast told her to fight.

"Dumb little dog. You're no match for me. Ah, how I remember the last time I saw you as a child. The smell of your mother's flesh burning purified the air, our coven safe from your dirty filthy family."

Gabriella released her anger, forcing a shift. Her paws gripped the turf, and she readied to lunge. The Alpha morphed to his beast and growled, warning the high priestess away from Gabriella.

Mao gave a maniacal laugh, and plunged all four of her fingers into Viktor's neck, tearing a chunk of flesh away from his body. Blood sprayed over the lawn as the vampire went limp in her grip.

"No! Viktor!" Quintus screamed. As he lunged for Mao, she transformed into an apparition, sending him crashing to the ground.

"The bone!" Lilitu demanded. The heavens opened from above, and a torrential rain bucketed down from the sky.

"Get out of my house!" Samantha straightened her back and held up the artifact. The high priestess of New Orleans snapped the bone in half, her eyes gleaming with hatred for the intruder.

"You're going to regret that," Lilitu sneered. Her head swiveled one hundred and eighty degrees to focus on the child.

Luca held tight to baby Kate as she cried, thrashing to get out of his arms.

"Come little one," Lilitu trilled. With a flick of her fingers, a burst of black magick rushed at Luca, shoving him to the ground. Kate rolled with him onto the slick grass.

Gabriella shook with rage as Lilitu reached for the toddler. The priestess conjured an athame, raising it high into the air. Gabriella lunged at the witch, her jaws clamping down onto Lilitu's wrist. Hunter attacked her from behind but was unable to thwart her as the high priestess shook off Gabriella.

Lilitu set her sight back on Kate. The knife sailed through the air towards the toddler, and Gabriella rolled in front of the child, shielding her. As the blade sliced into her body, Gabriella writhed, white hot pain shooting through her body. Expecting another blow, she braced herself, still protecting the child.

"Let her go," Sydney yelled, her gun drawn. Shots rang out and the high priestess dissipated into smoke.

Gabriella heaved for breath, the poison streaming through her body. Quintus' dark eyes met hers as her world spun into darkness. The sound of Kate's cries echoed in her mind. She succumbed to her sleep, comforted that the baby was still alive.

"Gabby," Quintus whispered.

The pain gnarled through her bones, and she struggled to breathe, her ribs aching with each rise of her chest. Her eyes fluttered open, awareness of her mate calmed her wolf, who lay whimpering.

"The baby." *Kate.*

"She's safe. I flashed you and Hunter out of Luca's…"

"But the baby. Samantha. Oh God…" Panic tore through her but as she went to shove up, a stabbing pain shot down her flank.

"You've been poisoned, Gabby. I need you to drink from me."

"No." She thrashed, naked on the bed. "I've got to go back."

"No, you're not going," he insisted.

"But Lilitu…"

"Lilitu's gone. Luca, Samantha and Kate are safe. Kade and Sydney too. Sam will take the necessary steps to keep her from getting in their homes. When we're outside like that…we were too exposed."

"Nothing works to keep her out. This is all my fault." Gabriella arched her back and exhaled loudly. She brought her hand to her side, and winced. As she raised her palm, her eyes widened at the sight of the blood. "That bitch stabbed me."

Quintus tore off his shirt, and pressed it to her wound. "She poisoned the athame."

"This is why I run from them…ahhh." She sucked a breath as he applied pressure. "She was going to kill the baby. Who does that? That woman is pure evil."

"The baby's okay, but…" Quintus shook his head. His eyes flashed in sadness and he quickly diverted his gaze. *Viktor.* His gut clenched in grief, but he attempted to hide his devastation from Gabriella.

"Oh Quintus. I'm so sorry. He's not…I mean…I know she hurt him but maybe he's still…" Gabriella lost her words as his grief twisted through her.

"No. I don't feel him." He blinked away the tears. "I don't know what happened. He's an immortal, but I think she killed him."

"He couldn't materialize away."

"I don't know what happened. I couldn't get to him. It was like a tunnel. I tried. Then Lilitu." Quintus' lips tightened, and he closed his eyes briefly, then met her gaze. "I failed him."

"But maybe Thorn…"

"He's a fucking demon. He brought Mao back from Hell. He did this. It's all been a set up."

"I'm so sorry…I can't believe Viktor is gone. We'll go look for him."

"I don't want to talk about it now. Look, Goddammit, I can't believe I let this happen to you."

"You didn't do this. If this is anyone's fault, it's mine. I brought Lilitu to New Orleans. She wants me dead. We've got to figure out how to use the bone." Gabriella moaned, holding her side. The pain subsided as numbness bloomed in its place. "Oh Goddess...where is it? The bone."

"Over here." Hunter lay on a black leather sofa.

Gabriella craned her head and caught a glimpse of the Alpha, his arm outstretched, holding a sliver of the first witch's sternum. Blood dripped from his hand. "Hunter. Are you all right?"

"I'm good," he replied.

"Don't lie to me," she reprimanded.

"What's the damage?" Quintus asked.

"Just a scratch. Samantha has the other piece. She shoved it at me right before you flashed us." The Alpha grunted as he shoved onto his feet.

"He's hurt," Gabriella said. She sensed something was wrong with the wolf but couldn't tell how badly he'd been injured.

"I'm fine," Hunter lied. He crossed the room and opened the door. "I'll be back. I just need something to eat."

"Are you sure you're all right?" she asked.

"The Alpha will live. You, however, are losing blood," Quintus said, his eyes narrowed in concern.

"I'll be okay. Just let me shift." Gabriella called on her beast. The animal crouched, refusing to transform. "I don't understand. I just did it. What's wrong?"

"I don't know, but you need my blood," Quintus told her.

"Where are we?" Gabriella asked. She glanced around the unfamiliar room. Flickers of light danced on its mirrored walls. A delicate art structure fabricated from blown glass and delicate crystals wove across the ceiling like a colorful web.

"Underground. My home in New Orleans has a chamber that I keep for emergencies. It's completely sealed from the outside. Fully stocked with blood and food. We stay here until you and Hunter are well and we hear back from Samantha."

Quintus dropped his fangs, his eyes locked on Gabriella. Her heart caught at the sight of his teeth. She went to reach for his face but struggled to move it, her arm paralyzed. "Something's wrong. Something…I can't feel my hands. Quintus. Help." Her expression tensed in anxiety. Her lips moved but no sound was released.

Quintus bit into his forearm, and pressed his flesh to her mouth. "Drink."

Gabriella's heartbeat sounded in her ears as her body went limp, the poison taking effect. His blood rushed into her mouth, the iron-tanged essence coating her tongue. Unable to swallow and paralyzed, Gabriella's eyes welled with tears.

Drink, Gabriella. The unspoken words echoed in her head. A drop of his blood dripped down her throat. Slowly, her mouth reanimated, allowing her to absorb the magick of her mate.

"That's a girl," Quintus said.

Gabriella moaned, her lips suckling, drawing a swallow. His magick began to flow through her, restoring her cells, healing her from the inside out. A prickling sensation teased her fingertips as her muscles came to life. With a groan, she reached for his arm and clutched to him.

Gabriella sensed his arousal. The sharing of blood, the exchange of magick and essence, flamed desire. Sucking harder, she draped her leg over his hip.

"Fuck…Gabby, now what are you doing?"

"Quintus." Gabriella's body lit on fire, his sweet blood bringing her to life. Everything dark in her life was erased, light blooming in her heart. Magick sparked through her cells, igniting passion. She lapped at his wrist and pressed her lips to his skin.

"Viktor's gone," he whispered.

"I'm so sorry." Words evaded her. Nothing would bring his brother back tonight.

"You're healed. Being with you is the only thing that makes me feel better."

She looked up into his eyes, and sensed both sadness and desire. "We'll find him. I promise," Gabriella said, unsure of whether or not Viktor was alive. It didn't matter. She'd spend the rest of her life helping him find his brother, so he could have closure.

"I need you," he growled.

His mouth crushed onto hers, commanding her wolf to attention. His strong lips sucked and tasted hers, and she responded, matching his kiss.

Goddess, she loved this vampire. Love. It seemed impossible to fall for someone so quickly, yet his kiss, the gentle way he held her face, tasting her as if he'd been starved for centuries, was as real as the sun. He was hers and she'd save him the way he'd saved her.

Filled with his strength, she gently guided him onto his back and straddled him. Her dominance rose, and she trailed her lips from his, peppering kisses down his throat. She splayed his arms to the side, trailing her mouth along his collarbone. Her lips moved to his chest, and traced a circle with her tongue over his flat nipple.

"Gabby," he breathed.

She released his hands, and reached for his shoulders. Ever so slowly, tasting and sampling, her lips grazed over the ridges of his abdomen. She raked her nails down his chest and placed a kiss to his hip as she settled between his legs. *Mine.* As she fumbled open his button and zipper, her eyes darted to Quintus, whose heated stare and curled lips told her he'd read her thoughts.

"Always," he told her, lifting his hips as she tugged off his jeans.

"It's time I take care of you." Gabriella lowered her eyes in submission. This man understood her feral nature. He sought to tame her, and she'd willingly submit to his lessons.

Her lips brushed his inner thigh and he shivered underneath her touch. She gently cupped his balls, teasing the sensitive crinkled skin. Her tongue swirled over the crown of his dick and teased his wet slit. Gabriella lapped at the broad head of his cock, her heated gaze drifting up to meet his. She released her power, and swallowed his hard length. With each moan he uttered, she suctioned her lips around his cock, stroking him in and out of her mouth. His fingers tunneled into her hair, but he didn't attempt to stop her as she took control. Her hips rocked up into the sheets, desperately seeking relief for her aching pussy.

As her mouth slid up and down his shaft, he trembled. She made love to him, and reveled in her control. Tasting her mate soothed her soul. So much darkness, yet this brief indulgence brought light into their world.

"Fuck, you're killing me," he hissed. "I need to be inside you."

Ignoring his demand, she swallowed him down to the root of his shaft, tightening her lips as she sucked his cock. Her hand gripped his dick, gently twisting as she lapped at his tip. She kissed his broad crown, the salty taste of him lingering on her lips.

"I need you too," Gabriella whispered, her voice husky.

Her long hair spilled over his thighs and chest as she crawled up his torso. She brushed her lips to his abdomen, her tongue darting over his hard ridges. As she swung her legs over his hips, straddling him, her palms pressed onto his strong shoulders. Gabriella's eyes met his in a heated gaze and she licked her lips, hungry for her mate.

"Gabby…"

"Shh…" Her hands cupped his cheeks. The vampire had put his life on the line for her. His brother had died, chasing a memory that she knew was somehow tied to her. His pain was hers, but she'd spend a lifetime healing him, filling the pit of his loss with her love.

"Quintus." She lowered her hips, his tip probing her entrance.

Gabriella gasped as his cock plunged inside her wet sheath. He withdrew slowly and eased back inside her, stretching her open.

"Ahh…yes." Her skin danced with magick as he took her breast between his lips and his tongue teased over her sensitive peak.

She sank down onto him, his shaft filling her. Lit with arousal, she rocked her pelvis against his, her nails digging into his shoulders.

"Fuck me." Primal, her wolf went feral for her mate. Her fangs released, and she dragged the sharp points across his chest.

"Jesus, Gabby. What are you doing? That feels so…" Quintus lost his words as she gently nibbled his chest. His firm hands gripped her hips as he plunged inside her to the hilt.

"Harder…yes!" Her pussy clenched down around his cock as he gave a jarring thrust. His fangs dropped, and her hungry eyes locked on his. A firm hand captured her mane, fisting it tight.

"Ah," she cried, a sweet sting on her scalp as he tugged her head away.

"You've teased me enough, bella," he growled.

She gave a small smile as he flipped her onto her back. He released her hair, his hands cupping the back of her thighs as he spread open her legs. Her body rocked with pleasure as he slammed back inside her pussy.

"Mine," he grunted.

"Ah…" As he pounded inside her, she trembled.

"You're everything," he told her, his thumb on her clit.

Her orgasm teetered. With each hard thrust, she surrendered to the pleasure spearing through her.

"Always."

"Please…Goddess…I can't." Her words rolled off her tongue, but her thoughts went blank as her climax exploded like fireworks. She screamed at the sweet slice of his fangs into her neck.

She pumped her hips, shaking in pleasure as the erotic waves rolled through her. Her beast howled in submission, at one with her mate. Forever she'd give herself to this man. Her vampire. Her mate. Her love.

"Quintus…Quintus…" she repeated as he made love to her.

"I'm not done with you yet, little wolf," he told her.

She gasped as he withdrew and flipped her on her stomach. The momentary loss was quickly replaced by anticipation as he lifted her hips, his hard cock brushing her inner thigh. She released a loud exhale as his finger slid inside her slick hole.

"Your pussy is so fucking beautiful. Do you know that?"

"Please," she begged.

"Always. I'll always be here for you, Gabby. This. What we have." He withdrew his fingers and slid them through her wet folds.

As his finger brushed over her clit, she shivered, holding her breath, waiting for his next move.

"Ahh…" Gabriella froze as his fingers played at her ass.

"I want all of you." Quintus circled the pad of his thumb over her puckered hole.

Gabriella's head lolled forward as he pressed his cock inside her. She lost her words as he eased his finger inside her ass. "I've never…Quintus…"

"Someday…I'm going to fuck you here too."

"Quintus." She gasped as he added a second finger.

"Easy, bella. Just breathe," he told her.

"Yes, yes, yes," she repeated as he plunged his fingers inside her back hole.

Gabriella's body lit on fire as he filled her, the unfamiliar fullness overwhelming her senses. As his other hand found her mound and flicked over her clit, she splintered apart, her orgasm rushing into her. Her body shuddered in release, and she clutched at the pillow, panting for breath.

As he gave a final thrust, she heard him groan in release. The weight of his body collapsed onto hers, and she settled onto the bed. Her heart open and vulnerable to her mate, the last shivers of her climax fluttered through Gabriella.

Her mind raced as exhaustion claimed her. This incredible man was hers. A lifetime she'd waited to be home, to belong to not just a place but to a person who loved her. *Love.* It was an emotion that had evaded her for so long she hadn't remembered what it was like to care for someone…until now.

She didn't know if there would be a future but if she died tomorrow, her life was complete. *Quintus. I love you.* The words drifted in her mind as sleep claimed her.

·❦· *Chapter Thirteen* ·❦·

Love. He'd heard the word as if she'd said it aloud. Quintus pressed his lips to Gabriella's head, inhaling the fragrance of her hair. His sweet little wolf had opened her heart, and he knew how incredibly scary that had to be for her. Unable to trust anyone for years, she'd surrendered her body and soul to him.

With her tight in his embrace, he recalled the horrific scene in Luca's yard. With a heavy heart, he called for his brother. *Viktor.* In the silence that followed, he bit back his sorrow, failing to sense his brother's presence. Death came for humans and supernaturals alike. But Quintus had kept his circle small, his heart protected. Now ironically, Mao had killed Viktor.

He prayed it wasn't true. If she'd taken him to Hell, it'd be unlikely he'd sense him. The obsession to find his brother would have to wait. Killing Lilitu had to be his utmost priority. With Gabriella in danger, he had to find a way to protect her. Lilitu had proven a worthy adversary, breaking through the wards at his home and again at Luca's, finding them in the catacombs. Her dark magick grew stronger and her death was the only option.

Quintus heard a rumble, and gently removed himself from Gabriella. Taking care to cover her with the blanket, he kissed her forehead. He padded quietly across the room to the closet and opened it, retrieving a bathrobe. As he dressed, he silently sighed, stealing one last glance at his sleeping angel before he exited the room.

He closed the door behind him, and stopped cold, sniffing the air. *What the hell?* Quintus rushed down the hallway and caught sight of Hunter standing over the stove.

"What are you doing?" The vampire pulled his robe tight and tied the belt.

"What does it look like I'm doing? I'm hungry. I'm horny. Figure I have a better chance with food." The wolf turned to Quintus, giving him a roll of his eyes and then focused back on stirring the concoction in his pot. "Y'all seriously don't keep much in this secret dungeon, but I found all the frozen and dry stuff."

"What are you making?" Quintus lowered his voice, already recognizing the delicious scent of the mystery meal.

"Jambalaya. Found some andouille and crawfish in the freezer. It's not fresh. But beggars…y'all get me."

"Fuck, wolf…" Quintus inhaled deeply and shook his head. "It smells amazing."

"You must have been a foodie in a previous life."

"No. Just a dumb young boy."

"Hardly a boy by the looks of ya."

"Yeah maybe. Even as an adult, I wasn't ready to grow

up." Quintus stretched his neck from side to side, easing the tension from his muscles.

"None of us are," Hunter agreed.

"I hardly remember now."

"Nor do I." The Alpha spun around, waving his wooden spoon and tilted his head. "It's something how the time passes."

"Yet all that matters is right now. The present."

"Gabriella?"

"Things went to hell today, si?" Quintus failed to hide the anger in his voice.

"I haven't had a whole helluva lot of experience with this shit. I mean out in Wyoming, I'm dealing with the occasional black magick fuck up. Usually a witch or some other supe trying to get their way. But this Lilitu bitch is a whole new level of fucking crazy. And Jiangshi? Yeah, they're not usually something I'm used to dealing with. To be fair, I'm pretty sure most wolves aren't. Pretty sure Tristan would have mentioned it in his holiday card. He's pretty detailed."

Quintus raised a silent eyebrow at the Alpha.

"Yeah. Okay. Sorry. Just fucking with ya. Tris doesn't do a card." He turned around and shrugged. He gave a wave of the spoon before setting it back into his epicurean delight. "But he does call me. The asshole likes to mess around. Once told me a mermaid showed up in his bar and I bought it for five seconds before I questioned the lack of an ocean in Philly. Or a mermaid. He got a good laugh. He's a dick like that."

"Your point?" Quintus shook his head. There was a reason he tired of wolves and their constant nonsense.

"Relax, Quint. Go with it. I think we're bonding here."

"What the fuck is your point?"

"You vamps need to learn how to relax. Ya know that don't you? Thousands of years here and you'd think you could have some fun. Indulge me."

"Fine. Just give me some food. Let's go. Plate up."

"How can you be hungry? You just fucking fed! You're like the three little piglets except you're one big piglet, eating all the human food too."

"None of your business, dog."

"Hold on there with the d word, ya pointy-toothed ancient." Hunter swung around holding his arms up, the spoon in one hand. A sly smile crept onto his face.

"Sorry." Quintus nodded with a sigh. "I just…there's something about human food. The day I turned, I swore I wouldn't lose that shred of me that made me human. I know full well that all I need is blood to survive…physically. But having a meal. The taste buds keep a memory. And today, this also will be a memory."

In a moment of weakness, Quintus' voice went soft, his thoughts drawn back to Viktor. "My brother. He…he was kind of a purist. We argued often. Every now and then I'd get him to try something human. It was as if he'd forgotten. I'd have to remind him of the flavor, spend hours convincing him to go to a restaurant. And when we'd finally go to one, he'd order the bloodiest piece of steak he could get."

"I'm really sorry, Quint. Maybe he's still alive. We could contact Absinthe. Find that weasel, Thorn," he offered.

"I don't feel him." Quintus' lips formed a tight smile. "I should feel him. For thousands of years, no matter how far he was, I always felt him. But there's nothing."

"What do you know about Hell?" the Alpha asked, his voice serious.

"That I don't want to go. I know that anything or anyone I've ever met who has been there is never the same. Demons. Succubus. The various demonic creatures that inhabit the underworld, they torture the pure souls who are trapped for any period of time. I've had the unfortunate experience of rescuing a friend or two over the centuries, but I was in and out. The ones who go for any amount of time...they change. I knew this guy...he was a genuinely nice vamp. Walt. Got mixed up with a succubus who convinced him to go."

"Lured was probably more like it," Hunter interjected.

"Yeah, well. You know how it is. It's not like anyone usually goes knocking on Hell's door without a reason. "

"Hot piece of ass."

"Hot as in going up in flames. Lucifer's plaything." Quintus shook his head. "Walt thought he'd get a favor from her. His heart was in the right place. His only living niece had died. Couldn't turn her because well...she was a kid."

"It's been done."

"Yeah, I know it has but it's not safe. Turning a kid...they don't grow up into normal adults. It's just not something you should do. There aren't many rules but it's one of the few words of wisdom I pass on to new vampires. Anyway, the point is, he wanted her back. His sister was distraught."

"Necromancy."

"It's never a good thing. I guess he could have gone in search of black magick. But instead he hooked up with Jasmine. Sexy little succubus convinced him to seek out the help of her friends. She looked innocent enough with her big blue eyes." He sighed. "Long story short. I knew he wasn't coming back but that bitch caught me on the wrong day and I went back in for him. We're lucky we got out. Poor slob was never the same."

"And his niece?"

"Oh they brought her back all right but naturally she was possessed. The exorcism killed her in the end. But she wasn't technically alive anyway. His sister killed herself."

"I heard Leo was under," Hunter commented.

"Yeah but they were in and out. Got lucky and killed the demon fast."

"Not everyone comes out right in the head." Hunter's voice was a monotone as he spoke, his eyes staring as if in a trance.

"You sound like you've had a trip."

"I'm just saying. If he's there…we can try to get him out."

"You volunteering?" Quintus asked, surprised at the Alpha's statement.

"Maybe I am."

"I'll contact Thorn. If Viktor is there, I can't leave him. But I can't go look until this thing with Gabriella is settled. Lilitu breaks wards. If she got to my house in New York and over at Kade's, she's packing some demon strength black magick. As safe as this place is, I don't trust staying here for too long. We can't risk it."

"Yeah, about that. I'm thinking we should hit the bayou."

"How's that?"

"I've got a place. You know this is my home." Hunter nodded.

"So you're thinking the bayou is safer? I don't know." Quintus shrugged and shook his head.

"Only Logan knows where my place is. A while back, when Ilsbeth was flying her broom high, I got her to whip me up a spell."

"Jesus, that woman gets around."

"Hey, now." Hunter spun to face him, raising an eyebrow. "I may have used her but not 'used used' her. No fucking way. Ya see where that got Dimitri. Not me. I've always known that Ilsbeth was one dangerous bitch. Don't get me wrong. I see why D got him some of that. She's a tempting one, all right. Beautiful. At least she used to be until she lost her mojo. But fuck if she won't throw a hex at your ass as fast as you can say broomstick."

"Your place. Tell me more," Quintus redirected. He of all people knew how Ilsbeth could throw a conversation off topic.

"It's basically invisible. I mean it's not infallible. A wolf will know I'm there if they bump into the damn thing. Out in the swamp, everyone's got their own place. The rest of the supes can't find it though."

"Lilitu might, but right now we're buying time."

"We've got the bone. Sam's looking at it too," Hunter said.

"You've got the other half, right?" Quintus asked.

"Yeah, but I'm not witch."

"I've been thinking about this. It's like I said, I don't think this is just black magick. And Mao showing up. She wanted that bone. It's all tied somehow. No, all this reeks of hell and demons."

"Lilitu isn't the only witch in that coven who has a stake to get the first bone back. They'll come at Sam and us."

"Lilitu sought a demon's help. She's got way too much power."

"Unless any demon buds owe you any favors, I don't think we've got a shot at stopping her." Hunter opened the cabinet and set bowls on the counter.

"Even half-demons aren't to be trusted. And Thorn? I'm going to tear the head off that asshole the next time I see him. He puts on a good show, but his hell game is strong. He's up to his eyeballs in this. He got my brother…" *Killed.* Quintus couldn't bring himself to say the word aloud, and continued. "I know a guy."

Hunter laughed and sank a ladle into the pan. "A good story always starts with, 'I've got a guy.' All right. All right. Let's hear it."

"Goes by the name of Kellan," Quintus began.

"Demon?"

"Fae."

"Jesus, Quint? A fairy? They're more dangerous than some of the fucking demons I've met."

"I know, but I'm done with the witches. Samantha means well, but she's fairly new."

"She's a high priestess."

"Technically, yes. But she's no Ilsbeth. No matter how strong her magick is, she doesn't have enough experience. What happened today…the baby." Quintus sighed. If Gabriella hadn't taken the blow, the child would have been dead.

"I've got to admit. That whole scene was a little out of control." Hunter set a bowl in front of Quintus and turned back to the stove. "Witches. Demons. They've got the market cornered on poison."

Quintus noted how the Alpha favored his right arm, his eyes narrowing on a white cloth peeking out from underneath Hunter's buttoned shirt. His fist curled into a ball. "What's going on with your hand?"

"Nah, it's nothing." Hunter continued his task.

"Uh huh. You sure?" Quintus suspected he'd been hiding the serious nature of the injury.

"Yeah, yeah. Hurt myself here in the kitchen is all. Knife slipped."

"You had the scratch before you started cooking, remember?" Quintus paused and lifted his spoon. "As I was trying to get Mao away from Viktor, I noticed you were close to Lilitu. You wouldn't have happened to get in the way of that athame she was carrying, would you?"

"Look, it's nothing. I'll be fine. I've run miles a whole helluva lot worse hurt than this. I told you. Just a scratch." Hunter turned to Quintus, averting his gaze as he set a second dish onto the table. "I'll be good after I eat."

"Let me see it." As Quintus spoke the words, he knew the Alpha wouldn't like being spoken to like a five-year-old child.

"Fuck you. Eat your Jambalaya," he grumbled.

"Nice. Yeah, okay, don't show me. But I'm going to kick your ass from here to New York if it gets worse, do you hear me? Gabriella, she went numb. Ya hear me asshole? Numb? Couldn't move." Quintus slid a spoonful of the food into his mouth and closed his eyes. "Mmm."

"The way she was stabbed? She's lucky she's breathing. Immortal is a relative term."

"This is…oh my…" Quintus lifted his eyes to meet Hunter's.

"We all can die given the right circumstances."

"So good. Excellent."

"What'd ya expect? The wolf has skills," Hunter joked, a small smile forming on his lips.

"Tru dat." Quintus nodded.

"So I take it Gabby's all right? I guess I already know the answer to that question."

"She's amazing." Quintus smiled.

"Yeah, I could hear how amazing she was. You know, one of these times, if you're looking for an extra player, I'm down." Hunter laughed and opened the refrigerator, retrieving bottles of water.

"I bet you are."

"I know you vamps. Not so good in the sharing department, but now that you're mated and all…let's just say it was tempting to help you out in there."

"I don't need any help, asshole."

"She's a wolf, Quint."

"Full moon's over. She's good." The vampire shook his head, continuing to eat.

"I'm just sayin'. We are a playful bunch. She's claimed. It's not like she's going anywhere. You guys are mated."

"I can't believe it," Quintus confessed, a broad smile crossing his face.

"You mated motherfuckers make me sick." Hunter laughed and twisted off a cap, sucking back the bottle.

"Sounds like you're a little jealous, Alpha. Which, hey, can't say you shouldn't be, but don't be a hater. She's mine."

Hunter released the water with a hiss. "No hatin' here. Just offering my services should you need them."

"I don't need your…" Quintus stopped speaking as soon as the door creaked open. *Gabriella.*

"What services?" Gabriella asked in a sleepy voice.

Quintus dropped his spoon and pressed to his feet, taking in the sight of his beautiful mate. Her messy curly hair tumbled over her shoulders, his oversized robe draped to the floor. She gave him a sheepish smile.

"Ah si, bella. You look beautiful." Quintus crossed the room to meet her, wrapping his hands around her waist. As his lips brushed hers, he resisted tearing off her robe. With her body crushed to his, his cock twitched in response.

"Hmm…I've missed you."

"Hmm…I've missed you too, baby," she meowed.

"Someone's missing something but I don't think it's either of you," Hunter commented, giving a roll of his eyes.

"Ah, sorry Alpha." Gabriella laughed softly, peeking around Quintus' arms to smile at the wolf.

"You feeling all right?" he asked.

"Yes. He helped me. I'm okay now," she told him.

Quintus gave her a knowing smile. He released her from his embrace and slid his hand into hers, leading her to the table. "Come sit. Alpha made us a delicious meal."

"You cook?" she asked, an element of surprise in her tone.

"I'm not just a pretty face. Here ya go." Hunter placed a bowl of Jambalaya in front of Gabriella then slid a bottle of water toward her.

"Thank you. It smells so good. I'm starving."

"You're lucky to be alive," he replied, sitting down to join Quintus and Gabriella.

She slid her spoon inside the thick spicy meal and paused, looking at them. "I couldn't let anything happen to that baby. I don't know Samantha. Or Luca." She shrugged and gave a sad smile. "I don't know any of them. But we brought this to their home. And Kate? She has a whole lifetime ahead of her. If anything had happened, I couldn't forgive myself."

"It's okay." Quintus gently placed a reassuring a palm onto her back.

"No. This has to end." She swallowed and set down her

utensil. "That day I found you." She smiled at Quintus. "Even if you'd said no. Even if you couldn't have helped me, I still would have given you my blood. I knew the vamps got off on it. I took a chance I could help you."

"You saved me."

"I never thought of the consequences. I put everyone in danger. Viktor…"

"That's not your fault," he insisted.

"We don't know that. Your house was set on fire. Both of you have been in danger because of me. In the catacombs. Now at Luca's house, the baby. It could have been any of them. Sam. Kade. Sydney. No, this has to end."

"It's going to. We're going to find a way to end it," Quintus said.

"But how? I need to talk to Samantha. If she doesn't have a spell or know what to do with the bone, I've got to go somewhere else to get help."

"Go where?" the Alpha asked.

"I don't know." She shook her head, her gaze fixed on the table. "I'll go anywhere to get answers. I'll keep running until I figure out how to use that damn bone. It'll destroy her. I know it and she knows it."

"You're not going anywhere," Quintus told her flatly.

"I can't put you guys in any more danger," she insisted.

"We're in this together," Quintus said.

"The three of us," Hunter added.

"You sure?" Quintus locked his eyes on the Alpha, who nodded.

"Damn straight. Gabby, you may have grown up alone.

But now you've got a pack. We're it."

"It's not fair to you," she protested.

"I'm not saying this isn't going to be dangerous, but I think we've got to approach this another way." Quintus reached for her hand.

"Another witch? Who else can we trust?" she asked.

"We can't really trust anyone as far as I'm concerned. My vampires, they're all as close to trustworthy as you'll get but I agree we can't wait on Samantha," Quintus told her.

"Then what?"

"Who," Hunter replied.

"Kellan. He's fae," Quintus began, still trying to convince himself this was a good idea. While it was dangerous, they didn't have many options.

"A fae? I don't know much about fairies, but my momma always said they were evil."

"Your mama be right," Hunter agreed.

"They can be difficult. They're not exactly demons but they know the underworld. With Kellan, there will be a price without a doubt. I did him a favor a while back. He's not likely to fuck with me."

"How can you be sure about that?" she interrupted.

"I'd call it eighty-twenty in our favor. He owes me and he's always looking for ways to get one up. I haven't talked to him in centuries, but I know how to reach to him."

"Why wouldn't Samantha just tell us to go to him?" she asked.

"Witches don't get involved with the fae. It's too dangerous. They aren't demons, but they definitely have some demonic-laced magick going on. Kellan's the only fae in New Orleans I'd trust. And even then I don't trust him."

"But you just said…"

"We're running out of options. We have to get Lilitu before she gets to you. This place here is only safe for so long before she finds you again. Hunter's got a place for us to move to after we blow."

"Wait…where's this Kellan dude?" she asked. "Does he live above ground?"

"He's got demon-like powers…qualities, but if you're asking if he lives in Hell, the answer is no. He's too much of a partier to let those assholes rain on his parade. He lives for Mardi Gras and fresh virgins."

"Fae have a special pass for Hell," Hunter said.

"What do you mean?" she asked.

"They can make a choice to go back into the netherworld, pass between the realms," Quintus explained. "But don't bring it up in front of him. Be very careful what you say. Any information he gives you, whether for small talk or otherwise, is considered a favor owed. We are in and out."

"I'd say wait for Samantha, but I don't want to put her in anymore danger," Gabriella said.

"We're going to do this together as a team. Don't go getting any ideas in that head of yours. I can see your wheels turning and you need to just accept my help. I'm not going anywhere," Quintus told her.

Gabriella nodded, yet Quintus wasn't fooled into accepting her silence as acquiescence. With her independent streak strong, he knew her wild nature couldn't be harnessed. While he admired that about her, he grew concerned her impulsivity would put her in more danger. With their blood mingled, she'd adapt, possibly taking on some of his own powers.

With no more words to be spoken, they ate in silence. One thing was clear. The end was coming. First he had to outwit Kellan.

"Fuck," Hunter groaned as they materialized into the back alley.

"You okay?" Quintus asked, aware the Alpha suffered.

"I think it's getting better," Gabriella said, panting. "It must be our mating. I'm not as bad. Not like…well, not like him."

Hunched over with his hands on his knees, Hunter spat onto the pavement.

"You okay, brother?" Quintus asked, his lips tight realizing the word he'd used to call the wolf. *Brother. Viktor.* When this was all over he'd go for him. But tonight, he needed to focus on their task.

"Yeah, yeah," the Alpha lied, holding his clenched fist to his chest.

"When we get back, I'm taking a look at your arm. You all right to keep going?" Quintus knew the materialization made wolves sick, but he grew concerned the Alpha was suffering from poisoning.

Hunter coughed and sucked a breath, standing straight upward and nodding. "Yeah, I'm good."

"There're a lot of humans out tonight. Let's do our best not to cause any sort of a conflict that would result in their untimely demise," Quintus suggested.

"Like what?" Gabriella's focus shifted to a homeless camp as they crossed the street. Nearly twenty men and women gathered on the grassy area between the roads.

As they passed, Quintus reached into his pocket, and set a wad of bills into the lap of an older gentleman leaning against the brick wall, his grey puppy sleeping alongside him. There were far too many humans sleeping on the streets, yet if he could help a few every now and then, he'd try. He couldn't save the world, but he was determined to get a few humans back on their feet.

Jazz music grew louder as they turned the corner onto Frenchman. He reached for Gabriella's hand, and a picture of him dancing with her flashed in his mind. He swore when all this shit was over, he'd take her on a proper date.

"Where are we?" Gabriella asked, walking into the light that flickered from the gas lamps that hung on the side of the building.

"Frenchman Street."

"These murals are beautiful," she commented, spying a painted cat on the wall of a two-story building.

Tinkling charms sounded, and Quintus slowed. Bells of various sizes dangled from the porch above. The unassuming establishment appeared to be a typical jazz club, but dark magick hummed in the air as a warning.

"Why do they have so many wind chimes?" Gabriella asked. "Do you feel that energy?"

"Yeah, I feel it. Those are bells," he told her, his voice low. "The fae use them to ward off other fairies. Evil fairies."

"But I thought they all had ties to Hell," she responded.

"They do, but some are far worse than others. It's like any other supernatural really. Take Samantha. Compare her to Lilitu. The fae, they are a devious sort. Tricksters. The bells are both a beacon and warning. For us? A welcome mat."

"Okay, let's do this," Gabriella said.

"Remember the rules. We stick together. Limit the information given and questions asked. If anything goes down, we're flashing out. Got me?" Quintus directed.

Hunter gave a nod, and reached for the brass door handle. "Ladies first."

"Whatever you see in here…keep in mind, it may or may not be real. The fae like to play with your mind. No matter what happens, stay with me," he told her, giving a squeeze to her hand. "That goes for you too, wolf. Stay close. I don't like what's going on with you."

"I'm good."

"Uh huh. Let's go." Quintus sensed the Alpha's pain but knew he didn't want to admit to his weakness. As soon as they were finished with the fae, he was going to heal him.

Quintus pushed the heavy wooden door open, and strode into the crowded bar. A heavy-set man played a trumpet solo while an older woman gently rapped her sticks on a high-hat cymbal. The bass player stared at Quintus but quickly broke eye contact as the dominant vampire strode through the bar as if he owned it.

The scent of frankincense mixed with sweat lingered in the air. Waitresses buzzed around a floor filled with small round tables, patrons talking and listening to music. Bartenders busily worked behind the bar, attending to the three-person-deep line waiting for their drinks.

It had been years since Quintus had seen Kellan, but as he listened through the din, he heard the familiar humming. The fairy had a distinctive habit that either lulled or annoyed his victims. As they made their way to the back of the darkened bar, Quintus noted the branches growing through cracks in the brick walls.

He stopped short as he came upon the arched exit. An intricate metal gate blocked his way. Quintus sucked a deep breath, steeling his nerves as he inspected the poisonous silver structure. Clever fae knew the metal would deter both vampires and werewolves alike. In contrast, the fairies couldn't bear the sight of iron, let alone touch it.

His eyes went to Hunter's and he nodded toward the gate. "Careful."

"Silver." The Alpha shook his head. "Does that prick really think he's going to keep us out of here with that shit?"

Quintus turned his head, giving a glance over his shoulder to see if anyone was looking. With a swift kick of his boot he smashed the door wide open and it clanged against the stone wall. As it swung back toward them, he shouldered it open, and ushered Gabriella and Hunter through the narrow doorway. "Don't let it touch you. He's a clever fae but not clever enough."

"What a dick." Hunter kept close behind Gabriella, taking care to shield her.

As they stepped into the courtyard, darkness morphed into a reddish hue, a bonfire burning in the corner. Quintus suspected oak doused with dragon's blood flamed within the fire pit. The distinct silhouette of the tall blonde fae sat in a chair facing them.

"You broke my fucking gate, you overbearing fanger," his rumbling voice yelled.

"You can replace it," Quintus told him. As they approached, he caught sight of Kellan's beady yellow eyes, his hands curled into fists. A topless woman knelt between his legs sucking his dick.

"My time, my time. You waste my time. You'll owe me," he told him. Kellan shoved at the woman's shoulders until she released his cock. "Go on. I've got business here."

The girl swiftly pressed to her feet and gave them a closed smile before scurrying back into the bar.

"I'll pay for your time. There shall be no debt," Quintus assured him, well aware everything came at a price.

"Why do you come here to bother me tonight? I expect payment, you understand this?" Kellan stuffed his dick into his pants and zipped them shut.

Quintus sifted through his pocket and retrieved several bills, fanning out five hundred dollars.

"Ah, then. I've got plenty of time to see an old friend." Kellan extended his hand, ushering them to sit.

"Of course." Quintus placed the bills into Kellan's palm

and nodded to Gabriella and Hunter. As he sat onto the rotted wooden chair, he flicked away a piece of the old paint that had flaked away from the armrest.

Quintus' expression remained impassive as he locked eyes with him. He wasn't fooled by the attractive fae's welcoming smile.

"Wolves," Kellan noted, leaning into the light of the fire.

"She's mine. The Alpha is under my protection as well, so I expect no harm will come to either of them," Quintus stated.

"Harm? Pfft. You're dramatic, vampire. I'm just sitting here drinking an ale and getting a blow job. Enjoying some music. Besides..." Kellan sniffed into the air, his gaze landing on Hunter. His nostrils flared. "He's already hurt. He's ill."

"He's not your concern," Quintus told him. His gaze darted to Gabriella who wore panic in her expression. *We'll deal with it later. He's fine.* Jesus, this wasn't going how he'd expected. He should have insisted on seeing the wolf's arm back at his home.

"And this one..." Kellan extended his hand to Gabriella. "It's okay..."

Gabriella's focus went to the fae, and she reluctantly placed her palm into Kellan's. Quintus gave a reassuring squeeze to her other hand.

"She's mine," Quintus reiterated.

"Yes, yes. I heard you the first time." Kellan turned her hand over, examining her palm. "She's so young. And you not so much. I feel her magick. It's fresh. So strong."

"That's enough, Kellan," Quintus told him, his face tensed, a tick pulsing in his jaw.

"Just saying hello is all. If you want answers, I must know who I'm dealing with." He released her hand and looked to Hunter. "The Alpha is sick. He's going to die soon if you don't do something."

"I'm fine. You're going to be the one regretting things if you don't mind your business," Hunter growled.

"Enough," Quintus snapped. While he agreed with the Alpha, he needed the fae's help. Arguing with Kellan in his realm would get them all killed.

Kellan smiled, the light flickering onto his handsome face. Quintus blinked and the fae transformed into a horned creature, its scaly yellow skin shining under the light. He moved quickly to diffuse the situation as Hunter jumped to his feet and tore at his shirt.

"Enough, Kellan!" Quintus shouted at the fae. He turned to Gabriella whose face had gone pale. Hunter's fangs had dropped, claws sprouting from his fingertips. "No shifting. This isn't real. He's fucking with you." The devilish creature began laughing maniacally and Quintus jumped to his feet. "Fucking knock it off, asshole. We have business. You want money or not? I'm flashing if you keep this up."

Kellan instantly appeared as his human form, and lifted the bottle to his lips, smiling. "Just having a bit of fun. No harm done."

Quintus' eyes flared in anger. Hunter fell back into his seat, releasing a loud sigh. The fucking fae was right about one thing. The Alpha struggled, and Quintus suspected he'd been unable to shift.

"This is Gabriella. She's a hybrid," Quintus told Kellan.

"I'm a witch," Gabriella offered, her voice shaking.

Kellan tilted his beer bottle and nodded. "That explains the magick. Tricky little hybrids. Mother Nature is a delight."

"We seek your assistance in exchange for payment." Quintus leaned toward Kellan, his eyebrows narrowed.

"What is the favor?" Kellan smiled at Gabriella.

"A purist coven. Specifically, a high priestess. We believe she's working demonic magick. She's been trying to kill Gabby since she was a kid."

"When I was thirteen, I shifted," Gabriella divulged the private information to the fae. "I've been on the run ever since."

"Her name is Lilitu. All I can share is that she's able to break wards," Quintus explained.

"Not here she can't." Kellan gave a proud smile. "The fae run the show."

"You haven't seen this bitch in action. I know you think you have it all figured out but she's the real deal." Hunter coughed, his arm held to his chest.

"At first we suspected black magick, but it's more than that. My home in New York? She somehow managed to break wards and set it on fire. Broke through wards at Kade's estate as well. And I suspect she's somehow involved with necromancy. There was someone once. We'd begun the bond but never completed it. She died. And when I say she died, I'm talking well over a thousand years ago. But a demon, goes by the name of Thorn…long story short she's back from the dead."

"Perhaps he's the one who reanimated her. I assume she's not exactly the same, huh?" Kellan laughed.

"The demon. He's a half-breed, and doesn't appear to have anything to do with the necromancy. But you're right in that Mao, she's not the same. Looks the same but clearly isn't. I suspect she's a Jiangshi."

"You don't see that every day, do you? Someone wanted to create the indestructible. Ah but for what?" Kellan asked, his tone thoughtful. His gaze settled onto Gabriella. "The wolf hybrid is your mate, yes?"

"She is."

"And this Jiangshi shows up at the same time you meet her?"

"Shortly after, yes."

"It's almost as if someone knew. A prophesy. Why does a demon create a Jiangshi? Why does one show up more than a thousand years later? And this high priestess? Instead of letting you run off, she continues in pursuit." Kellan pressed the heel of his hand to his forehead, humming quietly, then continued. "No…something about this. A high priestess who breaks wards can easily find the mouse. She tracks the mouse. She plays with the mouse. She was waiting."

"But she almost killed me. The other day, she tried to kill a baby. Her knife went clear through me. The poison."

A mischievous grin crossed his face, his eyes darting to

Hunter then back to Quintus. "Poison. We know what ails the wolf. But no mind. The wolf is but a casualty in the game. Many battles, many battles, but only one war. This high priestess has been patient. Waiting, waiting," Kellan sang. "But she's so close…close to what? What is it that she wants? How is the Jiangshi related?"

"They've been seen together but never spoke. Lilitu never even acknowledged Mao's presence the other day," Quintus noted.

"But what? What does she want? What is so special about you, little wolf?" Kellan stared into Gabriella's eyes, rubbing his palms together.

"I…I…nothing," she responded. "I'm a hybrid. She killed my mother."

"No, no, no. You're lying," he accused.

"I'm not lying. There's nothing special," she insisted.

"Liar!"

"What the fuck, Kellan!" Quintus jumped to his feet, resisting the urge to punch the fae.

"What the hell is wrong with you?" Hunter asked. "She just answered you."

"She. Is. Lying." Kellan sat back into his chair and steepled his fingers.

"I'm not lying…I just…" Gabriella trembled, and nervously twisted her hair. "I don't know. She's always hated me. I'm not pure. I'm a hybrid. Witches only. My blood. It ruins the coven. It's not meant to be. My blood, it taints their lineage."

"Ah…there you go, little witch." Kellan smiled.

"My blood," Gabriella whispered.

"Tell me. It will stay amongst us friends."

Quintus briefly shut his eyes and gave a loud exhale as he sat back down. *Gabriella's blood.* It was different than any other he'd ever tasted, but moreover it was the magick within it that was special.

"I...I...my blood. I used to sell it on the black market," she admitted.

"Vampires," Quintus added.

"So it's valuable?" Kellan asked.

"Only to vampires," she replied. "I mean, there's no other use for it."

"Demonic poisoning. A while back, Gabriella saved me," Quintus said.

"Ah, I love a good love story. Vampire meets witch."

"It was a crypt." She shrugged.

"Don't say romance is dead." Kellan's smile faded, and he focused on Gabriella. "What else? There has to be something else. Why, why, why does she want you?"

"I don't know. The vampires, they like my blood. It's like a special flavor. They're willing to pay for it."

"You're a donor. You let them bite you?" he asked.

"No way. I just, you know, I siphoned off a bit here and there. At first I started doing it in Boston when I was thirteen. I met a human woman on the streets who suggested I do it for money. She was a donor, and said they'd like virgin blood. It was popular, and I earned enough for a ticket to Miami. I got away.

"Then once in South Beach. I'd been selling my blood

for a few weeks to this blood club. The vampire who runs it, he tells me that the others, they want more of my blood. They wanted me to let them bite me for extra money. I said no, then ran to the next town because it was unsafe. I was able to stay some places longer than others. Sometimes years." Gabriella shoved her fingers through her hair and sighed. "But I never let them bite me."

"Any other surprises before we talk money? My help comes at a cost," Kellan said.

"We have something that supposedly can kill Lilitu. End the coven. But we don't know how to use it. We've consulted with another high priestess. We're coming to you. Name your price."

"Twenty-five thousand dollars."

"Is he out of his damn mind?" Hunter exclaimed. "We don't even know he can help us."

Kellan dug into his jeans pocket and retrieved a small business card and offered it to Quintus. The vampire snatched it out of his hand and promptly tapped at the screen of his phone. "Done."

Kellan's phone beeped. He picked it up off the armrest and nodded, a smile blooming on his face. "Well then. Looks like we're in business."

"Let's make it fast. You may think you're safe in fairy land, but we're not. Lilitu breaks all the rules." The Alpha scanned the courtyard.

"Fae realm," Kellan corrected.

"He's right. She could find us anytime. She's able to track Gabriella with little issue." Quintus took note of the sweat beading on Hunter's forehead. If he didn't get him out of here soon, he grew concerned he'd die.

"What do you have?" The fae cocked his head, staring at Quintus.

"Bone of the high priestess. Found it in the catacombs."

"How's that?"

"The short of it is it required Gabriella's blood and mine, but we got the bone. Lilitu has been after it ever since. It supposedly can kill her, but we don't know how to use it."

"Well, well, you are clever, I'll give you both that," Kellan said, his eyes lit with excitement. "So. Do you want to know?" He clapped his hands together, humming.

"Are you fucking kidding?" Hunter uttered, wearing an expression of annoyance.

"Yes, Kellan. I paid you, now out with it." Quintus blew out a breath. They were running out of time. Although the fae bar was cloaked, any of the patrons could have reported back to Lilitu if they were in need of favors.

"Blood! Blood is the answer. And a spell. Which I can give you for another fifty grand. And before you go getting rough on me, you know it'll work. We don't do business often, but I do not fail."

Quintus tapped at his phone. Money wasn't an issue, time was. "What else do you need?"

"Your blood is the answer. A potion. From the first witch to the blood of a hybrid, the witch must die through a sister of the coven. Your hybrid must be the one to destroy her. But she will never have the power without the bone inside her, the strength of the one who created the coven.

This witch. Lilitu. It sounds as though she's taken on demonic powers." Kellan turned to Gabriella. "She's waited for years for you. Years for you to be born. Years for you to find your mate so that you could find the first bone." He smiled and set his focus on Quintus. "I am afraid I do not have answers to your Jiangshi, however. I, too, suspect they are related. But the Jiangshi are rare. This thing may have been set off by your mating."

"Or the demon who made her could have a tie to Lilitu," Quintus suggested.

"Possibly, but you need to kill Lilitu to find out. If they're connected, perhaps it will weaken the Jiangshi. Demonic magick is very hard to defeat. While there is something special about Gabriella's blood, that in itself isn't enough." Kellan reached into the fire pit, lifting one of the logs. A red-hot handle protruded from the earth and he wrapped his hand around it and lifted it upward, revealing a small chest. He set it on a large boulder to his left and opened the metal box, retrieving a brass chalice and athame.

"What do you need?" Gabriella asked.

"Your blood." Kellan held up the knife. "There's always a sacrifice to be made and this time, it ain't money. You go first."

Gabriella stood from her chair and walked over to Kellan. She extended her hand and startled as he snatched it. "Come. This will only sting a bit, my lovely."

"Careful with her or I'll be using that knife on you, fae." Quintus hovered over them as the athame sliced into her palm. His brave mate bit her lip in silence as her blood dripped into the vessel. After several seconds, she yanked back her hand.

Quintus extended his wrist, glaring at the fae as he sliced him open, his sanguine essence mixing into Gabriella's. He glanced to Hunter whose eyes fluttered shut. *Fuck.* "We need to hurry."

"This will only take a minute." Kellan shoved away Quintus' arm and rolled up his sleeve. As his fingers stretched into the light, claws protruded from the tips.

"What are you doing?" Quintus reached for Gabriella's arm and gently sealed her wound with his tongue before healing his own.

"Demonic magick must be fought with the hell from whence it came. You and I both know the fae walk the earth, choosing Heaven or Hell. Yet the elements from our dark past are never too far. Fire is life."

Gabriella released an audible gasp as Kellan reached his hand into the fire pit, shoving the coals aside. His clawed fist buried into the earth while he hummed. Quintus caught her gaze and shook his head no, concerned as her fear escalated. *Don't move. It's okay*, he told her, knowing she'd hear his thoughts.

She looked to the Alpha, the light reflecting off the sheen that coated his face. *Hunter. We've got to get him out. Please.*

Soon. Quintus set his focus back onto Kellan who yanked his arm back out of the dirt, bright red flecks of the ash spewing from his fist. The fae laughed wildly as he sprinkled the mixture into the bowl.

"Ah yeah, baby! Hellfire and brimstone. Nothing like it

to get you revved up. Fuck yeah." He stabbed the athame back into the vessel, furiously mixing it. "Where is the bone? It is time."

Hunter grunted, uttering unintelligible words. Quintus leaned over him, setting a comforting hand onto his shoulder. "Hang in there, brother. We're out of here in a minute." He reached inside his front pocket and retrieved the small fragment. Offering it to the fae, his face grew stern. "Don't fuck this up. If you don't get this right, you're a dead man, understand?"

"I never make mistakes," Kellan insisted. "Give it to me now."

Quintus took solace in knowing that Samantha had the other half. He didn't trust the fae but he was a last resort.

Kellan turned to a mortar and pestle, dropped the bone inside, and set to pulverizing it. Within seconds, all that remained was a fine powdery substance.

"This." He held the crushed bone into the air in reverence. "It's very, very rare for someone to collect the first bones. They're usually destroyed. Make no mistake, your coupling is fate. Destiny drove the discovery. Perhaps it was foretold somewhere or by an oracle, but I believe the high priestess knew your mating would ultimately result in the discovery of the bone and possibly her demise. She attempts to control fate. She let you live all these years because she wanted you to find them. She knew you needed Quintus. Now…if the bone is in her hands, she'll be more powerful than any witches on the face of the earth. It's very dangerous for all who cross her. All the other covens will be at her mercy."

Kellan held the mortar over the bowl and began to chant. Quintus spoke over twenty languages fluently and recognized it as a blend of Old Norse and Fae. "Megin, megin, megin," Kellan repeated, his voice growing louder and louder.

Quintus tilted his head toward the sky as thunder rumbled overhead. Within the fae realm, they should be protected by the elements, but as lightning flashed in a red hue, Quintus questioned its source. *Lilitu.*

"Hurry," Gabriella cried. "She's here."

"I see you've brought the trouble to my home. This will be extra," Kellan growled.

"Whatever it is, I'll pay. Now finish the spell and tell us what to do," Quintus ordered.

"It's already finished, but I'm giving this to you with a warning. I will not be held responsible, vampire." Kellan retrieved a small vial from the chest and carefully lifted the bowl to its rim, pouring the bloody elixir inside it. Thunder rumbled and he startled, nearly dropping the glass. "Fuckin' witches." He fumbled with a cork.

"Hurry up, fae," Quintus demanded.

"She's here. We've got to go." Gabriella's body trembled as she stood, her foot tapping the ground. She looked to Hunter and went to him. Crouching, she set her palm on his face. "Please. He's dying."

Kellan extended his hand to give Quintus the vial but as the vampire reached for it, the fae clasped onto his wrist, yanking him to his chest. His face inches from Quintus', he issued a warning. "This magick. She needs to drink it, but it can only be done in the presence of Lilitu to work. Hellfire…not everyone can handle it."

"What the fuck are you talking about?"

"It can mess with your head. The illusions you see from me? This is the power within the fire. Within Hell. It is not meant for others."

"Are you fucking kidding me? But you want Gabby to drink this?"

"If you want the high priestess dead, then yes. I did as you asked. I owe you nothing more." Kellan released Quintus, shoving him backwards.

A bolt shot down from above striking the fire, and Quintus caught sight of Lilitu's face in the clouds. Her cheeks stretched the veil, like a fist pressing through latex. Her mouth opened wide, and her roar grew louder.

With his arms outstretched and frantic laughter, Kellan fell back into the fire pit, melting into the embers. As the veil broke, Quintus rushed to Gabriella and Hunter, throwing his body over theirs. Dematerializing them away, he prayed the next time he saw the high priestess, they'd destroy her forever.

Tears streamed down Gabriella's face. "He's dying. His pulse is weak."

"Goddammit," Quintus yelled as he sucked a breath.

He pressed onto his hands and knees and rolled the Alpha onto his back. Quintus tore at Hunter's shirt, exposing the hidden wound.

"What is happening to him? What is happening?" Gabriella repeated as she caught sight of Hunter's skin.

"It's the poison. It's like a flesh-eating bacteria. The demonic elements have attracted insects. They're part of death." Cream-colored worms oozed from a three-inch gash on his arm, the rotted skin peeling away from its edges. Quintus gently pressed down onto the wound with his fingers. Hundreds of maggots gushed from the opening, spilling down onto the carpet.

"No, no, no," Gabriella gagged. "I've never...oh my Goddess, I'm going to be sick."

"Turn on the shower," Quintus ordered.

"Where are we?" she asked as she pressed to her feet.

Quintus took in the sight of his surroundings. A log cabin in the bayou. He hadn't been certain of the location but Hunter had told him details, enabling him to materialize into his home. The interior was exactly how he'd described, a wide-open living room and kitchen area with cathedral ceiling. Off to the left was a thick wooden door, leading to the bedroom.

"Over there." Quintus pointed to an opened interior door. "The bathroom should be through the bedroom. Go look." He rounded behind Hunter and slid his arms underneath him, lifting him off of the floor.

Gabriella hurried to the bathroom, and turned on the lights. She turned the shower spigot, and water sprayed onto the white tiled floor.

Quintus followed, gently laid his body into the cold

spray and tore off his shirt. Gabriella reached for the shower head and yanked it out of its cradle. She directed the nozzle toward the wound and began spraying it clean of the insects and pus.

"I've got him," Quintus said, pulling the Alpha onto his lap. The vampire bit his arm, and pressed the flowing blood to Hunter's lips. "Come on, dammit. This has to work."

"His pulse is weak." Gabriella reached for his arm, inspecting the wound. "I can't believe this is happening."

"Come on, Hunter. Don't fucking die on me." Quintus rested his head against the cold tiles, willing him to drink. The imperceptible draws on his magick drained slowly, and the vampire sighed in relief. The cool water turned warm and his gaze caught Gabriella's.

"It's working. Look," Gabriella ran her finger over the new skin that had formed over his wound, "it's totally healed."

Quintus detected the Alpha's strong heartbeat but Hunter showed no signs of rousing. He pulled his arm away from Hunter's mouth, and lifted him closer, speaking into his ear.

"Come on brother. You're strong. Can you hear me?"

Gabriella reached up to the spigot and turned off the water. She dropped the showerhead and ran the back of her hand across her eyes.

"I don't know what's wrong with him. My wolf should be able to contact his, but he's not responding," she said. "Maybe he just needs some rest."

"Get his jeans off. We'll put him into the bed and see if

he can sleep it off. He may need more blood but I want to get him out of the damn shower first."

Gabriella unzipped his pants, and tugged hard at the sodden jeans, until they peeled away. Still holding Hunter in his arms, the vampire shoved to his feet and scooped up the Alpha with a grunt. Gabriella reached for a couple of dry towels hanging on a rack and followed Quintus into the bedroom. As he set Hunter onto the bed, she handed him one and began to dry off her face.

"Do you have the vial?" she asked, concern painting her face as if she'd forgotten about what Kellan had given them.

"Yeah, yeah." Quintus dug into his wet pocket and retrieved the cylinder. "Thank fuck it didn't break."

Gabriella began undressing. She peeled off her wet t-shirt and bra, then made quick work of shucking her panties and jeans. "Here. Give me your clothes. I'm going to put them in the dryer."

"I can go get some new clothes," he said. "But I don't want to go anywhere until we know he's all right."

"No, I don't think you should flash out of here for anything. We need to stay together. For as rustic as this place appears, I can tell by his fancy bathroom that he's got a washer and dryer. Let's use it."

"Was it the ten thousand dollar toilet that gave it away?" Quintus laughed, unbuttoning his pants.

"I've only seen one of those in my lifetime. Fancy hotel in New York. Heated seats," she laughed. "You're right. If he's got a bathroom like that out in the middle of the bayou, the man has a dryer."

As Quintus reached for a towel, he pulled Gabriella to him. "This is all going to be okay."

"I'm just glad we got the potion or whatever the hell it is. We have to text Samantha to let her know."

Quintus pressed his lips to hers, tasting his mate. "I want you to know how much I care about you, Gabriella. You are everything." His forehead rested against hers, lingering for moments before he reluctantly released her. She gave a sad smile and gathered the wet clothing, leaving the room.

Quintus glanced at the Alpha whose chest rose and fell steadily. They'd have to heal him further before going after Lilitu. Whatever mojo the fae performed had better work, he thought to himself.

He reached for the vial and held it up into the air, observing the luminescent flecks that sparkled within it. *Hellfire. Jesus Christ.* And Gabriella was supposed to ingest this shit? It wasn't as if he hadn't seen crazier things work in his lifetime but never had it been for someone he cared about.

Gabriella returned to the bedroom, a white towel wrapped around her body. His heart tightened at the sight of her. His tough little wolf had dried her tears but her reddened eyes gave her away. He took her hand and brought her over to the side of the bed.

Careful not to disturb Hunter, Quintus lay back onto the mattress. Gabriella fell into his embrace and he wrapped his arms around her. The warmth of her lips brushed his chest and he reasoned he could stay like this for the rest of his life.

"You okay?" he asked, already knowing the answer.

"I'm tired. I'm tired of running. I'm tired of the death," she responded, her voice soft.

"Someday when this is all over, I'm taking you on a date." Quintus gave a small laugh.

"A date?"

"Si. A date." Quintus smiled as he felt the corner of her lip turn upward, her hand brushing over his chest. "I know this thing between us…it's fate. It's finding someone that you're drawn to, but I want you to know I…" *Love.* "I care about you. I want a life for us."

"We're immortal."

"But you deserve more. You deserve flowers. And dancing. Breakfast in bed." He smiled.

"You miss being human, don't you?" she asked.

"It's not as though my life before being turned was easy. But I was brought up to believe certain things. A few thousand years go by and you still want the basics. A home. Someone to love."

"A family," she whispered. "I never really thought about it. My mom is gone. I don't have anyone else."

"You have me."

"You wanted children didn't you?" Gabriella asked.

"I gave up on that a long time ago. I'm vampire. I can do many things, but bringing a new life into this world isn't one of them." Quintus had accepted that he'd never have a child. A family wasn't part of the equation. He'd sire other vampires, but that was the only gift he could give to others.

"I'm part witch. For now anyway," she stated.

"You'll always be witch and wolf," he replied, stroking her hair.

"I'm just saying…Samantha…"

Quintus' chest momentarily stopped rising as his breath caught in his throat. Not one woman in his entire lifetime had broached the subject of having children. As vampire, Mao had been the only person he'd ever cared about and not once had they ever discussed having a family.

"Quintus." She tapped lightly on his chest with her palm. "It's just that if…I…I never thought of having kids. You know seeing the baby…I just thought…"

"No, it…it can't happen for me. I'm a vampire. This is something we must accept when we are turned. It's rare to…" Quintus fell silent. *Did Gabriella want children? Jesus.* He'd never thought that she'd want to have kids, that by completing the bond, he'd rob her of the chance to have a family.

"If you don't want a family," she paused, lifting her head off his chest, her eyes meeting his, "I understand. I wouldn't want kids with someone like me either. I've been nothing but damaged goods."

"Hey, no." Quintus' heart squeezed at her statement. "Look at me." He brushed a finger underneath her chin, until her gaze met his. "I want you to know something right now. You're not damaged goods. None of this is your fault. None of it, do you hear me? You were just a child. No, what's happening, this is all Lilitu."

"But it is my fault. I involved you in this mess."

"I wouldn't be alive if it weren't for you. Gabby, I'm

sorry for my reaction about children. It's just that, well, first of all, it's never been a possibility. What's happened with Luca and Samantha is unusual. I don't know of many witches or wolves or even hybrids bonded to vampires, but it's rare for one to get pregnant. Our magick keeps us alive, but we generally don't have the capability to create life. And second, it's not that I don't want kids. It's just that I can't let myself go there. It's just too…if it's not possible, it's not possible. But with you?" A sad smile formed on his face, his chest tight with emotion. "I'd give anything to be able to give you a child."

"Quintus," she whispered, tears filling her eyes. "I'd like that someday. If it's fate, it will happen. You're my family."

"And the Alpha." He glanced to Hunter who remained unconscious.

They needed to do more to help him, but Quintus had been reluctant to suggest his idea. Gabriella's blood teemed with magick, and he suspected her capable of healing many different creatures. He too needed to feed, but the nature of the bite stirred sexual desires. Although he'd shared women many times with Viktor, Gabriella was his. He considered her response to her spanking, aware she'd been aroused by the Alpha's touch. As he recalled the interaction, his cock stirred. Her gentle voice broke his contemplation.

"Yes. He's our family too." Gabriella pressed her lips to his chest, and reached for Hunter, placing her palm on his abdomen. "His wolf. I can feel him but I can't talk to him. I can't sense him…not the way I usually do. The poison did something really bad to him. If we had done something before we left to see the fae, maybe this wouldn't have happened."

"He's a man. No, what he is is an Alpha. He takes care of all others first. Including his pack. And you, Gabby, you're pack."

"We've got to do something," she sighed.

"There may be a way, but I'm not sure it's going to work. And if we do it, you need to be aware of the possible consequences."

"What can we do? I don't want to leave here yet. Lilitu seems to be able to find me everywhere I go. Everyone says they're protected by wards. But they aren't working. I'm not sure if it's because I'm a wolf or what but here, in this bayou, in the middle of nowhere I feel the safest I've felt in years. Something about it." She closed her eyes and breathed. "It's like home. I can't explain it. My wolf is finally calm."

"Soon this is all going to be over. But the next time we go out, it's to kill Lilitu. And we'll do it in New Orleans. Together. Do you hear me, Gabby? For whatever reason, you and I were brought together to defeat her. Neither of us could have retrieved the bone alone. And we couldn't have done any of this without Hunter, which brings us back to how to heal him."

"I wish I knew a spell, but antidotes to poison are not something I know about," she told him, frustration in her voice.

"I'm thinking your blood might be the answer. Usually I can heal wolves but the demonic magick she's used is too powerful. I'm sure Hunter thought he could handle the pain, because he's an Alpha. But whatever spread throughout his body, it brought on the necrosis. My guess is that I was able to heal you because of our bond."

"I've never given my blood to anyone besides a vampire. I don't know if it'll work."

"We've got to try it. I can risk moving him but I don't think it's a good idea. We'd have to go to Samantha or take him to another healer, and wherever we go Lilitu finds you. We don't have time. I also don't want to leave you here. No matter how safe this place seems, I'm not leaving you alone."

"I'll do it, but Quintus," She raised her head to face him. "When you've fed from me, it's…well you know."

"The bite, the feeding, it must be pleasurable. There is no other way except when done in anger and that, well, that is something you will never experience. Hunter already is connected to us. We don't have to go any further than the feeding but if that's something you want to explore…" Quintus waited on Gabriella to connect the dots. If she fed Hunter, it would not be without her total agreement. He believed it would heal the wolf but it had to be her choice.

"Let's do it." She nodded.

"This will be intimate. As intimate as it gets." A knowing smile crossed his face as he trailed his fingers over the back of her neck. "Do you remember the spanking?"

"Um what?"

"Your spanking. Do you remember, little wolf?"

Gabriella's cheeks heated against his skin and she averted her gaze. "It's kind of hard to forget."

"You liked it. Not just the pain but being watched, the Alpha's hands on your skin."

"I did," she replied, no hesitation. "I don't know why, but it just really turned me on. The more he watched the more I wanted him to watch."

"But this time? Not just watch," he said. It wasn't a question. He knew she'd have gone further had he let her.

"I've never done anything like that. Any of it. It was always just a fantasy, but I'd never trusted anyone enough to do it. The times I've been with other men, and there were only a few, it was nothing. I didn't have time for connections. I'd chosen humans. I know they're fragile but they're without complications."

"I can't predict exactly how Hunter will react."

"We can do this...together."

Quintus reached for Gabriella, pulling her onto him. As her warm lips brushed his neck, he waited patiently. She peppered kisses along his chin, slowly, until her mouth grazed his.

"Quintus," she breathed. "I need you to know that if anything happens, this thing between us is real. I never knew I could feel this way about anyone. I've never met anyone like you."

"Gabby, I..." Quintus kissed her with the passion he couldn't articulate. *Love.* He'd only told one other woman he loved her and she'd been killed. But he'd meant what he'd said, he'd give his life to protect Gabriella.

She straddled him, her slippery core gliding over his dick. His cock lengthened, his fangs dropping in response.

"Hmm…bella." He reached for her wrist and brought it to his mouth. "You're so fucking sexy."

Gabriella gave a small laugh, nibbling at his skin. "I want you inside me."

"Soon." He dragged his fangs along her wrist. "Hunter…"

"Yes." She nodded.

Quintus released her arm and set his hands on her waist. "As much as I want to be inside you right now…ah fuck." His body tensed as his cock slid through her slick folds. "Go to him."

Quintus set her gently onto the Alpha, her head rested on his chest while he sandwiched her between them. As he knelt behind her, his erect cock ached to sink inside her but he delayed his pleasure, set on healing Hunter first. He brushed a soft kiss to her shoulder, his lips grazing toward her wrist.

"Yes," she hissed.

"Gabby…" As his fangs pierced her creamy skin, she trembled underneath him.

Quintus suctioned the wounds, drawing her blood to the surface and pressed her wrist to the Alpha's mouth.

"Quintus," Gabriella mewled. Aroused, she gently rocked against the Alpha's hip.

"Can you reach his beast? Your wolf needs to call to him," he told her.

"Alpha," She pressed her lips to Hunter's cheek, her thigh brushing over his cock. "Yes, yes…oh Goddess, he's there. Can you feel him?"

The second Hunter began to move his lips and drink

from her, Quintus sensed the magick flowing in the air. The Alpha's eyes fluttered open and locked on his. "That's it brother."

"Hunter," she breathed as his hand clasped her wrist.

Quintus brushed his lips to Gabriella's then slid behind her, reaching his arm around her waist. His cock pressed between her legs, his fingers grazing over her clit.

"Yes," she cried.

Hunter released her arm, his tongue swiping over the bite. "Thank you. Holy fuck, I can't believe. I almost died."

"You're going to be all right," Gabriella managed, her hands trailing down the ridges of his abs.

"I'm sorry I put you guys in this situation." He shifted to move away, but stilled as the vampire spoke.

"Stay," Quintus ordered.

"I…are you both sure about this?" Uncertainty swam in his eyes as he searched for their agreement.

"Yes." Gabriella nodded.

"We both want this. Come feel her. She's so fucking wet, right now." Quintus reached for Hunter's hand and set it onto her mound. With careful control, he directed them. "That's it. Touch her."

Gabriella sighed as Hunter's fingers played over her clitoris. Quintus stroked his rock-hard dick, pressing its head to her entrance.

"Please," she begged, her lips gently brushing Hunter's. "It's okay."

This sight of his mate writhing on the Alpha spiked his arousal. Unable to restrain himself any longer, Quintus buried himself to the hilt, grunting as he filled her.

"Ah…yes," she cried. Her magick diffused, sparks of arousal crackling in the air.

As the Alpha took her taut nipple between his lips, Quintus thought he'd fucking come at the sight of his beautiful witch lost in the erotic moment. He caught Hunter's gaze, and gave a closed smile, his cock hardening at the sight of him pleasuring his mate. In all his years, he'd never expected to fall in love let alone share his mate with this Alpha. Her quivering channel pulsated around his cock, and he stilled inside her. Fuck, this woman would make him crazy, and he smiled, knowing he'd willingly surrender to the experience every day for the rest of his life.

Chapter Fourteen

When Quintus had suggested healing the Alpha, she'd have done anything to save him. With her mate's teeth sunk deep into her flesh, she quivered as her orgasm rocked into her. As Hunter's lips found her breast, Quintus stilled inside her. She smiled, realizing he'd been as aroused as she was.

Gabriella's body lit on fire, submitting to the only men she'd ever let close to her heart. Safe within her mate's control, she surrendered as he slowly withdrew his hard shaft and slid back inside her. His tongue grazed over his bite, and she knew this was only the beginning. She panted for breath, in an attempt to recover.

"Ah fuck," he grunted, his lips grazing her ear. "Hmm...you feel so good. You're so fucking tight. I like seeing his lips on your skin. But remember you're mine."

"Always," she moaned.

"Taste her pussy, while I fuck her," the vampire ordered.

Gabriella sucked a breath as Hunter gently bit her nipple, his tongue flicking over the sensitive peak. He dropped his head to her stomach, his lips grazing down to her bared mound. Sandwiched between them on her side, she mewled. The Alpha's tongue speared through her folds as Quintus thrust inside her from behind.

Quintus gently rocked in and out, fucking her as the Alpha stroked over her clit with his broad tongue. Her hips tilted onto his face, she accepted each wicked lash he delivered to her swollen bead. With each strong thrust Quintus gave, she gave a jagged moan, her orgasm mounting. Immersed in the sensation of two men pleasuring her, she submitted to the delicious torture.

"Oh Goddess…that feels so good…I need more. Just like that. Please, yes."

"Hmm…you taste so good, darlin'," Hunter told her as he wrapped her thigh over his shoulder. "I could eat you all day long."

"Sorry Alpha, but this pussy is mine. Sharing you isn't something I plan on doing very often, little wolf." His gaze went to Hunter and he smiled. "I think we need to show our Alpha a little love, si?"

A devilish glint in his eyes should have warned her of his next move but she still managed to squeal as he withdrew and grabbed her by the hips, flipping her over onto her stomach. Gabriella looked back to Quintus, her heart pounding as she took sight of her spectacular mate. He stood proud, stroking his shaft, his hungry eyes devouring her.

"Suck his cock." Gabriella's pussy flooded with arousal at the demand.

As Hunter moved onto his back, sitting up in bed, she

shoved onto her hands and knees, settling between his legs. Quintus tapped the head of his dick on the top of her bottom, teasing it toward her core. She shivered as he dragged the tip through her labia, teasing over her sensitive nub.

"I want to watch her suck you," he said to Hunter.

"You want this, darlin'?" The Alpha gave her a sexy smile, palming his hardened shaft in his hands.

Gabriella's pulse raced as her dark fantasy came to fruition. She glanced to Quintus for his approval and nodded.

"That's it," Quintus encouraged.

She reached for Hunter, but he corrected her. "Easy, now. Just open your pretty mouth for me."

The Alpha brought his cock to her lips, and she darted her tongue over his crown, tasting him. As he plunged his dick into her mouth, Quintus thrust inside her aching pussy. Hunter's fingers tunneled into her hair and she swallowed him down to his root.

"Fuck yeah," Hunter groaned.

With each thrust, Gabriella's body splintered in arousal. Surrendering to two men was more than she had ever imagined, the delicious sensations overwhelming her.

"You feel so fucking amazing," Quintus grunted as he slammed inside her.

Gabriella reveled in her control of the Alpha as he leaned back onto the headboard. She stroked the Alpha's cock, dragging her tongue along its sides. Quintus' fingers brushed over her puckered hole with his thumb, and she gave a ragged breath.

"What are you..?" Gabriella went still as his finger eased inside her back hole. "Ah…yes."

"All of you. Forever, my little wolf." Quintus nodded to Hunter, who reached over inside the night stand and retrieved a small container, tossing it to the vampire.

Relaxing into his touch, Gabriella focused on the Alpha, taking his cock between her lips. Her tongue swirled over his broad crown, eliciting a moan. Gabriella's head lolled forward as Quintus thrust inside her pussy, his finger slid deep inside her ass, stretching her bottom. He withdrew and added another finger, scissoring open her back hole as he continued to gently slide inside her core.

Gabriella went on alert as the cool liquid dripped down the crevice of her ass. Quintus withdrew from her pussy, and she released a small cry in protest. As he pressed his crown to her back hole, she tensed.

"I don't know, I don't know," she repeated, gasping for breath, her climax teetering out of reach.

"You must learn to trust me, bella. Easy now. Just breathe."

"You're all right, little wolf," Hunter told her, brushing a comforting hand over her hair.

"We're gonna take this slow," Quintus told her. "Press back on me, that's it."

Gabriella exhaled as his cock pressed through her tight ring of muscle.

"I…I…"

"You're okay?" he asked.

"Oh God…please Quintus…just…move…please."

Gabriella forced her body to relax as a twinge of pain passed through her and he settled inside her bottom. Hunter stroked her hair as she breathed into the sensation.

"That's a girl," he praised.

"I…oh Goddess…" With her body on fire, she ached for release. She relaxed into the dark intrusion, accepting him inside of her.

"Almost there…ah fuck. You're so…" Quintus lost his words.

"Please…" So full, she needed more, her pussy throbbed and she sought relief, wiggling her bottom toward him. "Fuck me."

As he slowly thrust in and out of Gabriella, she submitted, her body on fire with arousal. Quintus wrapped a firm hand around her waist and flicked fingers over her clitoris, applying more pressure.

"I'm…I can't…this feels so…" Gabriella failed to articulate the incredible pleasure weaving through her body.

Quintus gently rocked in and out of his mate. Gabriella's head rested on Hunter's thigh, his cock sliding into her mouth. Surrendering to her mate and the Alpha all at once, Gabriella reveled in an erotic experience she'd never thought possible. As Quintus applied pressure to her clit, circling it with his thumb, she splintered apart, her explosive release flinging her over the edge.

As her climax seized her, Gabriella screamed, writhing as the orgasm spiraled through every inch of her body. She stroked Hunter's cock with her hand, his seed spilling as he grunted loudly. Quintus gave a final deep thrust, coming hard inside her.

Gabriella panted for breath, her entire body tingling with pleasure. As Quintus gently removed himself, she trembled, the final erotic waves of her orgasm rolling over her.

Within seconds, Quintus had taken her safely into his embrace. She curled into his arms, her lips pressed to his chest. Goddess, she loved this man with every cell of her being. She knew right then she'd sacrifice her own life for him, and happily die knowing she loved and was loved.

Gabriella cuddled into her vampire, her heart crushing as she contemplated her next move. Wherever Gabriella had traveled, death and danger followed. She'd asked for Quintus' help after healing him, and he'd done as she asked, helping her find a way to kill the witch. But Lilitu was her responsibility.

Gabriella had never paid attention to potions, but she knew her mother often used them to help others. This one, though, would bring destruction. Merely touching the bone, she'd sensed its malevolent power. She imagined that nothing would be the same again after she ingested it, but if it was the only way to kill Lilitu, she was prepared to use it.

Quintus had warned her more than once not to go alone, but she couldn't put him at risk. Gabriella hadn't loved anyone since her mother died, and Quintus was the only light in her life. Hunter Livingston had guided her, become her Alpha. The two people she cared about the most would give their lives for her, and she couldn't let that happen.

Gabriella sealed off her thoughts and tightened her embrace around Quintus. Tears welled in her eyes as emotion consumed her. She shifted onto her forearm and gazed up at Quintus. Although his eyes were closed, she could tell from his heartbeat he wasn't fully asleep. She leaned forward and brushed a soft kiss to his lips.

"Hmm…" Quintus gave a sleepy smile.

"I'll be back, baby," she told him, and kissed him once more. Gabriella waited mere seconds before he drifted into a slumber. *I love you*, she whispered in her mind, trying not to wake him. *More than you'll ever know.*

She pushed out of bed and shoved onto her feet, glancing to the bed. Her vampire lay sleeping on his back, and the Alpha curled onto his side, facing away. She smiled, thinking of how lucky she was to have them in her life. *Caring. Loving. Protecting.* It was everything she could ever want or need in a mate and a friend. And this time it was her turn to do the protecting.

Gabriella pulled her dried t-shirt over her head, dressing. She'd finger-combed her wild mane into a braid and now stared into the mirror. She blinked, her eyes changing from blue to yellow, the wolf burning to escape. This, however, was a job for her magick.

She looked to the vial she'd set on the counter next to the sink. In the melee of leaving the fae's realm, she swore she heard him whisper something to Quintus about a warning. Instinctively she knew, after touching the bone with her own fingers, that the potion could harm her. But the power she'd gain would outweigh the risks. Kill or be killed. She had no choice but to fight, because Lilitu would pursue her forever.

No more than a spoonful, the elixir looked innocuous enough; however, given the ingredients and fae magick, Gabriella knew otherwise. She tugged at the small cork, easily removing the stopper. Within seconds, the room sparkled in black magick, the scent of sulfur filtering into the air. *Hellfire.*

Although they hadn't discussed it, Gabriella had overheard Kellan telling Quintus that it must be taken in Lilitu's presence. She recorked the vial and exhaled loudly. Lilitu would come for her no matter where she went. But this time, she'd trap her into her own death.

When Gabriella had retrieved her clothing from the dryer, she'd investigated her surroundings. After taking one look at the remote location of Hunter's cabin in the bayou and the rickety fishing boat tied to the dock, she determined she needed another means of travel. With very little knowledge of the swamps, navigating the murky alligator-infested waters would take her forever to get back to New Orleans.

Her only feasible option to escape would be to leave the same way they'd arrived. Very few vampires could flash from location to location. Although she was aware the skill was utilized by only the most advanced witches, Gabriella suspected she could materialize to a location. Ever since she'd mated, Quintus' magick had begun to merge with hers, and she noted that she was less and less sick each time they'd traveled.

Gabriella stuffed the vial into her front jeans pocket, and wrapped her fingers around the brass door knob, slowly turning it until it opened. She listened for movement and heard only the soft snoring coming from the bedroom. Quietly she padded through the hallway and into the kitchen, praying he didn't hear her. As long as she was on the property, with her emotions sealed off tight, Quintus would have no need for concern.

She glanced outside, noting the light of the waning moon glistening on the water. Without her phone, she'd lost track of time and suspected dawn would arrive within hours. She glanced over her shoulder before she reached for the lock and clicked open the deadbolt. As she put her hand on the knob, she heard his voice in her mind. *Come back to bed, bella. Rest. We'll go soon.* Her lips drew into a tight smile that didn't reach her eyes. She had to keep him safe. There was no other way, she told herself.

"Sleep, my vampire," she whispered, sending her magick to him, invoking a spell. "Somnium, sopor, nox. Blessed be." It was one of the early spells she'd learned from her mother. She'd used it several times on the coven children who'd had trouble sleeping at night. But for Quintus, she suspected the spell would only last minutes, then he'd chase her.

As she opened the door and closed it behind her, she

breathed in the swamp air. Crickets and frogs sang into the night. Spanish moss swayed gently in the cypress trees, a warm breeze blowing over the water. As she took a step onto the dock, a creak released from its wooden planks.

"I love you, Quintus," Gabriella whispered, firing up the energy within her soul. She closed her eyes, her palms upward to the sky, calling on the magick of the earth and moon. Imagining Lilitu, she focused on what she'd brought to the world. *Death*. A place where the veil between the living and the dead stretched thin, where grief and loss tore at its fragile fibers.

She called on her wolf, pleading for the powers of her mate, Quintus. Imagining her body dissipating into a thousand molecules, she siphoned his magick. Her pulse raced as the transfer began and she prayed she'd make it alive.

Within seconds, breath rushed into her lungs and she tumbled onto the gravel. She glanced up to the familiar pyramid-shaped tomb, its chalky white walls reflecting the street lights. A marble angel sat atop its peak, beckoning visitors who couldn't see over the brick walls.

Gabriella shoved up onto her hands and knees, listening for others. Although the cemetery's locked gates kept humans at bay at night, supernaturals found their way into the cities of the dead. She recalled her first meeting with Ramiel, standing on the corner off of Basin Street. She'd given him a sample of her blood, seeking to sell it.

Gabriella shrugged off the bad memory and pressed to her feet. She slid her fingers into her pocket and retrieved the potion. With dark energy sizzling around her, Lilitu would find her within minutes.

"Where are you, bitch?" Gabriella sniffed, cringing as she smelled the scent of urine in the air. "Is that you? Come find me. I'm here now."

Her boots crunched the stones beneath her feet as she proceeded with caution down a dimly lit path. Although she'd been in the same cemetery many times, she never shook the feeling she was a breath away from death.

Gabriella inhaled deeply in an attempt to calm her thoughts but they continued to race. Kellan had warned Quintus. The potion in her hand didn't exactly come stamped with FDA approval. Not only was she going to drink her own blood, she'd ingest the ancient bones of a witch and the earth of the devil. Fae magick was notoriously dangerous, its victims often dying a slow and miserable death. But it was too late to turn back and even if she could, she'd stay and face it. No more running; she was determined to protect others from the witch.

"Goddammit. Where the fuck are you?" Gabriella mumbled under her breath. She expected Quintus would wake up any second and come look for her. Although she'd kept her thoughts closed off, he'd break through her barrier within minutes.

"I know you can hear me, you shitty excuse of a witch. You've been following me my entire life. Get your fucking ass here now." With each step, the cemetery grew more silent. Crickets ceased to chirp, and no cars traveled the usually busy street. She opened her mind, allowing her wolf to filter the intermittent dark magick that morphed into a static current.

Gabriella ran her fingers over the cool stone of a crypt in an attempt to reach the dead. But even the spirits remained quiet in their sleep. A crackle of lightning struck a nearby mausoleum, and she ducked as rock blasted into the air. A jagged piece smashed into her back, forcing her to the ground. Her wrist snapped as she fell onto a pile of bricks. The vial slipped from her fingers and rolled onto gravel, disappearing underneath a crypt.

Stunned, Gabriella struggled to breathe and shifted onto her back. The chalky particles coated her tongue as she coughed, a cloud spinning like a dust devil through the cemetery. Panic superseded the pain as she realized she'd lost the potion.

"Where is the bone, wolf? I can feel it's here. If you give it to me now, I'll give you a quick death," Lilitu's voice cackled.

Gabriella shoved to sit up against a tomb. Cradling her injured arm against her chest, she reached with her other hand, fumbling blindly for the vial.

"Where's your vampire? The wolf? Are they off chasing his Jiangshi?" Maniacal laughter followed.

Gabriella's stomach rolled at Lilitu's words. *Mao.* Was she responsible for creating the hideous atrocity and bringing it into their lives?

"Maybe I'll just burn you like your mother. Your pathetic mate and Alpha will come running. Don't make me kill them too," she threatened.

Gabriella's fingertips caught the rim of the vial, but it rolled further into the crevasse between the bricks and the crypt. She turned her head and caught sight of Lilitu floating through the haze as if she were a ghost. The high priestess' dark magick grew stronger, and she sensed other witches in the distance. *The coven.*

Desperate, Gabriella rolled onto her knees, and with only one hand she felt for the potion. Despite the threats, she doubted Lilitu would kill her, not without her prize.

"What are you looking for over there, girl? A protection spell? An amulet? Whatever it is, it won't help you."

Gabriella swiveled her head, catching sight of the priestess. Dressed in black leather, she deliberately and slowly stalked toward her. *Focus, Gabby*, she told herself. Her fingers probed left then to the right, deep into the cracks in the earth. A scream tore from her lungs as a cockroach scampered up her arm and into her hair. She furiously shook her head, until the insect flew onto the ground. She loathed insects but couldn't stop searching until she found the potion.

"I always told your mother you'd be a disgrace to the coven. What kind of a witch is afraid of a little bug? You're pathetic." Lilitu stopped within ten feet of Gabriella, her eyes red with fury. She held up her palms, a cruel smirk crossing her face. "I want the bone. Maybe you need an incentive."

Gabriella shifted to her far right, tears welling in her eyes as her fingertips slid over the glass. As she gripped it and withdrew her hand from the fissure, hundreds of cockroaches swarmed over her arm. Determined, she jerked her hand away, holding tight to the vial. The insects scampered out of the ground, covering her body. Gabriella struggled to stand but stumbled.

Lilitu laughed uncontrollably then without warning ceased, pausing as she honed in on Gabriella. "I want the bone. I know it's here. I feel it."

"It's here all right," she confirmed, itching to kill the bitch.

"No one's going to stop me, not with the demon magick I have. You're all so pathetically weak. You're going to die tonight, so you make the decision. Give it to me now, and die swiftly. Or I'll pry it from your dead hands. And then I kill the vampire and the wolf. What's it going to be? Pick your poison, girl."

"I'm going to pick my poison, drink it and then use it to destroy you." Gabriella kicked off the roaches, and glared at the priestess. She lifted the vial and tossed the cork onto the ground. The putrid scent of the hellfire wafted into the air and she coughed back the vomit that rose in her throat. As she brought the rim to her lip, she caught sight of Quintus flashing next to a tomb nearly twenty feet away. The Alpha rolled onto the gravel, sick from materializing.

"Gabby, wait!" Quintus yelled.

"I love you," she whispered, her eyes locked on his. She didn't give him a chance to stop her as she tilted back the vial and opened her throat. Like acid, the caustic poison burned her mouth but she didn't stop until the tube had been emptied. She tossed it aside as the last drop hit her tongue.

Gabriella lost control, her body possessed with the spirit of the first witch. Demonic fae energy twisted the spirit through her body. She opened her mouth to speak, but no words came. Radiant light speared from every pore of her body.

"Potions won't hurt me…" Concern flashed across Lilitu's face at the realization that the first bone was no longer present. She wore a shocked expression on her face. "What did you do?"

Gabriella seized, her body flattened against a mausoleum. Quintus flashed to her side, but as he went to touch her, he was blown back several steps. Hunter ran to him, restraining Quintus by his arm.

"Give her a minute," Hunter told him.

"What! Did! You! Do?" Lilitu screamed.

"I don't give a fuck. I'm getting her out of here," Quintus insisted, ignoring the Alpha.

"You're not going anywhere," an eerie familiar voice echoed, stopping him cold.

Quintus whipped his head around and caught a glimpse of Mao gliding toward him. Her skin had begun to disintegrate. The stench of rotting flesh hung heavy in the air, flies buzzing around her torso.

"Quintus, darling. You cannot escape me."

"What the actual fuck is that?" Hunter coughed and looked to Quintus. "Sorry bro, but that bitch is next. I know you loved Mao, but that isn't her. That…I don't know what that is but it's going back to Hell."

"You stay with Gabriella, I'll go after Lilitu," Quintus told him.

"No, I'll go," Hunter yelled to him. "Gabby needs you."

"You're not strong enough. There's no way in hell you're going to beat demon magick."

Through a hazy tunnel, Gabriella watched them argue. Her mind spun with random words, but she couldn't understand what they were saying. Helpless to stop him, Gabriella watched as Hunter tore off his shirt and began to shift. His mighty gray wolf growled and leapt onto Mao. Paralyzed, Gabriella surrendered to the tremendous power of the first witch and focused on Lilitu.

"I don't know what you did, you little bitch, but I'm going to kill you," Lilitu screamed.

As the high priestess ran toward Gabriella, Quintus rushed to block her. He seized her by the shoulders and sank his fangs into her neck, tearing at her flesh. Lilitu conjured the athame that had nearly killed Hunter and stabbed it into his side. Quintus fell backwards onto the ground, the knife firmly rooted in his flank. He spat her demonic blood out, careful not to swallow it.

At the sight of her mate, Gabriella released a guttural howl that shook the ground. Light emanated from her eyes, the spirit of the first witch streaming through her body. Although conscious of Quintus, her attention focused on Lilitu, who began chanting a spell, her hands upward to the sky.

Hunter rolled on the ground, screeching as Mao sunk her rotted teeth into the wolf, ripping his fur from his body. Blood sprayed into the night, splattering onto a tomb.

"Help the Alpha," Gabriella told Quintus as light

streamed from her eyes. "Lilitu is mine."

With the Alpha compromised, Quintus nodded, and ran to Hunter's aid. The Alpha snarled, snapping his teeth into her arm. Thrashing his head, he tore at her decaying flesh until her wrist partially detached. The severed hand dangled by its ligaments, dripping green-tinged pus and blood onto the gravel. A fetid stench infiltrated the air.

"Get the fuck off of him." Quintus wrapped his hand around Mao's neck. He slid his fingers into her mouth, cringing as her forked tongue lapped over his palm. He grunted, prying open her jaw.

Freed from the zombie, the Alpha rolled to the ground, whining in pain, a section of his flesh and fur missing from his back. Mao gave a loud shriek, spinning around toward Quintus, her wild red eyes flaring in anger.

"I'm going to kill you all. It's just a matter of time." She broke from his grip, stumbled backward and rocked on her heels, finally finding her footing.

Quintus' heart pounded, taking in the sight of the woman he'd once loved, knowing he was about to kill her. But he knew, no matter how much this rancid creature looked like her, she wasn't Mao.

"I've killed Viktor." Her rotted brown teeth broke through her heinous smile. "Or have I?"

The mention of his brother hit him like a punch to the gut. Quintus sucked a deep breath, concentrating on his task. His gaze darted to Gabriella who continued to step toward Lilitu. Out of the corner of his eye, he saw Hunter shift to human and back to wolf again. With a fiery glare, he set his focus back on Mao.

His gaze dropped from her eyes to her bloodied stump, the broken white bone jutting from the wound. *The hand. Where the hell is it?* She'd flash back to Hell, taking it with her if he didn't move quickly.

"What are you doing, darling? Once the witch kills the cunt you mated with, you'll be mine again." Her long tongue curled out of her mouth, dripping with saliva.

"Who sent you?" Quintus eyed the torn hand lying on the ground.

"Hmm...you never can tell." She laughed, tilting her head. She ran her hand over her gown, its purple shredded velvet exposing her thighs. The skin beneath was riddled with seeping red boils. "They say the Goddess does all the work. It's a lie. It's demons who create, create, create."

"Who made you?" he asked, his feet edging toward the right.

"Prophets. Witches who need help. They all have a price for their work. Ramiel." Her eyes rolled upward in her head, revealing only the whites.

"Ramiel?" He'd been the vampire who'd paid for Gabriella's blood, had threatened to beat her. "He's no demon."

"Isn't he? Had you ever heard of him? Stupid, stupid vampires. The demonic magick is so strong we can easily fool you all."

"Why create you?"

"Your mating," Mao growled, her smile falling into a scowl. "It had to be stopped. Your bitch may live but you're coming with me to Hell. Someone must pay for Lilitu's debt... she's been a greedy, greedy witch. She owes. Viktor was payment but the demon wants more. I'm but his humble servant."

The earth shook beneath his feet. He caught sight of Gabriella. A blinding light streamed out of her fingers. Mao's gaze went to the severed hand and back to Quintus. He lunged for the rotting flesh, snatching it off the ground. As Mao rushed to retrieve it, he bared his fangs, and grabbed her by the back of her long hair. She screeched, writhing in an attempt to steal it back from him, and he sunk his teeth into her shoulder, tearing open her rotting flesh. As she struggled, he spat out the decomposing skin and shoved the hand into her mouth.

"This is for my brother, you evil bitch." Quintus swiftly flipped her onto the ground and with a knee to her chest, continued to stuff the severed fingers and palm down her throat. Her eyes bulged as he cupped his hand over her lips. Convulsing underneath his weight, her torso collapsed upon itself. The pus-filled cavity burst open and her flesh melted.

"She's a devil," he heard Hunter yell. As Quintus turned to Gabriella, he caught sight of his mate. Thick green horns curled out of her head into points. Fire spat from her mouth as she spoke.

"What the fuck did that fae do to her?" Hunter asked.

"Hellfire," Quintus responded. No matter how she appeared, there was no way she'd become a demon. He sensed her wolf, and exhaled loudly. "Fae magick. We're seeing an illusion."

"No, Quint. She's a fucking devil. Something isn't right."

"Back off Alpha." Quintus struggled to find his balance as the earth beneath his feet violently shook. The ground split open, forming a deep crevasse.

Gabriella's body illuminated with the energy of the first witch as she stalked toward Lilitu. Her eyes held a smile, watching as terror emanated from Lilitu's face. All the dark emotions she'd inflicted on Gabriella churned inside her chest propelling her omnipotent power.

Drawing on the ancient energy, she flashed five feet toward Lilitu. Gabriella would bring destruction. There had been a time, one more innocent, when she'd have granted mercy but not tonight. Only death existed, and she'd be the one to send Lilitu to Hell.

As Gabriella advanced, Lilitu held up her athame but fear shone in her eyes. A bolt of lightning struck within inches of Gabriella but she merely absorbed its energy and stalked toward the witch.

"Tonight is the end," she declared, scanning the cemetery for the coven witches who hid in the shadows. Light speared from her hands, the pure energy searing the ground, leaving a trail of ash as she walked. "The first witch, who lives inside me demands your sacrifice. She's sending you home to Hell. Tonight," Gabriella stepped within two feet of Lilitu, "you die."

Lightning blasted all around them, driving black divots into the ground. Lilitu lunged at Gabriella, stabbing the knife into her abdomen. Gabriella laughed and wrapped her fingers around its hilt. The power of the first witch was far too great for earth magick. Painlessly, she withdrew the blade and tossed it aside. Allowing the light to cease, she clapped her hands together and outstretched her arms toward Lilitu.

"And now." With every cell of her being, she focused on the first witch allowing her to seize her body. The beam of light streamed from her fingertips. Like a laser, it sliced clear through Lilitu. The priestess screeched wildly as blood gushed from her abdomen, her eyes bulging as the cavity grew wider and wider. "Everything you've done to me. To my mother. To your victims. It ends. You end." Gabriella closed her hands into fists and stretched open her fingers, tugging at the threads of energy, ripping Lilitu apart until her flesh exploded.

The rush of her power mushroomed into a storm of pure energy. Every ounce of magick flowed through her, destroying the demonic witch. Gabriella sucked a breath as the first witch exited her body and absorbed into the universe. She collapsed, curling into a fetal position.

Conscious but unable to move, she blinked away tears, her chest full with emotion. Gabriella knew the second she hit the ground her entire life had changed. Not only had she obliterated the entire coven, she'd destroyed the magick that had created the witches.

The sacrifice had been swift, her own magick disappearing in an instant. No longer would she be able to have a child. Her wolf howled for her mate, yearning to be in his arms. Her eyes fluttered closed, praying he'd understand.

❦· *Chapter Fifteen* ·❦

Quintus held tight to the ailing Alpha, as the blinding light tore through Gabriella. Although she looked to be demon, he was certain it was the fae magick playing tricks. As the light ripped the witch into thousands of pieces, Gabriella flashed back to herself. She crumpled onto the charred ground, and the entire cemetery went silent.

"Gabby!" Quintus released Hunter and rushed to her side, scooping her up into his arms. He lifted her off the ground and pressed his lips to her forehead. "You're going to be okay, bella."

"Quintus." Gabriella licked her lips, tears streaming down her face.

"You did it. She's dead. They're all dead," he told her, his voice calm.

"Tell me again," Gabriella whispered.

"She's gone. Mao's gone. The coven is destroyed." Quintus suspected his brother was dead too but aside from stepping into Hell to look for him, there was little he could do. He didn't dare mention it in front of Gabriella. Between the fae magick and first witch, she'd gone limp in exhaustion, her grief palpable.

"Something's wrong…" She swallowed and licked her cracked lips.

"Shh…it's okay." Quintus closed his eyes, tightening his embrace. He swore he'd never let her go. He reached for her mind, and her strong wolf greeted him. But something was off…her magick…it was gone. "I'm going to take you home now."

"I'm sorry," she said, burrowing her face into his chest.

"It's okay, Gabby. We'll find a way to get it back. I promise you," he assured her. He'd never met a witch who'd lost their magick. "Your wolf. She's there. It's going to be all right."

Quintus' gaze flashed to Hunter who shook his head no, his lips drawn tight in concern.

"You comin' with us?" he asked the Alpha.

"I'll stay here and clean up after this mess. With all the energy that just fired off, y'all know Logan's going to be fixin' to kick someone's ass. Kade will be showin' up here soon. And fuck if the humans aren't going to get riled up. Your girl there took out the whole damn coven but this is a cemetery for humans." He sighed. "Go on now. We'll meet up later at your place."

Quintus didn't argue and swiftly dematerialized. As they flashed into his bedroom and fell upon his bed, her sadness overwhelmed him. He could tell that with the little energy she had left, even in a state of sleep she'd shielded her thoughts.

"Whatever it is, it's going to be all right, Gabby." His heart constricted, her utter sadness threading through him. The fae had warned him something bad could happen, and this was far greater than the illusions he'd seen. Gabriella had given up her magick in order to destroy Lilitu; everything she'd been her whole life had been torn away. "I'm sorry about your magick, but I swear to you, you're never going to be alone again. I'll be with you. I'll take care of you as long as I walk this earth and beyond. I…"

Quintus closed his eyes, his lips grazed her ear as he whispered to her. "I love that you're brave. Not that you aren't scared but you'll do anything to make things right. To protect others. I might spank your ass for leaving like you did, but I know why you did it. I know how you think. But you don't need to walk alone anymore. I'm here. Hunter's here. We're your family. Gabby…I love you."

Quintus pressed his lips to her forehead and gently removed his arm from underneath her body. Gabriella needed rest. He slipped out of bed and stood, then removed her boots. Although her clothes were covered in dust, he didn't want to disturb her. He reached for a throw at the bottom of the bed and spread it over her, a long sigh releasing from his lips.

A voice called from downstairs, and he smiled. *Damn wolf knows how to get in my house.* He'd deliberately adjusted the wards so that Hunter could enter but he gave a small laugh at the irony of the situation. After a lifetime of keeping others at a distance, he'd fallen in love with an incredible woman and bonded in friendship with an Alpha within days. Quintus gave Gabriella one last glance, turned off the light and flashed to the kitchen.

He found the Alpha, fully clothed, sitting at his kitchen table and shoving food into his mouth. Quintus smiled, pulled out a chair and sat, his hands folded on the table.

"Where'd you get the threads so quickly? Not that I'm complaining. I've seen enough of your bare ass lately."

"I've got a hottie down on Chartres Street. It's a quick run. She, uh, dresses me every now and then," he laughed.

"I'm sure you've got a wolf in every town."

"It's in my nature. And I'm good with it, if you know what I mean. Don't get me wrong, you and Gabby are great together but that mating bullshit isn't for me. Why do you think I love Wyoming? It's remote. None of the females in the pack are my mates. They're more like playmates, if you know what I mean. Got my own place. Make my own rules."

"You're the Alpha. That's kind of how it works." Quintus raised his eyebrows, his gaze falling to the bag on the table. The delicious scent of baked goods wafted into his nose.

"Beignet?" Hunter held up the powdery treat and took a bite.

"I'll never be able to live on just blood." Quintus retrieved a pastry from the bag and sniffed before sinking his teeth into it.

"You can live on blood. You're a vampire. It's kind of how it works." Hunter laughed.

"Goddess, these are delicious."

"One thing that's not as easy to get at home."

"NOLA's the best." The fluffy dough covered in its sugary coating tasted like heaven.

"My life is good how it is. I've got a few regular *friends*, shall we call them, in New York and New Orleans." He shrugged and raised an eyebrow. "No complications. Wolves are easy creatures. We all know the score. If you're not my mate, you know it. And I know it. Neither of us is under any illusions we can have a permanent thing. A sex thing, yes. Anything else is a no go."

"You'll find someone someday. Take me for example. Viktor always said…" Quintus closed his eyes, the pain of the loss rushing to his chest. He took a deep breath, and raised his gaze.

"I'm sorry about your brother, man. If you need help getting him…"

"No. Don't go there."

"I'm just sayin'…he could be alive."

"You know how you feel your wolves? You just know they are there. Can sense their pain. Their presence," he sighed. "Well, I've got nothing. A few thousand years and nothing."

"We can search for him," Hunter suggested.

"I can't leave Gabby." Quintus shook his head.

"But we can't just leave him there," Hunter protested.

"First of all, I don't feel him anymore. Seriously, Hunter, that's like a doctor calling it. But let's say by some miracle he's in there, he won't ever be the same. No one goes into Hell and comes out unscathed. It doesn't happen. Even just a brush with it, of which I've had a few. It fucks with your mind." Quintus blew out a breath and set the beignet on the table. "I'm not saying I'm not going to look, but what I am saying is that I can't leave Gabby right now. She hasn't had stability in her life for nearly twenty years and before that, her life was a shit show. Aside from her parents, and we don't even know who the father is, she's grown up alone. Selling her blood. To fucking Ramiel, who is still out there, by the way. Who the hell knows if he's going to come at her again? No," Quintus shook his head again, his lips tense, "I can't go right now. We just bonded. She deserves some peace."

"You sure about this, Quint?"

"One hundred percent. I can't leave her. You know how it is in Hell. You step in, you can be gone five hours or five hundred years. I can't chance that right now. She's…" Quintus paused and stared at the Alpha, resigning to trust him with the truth about what happened in the cemetery. "She lost her magick."

"No man, her wolf is good. I felt it back there and I can feel her now."

"Her wolf is good. But her magick…you know…" Quintus gave a tilt of his head.

"Oh, that magick. Are you sure?"

"I guess between the fae magick and the first witch, she used everything she had on Lilitu. Honestly, who the hell knows what happened? Of course I'm going to check with Samantha but in my experience…well, it's rare a witch loses her magick for any reason, but the ones I've seen lose it, they didn't get it back."

"Good riddance. What the hell does she need it for anyway? She's a wolf. Not to brag but we're kind of awesome if you haven't noticed." Hunter laughed.

"You know, it's strange. Before this happened, I would have thought the same thing. It's not like I got the impression that she practiced very often. It's held nothing but bad vibes. She's never been part of a coven as an adult. But I'm telling you, she's really upset. She's blocking me. I'll ask her about it when she wakes up."

"Yeah, she's a true-blue wolf. She seems in love with you, happy to be mated. It would be one thing if she practiced magick, but she seems more in line with her lycan nature."

"It's natural to be upset over the loss but this is something more. I don't know. What did she get from witchcraft that was such a great loss? It doesn't make sense," Quintus said.

"I don't know. It's like I said. She has pack now. She has you. She's mated. Has a family."

"Family." It hit Quintus like a ton of bricks. *Children.* She believed her magick could make her like Samantha.

"What is it?"

"A baby."

Hunter went to shove the pastry into his mouth and stopped mid bite. "Oh, a baby. I just assumed that was a no go with you being a vampire."

"Yeah, it's not common." The thought of having a child with her had crossed his mind after their conversation, but he remained rooted in the reality that vampires couldn't sire babies. Luca and Samantha's child was a miracle.

"Sorry, man. I don't know what to say. Gabby had to know this when she mated with you. You could adopt."

"Yeah, it's tough. Look, I knew the score. When you're turned, the sooner you accept that you are vampire and everything that goes along with it, the better off you are. The less likely you'll end up like a shish kebab."

"It's all about food for you, isn't it?" Hunter laughed. "No offence but that part about accepting being a vampire, I figure you're about at ninety-nine percent. Seriously, you're kind of obsessed."

Quintus laughed with the wolf. Hunter knew far too much about him, and for once, he simply didn't care. The only thing that mattered was Gabriella and her happiness, and that too, made him smile.

He shrugged and stuffed another beignet into his mouth. *Goddess these things are good.* Tomorrow, he'd begin his mission to make every day of Gabriella's life happy. Evil and terror were a thing of the past. When he went to look for Viktor, he'd ensure that she was safe and secure, knowing she had family. He smiled, knowing he felt love and was loved.

Quintus stood, gazing out over the horizon. Lights twinkled off the buildings as the echo of car horns and music reflected the mood of the city. A lively Saturday evening beginning in the French Quarter.

Quintus scanned the rooftop, ensuring every detail was

perfect. Candlelit arrangements floated in the long rectangular pool. The fragrance of her favorite flowers, lilies, permeated the air. A table off to the corner had been set, awaiting a delicious dinner. A jazz quartet played soft music in the corner. He laughed, so cliché, yet exactly how he'd dreamed it would be.

He'd spent the last three weeks nursing his beautiful wolf back to health. She'd broken down, admitting she'd been devastated about not being able to have children. It had crushed him to see her in such pain, but there was little he could do.

Acceptance was forced on a vampire. In exchange for power and immortality, they drank blood to stay alive, sacrificed their human existence. You were born into a new family, vampires. When you bonded, your human mate accepted your limitations, everything you were and weren't. Biological children weren't part of that equation.

Quintus had put out feelers into the supernatural world, searching for his brother. When he'd gone to seek assistance from the fae, his realm was gone. Thorn, the half-demon, hadn't been heard of since he'd gone missing after the Mao attacked Viktor. Absinthe claimed to have no knowledge of his disappearance or how to reach him. Both Quintus and Kade had scoured New Orleans for Ramiel, but no one had seen him since the night they'd killed Lilitu.

Although he still couldn't sense Viktor's life force, Quintus vowed to find him, dead or alive. But Hell wasn't a place he could go until Gabriella was settled and he had established a solid plan to get in and out of the underworld safely.

The elevator dinged, drawing him out of his contemplation. His breath caught at the sight of Gabriella exiting from the elevator, seemingly floating on air. She was sexy as fuck without even trying, every curve of her body accentuated by her sheer fitted dress. Her hair had been pulled up, exposing the satiny skin of her neck. Radiant as the sun, she glowed. Her smile told him his surprise had been successful.

Tonight she'd find out how much she meant to him. As he approached Gabriella, his face beamed with pride.

"You're stunning," he told her. Lifting her hand upward, he spun her around, and she giggled.

"You look so handsome. A tuxedo? Sexy," she purred, falling into his embrace. "And this hotel…it's beautiful."

"Sorry, but you're the only beautiful one here. You're everything." His forehead rested against hers. "But interesting you should mention this hotel. You see." Quintus briefly pressed his lips to hers and led her toward the ledge, gazing onto a view of the Mississippi.

"Everything changes. This hotel, when it was first built, it was only five stories high. It was a great hotel at the time. But there was a fire, destroyed nearly the whole building. It had a good foundation, so they rebuilt it. And over the years, there were more renovations. Today, this hotel is over one hundred years old and more beautiful than ever. Visitors from all over the world flock here to enjoy the elegant ambiance of the restored lobby and its world class service."

"It's beautiful here. The view is amazing," she said, smiling as she gazed over the horizon.

"You. Me. Everything about us. We've been born. I've nearly died. Your magick is gone. We've faced trials. But we had good foundation," he gently placed his palm to her chest, "in here. Our hearts. Changed, si? But we prevailed. And tonight, with you by my side, I'm the happiest I've ever been in my life."

Quintus held her hand in his. "Gabriella, I know we're mated. This is what wolves do. But I…" he gave a small laugh, "I'm an old-fashioned man." He paused, looking onto the muddy river.

Gabriella smiled, tilting her head in confusion, but remained silent.

"You came into my life a month ago. The bonding, the mating, that was fate. Destiny…it wasn't in our control. Love, however is something we choose." Quintus reached for the small box in his pocket and flipped open the top, revealing the stunning rectangular diamond ring. "I love you, Gabby. I've never in my life felt this way about another person. I know neither one of us needs to do this, but I want you. I want you as my wife. Will you marry me?"

"Quintus." Gabriella's hands covered her lips in surprise. "Yes, yes…oh yes."

He slid the ring onto her shaking hand and as she rushed into his arms, he held tight to her. Quintus had never imagined he'd be whole again. That anyone could steal his hardened heart, claim it as her own. He captured her lips with his, his tongue sweeping into her mouth. Demanding and possessive, he kissed her with all the passion in his heart.

Gabriella broke contact, her eyes brimming with tears. "No, wait. Quintus. I have to tell you something."

⤙ Chapter Sixteen ⤚

Everything she'd ever hated was tied up into a neat little ball called 'magick'. Its dangling cords had strangled Gabriella, haunting her entire life. Even as a child, well before she shifted, she knew there was something different about her. She didn't want to be a witch, or have anything to do with her coven or the evil they represented.

A family wasn't ever an option. She dared not dream about the security of having a home or someone to love. But now…now her entire life was different. Mated, she'd fallen in love with an incredible man, lover…father.

She'd cried in the shower, her hands over her womb, grieving the loss of the dream of having his child. For but a second, she'd had a glimmer of hope upon learning, that on a rare occasion a witch's magick could create a child, allowing the vampire to sire a biological child. The odds were slim, but the mere chance was all that was needed to plant a seed in her mind.

When she'd swallowed the poison, she'd given no thought to her decision, determined to kill Lilitu. Gabriella never suspected the hellfire would rob her of her magick. When she'd destroyed the high priestess and coven, it had taken every iota of her energy, the magick released into the night. As soon as she blinked her eyes open, gazing at Quintus, the realization slammed into her like a freight train. Her magick was gone, smashing any hope she'd conceive.

A week had passed before she'd been able to admit to Quintus how devastated she was. She'd known he'd understand. He'd gone a lifetime accepting he'd never have children. Quintus had assured her that they could adopt a wolf, raising a child within the pack.

Days had morphed into weeks, and she'd begun to accept her fate. Quintus had gone to New York, while she remained with Lyceum Wolves. Although she loved Hunter, his pack was too far away for her to belong, and she needed to be able to run with a pack where she lived in New Orleans and New York. *Home.*

During her full moon run in New Orleans, the Alpha Logan's mate, Wynter, had pulled her aside. Careful to delicately broach the subject, she asked if Gabriella was pregnant. She'd been with the pack long enough to know when wolves were breeding with their mates, detecting the familiar scent. Given both mates wanted children, they'd conceive.

Gabriella had kept her secret guarded since yesterday, processing the realization that she could have children. An undetectable remnant of her magick remained and had manifested into a breeding cycle. Nervous, she couldn't be sure Quintus would want a baby right away. They'd only known each other a short time, but despite that, she loved him, desperately yearned for his child.

On the way up in the elevator, she'd smiled, wearing the elegant dress he'd left for her on the bed. He'd sent a limo from his house to pick her up to bring her to the hotel, telling her he'd meet her there. As the doors opened, her breath caught at the sight of Quintus standing gallantly in his tuxedo. He turned and gave her a sexy smile, and her heart melted. As she stepped toward him, her eyes widened in awe of the gorgeous rooftop setting. Hundreds of Asiatic lilies, their sweet fragrance kissing the twilight air, accompanied the soft lull of jazz.

Quintus took her hand and she fell into his embrace, her heart pounding. As he slid the ring on her finger and kissed her, she could no longer keep the secret.

"What is it?" he asked, smiling.

She averted her gaze, her lips drawn into a tight smile. Butterflies danced in her stomach as she reached for the words. "I...I...Quintus, I know my magick is gone. And I never really wanted kids or at least that is what I thought when I was running. I didn't want to subject anyone to the hell I was going through. But then I met you, and you're my mate. And the baby...Samantha's baby Kate. Something inside me. I love you and I just wanted to have a baby...your baby." *Fuck, I'm rambling.* She took a deep breath and blew it out.

"Hey, bella. We talked about this. We can adopt." He wore a confused smile.

"I'm sorry it's just…well…the other day I was running with Wynter. And I know you're not a wolf but maybe you know this. You see, I've spent a lot of the time with the pack. I discovered something. I…I…"

"Whatever it is, it's okay. You can tell me," he assured her.

"I'm in a breeding cycle," she told him, her voice soft. "I guess wolves, you know they can decide on when and if they have children - their magick allows them to get pregnant."

"I'm sorry…what?" Quintus cocked his head.

"It means…"

"But…no…" He plowed his fingers through his thick dark hair. "Your magick."

"Yes," she whispered.

"Yes?" He went still.

"Yes. I mean if you want this. I know it's so soon. We haven't had much time alone. If you don't want to have a baby…" Anxiety twisted through her.

"I…I never thought I'd be a father. It's just not something that happens to us. Are you sure? Really sure?"

"I'm sure. The other wolves. They know. I can't explain how it happened. Maybe it started before I lost my magick." She exhaled, holding her breath before releasing it again. "But if you don't want to it's okay."

"What? No. I mean yes," he said nervously. Quintus rushed to her, sliding his hands around her waist. "Yes." He brushed his lips against hers. "Yes." Quintus kissed her again.

"Yes," Gabriella repeated, her heart racing as she heard his word.

"I love you, Gabby. So much," he whispered into his kiss.

Gabriella lost herself as his lips captured hers. She melted into his arms, her mind afloat in a blissful state of love. Her life had gone from hell to heaven. Quintus was everything she'd ever want or need.

"Dinner," he murmured into their kiss.

"Hmm…this could be, maybe like an appetizer." Her body flared in arousal, her fingers dropping to his pants and fumbling with his belt.

"Si, I'll feast on you first," he told her. His fingers slid through the slit of her dress, his hand gliding between her thighs. "Fuck, I can't resist you. Not even a little bit."

With his button freed, she unzipped his pants, sliding her fingers around his swollen cock. She fisted his thick shaft, kissing him back with fervor, nipping at his lips.

"I love you," he whispered into her lips.

"I love you, too." She smiled and tightened her grip on his dick, running her thumb over its wet slit. "Now fuck me."

Quintus hiked up her gown and lifted her into the air. She wrapped her legs around his waist, and her mouth crushed on his. They stumbled into a cabana, and she eased back onto the daybed, pulling his body upon hers. His hand cupped her bare mound, a finger grazing through her slick pussy.

"Jesus. No underwear, woman?" he growled, his lips traveling over her chin and down her neck.

"I'm a wolf," she laughed, stroking his cock. "Fuck me now."

"You're a demanding little thing, aren't you? I'm going to fuck you all right, but first I want to taste you," he told her.

"No fair. I want you first," she giggled, refusing to let go of his dick. "This is mine."

"You sure you want to suck me first?" He speared a thick finger into her tight core.

"Ah…fuck. Yes. No," she panted as he plunged another finger inside her. "I mean, yes…I want you."

"Compromises pet, compromises." He laughed, biting at her neck.

Gabriella reached down with her other hand and cupped his balls. "You mean like this?"

"You play dirty, my devilish wolf."

"I want to suck your cock right now."

"Seems we're at an impasse because I'm going to lick your pussy until you come so hard all of New Orleans can hear you," he laughed.

Gabriella's hips pressed up into his hand as he stroked over her clit with his thumb. "Quintus, please."

"Begging. Now, that's a sound I like to hear." Quintus sucked her lower lip into his mouth, and kissed her again. "Compromises."

"Quintus," she breathed. "Yes."

He tore his lips from hers and her pulse raced as he gave her a sexy smile, shucking off his pants. She shuffled back onto a cabana bed, her knees falling open. As he stroked his magnificent cock, the ache between her legs blossomed.

"Hmm…what are you doing?" she asked with a smile as he crawled toward her.

Quintus rounded to meet her. "Lie back."

Her breath quickened as he straddled her face, the tip of his cock brushing her lips. She went to reach for him and he scolded her. "Ah, ah, ah…no going first. Together."

Starving for Quintus, she parted her lips as he slid his cock into her mouth. Her gentle laugh was replaced with a moan as his head fell between her legs. The soft brush of his lips over her mound sent chills through her body. As his tongue swept through her glistening folds and over her clit, her body lit on fire with desire.

The salty taste of his essence coated her tongue, driving her beast mad with arousal. She struggled to concentrate as he fucked her mouth, his strong fingers dipping into her pussy as he tortured her swollen bead. With each lash of his tongue, she thrust her hips up into his mouth while tasting his cock. When he raised his pelvis, she palmed his dick, moving it to the side. She opened wide, sucking one of his balls into her warm mouth.

"Holy fuck," he groaned.

Relentless, she teased her tongue over his crinkled velvety skin then without warning, plunged his cock down her throat, sucking him hard. She reached her hands up his thighs, gripping his firm ass as he slid in between her lips, the tip of him gliding down her palate.

She quivered as he took her clit between his lips, his fingers plunging in and out of her pussy. Her orgasm built as he dragged his talented tongue through her labia, flicking at her swollen nub.

"Oh Goddess," she managed, her words garbled. She

moaned, thrusting her hips upward, seeking relief.

"Fuck, Gabby. You taste so fucking good. Your pussy…" He lapped at her clitoris. "Now. In you."

"Oh my God…" Gabriella gasped as he removed his cock from her mouth, her heart pounding.

Quintus swiftly lifted himself off her and settled between her legs. Her eyes glazed in desire, her handsome vampire taking possession of her body. With a swift thrust he drove his cock inside her quivering channel. She released an audible sigh, as he buried himself deep. With their hips moving in tandem, she surrendered, every cell of her body in a state of arousal as he made love to her.

She tunneled her hands through his hair as he slowed his pace. On the precipice of orgasm, she heaved a jagged breath, gazing deep into his eyes. "I love you. I love you so much."

As his lips captured hers, emotion flooded her chest, and she poured her passion into their kiss. Her love for him, far greater than the ends of the universe, she had never understood the full magnitude of her mating until now. There was nothing more in this world she wanted at this moment than to have his child, raise a family with her mate. This incredible man, this vampire, was hers for all eternity.

He peppered kisses down the hollow of her delicate throat, grinding his hips to hers, and grazing his pelvis over her clit. His fangs dropped, teasing her alabaster skin.

"I love you, Gabby. Now and forever," he growled.

Gabriella bared her neck to her mate in submission and cried his name out loud as his teeth pierced her flesh. Her climax pulsed through her entire body, and she surrendered, riding the waves of ecstasy. As her core quivered, tightening around his cock, he thrust hard, long strokes. Quintus gave a final grunt, stiffening in release, coming deep inside her.

He rolled onto his back bringing her with him, still panting for breath. As they lingered in their blissful haze, she relaxed into his embrace. Still partially clothed, she gave a small laugh.

"I really like compromising. Just sayin' I could do this every day," she told him.

"I may have lived a few thousand years, but you may just kill me," he laughed.

"Quintus." She paused, her hand on his chest. "I hope we have a boy. I want him to be just like you."

"She's going to be beautiful like her mama. Running free and wild," he replied, in a dreamy tone.

"She?"

"She. He. Healthy. Happy. As long as I'm with you, nothing else matters, si bella?"

"I love you. I can't believe everything we've been through and here we are," she said. "Together."

"You're the best thing that has ever happened to me. Don't ever forget that, Gabby. I've never been more alive than I have in the past month. You are the reason." He kissed the top of her head, and reflected. "I can't wait for you to be my wife. I've waited a lifetime."

"Human traditions," she mused. "Our family, we'll make some together."

"I love you, little wolf." Quintus kissed the top of her head. "Always. Forever."

⤚❊ *Epilogue* ❊⤙

White hot pain slashed through Hunter's chest as he yanked at the silvered chains. The stench of burning flesh permeated the air, the echoes of tortured souls screaming in the night. Traveling to Hell had seemed like a good idea at the time. *In and out,* he'd told himself. *Yeah, genius, terrible idea. This was a very, very bad idea.*

Hunter wasn't new to Hell. It'd been a long time since he'd been subjected to the torture of the demons. The last time, however, he'd been tricked into going by the little she-devil herself, Ilsbeth. He'd owed her a favor, saving his brother from certain death. Although he'd never told Tristan, he'd accepted this fate, looking for a scale of a demon, repaying his debt to the witch.

This time, however, he'd gone willingly. Quintus had saved his life, bringing him back from the brink of death when he'd been too damn stubborn to admit he'd been ill. The cut on his arm had burned like a bitch but being Alpha, he'd hoped he could fight it on his own.

When Quintus and Gabriella had saved him, sharing

their blood, making love, he'd known then he was going for Viktor. He agreed that with Gabriella's past, there was no way Quintus could leave her.

After spending a week in Wyoming and checking in with his beta, he'd made the decision to enter Hell. He used the same spell Ilsbeth had given him a hundred years ago. Requiring wolf hair and a few other essentials, he'd waited until the full moon and opened the portal.

As always, entering Hell had been easy, but once he stepped inside the fiery demonic haven, his stomach had turned. Determined, he'd moved forward with his search into Lucifer's inferno. Although he didn't know Viktor Christiansen well, he'd made the sacrifice, refusing to accept his death.

The Alpha grunted, his spine aching from sitting on the cold stone floor. He estimated it had only been a week since he'd been captured. Ramiel had caught and flogged him, dragged him into the pits of his dungeon. He hadn't seen the demon for days, but knew it wouldn't be long before they came to torture him again.

A door creaked open, and rats scurried across the floor. Hunter shook his head, wondering what asshole was about to join him in his sardonic hell. A lesser being shuffled about, its hooves brushing sparks of hellfire into the air as it yanked the chains down onto the ground.

"Hey asshole, can I get some water over here?" the Alpha called to him. Fucking demons were evil but for the most part dumb as dirt. He'd kept an expulsion spell locked away in his pants. Although they'd whipped the hell out of his back, splitting open his skin, the fuckers had forgotten to search his jeans.

Hunter shoved his hands into his pocket, fingering the fine crystals he'd sewn into the fabric. One drop of water and he'd blast back to Wyoming and kiss the first bison he saw.

The cloven beast grunted, nodding toward the well. The water wasn't given for comfort; rather its purpose was to keep victims alive for future torturing. The never-ending cycle was perpetuated over time, an infinite universe where victims were tortured, roused, healed and tortured again. Hunter knew the routine all too well but this time was prepared.

The minion filled a chalice and shoved it through the silver bars. *Fuck yeah.* Hunter reached for the cup. As the chain stretched, the metal seared deep into his skin. His forefinger rimmed the glass. *That's it…just a little bit more.*

As he dipped his hand into the water, Hunter smiled. The chains snapped and the bars swung open, he shoved to his feet and scooped up the chalice. *Time to get the hell out of this fuck hole. Later homies.*

He brought the cup to his lips, readying to take the last step to open the portal, but stilled as he heard the cry. *Goddammit. Just leave, Hunter. Don't be an asshole*, he told himself. But curiosity won, and as he put one foot in front of the other, moving toward its source, he cursed. He cautiously approached the darkened cave, suspecting it had been plated in silver, ensuring its occupants would both suffer and weaken.

"Fuck." Hunter stopped in his tracks as he heard the female crying.

"Hunter," her voice pleaded.

"Sweet baby Jesus." His heart caught at the familiar voice. *No, no, no, this is not happening.*

The Alpha stepped closer to the cell, peering through the thick silver bars. His pulse raced as he caught sight of the almost unrecognizable vampire lying on the dirt floor, his body beaten and bloodied. *Viktor.* A diminutive female sat next to him, holding his head in her lap. Her familiar blue eyes blinked up at him and he swore. *Fuck it all to hell.*

"Ilsbeth."

Romance by Kym Grosso

The Immortals of New Orleans

Kade's Dark Embrace
(Immortals of New Orleans, Book 1)

Luca's Magic Embrace
(Immortals of New Orleans, Book 2)

Tristan's Lyceum Wolves
(Immortals of New Orleans, Book 3)

Logan's Acadian Wolves
(Immortals of New Orleans, Book 4)

Léopold's Wicked Embrace
(Immortals of New Orleans, Book 5)

Dimitri
(Immortals of New Orleans, Book 6)

Lost Embrace
(Immortals of New Orleans, Book 6.5)

Jax
(Immortals of New Orleans, Book 7)

Jake

(Immortals of New Orleans, Book 8)

Quintus

(Immortals of New Orleans, Book 9)

Club Altura Romance

Solstice Burn

(A Club Altura Romance Novella, Prequel)

Carnal Risk

(A Club Altura Romance Novel, Book 1)

Wicked Rush

(A Club Altura Romance Novel, Book 2)

About the Author

Kym Grosso is the New York Times and USA Today bestselling author of the erotic paranormal series, *The Immortals of New Orleans*, and the contemporary erotic suspense series, *Club Altura*. In addition to romance novels, Kym has written and published several articles about autism, and is passionate about autism advocacy. She is also a contributing essay author in *Chicken Soup for the Soul: Raising Kids on the Spectrum*. In 2012, Kym published her first novel and today, is a full time romance author.

• • • •

Social Media/Links:

Website: http://www.KymGrosso.com
Facebook: http://www.facebook.com/KymGrossoBooks
Instagram: https://www.instagram.com/kymgrosso/
Twitter: https://twitter.com/KymGrosso
Pinterest: http://www.pinterest.com/kymgrosso/

Sign up for Kym's Newsletter to get Updates and Information about New Releases:

https://www.subscribepage.com/kymgrossomailinglist

Made in the USA
Middletown, DE
02 November 2021

51210854R00212